MARSH MADNESS

A Miss Fortune Mystery

NEW YORK TIMES BESTSELLING AUTHOR

JANA DELEON

Design and composite cover art by Janet Holmes.

Created with Vellum

MISS FORTUNE SERIES INFORMATION

If you've never read a Miss Fortune mystery, you can start with LOUISIANA LONGSHOT, the first book in the series. If you prefer to start with this book, here are a few things you need to know.

Fortune Redding – a CIA assassin with a price on her head from one of the world's most deadly arms dealers. Because her boss suspects that a leak at the CIA blew her cover, he sends her to hide out in Sinful, Louisiana, posing as his niece, a librarian and ex-beauty queen named Sandy-Sue Morrow. The situation was resolved in Change of Fortune and Fortune is now a full-time resident of Sinful and has opened her own detective agency.

Ida Belle and Gertie – served in the military in Vietnam as spies, but no one in the town is aware of that fact except Fortune and Deputy LeBlanc.

Sinful Ladies Society – local group founded by Ida Belle, Gertie, and deceased member Marge. In order to gain membership, women must never have married or if widowed, their husband must have been deceased for at least ten years.

Sinful Ladies Cough Syrup – sold as an herbal medicine in Sinful, which is dry, but it's actually moonshine manufactured by the Sinful Ladies Society.

And confirmed what I had suspected.

They moved me to last because this entire hearing about Kitts was a farce. They really wanted to know about Dwight Redding, and they were hoping that calling Carter up first would get them something they could use to back me into a corner.

I clenched the arms of my chair as Carter rose, looking impeccable in his dress blues. Gertie, sitting to my right, took my hand in hers and squeezed.

I had no worries for myself. I'd been here before, and although I'd been hoping to never see the inside of this room again, it didn't scare me. I knew what to expect, and Alexander had prepared all of us for every potential situation, probably a few the DOD hadn't even thought of pitching. But I was worried about Carter. I knew he was going to lie, and I knew exactly what that was going to cost him. The only plus was at least it wasn't a trial, and he didn't have to swear on a Bible.

He didn't look remotely nervous as he took a seat in the chair in front of the long table of committee members, but I hadn't expected him to. Carter was Force Recon, and some joked that the only Marines who gained entry either were born with no nerves or the Marine Corps surgically removed them.

The chairman began his questioning, starting with the mission and why Carter had made the decision to scrap it. How he'd been separated from his men while attempting to get them all clear. Carter gave his testimony, which I'm certain matched what the other men on his team had said, and since the chairman didn't linger over any of those details, I knew he was just trying to ensure Carter was going to tell the truth. But when they got to his escape from the compound in Iran, some of them shifted in their chairs. Others leaned forward. Here was the real reason we were all in this room.

"You said that you heard an explosion, correct?" the chairman asked.

"Yes," Carter said. "I assumed someone had made a mistake handling one of the weapons they were dealing, but then a guard rushed in, yelling at me. I didn't understand him, but I think he said the word 'attack' or something similar. When I saw his panic, I thought it was the military launching a rescue, but then he cut me loose."

"Why would he do that?"

"I have no idea, and no amount of dwelling on it has given me one."

"And you're certain this was one of the compound's regular guards?"

"He was Iranian, dressed like the rest of them, and carried the same weapons, but we didn't exactly hang out like drinking buddies. And the beating I took the first day made my eyes swell shut. My vision didn't return to normal until after I got back to the United States."

"So this man set you free for no apparent reason that you can think of?"

"That's right. After he cut me loose, he was frantic, waving me out, so I ran. When I got to the door, I realized that a full-on battle was going on outside. There was gunfire and smoke bombs, which compromised my vision even more. I crawled around the building, away from the fire, and kept crawling until I reached the stables. The horses had halters on them, so I grabbed a rope from the fence to use as reins and I took that horse as fast as he could run into the mountains."

"You never saw who the terrorists were fighting?"

"No. I didn't care. My only concern was finding a US military unit, and there was nothing about that skirmish to indicate US involvement."

"And you went through the mountains alone?"

"It's probably more accurate to say the horse got me through the mountains. I was hovering on the edge of consciousness most of the ride, but obviously he'd traveled that path before and knew the way. When I got to the other side, I traded the horse for a ride to the port and stole a boat. The next thing I remember is waking up on a Navy submarine."

"You expect me to believe that a large, important part of your memory is completely gone?"

"What you believe isn't my problem. But I challenge you to go days without food and water, being tortured for hours on end, and let me know how functional you are. You don't look as if you've ever missed a meal or had so much as a hangnail."

"I don't appreciate the disrespect, Master Sergeant LeBlanc."

"Neither do I."

It was all I could do not to cheer.

"You have my medical records," Carter said. "Talk to my doctors—you know, the people who work for you. Ask them if I'm faking the condition I was in when I was recovered."

The chairman's face tightened, and I could tell he didn't believe Carter's story, not exactly the way he was telling it. But he didn't have a shred of evidence to prove otherwise, and the medical evidence supported every claim Carter made.

"You're dismissed, Master Sergeant. But we reserve the right to question you again."

"You can question me until both feet are in the grave, but my answers will never change."

Carter rose from the chair and headed back to our seats. I gave him a tiny nod, and he pinned his gaze on me. I could see all his anger, frustration, and worry right there in that single look, and I hated Kitts all over again for putting Carter in a position to have to lie to protect me. Death had been so much less than what Kitts had deserved.

Then it was my turn.

"Ms. Redding," the chairman said as I took a seat. "You've had an impressive career with the CIA."

"I'm aware. I was there."

"How did you get into Iran?"

"I didn't. I was in Khasab, on vacation."

"No one believes that."

"That sounds like a *you* problem. I'm certain you've seen the YouTube video from the Khasab marketplace. Are you suggesting that I made it across the Strait of Hormuz—twice—without being shot down or blown out of the water, freed Carter, and the next morning I was chasing a runaway camel in the marketplace? No one is that impressive. Not even me."

"Oh!" Gertie said. "I remember riding a camel. Wait—who do we know that owns a camel?"

The chairman shot a dirty look at Gertie, and she let out a dramatic sigh. I drummed my fingers on the arm of the chair and stared at the chairman, my behavior and silence conveying the words he didn't want to hear—*you're not getting anything else out of me*.

The chairman pinned his gaze on me. "This man who assisted Mr. LeBlanc with his escape—who was he?"

"How the hell should I know? If I was psychic, the CIA would have had to pay me a lot more."

"So you're stating, unequivocally, that the man who aided Mr. LeBlanc was not your father?"

"Again, I wasn't there, so I didn't see the man. But since my father is dead, I'm going with no."

"Ms. Redding, we're fairly certain your father's death has been...overstated."

I shrugged.

"So you refuse to give us information on your father."

I laughed. "According to the CIA, the man who donated biological material to me died when I was fifteen. He let a young girl with no mother and not a single other family member believe that he was dead. The CIA *told* me he was dead. We buried teeth and I collected life insurance, and a man who wasn't even related to me finished raising me."

I leaned forward and stared at him, now angry at him, my father, and every other person who crapped on people who cared about them.

"Do you really think a man who would do that to a child cares about me as an adult? The CIA told me he died in that blast."

"But they lied before."

"And? Take that up with the CIA. But hear me on this, you won't scratch the surface of *my* righteous indignation when it comes to Dwight Redding, and they never deemed me important enough to know the truth back then. So good luck."

The chairman didn't believe me, but he didn't have a basis for pushing his point. Not when all of us were denying any knowledge of anything at all. But I had a feeling he wasn't done—he was just going to attempt to tighten the screws from another angle. His next question proved me right.

"During your time with the CIA, were you ever inside the federal lockdown facility where Colonel Kitts was held?" the chairman asked.

"Why would I have been? When a mission was complete, the only place I could have visited my targets was the afterlife."

"You left one alive in your home."

"Only to get a name. And I don't give him long. Quite frankly, given your incompetence, I'm surprised he's still alive."

His jaw flexed and I could tell I'd struck a nerve.

"So you won't mind telling us where you were the night Colonel Kitts was killed?"

I shook my head at the absurdity of the question. "I was in bed with your other suspect in my house in Sinful, Louisiana. I had people over until about ten and Carter was on shift until midnight. Then we had a private sort of party. Do you want the details of that?"

"I do," Gertie said, and Harrison snorted. The chairman gave her a dirty look.

"No?" I continued. "Afterward we went to sleep. Carter got a call from dispatch at 6:00 a.m. and left, and my friends came over shortly after that with pastries and we had coffee."

The chairman frowned and I smiled at him.

"I suppose you're going to argue that my friends are lying, or Carter is lying, and I wasn't there the entire day and night. That I somehow traveled from Sinful to DC without being spotted at an airport, gas station, or toll road. That I entered a federal prison I'd never set foot in before and managed to do so without clearance or identification. Then I located Kitts's cell, dispatched however many guards you had assigned to him, killed him, waltzed out unseen, drove back to Sinful, and was sitting in my kitchen ready for breakfast. Does that sound ridiculous enough for you?"

"You have friends with access to a private jet. You didn't have to drive."

"You're right. I didn't. But I also knew what kind of man Kitts was when Carter returned from Iran. If I was going to kill him, it would have been then and from 1,000 meters away. People like Kitts aren't worth the risk to kill in federal lockup. Not to me. But *you* have known what Kitts was for years and never once lifted an eyebrow until now. I have to assume that's because the men and women he used to put all those fancy medals on his uniform weren't capable of causing you trouble like we are."

I leaned forward and looked him directly in the eyes. "Have you even checked toll and interstate cameras or security footage at airports or the flight paths for private planes? I'm guessing not. And the only reason people don't go looking for evidence in a murder investigation is because they already know who the perpetrator is. Maybe you saw him this morning when you were shaving."

The chairman's face turned red. "You are out of line."

"No, what I am is out of patience. Push me as your fall guy on this murder, and I'll burn you down. And trust me, you'll never see me coming."

The committee members all shifted uncomfortably in their seats.

"Is that a threat, Ms. Redding?" the chairman asked.

"I don't make threats. Consider it a warning. I don't usually give those, either."

"If you'll just tell us what we want to know, then this committee is happy to let you all return to your lives."

I rose from my chair, done with this sham of an investigation.

"If you think threatening me and my friends is going to get you a kernel of information on Dwight Redding, you're grasping at straws. Every one of you sitting behind that table probably knows more about the man than I do."

I pointed a finger at him. "*You* knew what Kitts was doing. Knew and did nothing. That puts the blood of every soldier who died serving under him on you. The man sent mercenaries to my home to kill me in my sleep, and the only thing you can find to worry about is a ghost? Who, as far as I know, never betrayed this country or the men serving it. I want you to think very carefully about the next thing you say to me. The only words coming out of your mouth should be *thank you*, because I spent my entire career cleaning up messes made by people like you."

I turned and started walking away.

"We're not done questioning you."

I didn't even turn around until I got back to my seat. "But I'm done answering. If you want to pursue me, go for it. But the story I have to tell will be immediately distributed to every major news outlet in the world. And if I or any of my friends should meet with an unfortunate death, same result. So I suggest you all get to praying that we live long, happy lives and die from natural causes."

"Are you threatening this committee again?"

"Don't have to. I'm holding all the cards."

Everyone stood, and Alexander grinned as he walked to the table and started handing documents down the line.

"What's this?" the chairman asked.

"You've been served," Alexander said cheerfully. "It's a class action lawsuit on behalf of the injured and fallen soldiers who served under Kitts. I only have sixty on my list now, but it's early days. It's interesting how they all have similar stories of questionable decisions made up the line. I suggest you review their statements and the price for their silence very carefully. Unless the rest of you want to go under the microscope alongside Kitts."

The chairman flung the papers onto the ground and glared at Alexander. "I'm ashamed that you're now serving the wrong side of things."

Alexander gave him a huge smile. "As always, I'm serving truth and honor. I find it distasteful that the most horrific of crimes were committed not by the enemy but by a decorated officer, and against his own men. I find it even more distasteful that it's not even the first time it's happened. What I don't find remotely surprising is that a group of politicians is attempting to shift blame and cover it up to save your own uncalloused lily-white skin. You've never spent a night of your lives sleeping on anything but designer sheets. Those men Kitts sent to their death were just as expendable to you as they were to him. You allowed a serial killer to not only occupy a commanding position but be decorated for it. Good luck with reelection."

The chairman's face turned beet red, and he jumped up and started yelling, but we no longer cared. We simply gathered our things and walked silently out of the room as he raged. We'd said our piece and as far as I was concerned, that was the end of it. Dealing with the fallout from Kitts was their problem.

CHAPTER TWO

Our flight back to Louisiana didn't leave until the next morning, but no one was in a jovial mood, so we all elected to head back to the hotel and order room service. Carter and I ate our dinner on the tiny balcony that looked out over the city, neither of us speaking the entire time. When we'd finished our meals and the plates were stacked inside on the tray, we sat out there again with glasses of wine.

"Do you miss it?" he asked, waving a hand toward the city.

"No."

"Not at all?"

"Not at all. This was never home. This was where I lived when I wasn't working. I could have been in a condo in Denver or a basement unit in the Bronx. It wouldn't have mattered. The only thing important to me then was what I did after I walked out my front door."

"So a fishing cabin on Number Two would have been perfectly fine."

"Well, travel is a problem, even to just the grocery store, so no. But the isolation would work fine for me. And the lack of people. I'd have to have a heck of a room deodorizer, though."

He smiled and for the first time in a long time, he didn't look as if he was forcing it. "I'm glad to hear it."

"That I don't want to ever live in the city again or that I don't want to live on Number Two?"

"Both."

I stared out at the city lights and sighed.

"What's wrong?" he asked.

"Nothing, really. I was just thinking that people used to say that when you were high up, the city lights looked like a million stars. But now, after being all over the world and living in Sinful, I feel sorry for them, because they've obviously never lain back and looked at a starry sky in the middle of nowhere. It's not even close to the same. The city lights are like cheap plastic diamonds compared to the real thing."

Carter nodded. "I'm glad I never had to spend too much time in cities. I don't think I would have liked it."

"Why do you think I had no friends except Harrison, no hobbies except shooting guns, and never left my condo unless I had an appointment or a mission?"

I shifted in my chair to look at him. "You know what the worst part is—I actually liked my life then. Or I thought I did. I thought I was doing what I was supposed to do and that being good at your job was all there was for anyone. I never understood when people talked about 'work-life balance' because work was my life, and I saw no imbalance."

"It was somewhat the same for me while I was in the Marines—the focus on the job, I mean. But different because I had the advantage over you of growing up in Sinful, so I'd already lived that other side of the coin."

He frowned and I knew what he was thinking. I'd been silent for so long, hoping that he worked everything out—giving him the space to do so without providing prompts. His healing needed to come from inside him. Not from external pressure. But now, with everything that had happened, it was time to talk about the elephant in the room.

"You know your career is above reproach, right?" I asked. "Every order you executed is because you trusted those giving them to be doing so in the best interest of this country and the men and women who served."

He nodded slowly, staring out over the city, then he reached over and took my hand in his and locked his eyes on mine.

"I know you've been worried about me," he said. "And I know you've been trying to give me room to sort out everything without pressuring me to 'forget about it' or 'move on' or all the other things that people didn't dare say, but I know they were hoping for."

"Oh, I definitely want you to do both, but I also know that neither comes easy. Putting pressure on you wouldn't accomplish anything but pissing you off. And as much as you refuse to believe it, I'm never *trying* to piss you off."

His lips trembled. "Even the time you kicked the mirror off my truck, so I'd be forced to arrest you along with Ally?"

I laughed. "Okay, I'll give you that one."

"You know I wasn't really pissed at you, even then. I was angry that I was going to be forced to arrest you on top of already being angry about having to arrest Ally. But I admired what you did. We would have made sure Ally was taken care of—Myrtle would have poisoned my coffee if I hadn't. But you being there with her was what she needed most. You're a good friend, Fortune. My *best* friend."

"So what you're saying is I have leverage... Soooooo, are you going to forget about it and move on?"

"No. I'm going to move on because it's time, not because of your assumed leverage. And I'll admit that Kitts being dead has helped spur that along. Not because I wanted revenge—

although I definitely wanted him to answer for his crimes—but because I know he can't ever abuse the trust of good men and women again. He can't sacrifice them at the altar of his career."

He blew out a breath. "But I will never forget. And I hope and pray that all of this has taught those running our military that no one is above scrutiny. I hope this lawsuit of Alexander's makes everyone with power take a harder look at what's really going on. That no one ever gets a pass again because of their length of service and their past accolades."

"You know they're never going to allow that lawsuit to go to trial. They can't afford to."

"I know, but they'll write fat checks to keep it quiet. And all parties to the lawsuit have already agreed that they'll only take what they need to put their families back whole. The rest will be used to start a charity to help injured soldiers and their families. Alexander is going to set it all up and said he'll be tapping the shoulders of every rich person he has dirt on to get donations."

"So...everyone he knows?"

Carter laughed. "Probably. He's a pretty impressive guy."

"I'm glad you think so, because I think when the dust settles, he and Emmaline might just see what those sparks flying between them ignite."

Carter's eyes widened. "What? Jeez, what else have I missed while I was mired in guilt?"

"Easter in Sinful this year was an Alfred Hitchcock film—*Attack of the Holiday Birds*," I joked. "And Good Friday was anything but biblical...except maybe the part where we almost started an exorcism."

He shook his head. "Those I remember. But seriously, my mom and Alexander?"

CHAPTER THREE

TWO DAYS LATER, I STROLLED INTO THE GENERAL STORE TO pick up my grocery order and maybe have a chat with Walter, if he wasn't busy. The store was empty when I walked inside—and I mean really empty. Walter wasn't even in sight. I called out and heard a muffled answer from the storeroom, but I couldn't make out what was said. I figured he'd be out soon, so I slid onto the stool I usually occupied when I took some time to talk and waited.

A couple minutes later, Walter and Ida Belle came out the storeroom door, both looking rumpled and red-faced. I raised one eyebrow and as Ida Belle started to talk, I lifted one hand.

"No," I said, just as she always did to Gertie.

"Oh good grief!" Ida Belle said. "It wasn't that! We're not uncouth like some people. I was trying to help Walter move some boxes back there, but they have proven to be too much, even for the two of us."

"I can help," I said. "Surely the three of us can manage."

Walter nodded. "Ida Belle and I only needed another 15 percent and we'd have been there. You'll be another 80 percent. We could probably throw the boxes across the room."

"I don't think shot-putting your stock is good for business," Ida Belle said as we headed into the storeroom.

Walter indicated the boxes in question, on a pallet outside the loading door, and where he wanted them inside, and we all grabbed a corner. The boxes were bulky and definitely had some weight to them, so I could see why the two of them had struggled, but with three of us, they were no problem. We got them all moved, then headed inside where Walter pulled us all out a bottled water and we sat around the register.

"I talked to Carter this morning," Walter said. "Alexander told him he expects a settlement offer quickly."

I nodded. "They don't want this to come out. If people knew what Kitts got away with all those years, it would be a really bad look."

"You think they'll accept an offer?"

"They won't be accepting the first offer, but they'll agree when Alexander tells them it's the best offer. They're all honorable men and women. They don't want to damage the military beyond repair, and that's exactly what a trial would do. They still believe that the men and women serving are doing it for this country and its citizens. They just want to make it painful enough so that men like Kitts can't get away with that level of treachery again, and so that they have the funds to help the soldiers and families of soldiers who are struggling because of service injuries and fatalities."

Walter nodded. "I can agree with all of that. Have you heard anything about that mercenary that you left alive?"

"Yeah, he's locked up. No bail."

"If it goes to trial, do you think he'll get life?" Ida Belle asked.

"He won't make it to trial. He'll end up like Kitts. I'm sure he had plenty of clients, and none of them are interested in the local things a little at a time. Then I can ride him everywhere like Sheriff Lee does his horse."

Since I'd seen Lee's horse in places and situations that he had no place being—and with consequences that weren't favorable to Sheriff Lee, the horse, or anyone else—that sounded more like a threat than an assurance.

"And just think," Gertie continued, "I'll be the only wise man with my own camel at the Christmas gala."

Ida Belle's look of dismay was priceless. "Because your bird wasn't enough of a problem? You figured introducing a camel to the Christmas gala would be an improvement on what? The terror? The potential for a lawsuit? Of all the things you've done before, this has got to rank second-worst decision ever."

"What was the first?" I asked.

"Bringing that gator home in her pants," Ida Belle said.

"Ah." I nodded. "Well, the camel is here now and the guy who sold him is gone, so he has to stay somewhere, at least until Gertie can find a place for him."

"Who the heck is going to take a camel?" Ida Belle asked.

"A stable?" I suggested.

Gertie brightened. "I'll tell them he's a Middle Eastern sort of horse."

"So that they'll think he's an Arabian and you'll show up with this?" Ida Belle shook her head.

"Well, while you stand here and stew, I'm going to try him out," Gertie said and strolled around to the other side of the giant brown beast, who looked as if he'd gone to sleep standing there.

Maybe Clyde and Sheriff Lee's horse had more in common than we thought.

"You are not riding that camel!" Ida Belle said.

"Too late." Gertie grinned as she swung up onto the saddle.

I peered around the side and realized that trailer guy had

left a stool next to the camel. Great. Fortunately, the camel still looked uninterested in moving from the spot, but that was all subject to change. It wasn't as if living, breathing things had an Off and On switch.

Or maybe they did.

We'd all forgotten today was tornado siren testing day. But it was clearly an On switch for Clyde. As soon as the first wails echoed through Sinful, the camel's eyes popped open and he bolted, Gertie clinging to the strap on his middle as he loped away.

I started to chase him, but Ida Belle ran for her SUV. "You're fast, but you can't outlast that camel," she said. "And he's got a lot more open space here than the one in that market did."

I jumped into the SUV and we took off just as the camel rounded the corner. I heard the sound of vehicles slamming on their brakes, but fortunately no sounds of accidents. When we turned the corner, I spotted the camel about to enter the park, Gertie still on board.

"At least he's moving for open land," I said.

"Open land with kids playing," Ida Belle said. "They're out of school today for teachers' training."

Ida Belle floored the SUV and we shot off for the park, but she had called it correctly. There were kids everywhere, and she couldn't follow the camel with the SUV. The rest of this would be a footrace.

I jumped out of the SUV before she'd even come to a complete stop and sprinted after the camel, who I could see now was well into panic mode. Kids and parents screamed as they ran to flee the charging beast, who made a quick turn every time he met with panicked people. Unfortunately, that had him going around in a bit of a tight circle, and I was amazed Gertie had remained seated through all of it.

When he finally stopped spinning, he loped off and looked as sturdy as Father Michael did after...well, pretty much any day after leaving his house. Good God. A dizzy, panicked camel was not a good look for a crowded park. Gertie pulled frantically on the reins but with the screaming kids and parents and the wailing siren, there was no way the camel was going to stop.

I was about twenty feet behind him when he made a hard left turn and ran back toward the road, but as he approached a swing set for the smaller kids, he was swerving so much that instead of missing the swings, he ran right through the center of them. The tripod structure had a regular swing on each end and an old tire hung in the center attached to the top of the frame for kids to hang off.

Unfortunately, it was the perfect height to catch the camel's head.

As he swerved toward the center of the swing set, his head hit the bull's-eye that was the tire, but instead of stopping when his head popped through it, he got even more scared and dialed things up, ripping the entire swing set out of the ground as he bolted.

With kids on the two swings!

CHAPTER FOUR

"JUMP!" I YELLED AT THE KIDS, BUT THEY CLUNG TO THE swings, laughing and screaming in delight as they swayed on each side of the running camel.

Good. God. They were as crazy as Gertie.

I turned up the speed, but a camel in an open space has the advantage. I saw Ida Belle running at an angle for the street, but she didn't even come close to intercepting. A couple of women were running behind me, screaming bloody murder, and I could only assume their kids were the two who elected to stay on the swings and train for the circus.

Ida Belle already had the SUV started and in gear when I jumped inside and we took off after the camel, who was already half a block away. The camel made a turn on the next street and took out the postman and a rosebush with one end of the swing set frame. I glanced as we passed, hoping the man was all right, but we didn't have time to stop and check. I dialed the sheriff's department but it was busy. No surprise. Everyone on the block appeared to be standing in their front yards, which meant news of the camel fiasco had already swept through town. Probably half the population was trying to reach the sheriff's department about now.

Mid-block, something caught the camel's eye and he swerved to the right, running onto the lawns. I saw Nora standing on her front lawn, wearing a string bikini—heavy on the string, light on the bikini—and a huge straw hat with flowers on it. She was holding her cat, Idiot, under one arm and waving to a dump truck that was pulling away...and scattering sand all over her driveway and the road as he went. The camel locked in on the sand and must have figured he was close to home, because he headed straight for Nora's driveway.

Ida Belle laid on the horn and as Nora turned around, I swear I could see her pupils enlarge from three houses away. Idiot, clearly sensing the danger, did a sideways spring off her body, as only cats can do, attempting to escape into a nearby tree.

He missed.

And landed on the back of the camel.

Nora dived into her azalea bushes, and all I could see was her feet sticking up as we drove past. I'm sure the cat's claws didn't even put a dent in the camel's thick hide, but the additional weight clinging to his rear probably didn't make him any less stressed. He turned up the speed and ran for the layer of sand, as if it would somehow save him from whatever ring of hell he currently found himself in.

I was praying that he'd stop when he reached the sand, but all hopes were dashed when he crossed the driveway and went around the house toward the backyard.

"Heaven help us all," Ida Belle said. "She put in a pool."

"At least she was wearing a bathing suit."

"Barely."

Ida Belle raced into Nora's driveway and slammed on the brakes. I was out of the SUV before it stopped and already running for the backyard. The fence between Nora and her neighbor's had been removed, and orange plastic construction fencing waved on the remaining posts on each side. I bolted across the trail of sand and into the backyard just as the camel barreled into the pool.

And the tornado siren stopped.

The kids let out a final scream of glee and jumped off the swings, then swam for the side. Gertie, remarkably, was still astride the camel, who was now swimming around in a circle, looking somewhat pleased, despite the swing set still hanging from his neck. Idiot had either jumped or been flung off the camel's butt when they hit the water and had clawed himself onto a foam float shaped like a flamingo.

Ida Belle ran up beside me and shook her head. "I told her that a zero-entry sand pool was a bad idea around here. Anything can wander into it."

"In fairness," I said, "I don't think she planned on a camel taking up residence. He probably thinks he found an oasis in the middle of the desert with sand covering a good quarter of her yard. What the heck is she building? A volleyball court?"

The kids, one boy and one girl, had made it up the slope of the pool and were high-fiving each other. I was glad they hadn't been hurt but couldn't help smiling. This was the kind of story that got retold their entire lives. And since they were probably about eight, that was a lot of years to recount their story of the runaway camel. Their mothers, on the other hand, would probably need Xanax and therapy.

"Did you see us go?" the boy asked. "Holy crap! That camel is fast."

"You can't say crap," the girl corrected, "but he really was. Our moms are going to have a fit. They're going to have to dip into their secret wine stash early."

"My mom said the secret wine stash is how we got my sister. I hope she doesn't drink any."

Nora came lumbering up about that time, scratched from top to bottom from the branches on the azalea bush and with leaves and flowers stuck in her hair.

"I probably have something for them that works better than wine," she said.

"No handing out your stash to beleaguered parents, Nora."

Carter's voice sounded behind me, and I turned around to see him walking toward us, his gaze locked on the swimming camel.

"Let's go tell our moms what we did!" the girl said, and the two of them flashed grins at us and ran out of the yard.

"Just when I think I've seen it all," he said and looked at Nora. "Please tell me you did not buy a camel."

"Not me," Nora said. "I have trouble keeping plants alive. Except weed. I've got the best weed in the South."

Carter closed his eyes and looked skyward, pretending that he hadn't heard a word she'd said.

"He's mine," Gertie said, still perched on the camel and beaming. "Isn't he awesome?"

"Get me a handful of that weed," I said before Carter could put his thoughts into words that were legal to say in public.

He stared at me as if I'd lost my mind.

"It's for the camel," I said. "We have to get that swing set off him before he takes out more than just the mailman. And since half the fence is down for this construction project, it's not like we can just close the gate and wait him out. So unless you've got a horse tranquilizer handy..."

"Oh, that's a great idea," Gertie said. "I had some of Nora's stash a couple weeks ago and was so relaxed I slept for two days."

"You told me you were sick," Ida Belle said.

Gertie nodded. "Sick of being awake. Best sleep I've had in years."

I motioned to her to get off the camel. "He's ignoring reining anyway, so you're safer off him."

Nora was back with a five-gallon bucket of her stash by the time Gertie had dismounted and waded out. Carter's look of dismay at the size of the bucket was priceless, but he just shook his head and started off for the other side of the pool.

"I'll just rescue the cat," he said. "If anyone asks, I know nothing about anything else going on here."

Nora perked up. "Something's going on? Tell me!"

He sighed and grabbed the pool brush to attempt to drag the float Idiot was on to the side of the pool. Nora opened her bucket and gave me a bud and I headed down the slope toward the camel, who was alternating giving me and the cat on the float a wary eye. I couldn't say that I blamed him where the cat was concerned. I had one eyeball on him as well, and for good reason. The last time I'd gone rounds with Nora's cat, he'd had a loaded gun.

The float was almost to the side when the impatient cat decided to make a leap for it. Of course, his leap sent the float backward and threw him completely off trajectory. He dropped about two inches from the float and a good foot from the side of the pool, clawing at the brush as he hit the water. He sprang up so fast that I swear his head wasn't even wet, then climbed on top of the brush and ran up the pole like a tightrope walker at the circus. Reaching Carter's arms didn't slow him down one bit. He ran straight up to his shoulders, then perched on top of Carter's head, claws dug in and dripping. Carter cursed as he tugged at the cat hat, trying to pull him off his head, but Idiot had attached for the duration.

Finally, he leaned over, figuring the cat would let go if he was hanging upside down, but he was just a tad bit too close to the side of the pool. His foot hit the pool brush as he bent over, and he went cat-first into the pool. Idiot decided his new perch wasn't good any longer and vaulted off Carter's head and back onto the camel. The startled camel shot halfway up the beach entry. Ida Belle and I ducked to avoid being taken out by the swing set, and Nora fell backward over a lounge chair.

Fortunately, the last place Idiot wanted to be was on the camel again, so he vaulted off and landed in the bucket of weed, which appeared to have the same effect on him as catnip did. He immediately flopped over and started rolling on top of the buds. Nora pulled herself up on a lounge chair and reach in the bucket to pluck the cat out. She grabbed her straw hat off her head, dropped the cat inside, and pulled the sides up, effectively trapping him. From the sounds he was letting out, I wouldn't want to be Nora later on tonight. After all, we already knew he could shoot a gun.

"That's why I had to start putting lids on the buckets," Nora said. "No one wants to smoke cat hair."

Idiot was still growling as she stalked off for her house.

I grabbed another piece of bud and approached the camel, who'd been warily eyeing us from a patch of sand that Nora had installed on one side of the pool. He didn't trust me, but he wanted what was in my hand. That's when I heard a cough behind me.

Andy Blanchet, who was filling in for Deputy Breaux while he had his wisdom teeth removed, headed toward me, shaking his head at the scene in front of him. We probably looked a ragtag bunch—Carter, fully clothed and climbing out of the pool; Nora, wearing a bikini and headed into her house with a yowling cat in her hat; and Ida Belle, Gertie, and me standing in front of a camel.

When he stepped up, he took one look at the lump in my hand and started laughing so hard he had to sit in a patio chair.

Carter walked up and looked down at Blanchet, who barely managed to stop laughing long enough to focus in on Carter.

"Since you're so amused by these three and their shenanigans," he said to Blanchet, "I'm delegating. This one is all yours and I was never here. I'm going home to shower and change and none of you are going to leave this property with anything that can be eaten, smoked, or drunk."

Everyone nodded except Gertie, who looked at the ground. Andy just grinned as Carter dripped his way out of Nora's yard.

"He seems pretty calm now that the siren's stopped," Gertie said.

Ida Belle reached up and grabbed the swing set frame, and the camel's eyes widened.

"Nope," I said. "He's still stressed, and it will take all of us to lift that swing set off him, so we need to make sure he doesn't take off running again."

I gave him a bud, which he downed in one chomp, then Nora came back outside and shook her head.

"That would work a lot faster if he was smoking it," she said.

"He doesn't even observe reining," Ida Belle said. "I hardly think he's going to play puff-puff-give."

Nora reached into her bathing suit top and pulled out a doobie the size of a cigar. Blanchet let out a strangled cry, but I wasn't sure if it was because of the size of the joint, where it had been stashed, or that Nora obviously intended to swap smoke with the camel.

"If you need to cut out, I'll totally understand," I said.

He shook his head. "No way in hell I'm missing this. Besides, I don't have an election or a job to worry about. But I'm beginning to understand why Carter tells me 'I don't know anything about that' when I ask about stuff."

Nora took a draw on the cigar joint so big her chest

strained the fabric on the bikini. Then she leaned toward the camel and blew the smoke in his face. At first, the camel wrinkled his nose and I thought he was going to back away, but then he must have gotten a whiff of something he liked because he moved forward, head up, sniffing the smoke.

Blanchet shook his head. "In all my years on earth... You aren't amazed by this?"

I shrugged. "I spent a lot of time in the desert among the, um...more questionable residents. How do you think I got the idea to use weed to calm him down?"

"Experience with high camels. That's one to put on the résumé."

Ida Belle snorted. "If Fortune had a résumé, it would read like fiction. No one would believe it except those of us who know her."

Nora gave the camel a few more puffs and Blanchet looked over at me. "How many does she need to do?" he asked.

Nora's eyes closed and she crumpled onto the ground, the cigar joint still between her lips.

"I think she's done," I said. "Jury's still out on the camel."

"If a couple of puffs took Nora out like that, the camel doesn't stand a chance," Ida Belle said.

"Is she all right?" Blanchet asked, staring down at Nora.

"She's a professional," I said.

I plucked the cigar joint from her mouth and stubbed it out before tossing it in with the bud and putting the lid back on. Ida Belle pulled over a lawn chair and sat down to wait. The rest of us followed suit, and it wasn't long before we could see that Ida Belle had called it correctly.

The camel started to sag a little all over, as though he had been hunching his shoulders and had stopped. Then his head lowered and his eyelids started to droop. He started swaying his head back and forth, as if listening to music that wasn't playing.

"When you hear the imaginary music, it's starting to kick in," Gertie said.

Blanchet raised an eyebrow but had apparently learned from Carter's example and wasn't about to ask a question.

I lifted one leg and poked at the camel's chest with my foot, but all he did was give me a sleepy look and I swear he was smiling.

"Okay," I said as I rose, "let's give this a whirl. Blanchet, you grab one end of the swing set and Ida Belle and Gertie get the other."

As soon as they'd all gotten a firm grip, I pulled my chair right in front of the camel's head and climbed up on it. I grabbed the tire with both hands and nodded.

"Start leaning the frame forward," I said. "When the tire pops off, let it fall. Don't worry about me. I'll duck, but I don't want him panicking and getting tangled up again."

They moved the frame forward and I pulled on the tire. It wasn't snug, so there was no wrangling involved there, thank God, and the camel helped me out by lowering his head as I pulled. Either he was so blasted he couldn't keep it up any longer or he had finally figured out we were trying to help and was tired of wearing a swing set.

As soon as the tire was clear of his head, I gave it a hard pull and ducked as the swing set crashed on the ground behind me. The camel didn't so much as flinch.

"Good Lord, he's trashed," Gertie said. "I wonder how long he'll be like that."

"Hopefully long enough to get him into a place with a solid fence," Ida Belle said. "And I don't mean your backyard. You saw what he did to that swing set. He would waltz right through a wood fence. You're already up for two potential lawsuits and at least twenty more complaints. And for all we know the mailman might not even be with us anymore, and tampering with the mail is a federal offense."

"Is that why he was walking around looking drunk?" Blanchet asked. "I saw him on the way over and he was trying to stuff a stack of envelopes into a woman's robe. She was *not* understanding."

"Start calling stables and farms and find someone who will board that camel," Ida Belle said. "We all agreed we'd stay on the straight and narrow until Carter was elected. I know Celia's been looking for another candidate and the last thing we need is someone who's friends with her getting the job."

"She doesn't have any friends," Gertie said. "Just women who are too afraid of her to tell her how awful she is."

"Valid," Blanchet agreed.

"But if she helps someone into the sheriff's position, then they'll owe her," Ida Belle said. "Debt usually demands a higher price than friendship."

"Also true," Blanchet said. "Well, ladies, if the entertainment portion of the day is over, I've got to head out to another call. I stopped on my way over because someone reported a camel in Nora's backyard, and I figured I'd better take a peek. But I've got a streaker at the Swamp Bar that needs attending to. Whiskey refuses to approach him. Can't say that I blame him—the guy's using a walker, and no one wants that good a look at another man's business."

"Is it streaking if you're doing less than one mile per hour?" I asked.

"Good question," Blanchet said. "Maybe I'll ask after I throw a tarp over him. See you ladies later!"

He walked off whistling, and Ida Belle shook her head. "It's amazing what retirement and not having to care what other people think can do for your mood."

Gertie snorted. "You've lived every day after 'Nam like it was retirement, and you've never cared what other people think. I haven't seen it improve your mood any."

"Oh, this is me being pleasant," Ida Belle said.

I nodded. "I understand."

THE NEXT AFTERNOON, I WAS LOUNGING IN THE HAMMOCK I'd strung in the huge tree near the bayou and reading a book when I saw Merlin rise from his sunny spot in front of me. He fixed his gaze behind me before relaxing again in the warm grass and going back to sleep. I heard footsteps but there was no way to twist enough to see who was coming up behind me, and I was too comfortable to get out of the hammock. Besides, if Merlin wasn't concerned, neither was I. His list of people he liked was even shorter than mine.

A couple seconds later, Blanchet moseyed in front of me, hands in his pockets and a big grin on his face. He was the only person I knew who managed to be incredibly active while simultaneously appearing as if he was expending no energy on life at all. I hoped someday to reach that level of relaxed, but I was fairly certain it would only come in the grave.

"Has Cheech and Chong's camel found a place to live?" he asked.

I nodded. "A local horse breeder, River Hayes, agreed to take him in. At least until we can convince Gertie to get rid of him. That camel has no business being in Sinful."

He raised an eyebrow. "I've heard of Hayes. She's a pretty big deal in the horse training world. I can't believe she agreed to take on a camel."

I shrugged. "She might feel she owes me."

He laughed. "I have a feeling a lot of people around here are carrying the same marker."

"I'll never tell. So what's up?"

"I can't just drop by to visit a friend?"

"Sure, but that's not why you're here. You're practically vibrating. CIA, remember?"

He grinned. "I bought a house!"

"You already own a house."

"I'm selling it. I bought a house in Sinful."

I bolted upright, which is always a bad move in a hammock, and struggled for a moment to keep from pitching out of it. Finally, I got my feet planted on the ground and my butt perched on one side. Blanchet never made a move to help. His grin just widened.

"You bought a house in Sinful?" I repeated, not certain I'd heard him correctly.

"Yep. I bought Jenny Babin's house."

Jenny Babin's husband had died from an accidental overdose—or an intentional one, depending on who you asked—and she'd left town as soon as she could.

"But there was a body buried under the porch," I said.

"It's been gone for months and hadn't smelled for decades," Blanchet said. "Besides, do you know what kind of deal you can get on a property when someone was murdered and buried on-site? Not that I took advantage. I paid asking, but it was considerably lower than what the house would have been worth if the dead guy hadn't been there."

I laughed because I got it. It wouldn't have concerned me in the least to have had a corpse in my backyard. In fact, on my first day in Sinful, I'd turned up a body a couple feet from where I was currently sitting. But that didn't explain why Blanchet was selling his home that he'd lived in forever and moving here.

"Why are you moving?" I asked.

"You don't want me here?"

"Of course I want you here. I love having you around. You are a great help to Carter, and you don't give me grief for doing things a bit unorthodox."

He laughed. "'Unorthodox' is a pretty weak word to describe your methods. Your solution to yesterday's escapades was getting a camel high."

"I call that efficient and inventive. Seriously, though, that's great. I'll love having you live here. But what about Maya?"

"She thinks it's a fantastic idea—and yes, she knows about the whole patio-body thing. But Lara is staying in Mudbug and this way, she's close."

"So Maya's officially moving in with you?"

Twenty years ago, Maya had disappeared shortly after beginning a relationship with Blanchet. When he'd come to Sinful to fill in for Carter while he was on his mission in Iran, we'd landed in the middle of a decades-old secret that had not only exposed human trafficking but had returned Maya to him. Seeing their reunion was one of the highlights of my life thus far. Lara was Maya's now-grown daughter, and there was an adorable and funny granddaughter now as well.

Blanchet grinned. "I think we've waited long enough, don't you? I'm pretty sure our relationship can survive living together. God knows, it's survived worse."

"I'm really happy for you. Both of you. You deserve a wonderful life together."

"I agree. So... What about you and Carter?"

"What about us? We're already living a wonderful life together, especially now that the whole Iran situation is in our rearview mirror."

He nodded. "Carter does seem a lot better, but I meant

your living situation. You two ever talk about making things more permanent?"

"No. Don't get me wrong, I love going to bed with Carter and waking up with him—for all the obvious reasons."

Blanchet chuckled. "Yeah."

"But if we lived together, Carter would have to work a lot harder at not knowing what I was up to. Not knowing is probably what's saving us."

"It's none of my business, but I think you're underestimating just how much grief he's willing to tolerate. He loves you, Fortune. Completely and deeply. I know the look because I wear it every time I look at or even think about Maya. I'm not saying you should rush into anything you're not ready for, but don't be afraid to take that leap when it's time, either. None of us are guaranteed tomorrow. Well, I gotta run and pick Maya up. We're furniture shopping. Mine is horrible, and Maya literally came with the clothes on her back, so we've got a lot of ground to cover."

"Have fun. And congratulations, Blanchet. I look forward to having you here. You and Maya."

He gave me a wave and headed off. Merlin got up from his nap and rubbed against my leg, probably thinking it was getting close to dinnertime. He wasn't wrong. I pushed myself out of the hammock and headed for the house, but the whole time, Blanchet's words were running through my mind.

None of us are guaranteed tomorrow.

It was something I'd always known. I'd been the person who made that lack of guarantee a reality for a lot of bad people. But it was only since the situation in Iran that I'd begun to feel that weight when it came to myself and Carter.

Was I ready to take the leap? Was Carter?

I still wasn't sure.

CHAPTER FIVE

I WAS POURING MY FIRST CUP OF COFFEE THE NEXT MORNING when my phone rang. I frowned because Ida Belle and Gertie didn't call. They just showed up. And Carter had been out the door early to help the game warden catch some alligator poachers. No one else would call this early unless it was an emergency.

I grabbed my phone and blinked when I saw the display.

Bayou Inn.

"Hello?" I answered.

"Thank God you're up!" Shadow Chaser's frantic voice said. "I need to hire you. It's a dire situation over here."

"Is someone dead at the motel? Because that's a thing for the ME and maybe the cops, depending on how he died."

"No one's dead here. At least I don't think they are. It's a family situation. I'm on shift today. Can you come up here so I can hire you and you can fix this? I don't do dead people."

"Let's not get ahead of ourselves until I know what needs fixing. Give me some time to have coffee and get dressed and I'll head over."

"I have coffee, but I don't have women's clothes—regardless of what you might find about me online—so definitely get dressed. And hurry!"

He disconnected and I dropped my phone on the table and took a sip of coffee. He sounded like he was in heart attack range, which for Shadow Chaser might mean he'd been stuffed in the trunk of a car by a murderer or he'd accidentally seen a motel patron naked. His dismay had been pretty much the same for both.

I sent Ida Belle a text telling her to round Gertie up and head to my house. That we either had a case or a nervous breakdown we needed to address. I downed my cup of coffee and headed upstairs to change. By the time I had consumed two more cups of coffee and had some breakfast, they were walking in.

Ida Belle looked as if she'd been up for hours, and my guess was she probably had. The woman managed to accomplish more before breakfast than most people did in an entire day. Gertie, on the other hand, looked as if she could have used another week or two of sleep. She was dressed but lacked her usual flair, except for the T-shirt that read *Fueled by Coffee and Chaos*. I wasn't sure if that was directions or a warning.

She sank into a chair. "Whatcha got? I'm starving and still half asleep."

"We can stop by the bakery on our way out and fill up a travel mug with coffee for you. That satisfies the coffee part of your T-shirt. Chaos is guaranteed because Shadow Chaser called me this morning in a panic saying he needs to hire me. Apparently, someone is dead, but not at the motel, and that's all I know."

Gertie perked up. "We've got a case?"

I put my hands up. "It's Shadow Chaser. We won't know until we get the details."

Ida Belle shook her head. "That boy is so drama. He's going to have a heart attack before he's thirty."

"He sounded like he was well on his way," I said. "So I figured we shouldn't keep him waiting any longer than we had to. I'm scared to think of what might happen if Mannie shows up to conduct motel business with Shadow wound up like a spring."

Gertie nodded. "If he's all het up, Mannie giving him a good hard stare might be enough to tip him over the edge. I guess we best hit the road and see what this is about. But I'll take you up on that coffee thing."

"Date night?" I asked.

She shook her head. "Jeb threw his back out with that whole sexy swing debacle. I'm afraid we didn't do any better inside than we did in the tree. The only plus is the ceiling was lower and he dragged the mattress off the bed for me to fall on when he cut the strap. But that mattress thing did him in. He was bedridden for days—and not the kind of bedridden you want, if you know what I mean. There was this one time—"

"No," Ida Belle said.

Gertie waved a hand at her. "Anyway. No date nights for a while. I was over at Nora's house trying out the new pool, and she whipped up a batch of Jell-O shots. I can't remember if we had dinner, but I'm going with probably not. I think the problems started there."

"The problems started when you went to Nora's house and consumed something she made," Ida Belle said.

"She said the shots would take away my leg pain and help me sleep."

Ida Belle snorted. "Death would certainly solve the problem of leg pain."

"I think staying out of that swing would solve the leg problem," I said. "No need to roll the dice on Nora's concoctions."

"Those shots work a lot better than Aleve," Gertie said. "After an hour in the pool, I couldn't even feel my legs anymore."

Ida Belle stared. "Lord help. I hope you weren't driving."

"Of course not. I'm adventurous but I'm not an idiot. I walked over and I guess I walked home."

"You don't remember?" I asked.

She shrugged. "No. Like I said, they worked great for the pain and the sleep. Must have sleepwalked home. But the dreams were crazy. I had this one about me being Tarzan, except the female version. Then I was one of King Arthur's knights in a swordfight. It was all entertaining but also exhausting."

I shook my head, trying to fathom being so out of it I couldn't remember. I wouldn't like it. I hated when I wasn't aware of everything. I was on guard even while sleeping.

"So you just woke up at home in bed?" I asked.

"In my bathtub, actually. Apparently I needed a shower. And I have a rash on the back of my legs near my butt. I must have gotten into something in Nora's backyard. Looks like poison ivy. I lotioned it up good this morning."

"Next time Jeb throws his back out, maybe you should just stay home and watch a movie," Ida Belle said. "Let's get this show on the road before Gertie starts scratching her butt."

We stopped at the bakery for coffee and pastries to go and as we were headed out, Carter crossed the street, shaking his head.

"It's early to be wearing that look," Ida Belle said.

"Why do you think I'm headed to the bakery?" he asked. "I'm hoping to load up on enough sugar to improve my morning."

"What's going on?" I asked.

"I've had five calls already from upset residents. Three of

them reported a half-naked old woman climbing trees in their front yards. One said the woman climbed onto their kid's tire swing and was doing bird calls. The last one said someone ripped a picket out of their fence and hacked one of their bushes up with it. The whole thing has been flattened. It looks like whoever did it fell on it when they turned to leave."

"Couldn't have been that old if she was climbing trees," Gertie grumbled in her coffee.

"No one called the sheriff's department last night?" I asked.

He shook his head. "They didn't call the sheriff's department because they didn't want Deputy Breaux to have to tackle an old, mostly naked lady. And she was acting so bizarrely that they were all afraid to leave their homes and confront her themselves."

"Crazy isn't contagious," I said.

Ida Belle frowned. "Hmmmmmm."

"And no one recognized her?" I asked.

"Apparently, she was wearing a mask," he said. "But she left her shirt and pants scattered down the block, and that bush she fell in was full of poison ivy. Shouldn't take long to figure it out."

"I'll bet you're already close," Ida Belle said.

Gertie mumbled something and headed for the SUV.

Carter looked at Ida Belle, then back at me and groaned. "It was Gertie, wasn't it?"

"Since we were at home sleeping, like all decent people," Ida Belle said, "we cannot confirm or deny, but I'd watch for butt-scratching the next couple days."

Carter sighed. "I don't even want to know. I've still got PTSD from that swing thing."

"This one wasn't nearly as scandalous," I said. "She had Jell-O shots at Nora's."

"Holy crap. I'm about to double my bakery order. Then I'll go collect the clothes, take statements, and put this one in the unsolved file."

"Don't unsolved cases go against your record?" Ida Belle asked. "I'm thinking about the election."

"I'd rather lose the election than question Nora or have Gertie tell me about her itchy butt. Why are you out this early, anyway?"

"We might have a case," I said. "Unless Shadow Chaser is being overly dramatic and exaggerating the problem, although he did mention a dead person."

Carter shook his head. "I can't take Shadow Chaser's nonsense on top of Gertie. I haven't gotten any calls from the motel, so I'm going to pray his issue is personal and in another parish, maybe even another state."

"One can only hope," I said.

We climbed into the SUV and Ida Belle looked in her rearview mirror at Gertie, shaking her head. "You left out the part of your story where you were naked in all those 'dreams.'"

"He said 'almost,'" Gertie argued. "I woke up in the bathtub with my undergarments on. How the heck was I supposed to know that was all I was wearing when I got there?"

"Because the clothes you left the house wearing weren't on your body or in your house the next day?" I suggested.

"I was never one for logic problems," Gertie said.

Ida Belle threw her arms up. "Then how about because you're supposed to know what you're doing when you're awake? You're not supposed to be wandering the neighborhood in your skivvies killing bushes and frightening people with your itchy butt."

"It didn't itch until this morning."

The look of dismay on Ida Belle's face almost matched

Carter's, and I couldn't help but laugh. Don't get me wrong, I didn't want to see skivvies or butt-scratching either, but if that was the worst thing I was going to hear today, I'd be thrilled.

But given the absolute panic in Shadow's voice, I had my doubts.

SHADOW CHASER MUST HAVE BEEN WATCHING FROM THE office window because he bolted out the door like a well-tipped valet at an expensive resort as soon as we pulled in. He flung the passenger door open and started motioning like we were about to miss last call for the champagne brunch.

We headed inside and took seats in the old metal chairs in what served as the lobby, which wasn't much bigger than an average bathroom. Shadow Chaser paced the length of the room—three steps one way then three steps the other, brushing our knees every time he passed—until Ida Belle held her hand up to stop him.

"If you pivot and pace one more time," she said, "I'm just going to stick out a foot and let you eat that wall."

"Why don't you tell us what happened," I said.

"Don't you think I'm trying? There's just so much, I don't even know where to start. And it's all important and it all needs fixing and Oh. My. God. How is this happening?"

Gertie pulled a lunch bag out of her purse, and I marveled at how absolutely nothing got in the way of her appetite. But then she dumped the sandwich in her lap and thrust the bag at Shadow Chaser.

"Breath in that before you pass out," she said.

Shadow grabbed the bag and started huffing in it, likely making everything worse. I checked the weather on my phone, and Ida Belle pulled out her pocketknife and started cleaning her fingernails. Gertie, figuring she wasn't going to get her bag back anytime soon, and likely wouldn't want it after all that huffing, started eating her sandwich. I really hoped he got a grip by lunchtime because my breakfast was already wearing off and I had made it a policy to avoid food from Gertie's purse ever since she started getting some of her 'groceries' at Nora's.

Finally, he lowered the bag and started blabbering.

"So there's this dead guy and they're saying it's accidental but that can't be because then it would be my great-uncle's fault and there's no way he made that kind of mistake. And he and my aunt can't afford bad press because this is their only way of making it and it was all my idea so it's all my fault, so you have to fix it."

I waited for something more—like an actual description of the problem—but Shadow just stared at me, wearing an expectant look.

I glanced at Ida Belle and Gertie, who both shrugged.

"I'm going to need a little more information," I said. "Real information. Starting with, who is the dead guy?"

"I don't know. Some guy."

"Okay, let's try again. Who are your aunt and uncle, and how do they know the dead guy?"

"They don't *know* him. Aunt Petunia and Uncle Corndog have a B and B. The dead guy rented a room along with some of his friends. They're having a class reunion or something like that and met up early. He died night before last and they found him yesterday, but my aunt and uncle didn't tell me about it until this morning, and now I'm freaking out."

Finally, we were getting somewhere.

"How did the customer die?"

He glanced away. "Sort of natural causes."

"I catch killers. If you're trying to catch natural causes, you need the medical examiner or a doctor, but I have a feeling you already knew that."

He blew out a breath. "They said he had an allergic reaction to something he ate the night before and suffocated."

"So anaphylactic shock. What was he allergic to?"

"Peanuts. And they're saying that my uncle used peanut oil to fry the fish he served that night, but there's no way he would have made that kind of mistake. My aunt and uncle knew he had a peanut allergy and Corndog knows how serious it is because his mother had one."

Thing started to fall into place.

"Are the police saying they're going to press charges?"

"No. I think they're going with it being a horrible accident for the moment, but what if that changes? What if the dead guy's family sues? They don't have any money. Why do you think they've been seeing after strangers in their own home? They even gave up their bedroom and moved into the servants' room off the kitchen just to make more profit. They'd slept in that room for over forty years."

Shadow was now on the verge of tears, and I really didn't want to see a grown man cry. Not even a wimpy one.

"Where do your aunt and uncle live?" I asked.

He handed me a brochure and my eyes widened. "The Voodoo Island Inn—a haunted B and B experience."

Gertie perked up. "Your aunt and uncle own the house on Voodoo Island? That's awesome."

"Not at the moment, it isn't," Shadow said. "Even if no one sues, the bad publicity will kill their business, and without the business, they can't afford to keep the house. Everything has gotten so expensive, and they don't have much left except the house. That's why I suggested they convert it into a B and B. I figured at least that way they'd make enough to cover their expenses and they could still live there."

I frowned and looked down at the brochure again. "It says here that 100 years ago, five people were killed in the house by an axe murderer. Seems to me that a peanut death pales in comparison."

"That's just for advertisement," he said. "You know, to create atmosphere?"

"What atmosphere is that creating?" I asked. "The don't-take-a-shower kind?"

He blew out a breath. "Look. All rentals can't indulge in the no-tell-motel business model and make a profit like this place does. And besides, I didn't want those kind of people in the house with my aunt and uncle."

"Criminals, people cheating on their spouses, or dead people? Because you got one of those for sure. Who knows, maybe all three."

His eyes widened. "Are you saying someone killed him?"

"What if a ghost killed him?" Gertie asked.

"Then he'd need an exorcist," I said. "Look, I'm saying I don't know enough to say anything at all, but let's play the guessing game for a moment. You said the customers were here for a reunion. Don't sparks fly between old lovers at reunions? So maybe the dead guy decided to have a fling with one of his classmates, his spouse found out, murdered him, and pinned it on your uncle."

"You think that's what happened?"

I threw my hands in the air. "No. I don't think that's what happened. I don't think anything at all because I barely *know* anything at all. I'm a detective, not a clairvoyant."

He looked disappointed but finally nodded. "I know it's not an attractive look, but I'm begging you to help. Even if my aunt and uncle avoid arrest or a courtroom, I don't want them to get those insufferable sideways looks and the 'bless your hearts' and all the rest of the cold shoulder moves that the South is famous for. And I don't want them cast out of their own home because of a foolish idea of mine that was meant to save it. So will you take the case?"

"The case to find out if there's actually a case? Sure. I'll ask some questions and see what I come up with."

He grabbed my hands and started shaking them. "Thank you! I don't know how I'll ever repay you...or pay you, actually. Do you offer payment plans?"

I managed to extract my hands from his. "Don't worry about it. Given all the trouble we've caused here, I figure I owe you."

He grabbed my hands again, then sank onto his knees and started sobbing. About that time, the front door opened and Mannie walked in. He paused and raised one eyebrow.

"I'm not trying to tell you how to conduct your personal affairs, but I don't think the sheriff will appreciate you proposing to his girlfriend."

Shadow jumped up from the floor like it was on fire. "No, I wasn't...I would never..."

Mannie smiled, which only seemed to scare him more. Maybe he wasn't as big an idiot as I thought.

"I would hope not," Mannie said.

"Shadow's aunt and uncle are in a bind, and I'm going to look into it for him," I said. "As a favor for all the times he's helped me with cases."

Mannie's smile widened as he stared at his clearly flustered manager. "You've never told me you helped Fortune with her investigations. You'll have to fill me in sometime."

Shadow's eyes widened and he paled. "I, absolutely, that would be great, I'll pencil it in. If you'll excuse me, I think I left my car door open."

He practically sprinted out of the lobby.

"You know he's scared when he's running for daylight," Gertie said.

Mannie nodded. "That and he doesn't own a car."

We all laughed.

"Moped?" I asked.

"Got it in one," Mannie said. "This thing you're looking into for him, let me know if you need any help. Despite the fact that he wants to flee every time he sees me, I kind of like the kid."

I nodded. "He's growing on me."

"How's Carter doing now that you put the Arms Committee in their place?"

"Much better. I think Kitts's dying was a big weight off his shoulders. He can't change the past, but at least it can't happen again. Not with Kitts, anyway."

Mannie nodded. "And hopefully Kitts was a lesson and they'll be watching a little closer from now on."

"Carter said the same thing."

Gertie narrowed her eyes at Mannie. "Hey, how come you didn't ask how any of us were doing?"

"Because the three of you probably enjoyed making them crazy."

I laughed. "Busted. It was pretty spectacular. I'll swing by soon and fill you and the Heberts in on everything. Sorry I haven't been by already. I've been trying to detox from it all."

Mannie gave me a single nod, and given his past as a Navy SEAL, I knew he understood exactly what I was saying.

"We better get going," I said. "I need to talk to Shadow's aunt and uncle and see if there's anything we can do. And if he stays outside any longer, he won't get rid of that sunburn until fall."

Mannie gave us a wave and we headed out. Shadow must

have been lurking in the breezeway because he hurried over as soon as we walked to the SUV.

"Is there anything I need to do?" he asked. "To help, I mean."

I nodded. "What are your aunt and uncle's names?"

"Aunt Petunia and Uncle Corndog."

I stared. "I mean their real names."

He looked confused. "That's the only names I know."

"Never mind. I'll figure it out. Please call Petunia and Corndog and let them know we're coming. I assume we'll need a ride onto the island? Or is there a bridge?"

Ida Belle and Gertie both laughed.

"No bridge then," I said. "So unless there's a Water Uber out there, we're going to need someone to pick us up. Text me contact information and I'll call when we're getting close."

"Thank you," he said. "Seriously. Thank you. I know I panic every time I see you drive into my parking lot and fear a lot for my life and my sanity, but you're good at your job. I mean the investigating one, not whatever you did for the CIA. Please don't CIA my family."

"I'll try to contain myself."

CHAPTER SIX

Ida Belle was still chuckling at Shadow Chaser when she pulled onto the highway.

"Okay, so where is this Voodoo Island, what is it haunted by, and why do people accept a nickname like Corndog and carry it into their senior years?"

"Voodoo Island is about an hour southwest of here," Ida Belle said. "It's basically a blip on the map in the middle of a swamp close to the Gulf. I've never heard anything about it being haunted, and my guess is that was Shadow's marketing take, figuring an isolated, creepy old house with a ghost would be a bigger draw than an inconvenient old house surrounded by dirty water and bugs. And that last question is too much to unpack in this lifetime, and I'm not certain I have an answer, anyway."

"Have you ever been there?"

They both shook their heads.

"It's always been a private residence," Ida Belle said.

Gertie nodded. "And far as I know, there's only the one house on the island. It really is small—a couple acres at the most—and surrounded by a swamp full of alligators. Boats are the only way on or off because one person could not afford to build a bridge with the engineering it would require. It's a good quarter mile from the island to the bank."

"Why in the world would someone build a big house out there?"

"Rumor is it was built by pirates as a hideout," Ida Belle said. "Someone—a relative of Shadow's maybe—bought a bunch of swampland down there probably eighty or more years back, and they discovered the house on the island. It was covered with vines, and it's completely hidden from the bank by cypress trees."

"I can see why pirates would like the location," I said. "If the only access people had were boats, and you couldn't spot it just passing by in one, then it would be the perfect place to lie low while conducting business. But how has it stood all these years without a hurricane taking it out?"

"Ah, that's where the voodoo thing comes in," Gertie said. "The rumors also say that the pirates had a voodoo priestess cast a spell of protection on the island, and that's why the house has weathered all storms."

"Apparently, that doesn't apply to the occupants," I said.

"You can't win them all," Ida Belle said. "But the real answer is likely that the center of the island is a good twenty feet above sea level. And from what I've heard, the house is raised another five feet or so, which means the storm surge would have to be over twenty-five feet to get inside. Being surrounded by ancient, thick trees gives it protection from the wind. And then there's the fact that everything was built better back then, especially for people with the money to put into the construction."

"Well, I can't wait to see the place. I assume since Carter wasn't called about the death, it's in a different parish than Sinful?"

"Yeah. The sheriff over there is a fool," Gertie said.

"Fool is far too polite," Ida Belle said. "That man is a waste of oxygen."

I raised an eyebrow. "Tell me how you really feel. So who is this man, and why should we cut off his air supply?"

"I retract part of my statement," Ida Belle said. "He's not a man."

Gertie nodded. "His name is Bryce Benoit. And he— Well, heck, I was going to say he grew up in Sinful, but that won't work because he still hasn't matured. And saying he was raised in Sinful doesn't work either because if he'd had any raising he might not be the biggest douche in the state."

"How old is this guy?" I asked.

"A year younger than Carter," Ida Belle said. "And there's always been a rivalry there—one-sided, of course. Carter wouldn't pee on Bryce if he was on fire. But Bryce always had this attitude like Carter was somehow preventing everyone from seeing his greatness."

"And he was the laziest human being in the world," Gertie said. "Even as a kid. He used to promise the, uh, unpopular girls dates if they'd do his homework. Got caught cheating on his tests all the time, which was no small surprise since he'd never read the material and mostly slept through class."

"Then how did he graduate?"

Gertie rubbed her fingers together. "His parents inherited some money, and since their number one goal in life was not dealing with anything unpleasant, they threw money at whatever problems Bryce created."

"So they didn't like adulting but thought it was a good idea to have a kid?" I shook my head, marveling at the superbly flawed logic.

"I don't think they intended to have one," Ida Belle said. "My guess is they were as lazy about prevention as they were about parenting. Bryce comes by his dedication to doing nothing honestly."

"Do I know his parents?" I was searching my mind for a Benoit that might have fit the bill but hadn't hit on one.

"No. They practically fled the state the day he turned eighteen," Gertie said. "He hadn't even finished high school yet, but that's when he got a hold of his trust. They just signed over the deed to the house, packed their personal things, and waved as they were driving out of town. It was all rather cold."

I shrugged. "My father faked his own death—twice. I'm afraid it will take more than disinterest with an open checkbook to make me believe he didn't have a choice in remaining useless as an adult."

"Bingo," Ida Belle said. "After high school he went to the police academy. Worked in three different cities for a matter of days before they fired him. Then his reputation preceded him, and he couldn't get hired. So he came back to Sinful and got a job with the sheriff's department."

"Why on earth would Sheriff Lee hire him?" I asked.

"He didn't," Gertie said. "Lee was out with something—gallstones, kidney stones—anyway, Mayor Fontleroy hired him because he'd been buddies with his father. And we all figure the mayor cashed a nice big check for his trouble."

Ida Belle nodded. "Then he proceeded to crap on that job. If he went out on a call, he'd try to convince people not to file a report because he didn't want to bother with the paperwork. If they did file, he'd just stack the folders on his desk and never work them. When he got called on it, he started paying other deputies to work his cases and let him take the credit."

"There's useless and then there's Bryce Benoit," Gertie said. "He tried for years to get out of Sinful and back into the city. That's where he really wanted to be, but the cities already had his number. Then he set his sights on being sheriff, figuring Lee wasn't long for the saddle. It was the only way for Bryce to get the authority to lord over more people."

"Then Carter came back and all bets were off," Ida Belle said. "Everyone loved and trusted Carter, and Carter is actually good at the job. Bryce knew he'd never win an election against him, so he bounced to the parish next door. Shortly after, the sheriff there—who everyone thought would die in his office chair—announced his retirement, endorsed Bryce as his replacement, and bought a new bass boat."

I shook my head. "What are the chances this death will get anything more than a cursory look by the illustrious sheriff?"

"Less than none," Gertie said.

"What about the medical examiner?"

"Fired from as many places as Bryce and reputation about as good," Ida Belle said.

I sighed. "So we have a collection of castoffs who aren't employable anywhere else. Great. Any chance this idiot *hasn't* heard of me and my relationship with Carter?"

"Also less than none." Gertie said. "Bryce is still trying to one-up Carter. You can bet he knows every move Carter makes."

"You know, this whole elected cop thing has some flaws," I said. "Except in Carter's case."

"Definitely," Ida Belle agreed. "On the plus side, there's a lot of low-key complaining about his lack of care. And even more talk about him taking money to look the other way when people's spoiled kids are problematic."

"So he's become his own parents, except his kids are everyone in the parish who has money to buy his complicity. Good. God."

"It might be his undoing," Gertie said. "The election's coming up, and I wouldn't be surprised if Bryce is out. I've heard that trust fund is running low, and those without big bank accounts are tired of a handful of rich people buying their way out of trouble."

"It doesn't sound like he's capable of real police work, even if he wanted to do some. If this does turn out to be a murder, and he can't solve it, maybe it will be the final nail in his coffin."

Ida Belle nodded. "Unfortunately, he'll be nailing Corndog in there with him."

GIVEN MITIGATING FACTORS—MOSTLY CARTER'S HISTORY with Bryce and Gertie's history with boats—I figured it was probably best if I let Carter know where we were going. It was an island, after all, and I'd already been warned that cell phone coverage would likely be spotty, especially if a storm cropped up. I didn't even want to think about the weather, since I'd also been informed that the shallow water and cypress knees prevented anything bigger than small flat-bottom boats getting across it. I didn't want to imagine how long construction had taken, hauling only a handful of two-by-fours at a time.

Carter sounded a bit better when he answered his phone than he had when we'd left Sinful that morning.

"How's the case of the near-naked tree-climber going?" I asked.

"Depends on who you're asking. Since no one could identify the woman by her underwear, and I have refused to search everyone's home or person looking for pink-and-black leopard-spotted undergarments, it's going fine for me. But the destroyed bush people were not happy with my refusal to dig through underwear drawers or strip-search women in the street."

"They're just being ridiculous. Tell them you received an

anonymous envelope of money to cover the cost of a new bush and fence repair and they'll be fine."

"That's actually not a bad idea. Thanks! Tell Gertie I'll be billing her with an upcharge. She can consider it a processing fee in lieu of the fine she'd get if I was being honest with my residents."

"I heard that," Gertie said. "And all of it is speculation."

Ida Belle and I looked at her.

"Fine, I'll drop cash off as soon as we get back," she said.

"Back from where?" he asked.

"That's what I called to tell you—we caught a case. Well, sort of a case. I'm looking into this situation of Shadow Chaser's as a favor."

"Just curious, why would you do him a favor?"

Since most of the reasons I felt we owed Shadow were the same things we'd sworn to Carter that we'd had no part in, I couldn't exactly tell him it was because we regularly destroyed hotel property, spied on guests, broke into rooms, blew things up, or anything else that might compromise his position as sheriff. Besides, if Shadow was keeping mum about it all, why would I volunteer incriminating tales?

"He's not a bad kid," I said. "And his aunt and uncle are in a sticky situation. Since the motel is one of the properties Mannie has taken over, I don't want Shadow so distracted he gets on Mannie's bad side. And I don't want Mannie dealing with issues he wouldn't otherwise have to."

Since Mannie had been crucial to rescuing Carter, I knew he wouldn't question my involvement given the SEAL's tangential association with the motel manager.

"Hmmmm. You never call when you've taken on a new case. Why the warning this time?"

"Because we're headed to Voodoo Island, which is where Shadow's aunt and uncle live. If we get stuck there for whatever reason and cell phone service is crap, I wanted someone besides Shadow to know where we were."

"You mean if there's a Gertie situation, and you can't call for help, you want me to come looking for you if you're not back by dinner."

"Yes," Ida Belle said.

"Ha," Carter said. "That's what I figured. Please tell me this case doesn't involve anything criminal."

"I was led to believe that nothing that happens in that parish is listed as 'criminal.'"

"Yeah, that's the problem. Do me a favor, make every effort to avoid Bryce Benoit. He's looking for any possible reason to get something on me."

"The DOD couldn't get anything on me. Do you really think that loser stands a chance?"

"No. But he could lock you up just to cause trouble, and I don't want Alexander getting his Rolls dirty, driving it down to Bryce's territory to deal with his high school grudge."

"You know I avoid law enforcement if possible. And it doesn't sound like this one is interested in working, so maybe he'll stay away, and I won't even have the displeasure of meeting him."

"If he hears you're there, he'll find you. Bet on that. I've got to run. One of Fred's cows got loose and just made her way into the flower shop. She's eating the profits."

Gertie shook her head as I slipped my phone back into my pocket. "Carter is spread too thin. I'd hoped he'd take some time off after DC, but he just jumped right back in the next day."

"I think he's better if he's working," I said. "Too much time sitting around is just more time to dwell on things that can't be changed."

Ida Belle nodded. "I agree, but Gertie's not wrong. He *is*

spread too thin. I know adding Harrison has helped, but the parish is growing quickly. A lot of people are leaving cities for a slower pace, even if they're still working in them. They're fine with the commute as long as the quality of life after they clock out is better."

"But it's not all the time," Gertie said. "Last week, I was dropping off a casserole to Myrtle and they were playing charades. How do you justify the payroll for another full-time officer when the problems seem to happen all at once or not at all?"

"There might be a solution on the horizon," I said.

Then I told them about Blanchet buying Jenny's house.

"When Blanchet moves to Sinful, he'll be available for contract work, and since he's already approved by the system, it shouldn't be a problem bringing him last minute to help out."

Gertie and Ida Belle were both smiling, and I knew they were as pleased as I was that Blanchet was going to be a Sinful resident.

"That's awesome news!" Gertie said.

Ida Belle nodded. "That is the perfect solution to Carter's staffing problems, and we couldn't ask for someone better than Blanchet to close the gap."

"Especially since he likes us," Gertie said. "And doesn't complain about our methods."

"That's because he doesn't have to worry about elections," Ida Belle said. "Carter doesn't have the luxury of being amused at our shenanigans."

I nodded. "I know, and I've been thinking. We've gotten a little lax in that whole hidden-agenda thing. I think we need to be a little more covert with our less-than-legal stuff."

"So go back to making up outrageous lies that Carter pretends to believe?" Gertie asked.

"Good idea," Ida Belle said. "Walter is smart enough not to ask questions he doesn't want to hear the answers to, but given that it's Carter's job to ask, he's between a rock and Fortune. And no offense, but you make the rock look like a pillow."

"I take it as a compliment."

Ida Belle grinned. "Which makes my point."

"I'm fine with telling stories," Gertie said. "I've got plenty of real-life stuff to draw off of. God knows, people wouldn't believe most of what I've done. Except you two, of course."

"That's because we're usually there rescuing you," Ida Belle said. "I could do with a little less knowledge of some things."

Gertie shrugged. "Even if I become the model of decorum, you have Ronald to deal with now. He's no slouch in the outrageous department."

"Don't remind me," I said. "I'm still seeing that superhero unitard in my nightmares. Carter walked into my house the other day, and a Marvel movie was playing on the TV. He actually flinched before I changed the channel."

I looked up as we passed a sign indicating that the town of Curses was only two miles away. Since we'd been driving almost an hour, I had to assume we were getting close to Voodoo Island.

"Curses?" I asked

"Seemed befitting," Gertie said. "Voodoo Island and Curses. The town council voted to make curses illegal though."

"Of course they did," I said.

Living in Sinful—where mostly everything that equated to a sinful behavior was illegal—I already had some experience with bayou town lawmaking.

"But there's a twist," Ida Belle said. "When they drew up the laws and voted on them, the document hadn't been proofread, so instead of making curses against the law, they actually voted to make cursing against the law."

I stared. "No one is allowed to curse—in any form—in Curses?"

"Exactly."

Fascinating. "So who decides what the curse words are?"

"That's been a hot debate for years now, but most people just err on the side of caution and don't say anything they wouldn't use in church."

"Good. God." I shook my head. "Can I even say that?"

They both shrugged.

As we pulled into Curses, I took a look around. It was tiny—I mean it made Sinful look like a metropolis. There was a total of three buildings, all of which had seen better days. A gun shop, a church, and a bait store, which according to the signage also served as boat repair, general store, and a restaurant.

"Well, I see they have the three most important things covered," I said. "No sheriff's department?"

"It's in Meditation—north of here and closer to Houma," Ida Belle said.

"Should I even ask?"

"A bunch of years back, someone hired a yogi to move here and break the curse on Voodoo Island," Gertie said. "He convinced people he was blessed with special powers that kept the curse away, so he stayed. The town used to be called Tackle & Bait but in appreciation for his services, they voted to change the name."

"Uh-huh. And how much money did this yogi bilk them for?"

Ida Belle snorted. "A house, maintenance, cooking, cleaning, and whatever money they could come up with for his 'fees.'"

"How long did that go on?"

"Until Number Three hit."

I knew what number two was and the island that shared the name had been dubbed so for a reason, but I was almost afraid to ask what a Number Three was.

Ida Belle must have noticed my confusion. "A hurricane. 1926. They didn't really start naming them until the '50s. Blew the whole town away, including the yogi's house, so they figured the hurricane was sent to expose his scam."

"Then why not change the name back?"

"Because it's a hassle and an expense to get everything changed," Ida Belle said. "Lawyers, paperwork, business registrations, driver's licenses, street signs. They put it to a vote and the people said enough."

"Is cursing allowed in Meditation?" I asked.

"Since Meditation copied Curses' laws to save money on drafting their own, no."

"But Meditation added an amendment," Gertie said. "You can curse when sitting cross-legged. I saw a bar fight there once. Looked like a bunch of drunk Russians dancing, except without the kicking."

I considered this for a moment and decided it was just ridiculous enough to warrant an in-person viewing. "We might just have to make a side trip to one of those bars on the way home."

"There's only one," Gertie said.

"Less things to have to choose, right?" I said as Ida Belle pulled into a clearing that was little more than a patch of dirt in front of a rickety dock.

Two newer-model SUVs were already parked there, so she squeezed in beside them and I climbed out and surveyed the pier.

"That thing looks like it's going to fall over at any moment," I said. "Is this really where they launch their boats?"

If the pier was in that bad of shape, I didn't even want to

know what was going on with the ramp. For all I knew the only part left might be the piece I saw descending into the murky water.

"It does look rough," Ida Belle agreed. "We probably shouldn't all stand on it at one time."

"I can't believe people want to stay in a haunted house enough to do this," I said.

"I can," Gertie said. "I've always wanted to see the island and the house. It's the stuff of legend in these parts."

"It's also the stuff you can get to by boat," I said, "which everyone over the age of five seems to have access to around here. Why didn't you jaunt out there and look around?"

She looked at me as if I was crazy. "Because it's cursed, remember? You don't want to risk bringing that sort of thing home with you."

"You went to Harrison and Cassidy's house and everyone swears it's haunted," I pointed out.

"That's ghosts," Gertie said. "Ghosts and curses are two entirely different things. Ghosts are like bringing home some drunk guy you met at a bar. Curses are like bringing home an STD."

"You're going now."

She shrugged. "I think I can handle a curse now."

I wasn't about to ask why that was the case.

"I don't subscribe to any of that nonsense," Ida Belle said. "And I mean all of it—ghosts, curses, STDs—because I don't believe in the first two and wouldn't expose myself to the last one. But there's a lot of superstition in this parts, so most probably believe there's some truth in the old tales of curses. Someone dying out there is only going to fuel that fire."

I heard a boat engine and looked over to see a small bass boat approaching.

Early seventies. Six foot two. Thin and wiry—which described his physique as well as what was left of his hair. His overalls strap bunched on the left side and the lowered shoulder indicated some arthritis. No glasses. Threat level nil unless he actually needed glasses, especially since he was driving the boat.

We started toward the rickety dock, but instead of pulling up beside it, he drove right for the ramp. Holy crap! We all stared for a moment, then scattered. We'd seen boats launch up ramps and embankments more times than we wanted, and it never ended well for the boat or anything in its path.

But just before he reached the ramp, he cut the motor and the boat turned sideways and pulled up right beside the ramp. Holy crap. The entire thing really *was* missing below the water line. He looked over at me and squinted, calling into question that whole no-glasses thing, then smiled.

"You must be Fortune," he said. "My nephew told us you were as smart as you were annoying, but he didn't mention how pretty you are. Or young. Are you old enough to drive?"

"Did your nephew fail to mention that I used to work for the CIA?"

He frowned. "No...wait. Yes, I think he did mention something of the sort. My memory gets the better of me sometimes. Anyway, we got a surprise storm moving in, so if you're ready to go, let's do it. You don't want to get caught out in a storm in these swamps. A couple months ago, I got hit by one coming back from a grocery run. It pushed me so far into the backwaters I didn't even know where I was. Took me two days to work my way out, and I was darn near out of gas before I found the dock again."

He grinned. "Boy, Petunia was mad. Not only did her milk spoil but I ate all the potato chips. Anyway, best get going."

Since all we had on us were weapons and whatever was in Gertie's purse and bra, getting stranded for two days in a small boat didn't sound like an adventure I was interested in. Especially since I knew Gertie's purse was already down one sandwich. So we all stepped into the boat and scooted around to find seats on the two benches.

"How many bedrooms do you have?" I asked as he pushed off and began our slow trip across the swamp.

"Eight. That doesn't include our suite off the kitchen. There was one more, but it's so small it wouldn't have fit more than a twin bed, so we turned it into a linen closet."

Eight rooms. Jesus. I wondered briefly if this was how Corndog transported his customers and their baggage, because every time a new person had stepped onto the boat the whole thing had swayed as if it was going to tip over. If this was his only transport, then it must take him half a day to get them all over to the island if they were full and they had a lot of luggage.

"And how many were booked when the unfortunate event took place?"

"Six. They're all old friends here for a class reunion this weekend in Houma and figured they'd come early and visit amongst themselves before the reunion kicked off."

Ida Belle raised her eyebrows. "So everyone staying there knew each other, including the one who died?"

Corndog nodded, his expression sad. "Poor guy. They were having such a good time that night—least it seemed that way when we was out there, and the racket didn't dim any when we left. But Petunia and I learned a while back to get earplugs, so we just finished with the cleanup and headed to bed after we was all done eating."

"And the ME said it was anaphylactic shock that killed him?"

"That's what he said, but I swear, I didn't cook anything in peanut oil. They told me about his allergy before they made the reservation to make sure we could accommodate him. Not like you can head out to a restaurant or order up one of them deliveries on the island, so what we serve is what you've got to eat. And I might not remember everything as good as I did when I was twenty, but I darn sure know the difference between peanut oil and vegetable oil. And my momma was allergic, so I've always been careful-like."

"What did you serve?"

"We had a fish fry. They're popular, especially when the house is booked by a group. They enjoy being outside around the fryer, drinking and talking. It gives people who never lived in these parts a new experience and gives the ones who had to move to cities to work a visit down memory lane."

"I can see that. Is there a chance that he brought something in with him that had peanuts in it?"

"I don't see why he would. The man's been living with this allergy all his life. If he'd made it to adulthood without making bad choices, I don't see as how he'd make them now."

"But you said he was drunk, right?"

"Drunk as skunks when Petunia and I headed in, but unless one of his friends brought something and was fool enough to give it to him, I don't see how he could have come by it. We checked our pantry and there's nothing missing."

"Do you measure the peanut oil left after using it?"

"Why on earth would I do that?"

"You wouldn't, but my point is while food might not have been missing, oil could have been."

"Well, unless he drank some out of the jug, which even being drunk wouldn't explain, I don't see how it matters."

I shrugged. "Just covering all bases. Did the cops ask you any of this?"

He snorted. "That boy is not and never will be a cop. He should be ashamed to wear the badge, but that's what happens when someone goes their whole life getting everything they want. That nephew of mine might lend himself to drama, and I don't understand why he doesn't put down that computer and go fishing, but at least he works. He came up with this whole B and B idea. Did he tell you?"

I nodded. I had a million more questions, but they could wait until I got to the house and got the lay of the land. It helped to actually see a place to get things into perspective, and I wanted to meet Petunia as well and make a decision on her credibility. So far, I didn't doubt anything Corndog had said, but that didn't necessarily mean he knew everything about the situation or that his recounting was accurate. Two sets of eyes were better than one, especially older eyes.

"His plan's been working just fine," Corndog continued. "We got caught up on our taxes and paid for a few repairs. Based on the reservations, we should have been able to get the roof done this summer, but now, we just don't know."

His expression was bleak, and I couldn't help feeling sorry for him. To face losing your home this late in life was a tragedy, and to have come this far and then lose right before the finish line—so to speak—would be even harder. Small successes had already been celebrated. Hopes had already been raised.

"Unlessin' folks has got a garden and like sittin' in the dark, I don't know how they can afford to eat these days," he continued. "Didn't no one plan on all us old codgers living this long—least of all the government. You seen a Social Security check? Couldn't support a house cat."

Gertie nodded. "We've had several of our Sinful residents who had to sell and move off to live with their kids. Killed them to do so, but with trying to maintain the properties and the way expenses keep going up, it got to be too much. And they had a community helping when they could. You don't even have that out here on this island."

Corndog nodded. "We didn't think about it when we

moved in. We was a lot younger and just excited to be here, and still are, truth be known. We love the house, the island, everything about it, really. I don't know what we'd do if we lost it."

"Try not to worry about it," I said. "I know that's impossible, but let me do my job. I'm good at putting the pieces together, and Ida Belle and Gertie are good at ferreting them out. We don't want you to lose your house either."

He sniffed and nodded. "I can't tell you how much I appreciate this. I don't know how I'll ever repay you."

"It's a favor for your nephew. He's helped us out with investigations a few times. That motel he works at tends to attract some of the people I end up hunting."

"That place has always been more than a little unsavory. He claims the new owners are going to improve the place and the reputation though."

"That seems to be the plan."

No way I was going to tell him that Big and Little Hebert were the new owners. He'd probably have a heart attack right here in the boat.

"There she is," he said and pointed.

I looked over and got my first glimpse at Voodoo Island.

CHAPTER SEVEN

THE ISLAND SEEMED OUT OF PLACE IN THE SWAMP. ALL THE surrounding land was low and flat with only marsh grass covering it. But this tiny patch of land rose out of the swamp as if it had been summoned there, trees so dense you couldn't see more than a couple of feet past the first wall of them.

Storm clouds had picked up overhead, and everything had gotten dim. There was a fine mist around the entire island that looked almost like fog. With the heavy moss hanging from the trees lining the edge of the island and the voodoo doll tied to a post on the pier, it looked like a scene from a scary movie.

Gertie, clearly excited, leaned over and whispered, "If the dock is this spooky, I can't wait to see the house."

Corndog tied off the boat, and as we climbed onto the dock, he lifted Gertie's purse out of the boat and his eyes widened.

"Lord help, you got an anvil in here?" he asked. "You best let me carry this for you. It's a bit of a walk, and luggage service is something I'm responsible for."

I thought for a minute Gertie might argue, but then I remembered we were talking about a Southern man of a certain age, and our host. She just nodded and thanked him. He picked up the purse straps, still frowning over the weight, and stepped off the pier and onto a dirt path.

"Rain's coming in fast," he said as he lifted his head and sniffed the air. "We best get to the house before it gets us. They was all in the library when I left."

"Wait...they're all still here?" I asked as we set off up the path.

"Yep. They prepaid and said they saw no point in trying to find another place and hauling out of here just for a couple nights. I figured some of 'em might be staying with family in Houma for the reunion and probably don't want to be there any longer than they have to be. Family can be a blessing or a curse."

"Seems an appropriate statement in this case," Ida Belle said.

I nodded. So given the choice of spending a couple extra nights with family or staying in a 'haunted' B and B where your good friend died, they'd all chosen the B and B. That said something about the people I was about to meet, but I didn't know what. Not yet, anyway.

We were about twenty yards into the trees when the thunder started overhead. Corndog and his sniffer had apparently called it correctly and the storm was about to hit. He picked up his step, as did Ida Belle, who was right behind him, but instead of going faster, Gertie came to a complete stop, and I almost ran into the back of her.

"Is that hosta growing out there?" she asked.

Corndog stopped and turned around. "Yes, ma'am. Petunia has been planting it in different areas. We don't get a lot of sunlight around the house, so she's been testing it for sun and saturation tolerance. That's about as close to the bayou as she's been able to get, though. Too close to the salt water and it doesn't seem to do as well, even with a bit more sunlight."

"What variety is it?" Gertie asked, and stepped off the path, headed for a clump of plants that I assumed were the ones that she'd risked being caught out in the rain for.

"Don't—" Corndog yelled, but it was too late.

I saw the snake drop from the thick moss above her, landing right on her head. Gertie let out a scream that could probably be heard back in Sinful and whirled in circles, frantic to get the snake off her head. She managed to toss it off into the trees with one of her arm swipes, but when she did, she backed into a thin tree trunk and another one fell to replace the one she'd just lost.

She started spinning all over again and then took off running down a narrow path in the trees, but not the path we were on.

"Stop!" Corndog yelled and hurried after her.

But Gertie disappeared in the thick growth, not slowing one bit. Corndog had sounded panicked when he'd yelled at her to stop, which I took to mean there was more wrong with the situation than what I could see. So I took off after her. It only took me a couple of strides to pass Corndog, and I spotted a flash of Gertie's yellow shirt ahead of me. Then I heard another yell and a splash.

I spotted the drop-off at the last minute and threw my arms around a cypress tree at the embankment to prevent myself from going into the bayou along with Gertie. A big hunk of the embankment had been torn off and was still sending pieces into the water. Corndog and Ida Belle hurried up beside me and we carefully peered over to see if we could spot her.

"There!" Ida Belle pointed off to our right, and I saw a patch of yellow clinging to roots below the overhang.

I hurried over, and Corndog called after me to be careful because the embankment wasn't solid. A warning that came a second too late. I stepped to the edge of the embankment, intending to climb down the roots and help Gertie out of the water.

Then the bank I was standing on collapsed.

I curled my body as I dropped, trying to protect my face and stomach from impact on the roots below, and had a second of relief when I hit the water. I popped back up immediately, dirt and moss still dropping onto me from above.

And that's when Corndog yelled the one word I didn't want to hear.

"Gator!"

I dropped my legs down, hoping to hit roots, but my feet plunged into the slimy, gooey mud that made up the bottom of the bayou. I whirled around and saw Gertie about ten feet away, the back of her T-shirt hooked on a cypress knee. She was trying to lift herself off it, but there were no other stumps nearby for her to use to step on, and she couldn't reach behind to push herself off the root.

The gator was twenty feet behind her.

I shoved off a root and started swimming for Gertie as a shot rang out above me. Then a second later, I heard a yell and a huge splash as more of the embankment tore away, and I figured Ida Belle had joined us for a dip.

The alligator had gone under just before she fired the shot, either to hide or to approach in stealth mode, preparing to snag Gertie underwater and pull her down for a death roll. Given that it was mating season, and gators seemed to be looking for a fight during that time, I was betting on the latter.

There was no way Ida Belle could get a shot from the water, assuming she hadn't lost her pistol when she fell, and I had no idea if Corndog was packing. I was going to guess yes, because this was Louisiana and he lived on an island surrounded by predators. But given his questionable vision and the gator's proximity, I was hoping he had opted for praying instead of opening fire.

"Duck out of the shirt!" I yelled to Gertie as I swam.

Her eyes widened, and she must have realized why I'd just told her to strip because she put her arms up and went below the surface. I covered the last five feet, praying she was going to pop back up.

Then the gator surfaced right next to the dangling T-shirt and raised his head up to nudge at the fabric blowing in the wind. I was just about to dive when Gertie surfaced next to me, sputtering water everywhere. The gator swung his giant head around and made eye contact with me, then sank again.

"Swim!" I yelled.

Gertie set out for the bank with me right on her tail. I could hear Ida Belle and Corndog yelling, but their words were all garbled with the boom of thunder overhead and the sounds of Gertie and me swimming. Gertie reached the mass of roots where the bank had collapsed just ahead of me and scrambled up a root, just out of the water.

Then she let out a yell like I'd never heard in the two years I'd known her.

I twisted around just as the gator surfaced right in front of me, his jaws wide open. I saw the flash of teeth and before I could pull my weapon, he lunged. So I did the only thing I could do.

I punched him right in the face.

The blow hit him between the eyes and I twisted out of the way as I let my fist fly. I felt his teeth scrape my side and knew he'd broken the skin, but I'd startled him enough that he'd disappeared below the surface again. I prayed he was headed off to find an easier snack.

I scrambled up the roots and pulled myself up to the destroyed embankment just in time to see the gator surface again inches below where I stood. One lunge was all it would take for him to pull me off. I spun around on the giant root I stood on and leaped for the bank, just as the gator launched himself out of the bayou. He grabbed my tennis shoe, and I grasped the roots that were holding the remaining embankment upright. I yanked my leg as hard as I could, but he had his teeth sunk into the rubber sole in a firm grasp, and my hold on the roots was loosening by the second. Just as I was going to slip my foot out of it, he let go and dropped back into the water.

Gertie was already climbing, and I set off after her, but when I drew close, she slipped. I reached down and grabbed the only thing available—the back of her sports bra. I twisted my fist in it, praying it was new and the fabric would hold, and yelled for Gertie to drop her arms. If the bra slipped over her head, she'd go crashing back down into the bayou, where I had no doubt the gator was still lurking.

She dropped a good couple inches, and I steeled myself for the giant jerk I knew was coming when the bra reached the end of its stretch capacity. I barely managed to keep hold of her and saw that the bra had come up over her chest and was now tucked under her arms. I heard something splash and Gertie sighed.

"There goes my bag of Skittles," she said.

So there we were—me clinging to a tree root on the side of the embankment, praying it held. Gertie spinning below me, suspended by my hand clutching her bra, flashing her boobs to the wildlife.

And it wasn't even Mardi Gras.

The alligator popped up below us and I was about to tell Ida Belle to shoot, but then he appeared to look up and decide we were too much to bother with. He gave a giant swish of his tail and headed off in the other direction.

"You've scared the alligator," Ida Belle said. "Flashing your wares and all."

"I can't dangle here all day," Gertie said, her arms still clamped to her side to keep the bra on. "And I'm starting to get dizzy."

"Yeah, well, my rotator cuff is going to move out of my shoulder soon," I said. "When you're facing the embankment again, prepare to grab hold. I'm going to swing you toward it. Do not miss!"

What I didn't say is that it wouldn't be a polite or gentle swing. I only had one shot at this. If Gertie lifted her arms and wasn't close enough to grab the roots, then she was going down again, and I had no doubt our reptilian friend would be happy to make a U-turn. I could feel my shoulder starting to burn as she slowly spun around, and I prayed I could not only hold out but muster up that final burst of energy that would be needed to get her those two feet back to the embankment.

Just as she turned to face the bank, I swung her out to gain momentum, then pulled as hard as I could for the bank. Gertie stuck her hands out just as she collided with the bank. Her face planted in a crumbling patch of dirt, but she managed to grab hold.

"Are you stable?" I asked.

"Yes, but I think this bra cut off the circulation to my lower body."

"Worry about it later. Get to climbing."

"I'll be flashing Corndog, and there's no way to pull my bra down hanging out here."

"You're probably covered in mud, and I'm guessing Corndog is old enough to have seen boobs before. What he probably hasn't seen is someone eaten by an alligator."

"Actually," he called out, "there was this one time over in Mud Bayou... You know what? I'll save that story for dinner."

"Perfect," I said. "Go!"

"Hurry up!" Ida Belle said. "If this storm hits while you're still hanging there, that embankment is going to be a slick piece of work. And your friend is still out there swishing around. Corndog has had his eyes closed since Fortune punched the gator. He couldn't watch anymore."

"Fine," Gertie said and started inching up.

I waited until she was a body length ahead of me then set out myself, warning Ida Belle and Corndog to step back several feet for fear that all our weight on the edge would send more of it down into the bayou.

Gertie finally managed to crawl over the edge and a couple feet to firmer ground, where she yanked the sports bra down to cover her goods, then fell back down to the dirt. I pulled myself up and over and practically sprang three feet from the edge to ensure I was solid. I heard a rip and looked back to see the gator tearing Gertie's T-shirt from the cypress knee.

Gertie sat up and groaned. "That was a brand-new shirt."

Her face and body were covered with mud, and there were bits of moss and twigs stuck in her hair and her bra. She looked like a forest creature. But then, I probably didn't look much better. I hadn't eaten the embankment, but I still had mud all over everything but my face. Ida Belle was dripping from her dip but looked otherwise unharmed.

"I dropped my pistol when that embankment collapsed," she said and sighed.

Correction. Ida Belle had sustained the biggest injury of us all. She'd lost her weapon.

"Do you have a spare shirt in your handbag?" I asked Gertie.

She shook her head. "I gave it to Sammy for his Great Pyrenees."

"Why did a dog need a shirt?"

"He'd been to the groomers and they messed up the orders. Shaved him within an inch of his life. I saw him on Main Street, and the big guy was so embarrassed he wouldn't even take a hot dog weenie from me. He perked right up once he was wearing the shirt."

Ida Belle shook her head as she pulled off her blue plaid shirt that she wore over a white tank and passed it to Gertie. "Put this on so Corndog can open his eyes and get us to the house."

Gertie silently took the shirt and wisely donned it without a single peep about fashion. Ida Belle might have lost her gun, but my money was on her in hand-to-hand combat. And losing one's favorite weapon had a tendency to bring out your fighting spirit.

"Everybody's up to biblical standards," Ida Belle announced. "You can open your eyes, Corndog."

Corndog slowly opened one eye, as if to ensure he wasn't being fooled, and his shoulders slumped with relief when he saw us all standing there, clothed, if not presentable. He gave me a look of sheer amazement.

"You punched a gator," he said. "Just walloped him right in the face. I've never seen anything like it before. When my nephew said you were deadlier than a serial killer, I just thought he was being dramatic, but I sure wouldn't want to fight you. Not even when I was younger."

"And you didn't even see the bra-dangling save," Ida Belle said, and Corndog blushed.

She turned to glare at Gertie. "Why the heck did you take off running? That was a rat snake. You almost got yourself, me, and Fortune killed, and you owe me a new pistol."

"He was on my head," Gertie said. "I couldn't see him and didn't think about asking him if he was venomous or not."

"You could have asked me," Ida Belle said. "And why did you head down the wrong path?"

"I thought I was on the one to the house. Spinning around must have gotten me mixed up."

Ida Belle shook her head. "So you're telling me that failing to identify a snake you've seen a thousand times at least and running down a path that doesn't look even close to as traveled as the one you were on has nothing at all to do with your eyesight."

"Fine! I'll go get new glasses when we get home. I think I broke these anyway, and they're my last pair of the old prescription. I'll have to put a bit of tape on them until we get home."

Since Gertie had destroyed an untold number of glasses since I'd known her, I didn't even want to ask how many pairs she'd purchased.

"You've been on your last pair for five years now," Ida Belle said. "I swear, if you don't get new glasses next week, then Fortune is going to stop using you for investigation. Between your vision and your purse, she can't afford the liability insurance."

Ida Belle turned around and stalked off. Corndog gave us a nervous look as a peal of thunder shook the ground.

"We best get going," he said. "If the bottom drops out before we get to the house, we might all be wearing a snake hat. They don't like these big storms—drop right out of the trees and scurry for cover."

Gertie hopped right up, as if she had not nearly died, and we set out after Corndog. None of us were necessarily scared of snakes, but we didn't want to wear them on our heads either. Ida Belle was back on the main path and yielded the lead to Corndog, who set out at a surprisingly fast walk. We hurried behind him, and I glanced up when there was a break in the trees to look at the angry clouds swirling overhead. I'd seen this kind of storm a million times since I'd moved to Sinful, and they always hit with a huge downpour. But at this point, all of us but Corndog could use a bath.

"Here we are," Corndog said as we broke through the trees and into a small clearing.

The house had the dock beat for atmosphere, hands down. It was indeed an uphill walk to get there, and if the cypress trees hadn't been so old and huge, it probably would have been visible from a distance, but the ancient, enormous trees surrounded the house, eclipsing it completely from sight until you were standing right in front of it. They also eclipsed most of the natural light, leaving only a small clear area that would get direct sunlight only when the sun was right overhead.

Right now, of course, the storm clouds were rolling in and it wasn't the time of year for the sun to be positioned over the house like a spotlight anyway, so it looked more like dusk than the middle of the day. And although there's no way in hell I'd live out here, cut off from an easy jog to a café or bakery, I could appreciate why Corndog and Petunia were desperate to hold on to their home.

It was a huge Victorian, painted in shades of dark blue and green and with copper tops on the turrets. It was easily double the size of my own home and since I knew what that one cost to maintain, in an established township, with easy access to supplies and people, I could only imagine what kind of costs they were looking at to keep the place up. Ultimately, I figured it was a losing proposition. As soon as you couldn't do a lot of maintenance yourself, all bets would be off owning a place like this. And I had an idea that Corndog, with his arthritis, wasn't rushing to climb a ladder anymore.

"Wow!" Gertie said, echoing my thoughts. "This is incredible. Who would have ever thought it was hidden back here?"

Corndog looked pleased at her compliment. "She's a beauty, all right. I'm just glad my great-grandpa bought her. Paid three thousand dollars back then, which was a king's ransom, but that wouldn't pay the light bill for a year these days. She needs a lot of work, but she's still magnificent. My whole life, I spent every spare hour I had out here helping him with the place. That's why he left the house to me. He knew I loved it as much as he did."

Even Ida Belle looked suitably impressed as we both nodded.

A huge drop of rain landed on my cheek, and Corndog gave us a once-over. "We best go in the side door to the kitchen. I got a hose just outside the door, and at least you can take off your shoes there. Will save having to clean the rugs in the entry."

Corndog headed for the side of the house and we hurried to follow. There was a set of cement steps that led to a side door. He made a move for the hose, but it turned out we didn't need it. The downpour hit just as we arrived at the entry, so Gertie and I stood under the roofline and caught a big wave of water as it barreled down the roof. It wasn't a great shower, but at least we were no longer covered in mud.

When lightning struck just past us in the trees, we decided we were clean enough and hurried inside. There was a small entry hallway and just past that, we found ourselves standing in a nice-sized kitchen with a large island. The room was a craftsman's showplace of hand-carved wood. Even the wall panels had decorative etchings on them. And if the kitchen was this fancy, all I could think was I couldn't wait to see the rest of the house.

"According to the legends," Corndog said as I studied the

floral etchings on a wood panel, "the pirate who built the place was a craftsman and artist, and he's the one who did all this work. Don't know if it's true, but it makes for a good story for guests."

"It's incredible," I said.

A woman wearing an old-fashioned, pale yellow dress with tiny blue flowers and a million pleats came bustling out of a door off to our left, wiping her hands on a dishrag hanging from her apron string.

Seventies. Just under five foot. Ninety-five pounds, with the apron and shoes. Arthritis in her hands and knees. Thick glasses and still squinting, so probably went Gertie's route on addressing her vision. Zero threat, unless she'd used peanut oil in something that killed the allergic guest.

"Sorry," she said as she approached. "I was looking for my baking sheet in the pantry and didn't even hear you come in. Darn thing was on the wrong shelf. I'm Petunia. You must be Fortune, Ida Belle, and Gertie."

Then she got a good look at us and exclaimed, "Oh my word! What happened? Are you bleeding?"

"There was a snake, end of trail, collapsing embankment, alligator, bayou accident," I said.

Her face immediately cleared in understanding, and she nodded, making me wonder just how many times it had happened before.

"And your side?" she asked.

"Just a scratch," I said.

"Well, you can't just drip the whole time you're here," Petunia said. "And I know mud is supposed to be good for the skin, but it's not so welcome on my carpets."

"We tried to wash off in the storm," I said.

"I think we can do better than that," Petunia said. "You all need a shower. I'll get your clothes on to wash, and in the meantime, I've probably got something you can borrow while I get them clean."

Ida Belle eyed the slim woman and shook her head. "Not for all of us."

Gertie glared at her and Petunia laughed.

"I've lost some weight as of late," Petunia said, "and took in some of my dresses so I didn't look like a slouch for guests. But I have some from when I enjoyed my own cooking more. Something that's not fitted and has a little give will work just fine."

She gave Ida Belle a critical look. "I'm afraid my dresses might be a little scandalous on you given the height difference."

"If Corndog has another set of overalls and a T-shirt, that will work fine for me," Ida Belle said.

"Perfect," Petunia said and eyeballed me. "I think our nephew left a pair of sweats and a T-shirt here last time he stayed over. They might be a little short with your long legs, though."

"I can make them work," I said.

At that point, I'd have worn anything but a scandalously short dress with pleats.

When I'd taken the case, it hadn't occurred to me that the reunion party would still be here. But since they were, that gave me an idea.

"You have two rooms available, correct?" I asked.

Corndog nodded. "That's right. The cops said to hold off renting the, um, dead guy's room for a bit in case they needed to check something, but I've got one room with a queen bed and one with two doubles."

"Good. We'll take them."

CHAPTER EIGHT

Gertie started clapping her hands. Ida Belle just sighed.

Corndog and Petunia just looked confused, so I explained. "I think we will get more out of the others if they don't know we're investigators. We'll just be guests."

Corndog's eyes widened. "You're going undercover. You *are* smart. I'll add you to the register just in case someone checks, but I ain't taking your money."

He scratched his head. "But you don't have any stuff to stay overnight, and it doesn't look like that storm is going to break in time to get you back to the mainland to get supplies and get back before dark. I don't take the boat out after dark."

"I have bathroom supplies," Petunia said. "I keep sample sizes on hand because so many forget something and it's not like you can just pop out to the store. I'm going to find you some clothes to change into and I'll get your stuff in the washer straightaway, then I'll bring up some bandages, peroxide, and ointment for those scratches."

I nodded. "Great. We'll wear whatever you come up with today and then have our own stuff to change into tomorrow."

"Not unless you want me to go around wearing nothing but my sports bra," Gertie said.

"Good point." I looked at Petunia. "Do you have an extra T-shirt as well? The gator ate Gertie's."

"Preferably something from back in those enjoying-your-own-cooking days," Ida Belle said, and Gertie scowled.

"I think I have a Mardi Gras T-shirt somewhere," Petunia said.

"Perfect," I said. "We'll head upstairs for a shower and change and bring our clothes back down to launder."

"What about your shoes?" Petunia asked.

"We left our tennis shoes in the entry," I said, "but they'll take too long to dry if you wash them. If you have a trash bag I can use, we'll just wipe them up best we can."

Petunia didn't look convinced. "I was bringing Gertie a dress—that's really all I've got that might work for her."

"No worries," Ida Belle said. "I see women wearing dresses and tennis shoes all the time. We're well past trendy heels."

"Speak for yourself," Gertie said.

"We'll make it work," I said to Petunia. "But we should get going before we make a bigger mess of your kitchen floor."

Petunia fetched a trash bag for our shoes and another for our clothes. We all pulled off our socks and stuffed them in the dirty clothes bag to send down with the rest of our things after we'd showered and changed.

Corndog looked excited. "I can't believe I'm going to get to play undercover investigator with you. Wait, what should I call you? Ida Belle and Gertie are probably fine, but my nephew says you've made a bit of a name for yourself in these parts, Ms. Redding, and Fortune ain't all that common."

"He has a point," Ida Belle agreed. "Probably best to choose a different name."

"What name would be easy for you to remember?" I asked

Corndog, given that he'd already admitted his memory sometimes failed him.

He smiled. "You kinda remind me of Petunia's sister Rose—God rest her soul—when she was young."

"Then Rose it is," I said. "Go ahead and show us to our rooms, and we'll pretend to get settled, then we'll wander back down to find the others."

"I'll find those clothes and bring them right up," Petunia said.

"What do you want Petunia and me to do after we get you settled?" Corndog asked.

"Whatever you normally do. We're just more regular guests."

"What if they see you dressed like this on the way to your rooms?" Petunia asked.

"We got caught out in the storm," I said. "And Gertie fell, then I helped her up. It's the truth, of sorts."

They both looked a bit nervous and so I asked Petunia, "You said you were checking flour. Are you baking something?"

"What?" she asked, momentarily confused. "Oh, some cookies. Traditional chocolate chip, from scratch, of course. I have baked goods every afternoon we have guests for a snack, but I've been a little off my game ever since...you know. Couldn't find my cookie sheet and looked high and low and it was right in front of my face, just on the wrong shelf. I guess stress has got the better of me."

"Let me worry about all of that now," I said. "You two just treat this like any other day with a full roster of guests."

Petunia gave us a nervous smile as Corndog motioned for us to follow. We headed out of the kitchen and into the entry. I gave the giant spiral staircase an appreciative look. It was the kind of thing you only saw in movies or magazine ads. This place must have cost a fortune and taken forever to build.

"Your rooms are on the south side of the house across the hall from each other," Corndog said as we headed upstairs. "They get the most noise from bad weather, I'm afraid, which is why we put people in them last. The one with the queen bed has a small bathroom with shower, but the double beds share the bathroom down the hall with other guests."

"They can use mine," I said. "That way, no one will catch any of us walking down the hall looking like Swamp Thing."

Corndog opened the door to the room on the left first and I walked in, taking in the double beds. It was small and the curtains and bedding were definitely from a different era, but it was neat and clean and had that old-world pretty look to it. The furniture was as ornate as the walls and banister, and I knew in an instant it was solid and heavy.

"The key's in the lock," Corndog said, and pushed the door closed enough to show us the giant iron key slotted in the inside lock. "You pull it out when you leave and lock the room with it from the outside. Twist it on the inside to lock yourself in at night."

"That's rather an interesting piece of history," Ida Belle said.

Corndog nodded. "The guests seem to appreciate it, so I'm sure glad we never changed them all out for something more modern. 'Course, we had no need to lock the doors until we started taking guests. We kept the unused rooms closed up so as not to waste air conditioning and heat on them, of course, but everything is pretty much the way it was when I inherited the place."

"I'm just glad you have air conditioning," Gertie said.

Corndog nodded. "Cost a pretty penny with all the maneuvering they had to do to get it to the lower floors. And I wouldn't let them touch the woodwork, so it took some doing. But that was back when I was still working for the oil companies and money was flowing like petroleum in the Gulf back then."

He walked across the hall and pushed open the door to the other room. The bedroom was roughly the same size as the other but with a queen bed and an attached bathroom. Both rooms were so small that the four of us standing in them took up all of the available floor space. But they were fine for our purposes and were a far sight better than the places we'd had to sleep in our past careers with the CIA and the military.

I looked back at the open door and the key in the lock and frowned. "Was the dead guy's room locked?"

I'd seen what looked like damage to the doorframe when we'd passed the door with police tape on it.

Corndog nodded. "When it got close to noon and they still couldn't raise him, they asked me to open it, but there's only the one key. I guess I need to figure out something on that, but to be honest, we've never had a problem before."

"So the keys only work for one door each?"

"That's right. Wouldn't be very secure if they was universal. Well, except in cases like this I guess, and I'm rather hoping we don't have that happen again. Still, a spare key would have saved me replacing a doorframe, so I'm going to check with a locksmith about having some made. The big guy—the one who's in charge—he forced it open along with the skinny one."

"And you found the key inside the room?"

"Yep. On the floor right next to the bed. Figure that's where he dropped it before he passed out."

Ida Belle cut her eyes at me, and I knew she was thinking the same thing I was—a locked room with the only key on the inside meant no one had sneaked in and murdered the guy unless they'd left through a window. I'd check on that possibility later.

"Thanks, Corndog," I said. "We'll get showered and

changed and head downstairs. Hopefully, the others will still be hanging out and we can get them to talking. You go back to whatever you would normally be doing. Just remember that I'm Rose and we're from Belle Chasse. We'll try to get a chance later tonight to talk to you more about everything."

"Got it," he said. "I'll head to the kitchen and get the coffee going for when those cookies are done."

"You'd better let Carter know we're staying over," Ida Belle said as soon as he left. "Otherwise, he might send out the posse when we're not back by dinner."

Crap! All three of our phones had just taken a dip along with us in the bayou.

The thought must have occurred to them at the same time it hit me, and we all yanked them out of our pockets.

"Still works," Gertie said. "Thank God for waterproof phones."

I nodded. One thin bar flickered off and on, which wasn't surprising given that the storm still raged outside, but at least it appeared to be working. I figured I'd never be able to get a decent call to stay connected in this weather, so I sent a text.

Staying overnight. Tell everyone. Big storm. Bad cell service here.

I hit Send, and we all watched the phone and waited. It took a bit but finally showed delivered.

"At least it went through," I said.

With all three of us texting different people about our overnight stay, word should get around as needed. In my case, I needed Carter to pop in to my house tonight and feed Merlin. Ida Belle needed Walter on Rambo duty, and Gertie had a bird and now apparently, a camel to consider.

The situation in Sinful now handled as best it could be, I turned my attention to our current problem.

"How long does it take someone to have an allergic reaction to food?" I asked.

Ida Belle shrugged. "Depends, of course, on the severity of the allergy, the type and amount of the allergen consumed, and how. In the case of ingestion, reaction time can be minutes to an hour maybe."

Her eyes widened as she latched onto my train of thought. "If those fish had been fried in peanut oil, you're thinking he would have had a reaction before he went to bed."

"Maybe," I said. "Depends on how long after eating they stayed up."

Ida Belle frowned. "There's also biphasic anaphylaxis."

"What's that?" I asked.

"It's the second act, of sorts. It can happen hours after the first episode."

"But there still would have been a first episode, right?"

"Sure, but symptoms include things like shortness of breath, rash, upset stomach, being lightheaded..."

"All symptoms of being insanely drunk," I said and sighed. "Can the second act kill you?"

Ida Belle nodded. "I wouldn't say it happens that often, but metabolism and response are a pretty individual thing. For all we know the alcohol could have played a role in it as well."

"Crap," Gertie said. "So Corndog might still be on the hook."

There was a knock at the door, and Ida Belle opened it to let Petunia in, clothes draped over her arm.

"Good Lord, one of those friends left the library just as I stepped out of the kitchen with the clothes, and I almost twisted my ankle ducking back inside," Petunia said. "If these don't work for you, one of you come down and get me and I'll try to drum up something else. And don't forget to bring me your wet things and I'll get them on to wash right away."

She placed the clothes and a first aid kit on the bed and

hurried out, still looking stressed over all of it. Gertie picked up the dress on top of the pile, and Ida Belle started laughing.

"It looks like my aunt's kitchen drapes," Gertie said.

"Your aunt had awful taste then," Ida Belle said. "Were your aunt's drapes also too short for the window?"

Gertie glared. "You know good and well they were since you spent just as many hours eating cookies in front of those drapes as me."

I had to agree, the pattern of the fabric and the cut of the dress were both less than stellar. The dress kind of looked like a box. I was sure Ronald would know what the style was called, but I was going with Awful Box Style. And the length—it was probably fine on Petunia, who was a good couple inches shorter than Gertie, but it would verge on questionable for what women Gertie's age were expected to be wearing since her knees were sure to show. She definitely couldn't wear it to church without causing some kind of uproar.

Then there was the material. It was something clingy, and stretchy, although on the thinner Petunia, it probably just hung there since there wasn't much to cling to past her shoulders. But the real statement of the piece was the pattern. A putrid shade of green made up the background and giant purple petunias the size of my head were splayed all across the dress. I couldn't imagine someone deliberately purchasing it and was going to assume the store was paying people to take them.

Ida Belle started chuckling, and Gertie glared. "I can't wear this. I'd look less obtrusive walking in there naked."

"No! You would not," Ida Belle said. "So it's a little short and a little loud—how is that a problem? God knows, we've both seen you in worse."

I nodded.

"It's hideous," Gertie said.

I nodded again.

"You're not helping," Ida Belle said to me, then turned back to Gertie. "Look, you're the one who went diving over a snake. And a harmless rat snake at that. You could ask for something else, but I don't think it's going to get much better. Either you dress like your aunt's drapes or Petunia might have something like what she was wearing. Would *Little House on the Prairie* look be more to your liking?"

Gertie sighed. "You know how much I hate pleats, and the whole bodice of her dress was covered with them."

"You also hate not breathing," Ida Belle said, "and those dresses are not stretchy like this one. Make do until your clothes are laundered. Then you can change for dinner."

"Why would I take off such a festive dress and change into jeans and a T-shirt for dinner?"

"You could say you were cold," I said.

Gertie raised one eyebrow. "You mean like *old* people do?"

"Let's not start pretending we're the same age as Fortune," Ida Belle said. "We already have big enough roles to play without making them impossible. It's the South. You're eccentric. Those people are from here. Trust me, they won't bat an eye."

I nodded. Given the things I'd seen people wearing in downtown Sinful, Ida Belle was definitely right on that one.

"Great," Gertie said. "So now I'll be the crazy old aunt."

"*Spinster* old aunt," Ida Belle added. "Talk a lot about your cats."

The next set of clothes were the sweats and T-shirt that Shadow had left behind. The sweats were skinny and clingy, which I hated, and had bands around the ankles. As soon as Gertie lifted them up, I could tell they were going to be too short.

"I can solve two problems at once," I said as Gertie chuckled.

I motioned to Ida Belle and she handed me her knife, anticipating where I was going with it. I made a clean cut right above both ankle cuffs and threw the offending elastic in the trash.

"I'm afraid you don't have that option on the T-shirt," Gertie said and held it up.

It was black and had a sort of golf ball-looking object on it. "What is it?"

"It's the Death Star," Ida Belle said. "From *Star Wars*."

"Ah," I said and nodded. "At least I've seen that movie, and I don't have to wear a dress. Not that Petunia had anything that would have looked remotely normal on someone my age."

"I'm glad I requested Corndog's overalls," Ida Belle said. "If I wore one of Petunia's dresses, everyone could see the brand of my drawers. Not that I'll be wearing any until our clothes are laundered."

I nodded as Gertie picked up the overalls and held them up next to Ida Belle.

"They're way too long though," Gertie said.

"I'll roll them up at the bottom," Ida Belle said.

"If this dress makes me the spinster cat lady, then who the heck are you?" Gertie asked Ida Belle.

"I'm the aunt who had a lifelong 'roommate' until she passed a couple years back."

"Ah," Gertie said and nodded. "That's not bad. I suppose stereotypes are best when doing undercover work. We should probably both show proper disdain for men."

"We kind of do that already just by being honest," Ida Belle said. "Most men give us plenty to work with."

"True," Gertie agreed. "I probably need to create some cat names."

"Don't go making up a bunch of stuff I have to remember,"

I said. "I need to be figuring out if a crime was committed, not worrying about roommates, knitting patterns, and cats."

"Don't worry about it," Ida Belle said. "You're the disinterested young person who's forced to haul her aging relatives around. Just spend a lot of time looking at your cell phone and ignoring us and you'll blend right in."

"What if I don't have a signal?"

"Then frown a lot and mutter like the world is ending."

I sighed.

"That's it," Gertie said and nodded. "Just like that. They *are* people about your age."

"But not her peers," Ida Belle said.

"Good point," Gertie said. "But maybe just this once, you could pretend to be an average thirty-year-old."

Since I had no idea where to even start with that task, I shook my head. "Let's not complicate this any more than it already is. I don't think we'll need to offer up much backstory, but I probably do need a job. Any ideas that won't get me more questions or expose me as a fraud?"

"Insurance processor," Ida Belle said. "You work from home. It's beyond boring so no one will ask."

"That's good," I said. "My guess is if they're interested in conversation at all, they'll probably talk about their friend or just talk among themselves and ignore us. Either is fine. If it comes up, then we're from Belle Chasse—I know it well enough to fudge some things if I have to—and you two heard about Voodoo Island from a palm reader and wanted to come out here as you're into the paranormal stuff."

"That last part's true enough," Gertie said.

"Not for me," Ida Belle corrected.

I pointed a finger at her. "*You* don't drive."

Ida Belle snorted.

"It's called undercover for a reason," I said. "You not driving explains why I'm here with you."

"I've had to pretend to be a lot of things, but me pretending not to drive might just be the biggest stretch I've had to cover," Ida Belle said.

Gertie nodded. "For me, it was being the nun."

"You played a corpse once," Ida Belle said. "One would hope that was the bigger stretch."

"Have you ever tried running in a habit? Corpses are never asked to run."

Ida Belle shook her head and looked at me. "What do we ask them, if anything?"

"You know how I work—all information is good information. I need to get a feel for these friends, especially for the one who died, and we're not going to get that information from him. So do the normal nosy, er...middle-aged lady thing."

Ida Belle snorted again but wisely didn't comment.

"It would look stranger if you *didn't* ask questions," I said. "I'll just attempt to look bored and aggravated over the sketchy internet. If they give me an opening to ask questions, I'll run with it, so just go along. But let it all play out as naturally as possible and keep our personal information light so we don't contradict ourselves later on. Go heavy on the weather and television shows. Things it would be hard to trip you up on."

Gertie sighed. "There is nothing natural about me in this dress."

"Why don't you hit the shower first since you're the worst off," I said.

Gertie gave the dress another hard look. "At least it's not tucked in at the waist. I have somewhere for my boobs to occupy because without a bra, they definitely won't be up where they're supposed to be."

"No one needs to hear about your boobs," Ida Belle said.

"Then I guess you don't want to hear about the four Slim Jims and stick of dynamite that I lost," Gertie said.

"I thought you said that was Skittles," I said.

"Them too," she said as she headed into the bathroom, hideous dress in tow.

I sank onto the floor in order to avoid getting mud on the bed. Ida Belle shook her head and dropped next to me.

"That woman's bra and purse are a menace," Ida Belle said. "Do you think we should see what she's got in there?"

"I'm less stressed living in ignorance. Send me the bill for your new pistol. You're here on business, so it's a business expense."

She shook her head. "Seems a shame we're racking up expenses but no income. Still, I feel bad for Corndog and Petunia. They seem like good people."

I nodded. I liked them too, but I was worried that we wouldn't be able to help them. Corndog had already mentioned his memory wasn't great all the time and I'd seen him squinting several times. Both supported the theory that a mistake had been made.

Which made what happened a tragedy, not a murder.

CHAPTER NINE

THIRTY MINUTES LATER, WE'D ALL SHOWERED AND MANAGED to get our hair a semblance of dry, if not styled. Ida Belle's short do was not an issue, and I simply pulled mine back into its usual ponytail. Without her curlers, Gertie's hair was a bit flat and looked as if it had been plastered to her head, but we had arrived during a storm, so it was easy enough to explain away. And although I thought it impossible, the dress looked even worse on Gertie than it had on the hanger.

The tape around the center of her glasses just set the whole outfit off even more. Gertie had shown a proper amount of dismay at the whole ensemble, but Ida Belle had pointed out that it was also perfect for undercover, which she seemed to accept. But she'd threatened us with our lives if we took pictures and took that a step further and said she'd haunt us after her death—wearing only sexy-time outfits—if we showed pictures to Ronald.

We'd done our best to wipe down our shoes and dry them with the blow-dryer. They were still damp but would do, especially with our whole 'caught out in the storm' story. We headed downstairs and I realized we hadn't asked where the library was, but then I heard laughter coming from double doors off the back of the entry and figured that must be it. Ida Belle raised one eyebrow as we walked, and the laughing got louder.

"They don't appear to be in mourning," she whispered.

"Everyone grieves differently," Gertie said.

A giant wave of laughter broke out in the room that could probably have been heard over on the mainland, and Ida Belle shook her head.

"There's a different kind of grieving and there's that," she said. "They sound like they're in the Swamp Bar."

"If they're drunk, they'll be easier to get information out of," I said as I pushed open the door.

The laughter ceased immediately, and I paused in the doorway, acting uncertain as I made a quick assessment.

Six people. Three men. Three women. All late twenties. One man was buff and clearly worked out. One was skinny and all arms and legs. The third was fit but didn't look like the sort that went in for gyms or sports. All three women were trim and muscular. They all spent time on their fitness. Threat level undecided since they were still all suspects until I determined exactly what had happened here.

"I'm sorry," I said. "We didn't mean to interrupt, but Corndog said they would be serving afternoon snacks in here?"

"Are you new guests?" one of the women asked. "I didn't think anyone else was staying here this week."

I gave her a forced smile as we stepped into the room. "My aunts have been begging me for months to bring them and I finally had time..."

Since Ida Belle and Gertie were walking in a bit behind me, I rolled my eyes as I explained, and she gave me a knowing smile.

"Sorry we're a little rumpled," Gertie said. "We got caught in the storm on the way to the house and had to change, but only had the one pair of shoes. It was a doozy. We don't get storms like that at home."

"Of course we do," Ida Belle argued. "You're just surrounded by a ton of brick and concrete instead of standing right in the middle of the darn thing."

Gertie glanced around. "All that hurrying made me hungry. Are the snacks here yet? I smelled cookies baking when we came in."

"Not quite yet," one of the women said. "I think they'll be here soon."

"Good, 'cause I'm starving," Gertie said. "Dinner can't come fast enough after all that walking."

"I hope none of you are allergic to peanuts," the skinny man said.

The others glared at him and he gave them an innocent look.

"What?" he asked. "Too soon?"

I bit my lower lip, taking advantage of the opportunity. "Do they serve a lot of peanuts here? My allergy isn't horrible, but they do strange things to my stomach and make me feel itchy."

They all glanced at one another, and I could tell they were trying to figure out what or how much to say. Maybe because they had something to hide. Maybe because they didn't want to scare us. Or maybe simply because it was personal, and they didn't feel like talking about a death that had just happened on their mini reunion.

The buff guy stepped forward and extended his hand. "I'm Daniel Stout. The beautiful blonde in the teal chair is my wife, Brittany. The joker on the couch is Tyler and the woman next to him is Nicole. On the other two chairs are Morgan and Amanda. We're all high school friends from Houma, having a little get-together here before we attend our ten-year class reunion."

I shook his hand and nodded. "I'm Rose, and this is my Aunt Ida Belle and Aunt Gertie."

"Are you from around here?" Morgan asked. He was thinner than Daniel and had less muscle tone and skin color than the others, and a habit of pushing his glasses back up his nose. I took him to be the studious one.

"Belle Chasse," I said. "They heard about Voodoo Island from a palm reader and have been pestering me to come here ever since."

"Not pestering, dear," Gertie said. "Young people..."

Ida Belle sighed, and some of them struggled not to smile.

"So is there a problem with peanuts?" I asked. "Should I skip the cookies? I was rather looking forward to them."

I cringed at my tone, which was slightly whiny, but I knew it would convey what I wanted, which was that I didn't want to be here, and cookies were one of the few perks I saw in this for me.

They all sobered and looked at one another. Finally, Daniel, who seemed to serve as the leader of the group, spoke.

"One of our friends passed away sometime night before last," he said. "Anaphylactic shock."

Gertie gasped, and Ida Belle covered her mouth with her hand. I let my eyes widen and my jaw drop before responding.

"I am *so* sorry," I said. "I can't even imagine... And the owners made a mistake? Is that what Tyler meant?"

Daniel shook his head. "We don't know for certain what happened, but there isn't really another answer. I can't imagine Justin—that was our friend—brought anything with him containing peanuts, and all of us knew better than to offer him anything with them. We'd gotten so used to dealing with it in high school that we automatically ditch everything with peanuts when we're going to be around him. Old habits."

"What do you think the peanuts were in?"

"We had banana pudding for dessert, so not that," Brittany said. "Our guess was the fish was fried in peanut oil. Corndog swears it was vegetable oil because of Justin's allergy, but we figure he made a mistake and used what he always used."

"But surely, someone could check the oil and know."

"He threw it away," Amanda said.

"After one fry?" I asked. "That doesn't sound right. I'm not a good cook, but can't you use oil more than once?"

I looked over at Ida Belle and Gertie, who both nodded.

"I have a Crisco can on the back of my stove," Gertie said. "Nothing like collecting bacon grease to add some flavor to other things."

Ida Belle frowned. "But if he didn't normally cook with vegetable oil, that's probably why he got rid of it. Might be turned before he'd use it again."

"True," Gertie said. "What about the fish? They could test the leftovers."

"There weren't any," Daniel said.

"That's not true," Morgan said quietly. "I helped them carry everything inside when we were done. There was a plate of fish left that night."

"Did the cops come?" I asked. "Did you tell them that?"

Morgan gave me a slightly indignant look. "The sheriff came and of course, I told him. But the fish was gone and the plate was on the drying rack next to the sink."

"Who ate them?"

They all glanced at one another and shook their heads.

"Probably Corndog and Petunia," Tyler said.

"They said they didn't," Amanda said.

"Would you admit to eating the evidence if you'd accidentally killed someone?" Tyler asked.

"Tyler," Brittany hissed. "You shouldn't say things like that. We were all drunk, and I've seen you eat an entire box of Krystal burgers and a bag of doughnuts in one sitting and not remember a single bite. Anyone could have headed for the kitchen that night and eaten that fish. It's not like the refrigerator has a lock on it."

"Then couldn't Justin have gone in there and eaten something he shouldn't have?" I asked.

Brittany frowned. "It's possible. Just not very likely. Justin liked his whiskey, but he's made it this long without making that kind of mistake."

"She's being polite," Tyler said. "Justin was a drunk. I would say a professional alcoholic, but his stumbling around and insulting everyone until he passed out was anything but professional. He was just sloppy and pathetic."

"Tyler!" Brittany said.

"What?" Tyler challenged. "He had an EpiPen right on his nightstand, for Christ's sake, and didn't even use it. The only explanation for that is he was so passed-out drunk that he didn't even wake up when he was dying."

Daniel banged one hand on the side table and glared at Tyler. "Enough. Our friend is dead, and I won't listen to you run him down. It's in extremely poor taste and not remotely befitting of how a man should behave."

Tyler immediately looked away, but I could see his jaw clench.

The others glared at him as well, and I wondered if they were irritated at what Tyler had said or the fact that he'd said it in front of strangers. The only one who didn't glare was Morgan, who just studied Tyler, a contemplative look on his face. I pegged Morgan as the one who didn't lead with emotion, but I figured I would have to get him alone to get anything good out of him.

The door to the library swung open, and Petunia walked in with a tray of cookies, Corndog right behind with two pots of coffee that he placed on a table against the far wall next to the cookie tray.

"As some of you already know, there's soda and water in the fridge," he said, and pulled open what looked to be a cabinet but was actually the door to a small refrigerator. "There's dishes, cups, and straws in the cabinet above, and if anyone wants it, I can bring in a bucket of ice for setups if anyone's ready to hit the whiskey."

Everyone shook their heads.

Petunia opened the cabinet Corndog had indicated and took out a small tray of sweetener and straws. "There's cream in the refrigerator as well," she said. "Is there anything else you need?"

"No, thank you," Brittany said. "The cookies smell delicious."

Amanda rolled her eyes, and Nicole elbowed her. I hadn't really paid much attention to Amanda since she hadn't spoken often and was angled somewhat away from me, but as Petunia and Corndog left the room, she twisted around, staring at them as they left, frowning. It was then that I realized that another woman in the room was wearing the same face.

"You're twins," I said, gesturing to Amanda and Brittany.

Tyler hooted. "You've done it now. Those two insist they don't look anything alike."

"We're identical twins, you idiot," Brittany said. "Of course we look alike, but our styles are completely different."

That was definitely true, and her wrinkled nose left no doubt as to whose style she found lacking.

Despite being on a cursed island that you could only get to

by boat, Brittany wore cream-colored slacks and a pale pink shirt made of silk. Her five-inch stilettos were as out of place here as anything in Ronald's closet would have been. Her hair was styled in long blond waves and didn't appear to have a single strand out of place, and her makeup looked as if it had been done on a Hollywood set. When she rose to get a drink, I swear she didn't have a single wrinkle in her clothes, despite having been seated.

Amanda, on the other hand, wore yoga pants and an oversize tee that hung off one shoulder, revealing a sports bra. Her feet were completely bare, and her matching blond hair was straight and pulled back in a messy ponytail. Her face was completely devoid of makeup and her bored expression likely matched the one I wore a lot of the time.

"This," Amanda said, as she rose and motioned to her body, "is not a *style*. This is me not trying to look like something I'm not. You're a masquerade, pretending to be all polished when your life is just as messy as the rest of ours."

Amanda turned and strolled out of the room, leaving Brittany staring at her retreating back, her face flushed and her eyes flashing with anger. Daniel stepped over and put a hand on his seething wife's shoulder, but she shrugged it off and jumped up.

"I'm going upstairs to read," she said and stalked out.

Daniel watched as she exited the room, then sighed. "I guess I better go after her."

"Only if you don't want to be sleeping on this hard couch tonight," Tyler said. "Because apparently, all the rooms are now taken, unless you want to sleep in the bed Justin died in."

Nicole sucked in a breath, and Daniel glared at him before taking off after his angry wife.

"More cookies for me!" Tyler said as he popped up.

Nicole pursed her lips. "Why do you always have to be that way?"

Tyler crammed an entire cookie in his mouth and asked, "What way?"

Nicole waved a hand. "That way! Making inappropriate comments. Shoving entire cookies into your mouth and then talking with it full. We're about to attend our ten-year reunion, Tyler, and it's like you never graduated from high school. Justin was Daniel's best friend. I would think even someone like you could manage an ounce of empathy, just this once. If you're so far gone that you can't muster it up, then do us all a favor and pretend."

"Please. Justin and Daniel went their separate ways after high school. And you want me to pretend that Justin was an awesome dude and I'll miss him? That's a stretch."

Nicole narrowed her eyes at him. "You're a used car salesman. You pretend that a wreck is a new Mercedes every day. Just apply the same skill set here."

Tyler shrugged and turned his back to us, ostensibly to fix himself a coffee, but I'd caught his look before he turned and could tell her words stung, more than just one friend to another. I glanced over at Gertie who nodded. Oh good. I was getting better at this. Tyler had a thing for Nicole. And clearly, Nicole didn't feel the same.

Nicole shook her head at his turned back and rose. "I think I'm going to get some air. The storm outside appears to be less temperamental than the one in here."

She gave Morgan a nod and headed out. Tyler turned around and looked at Morgan.

"I guess you think I should apologize to her," he said.

"I think you should apologize to everyone who's had the displeasure of meeting you," Morgan said. "But you could start with Nicole before you move on to Daniel and Brittany."

Tyler flashed an angry look at Morgan, but the other man held his gaze with a very calm expression. Finally, Tyler broke eye contact and left the room, clearly defeated but not looking remotely sorry for the ruckus he'd caused.

"I'm sorry if I set this all off asking about the peanuts," I said.

Morgan shook his head. "This was set off over a decade ago when this group of ill-suited people became friends. Justin's death has everyone on edge, and I'm afraid the worst of us is showing. For some, that means they're well beyond tolerable levels."

"You seem to be holding it all together," Ida Belle said.

He pulled off his glasses and began rubbing them with the bottom of his shirt. "Because that's what I do. It's what I've always done. Need a designated driver? Morgan will do it. Need help writing your term paper? Morgan is your guy."

"Seems like a lot of work," I said.

"You have no idea." He put his glasses back on and gave me a hard look. "You probably really don't have any idea. You look like the rest of them—high maintenance."

Gertie snorted. "Don't confuse natural beauty with high maintenance. Her mother had to pay her to wear a dress to prom, and that was *after* bribing her with more car privileges to even attend."

Ida Belle nodded. "Her idea of makeup is lip balm, and one day, her hair is going to break off because of that ponytail band."

I shrugged and grabbed a handful of cookies before sitting down. "Amanda doesn't look as bad as the others. Her sister looks like she's got an Instagram filter force field surrounding her."

Morgan stared at me for a moment, then laughed. "Maybe I was wrong about you."

"It was kind of a tacky thing to say though," Gertie said, giving me the disapproving look that I'm certain her students used to get.

Morgan waved a hand in dismissal. "It's honest. I'll take the truth over polite any day. It's just that Tyler takes things too far."

"I'm really sorry about your friend," I said. "Justin, right? Do you think it was the fish?"

Morgan shrugged. "Maybe it was the fish. Maybe his luck finally ran out and he got so drunk he ate something he shouldn't have and couldn't manage to use his EpiPen."

"Are they sure...I mean, they're absolutely sure it was anaphylactic shock?" I asked, attempting an uneasy look.

Ida Belle put her hand on my leg and squeezed. "Now, honey, we've already told you that was a fluke. Those things don't happen all the time. You were just unlucky."

Morgan gave me a questioning look and I shook my head and looked down, not sure where Ida Belle was going with this one.

"Poor Rose used to have an apartment in one of those historical homes that was remodeled for multifamily living," Ida Belle explained. "She'd become good friends with one of the other residents and the poor girl was killed by her boyfriend—poisoned."

Brilliant, I thought. There was no better way to create a bond than empathy.

I sniffed and looked up at the obviously sympathetic Morgan. "Penny was so nice. I didn't like her boyfriend, but I never thought..."

"Of course you didn't, dear," Ida Belle said. "Who would? Anyway, ever since then, random deaths, especially of young people, bother her. I'm sure one of your generations' newfangled doctors would say it's PTSD or something to that effect."

"That's horrible," Morgan said. "But Justin definitely died of anaphylactic shock. He essentially passed out face-first on the bed. He went into shock because of his allergy, but the ME said he was probably so far gone on booze that he didn't wake up. He simply suffocated. I guess we should at least be grateful that it was peaceful."

"He wasn't sharing a room with anyone else?" Gertie asked a bit hesitantly.

Morgan caught on immediately and shook his head. "No. The only couple in our group is Daniel and Brittany. Justin was the original ladies' man. High school quarterback, prom king... He had a different girl on his arm every week, and from what he posted on social media, that didn't seem to change much as an adult."

"So no wife and kids?" I asked. "I guess that's a plus."

"Definitely no wife," Morgan said. "And as far as we know, no kids."

"Does he still have family in Houma?" I asked.

"Not to speak of. His father was an abusive drunk and a con artist. He's in prison for the latter of his offenses, assuming his kidneys didn't give out on him. I don't think anyone checks because no one cares. His mother couldn't handle the stress of being married to him but wouldn't leave, either. She drank herself to death. Died shortly after we graduated. I guess the only positive is they didn't have more kids."

"No other family?" Gertie asked.

"Not that I'm aware of," Morgan said. "But then, a man like Justin's father tends to alienate everyone. I'm afraid Justin appeared to have some of the same characteristics."

I bit my lower lip, trying to look nervous. "Then what happens...I mean, with the body..."

Morgan frowned. "I'm not sure. I hadn't thought about it,

but I suppose if no one offers to handle the burial then the parish takes care of it, maybe? In this case, Daniel will probably volunteer to handle things and we'll all pitch in. The least we can do, I guess."

Ida Belle shook her head. "It's all really a shame. Such a young man and lost to drink, but they say it's a genetic thing—alcoholism, I mean. With his mother and father both being tied to the bottle..."

I nodded. "I had one friend who used to drink like that. His parents were alcoholics too. He had an accident and ended up in a wheelchair for a while. Got clean after that, so I guess he was lucky in the big scheme of things. I'm truly sorry for your loss. For all of you."

Morgan gave me a grateful look and nodded. "This was supposed to be a happy time of remembrance. That's what we were doing when you walked in. Daniel had recounted a story about a fishing trip and for a moment, we were all back there... when things were simpler."

He shook his head, bringing his faraway look back to gaze at me. "Anyway, Tyler's not always a jerk. He tries too hard for attention and tends to cross the line between humor and poor taste."

"You're a very observant young man," Gertie said. "I had many Tylers in my classroom over the years. I had many of you as well. I'm guessing you're the smart one."

Morgan gave her a small smile. "Did the glasses give me away?"

Gertie laughed. "Well, I'm wearing them, and I don't think anyone is going to attribute an elevated intelligence to me, so no. But you did mention helping with homework."

"So I did," he said. "Yes, I was the brainy, geeky one, if we're casting a Hollywood movie. Still am, really. Justin and

Daniel were the big men on campus—the football stars. They even looked so much alike that people thought they were brothers. Some people pushed for Amanda to go out with Justin so that they could be a twinsie set, but Amanda wasn't having any of it. Way too smart to get caught in Justin's net. Plus they were on two different paths. Brittany was head cheerleader, prom queen, and leader of the mean girls."

"Was she really mean, or are you just running with the cliché?" I asked.

He smiled. "Caught me. No, she wasn't mean. She's actually a nice person but I think she prefers people don't know that. She's very guarded, very private. But she was and seems to still be a massive snob. Not so much that she thought she was better and spent all her time looking down on people but more like anyone outside of her clique simply didn't exist. I suppose that might have been considered cruel by those who wanted to be part of her group, but she never deliberately sought to make others feel bad or uncomfortable."

He frowned for a moment, as if remembering.

"Amanda had no interest in following in Brittany's wake," he continued. "But Nicole volunteered for it. She's their cousin, and she and Brittany have been BFFs since the crib. Dance class, gymnastics, piano lessons...if Brittany did something, Nicole was right there with her. Tyler, you have probably already guessed, was the class clown. And that's us in a nutshell."

He blanched. "That was a poor choice of words. I'm starting to sound like Tyler."

I shook my head. "It wasn't intentional. That's the difference."

He gave me a grateful look as he rose. "Thank you for listening to me ramble. I suppose I better go do what I always do—put things back together. Otherwise, dinner is going to be an uncomfortable situation for everyone."

As soon as he'd left, Ida Belle looked over at me. "Well, that was interesting."

I nodded. It certainly was.

CHAPTER TEN

SINCE EVERYONE HAD FLED THE LIBRARY, I DECIDED WE should split up and conquer. Ida Belle and Gertie were going to wander around the house, taking pictures and seeing if they could overhear anything. I grabbed a couple of cookies and headed outside, hoping to catch Nicole and see if she was interested in talking. Morgan was just walking back inside as I left the library. He gave me a brief smile before heading upstairs.

I waited until he was out of sight before stepping out onto the porch, holding my cell phone up and frowning. As I turned around to close the door behind me, I pretended to catch sight of Nicole, who was sitting in a rocking chair at the far end.

"Sorry," I said. "I didn't know anyone was out here."

She shrugged. "I don't own the porch."

I shuffled her way, still looking at my phone, then sat on a couch near her.

"Cookie?" I held out my hand.

"No thanks," she said. "I'm type 1. I avoid refined sugars most of the time. I'd rather save the insulin for my favorite chocolates and the rare glass of wine or champagne."

"Okay, I definitely need to know what chocolates are worth a shot of insulin."

She laughed. "Bayou Betsy's Chocolates. She's a chocolatier in Baton Rouge so at least they're not readily available in NOLA, and shipping chocolates is risky except in the winter. Fortunately, Tyler remembered the exact flavor I love and brought me some."

"And that is?"

"Lava chocolates. Think of Valentine's-style chocolates but with a lava cake center."

"Jeez. I might need some of those." I tapped in the name of the chocolatier on my phone and frowned. "I was hoping I'd get a signal out here, but no such luck. Do they have Wi-Fi?"

"Yeah, a satellite system, but I think it's out because of the storm."

I let out a hugely dramatic sigh and shoved the phone back in my jeans.

"I don't get it," I said to her. "What's the draw with this place? I understand why my aunts wanted to come—they're into all that supernatural nonsense—but it doesn't seem like your group's cup of tea any more than it is mine."

"It's not. I mean, I can appreciate the architecture—I'm an interior designer for a custom home builder—and you don't find this sort of detailed woodwork just anywhere. Still, I'd have been happier with the hotel when it comes to comfort and access to things, but Brittany set it all up. She wanted more of a family feel for our private get-together and had been wanting to see the place. Their house isn't big enough to host us all, and at the hotel, we would have been surrounded by other people, and renting a meeting room seemed so impersonal..."

I nodded. "But cooking outside and sitting in a cozy library was more like reliving the past. That makes sense. Still, this is beyond out of the way, and inconvenient if you want any connection with the outside world."

Nicole smiled. "That's the only perk for me. I usually get work calls all day long even on vacation. This way, I get a genuine break."

"Your work sounds interesting, but yeah, I wouldn't like a bunch of calls on my days off."

"What do you do?"

"I process insurance claims. The pay isn't all that great, but the benefits are good and I work from home. Sometimes that's not the best because there are days that I feel like I never left work, you know?"

She nodded. "I have a home office and do most of my design work from there. Obviously, I'm on-site a lot, but it can be hard to turn off the job when it's just on the other side of a wall."

I nodded. "We have quotas, and I have a fire-breathing dragon as a boss. I tell people that glaring at my office door from the couch while drinking a beer is how I wind down every night."

"You would have fit in with our group well. We're big on cynicism, although we wouldn't all admit it."

"Really? Brittany seems like Miss Positivity."

"Brittany is definitely the cheerleader of the group. Has been her entire life, and I've known her practically since birth since we're cousins. She wants everyone she cares about to be their best self and get the most they can from life."

"She sounds exhausting."

Nicole blinked and then laughed. "You know what, she definitely can be. I love her to death, but I'm afraid I don't have a lifetime pass on the glass-half-full train. I'm solidly in Morgan's camp—living in reality."

"Which is sometimes very, very negative," I said and

sighed. "I'm really sorry about your friend. I didn't mean to set everyone off with my questions earlier."

"You didn't know. I'm sure it's not the sort of thing that Petunia and Corndog are going to spill the beans to guests about, especially when it looks like their mistake caused his death."

"No, probably not. But I still feel bad for all of you. I know this wasn't what you had in mind when you all decided to get together for a fun time."

She gazed out into the trees, seemingly lost in memories for a bit, and I could see tears forming in her eyes.

"Maybe it's best not to revisit the past," she said as she rose. "If you'll excuse me, I think I'm going to have a nap before dinner."

I watched as she went back inside, wondering what her cryptic statement had meant.

IDA BELLE AND GERTIE WERE IN THEIR ROOM WHEN I WENT upstairs. I had given Justin's room a longing gaze as I'd passed, but the police tape was still up, so I couldn't risk going in. I had no doubt I could search the room without raising the alarm to the two-bit sheriff, but if any of the reunion group saw me, there was no explanation that would suffice, especially given the story Ida Belle had provided for me concerning my friend's death. Normal people didn't go poking around the room a stranger had just died in.

"Let's head over to my room," I whispered when I poked my head in their bedroom door.

As soon as we were enclosed, I explained, in a low voice. "Your room shares a wall with someone. The ornate wood downstairs will prevent voices from carrying but I figure the walls up here are thin and they're only covered with wallpaper. I've got the bathroom separating me from the next room."

Ida Belle nodded. "You can definitely hear through them. Daniel and Brittany are in the room next to ours, and they had a good row just before you came up."

"What about?"

"Brittany is unhappy with Tyler and his mouth and told Daniel that if he had a backbone he would have put his pet in line a long time ago," Gertie said.

"Harsh," I said. "What was Daniel's reply?"

"He said Tyler was a grown man and there was nothing Daniel could do to change him, nor was it his job to try," Ida Belle said. "Then Brittany said there wasn't an ounce of man inside of Tyler—that he was still just as moronic as he had been when they were teens. Then she said this whole mess could have been avoided if Daniel hadn't insisted on including Tyler. That putting Justin and Tyler together in the same space was a bad idea from the start."

"Then Daniel told Brittany that she knew exactly why he'd invited both of them and he wasn't going to stand there and take insults from her when there were so many other people offering them up. That he was already dealing with enough. Then he left. We didn't hear the door open again, so I assume Brittany stayed behind."

"Anything else?"

"When we first left the library, we spotted Tyler headed down the hallway for the rear of the house which is where the dining room is," Ida Belle said. "We thought he was following Nicole so we tailed him, but it was Amanda who was on a small back porch. There was no way to hear what they were saying through the exterior walls, but we peeked through the blinds, and it was clear they were arguing. Amanda was pointing her finger at him and poked him in the chest."

"I wanted to sneak around and listen," Gertie said, "but there was no way to get around the house without going across the front porch, which by then, we'd assumed was where Nicole had gone. But we wouldn't have had time anyway. After the finger poking, Tyler got beet red and stalked back inside. We barely made a dive behind a serving cart when he flung open the door and practically ran back down the hall."

"Seems like Tyler is making everyone unhappy today," I said and shook my head. "You have to wonder why they bother being friends with him at all. Seems like this reunion would have been better without him."

"Seems like," Gertie agreed. "He's in love with Nicole."

Ida Belle lifted her eyebrows but I just nodded.

"I caught that," I said. "Finally. I might be getting better at reading normal people emotion. She's definitely not on the same page though. Brittany seems to be her only focus."

"Interesting," Ida Belle said. "I wonder if that's the way things were in high school. Seems like none of the others were a couple, at least not that they're admitting."

"No, but I did have an interesting conversation with Nicole."

I told them about our chat and her cryptic statement at the end.

"I wonder what she meant," Gertie said.

"Hard to say," I said. "Could be she thinks all of them getting together was a mistake because Justin died, or it could be because they're all arguing. Maybe it wasn't that different in high school, but glass-half-full Brittany wanted to relive something she refused to see as problematic. Because clearly, they're not a cohesive unit now. I wonder if they ever were."

"Their friend *did* just die, so no one is likely acting normally because nothing is currently normal," Gertie said.

Ida Belle frowned. "She's right. Obviously, there were some

issues among them—old grudges and petty jealousies, most likely—but so far, we haven't turned up any good reason to suspect Justin was murdered. If his death was really an accident, then there's nothing we can do about it."

I nodded. "I know. Between Corndog's admitted memory lapses and his squinting, could be he forgot about the allergy and followed his normal routine for the fish fry."

"Which would have been peanut oil," Ida Belle said. "Or he could have grabbed the wrong jug of oil from the shelf if his vision isn't up to snuff. I noticed the squinting too."

Gertie sighed. "I don't want to think he made a mistake like that. I get the impression neither of them will live with it too well."

"Good people wouldn't," Ida Belle said. "But we can't drum up a murder where there's not one just to make them feel better."

"We've got about thirty minutes until dinner," I said. "Let's head back down to the library in case any of the friends are down there. Maybe we'll get more information."

Gertie put her hands up. "To what end?"

"Maybe no end," I said. "But come tomorrow morning they'll be gone, so we need to find out as much as we can now on the off chance this isn't the horrible accident it appears to be. Tomorrow, I want to see that room before I call the whole thing quits."

NONE OF THE FRIENDS EMERGED UNTIL DINNER WAS ON THE table, and everyone was painfully quiet as the food was being served. Corndog and Petunia didn't eat with us, instead tending to things as servers in a restaurant would, but Ida Belle and Gertie's attempts to spur conversation were mostly met with short answers from one person and a complete lack of acknowledgment from the others.

Even the inappropriate Tyler appeared to have had his tongue clipped. As he kept sending sideways glances to Nicole, I had a good guess at what had him on his best behavior. Nicole, however, didn't seem to notice. She spent most of the meal casting looks across the table at Brittany, who spent a lot of time moving her food around on the plate but not actually eating more than a couple of tiny bites.

Ida Belle, Gertie, and I kept up the idle chatter among ourselves—mostly Gertie telling us about 'local' gossip—all made-up names but real stories. And she described a blanket she was knitting in excruciating detail. By dessert, I was so bored I decided to just start asking questions of the others, figuring they'd either answer or excuse themselves.

"So you guys are here for a reunion, right?" I asked. "I can't even imagine still being friends with people I went to high school with. That's kind of cool. Do you do this often?"

For a couple seconds, there was absolute silence, then I guess cheerleader Brittany found not replying too rude and shook her head.

"Not really," she said. "No one lives in Houma anymore except Daniel and me. Amanda and Nicole are in NOLA, Morgan and Tyler are in Baton Rouge. And Justin had ditched Louisiana altogether in favor of Miami."

"More gullible women," Tyler said, and all the schoolmates glared at him. "What? It's the truth. Justin was a player. I see no point in rewriting history."

"No one's asking you to rewrite it," Morgan said. "But perhaps not volunteering it when Justin's not here to defend himself would be the classier move."

Tyler snorted. "Seriously? If Justin was here, he'd have

spent this entire miserable dinner telling us all about his conquests."

"Or ragging on you," Brittany said. "But you're the big man with the big mouth now that he's no longer here."

Amanda shrugged. "Tyler's not necessarily wrong, you know. I'm not saying we should run Justin down, but I'm not going to pretend we'd have been having a discussion about theater or art if he was here. God knows we heard plenty about his Miami conquests the night we arrived, so it's more likely he'd have spent his time tonight trying to hook up with Rose. Especially since Nicole and I had to remind him within ten seconds of seeing him again that it was never going to happen with either of us."

Tyler raised his eyebrows when Amanda first started talking, apparently surprised that someone else had agreed with his take. But I saw his jaw clench when Amanda mentioned Justin hitting on her and Nicole. When she finished talking, Tyler gave me a once-over as if noticing I was a female in their age range for the first time.

"Yeah," he agreed. "You would have been just his type. You got a boyfriend?"

"Would I be here if I did?" I asked, hoping I'd put just enough disappointment in my voice to illicit some sympathy.

Tyler grinned. "Maybe I should take up Justin's banner."

"The world doesn't need more men carrying that banner," Amanda said. "*Women* especially don't need it."

"I'm going to follow in my aunts' footsteps," I said. "Maybe even take up cats and knitting at some point. Men are too much trouble."

Amanda lifted her wineglass. "Preach it, sister."

Tyler rolled his eyes. "Amanda went to Berkeley and they made her a lesbian."

"You just say that because you know my answer to you would also be no," Amanda said and smiled.

"Since I don't have any interest in you, there are no questions to answer," Tyler said.

Amanda gave him a knowing grin. "But you have questions for one of us, don't you? Poor Tag-Along Tyler. Always in that number three slot and never a shot at the prize."

Tyler flushed, and I could practically feel the tension among the dinner guests.

"Amanda," Daniel said, his tone issuing a warning.

Amanda, who I now realized was getting a little tipsy, looked over at me. "I've got a group of girlfriends who meet every Wednesday night at the After Party in the French Quarter. Do you know it?"

"Sort of," I said. I didn't, of course, but I didn't figure there was going to be a quiz. "I'm afraid I'm more of a homebody."

"Come by anytime you want," she said. "We usually get there around seven. The owner expects us and reserves a private booth for us at the back, so we've got room. You don't have to go out with a guy to get out of your house. Just sitting around drinking and bitching with the girls is great decompression."

"Thanks. I appreciate the invitation."

Morgan smiled at me. "Did you grow up in Belle Chasse?"

While I appreciated his desire to shift the conversation to something more comfortable, I had hoped I'd get through the night without having to talk too much about myself. But I was a pro, and when a pro was undercover, they did two things—made up things that were so mundane no one would ask more questions about them, and used real-life examples for certain things in case they were questioned for more detail.

"Idaho," I said, figuring that would eliminate any potential issues with my lack of knowledge on NOLA schools, locations, and people.

He blinked and I laughed. "I know. It's one of those places that you never know anyone from, which is why people want to leave. My aunts were in New Orleans and hooked me up with a place to stay while I looked for a job. I thought I'd have a big adventure, but I'm not really the big adventure type, so it was just the same life with better food and views. A couple years ago, they started letting us work from home, so I'm just as big a hermit now as I was back in the potato fields."

"You've got a good tan for a hermit," Nicole said.

I nodded. "I like to sit outside and read. I'm an early bird and we don't have set hours, so I'm usually done with my quota by noon or a little after. If the sun's out and I'm not working, I'm sitting in it."

"What are you reading now?" Morgan asked.

"Aunt Ida Belle gave me some old books of hers—the Dragonriders of Pern? I'm really enjoying them."

"Nice," Morgan said. "If fantasy's your thing, I'm surprised you're not all over the hot social media fantasy stories—*ACOTAR? Fourth Wing?*"

I shrugged, indicating I wasn't familiar with those series. "I'm not on social media."

Tyler stared. "How can you not be on social media?"

"Hermit, remember?" I said, looking down. I figured if I appeared slightly uncomfortable, then this line of questioning would cease.

"What about you, Ida Belle?" Morgan asked. "We know Gertie is into knitting and her cats—do you knit too?"

Ida Belle stared at him as if he'd lost his mind.

"Heavens no!" she said. "I like to fish. Back before my knees got shoddy, I liked to duck hunt. But my days of tromping through the marsh in hip waders are over, I'm afraid.

And my roommate was my hunting buddy—lived and hunted together for forty years. Since she passed, I haven't felt much like going. Can't talk Gertie into it, and she wouldn't be much use unless I wanted to knit the deer a scarf."

The others gave each other a knowing look at her 'roommate' comment and smiled at her knitting reference.

"I'm sorry about your roommate," Amanda said.

"Thank you," Ida Belle said. "So are there big doings planned for your reunion?"

"Ha!" Tyler said. "They'll have cheap finger food in a conference room at the hotel with even cheaper decor and call it a party. It's not even open bar. Not sure how much planning goes into that."

Brittany flashed a dirty look at him. "If you'd like a fancier event, then you're welcome to be committee chair at our twenty-year, which includes fundraising. That is, of course, if no one has taken you out by then because of your mouth."

Daniel winced at her 'take out' comment, which I agreed was a bit in poor taste. At least, for normal people it was. I didn't care, but my standards for death references were set by the CIA, so...

Brittany apparently realized her faux pas and tossed her napkin on the table as she jumped up from her chair. She glared at Tyler, clearly blaming him for her mistake, then strode out of the room. Nicole gave everyone an apologetic look and hurried after her.

"Always the dramatic exit, our Brittany," Tyler said. "But then, she never could stand to lose and with Justin dead, that's one less admirer."

"I'd watch what you say about my wife," Daniel said quietly. "Or I can accommodate her wishes."

Tyler smirked, but I saw him swallow. Regardless of his posturing, he was obviously leery of Daniel and realized he'd taken things too far. Daniel held his gaze for several seconds, then shook his head in disgust and headed off, presumably after his wife. Again.

"Congratulations, Tyler," Amanda said. "You're still the biggest douche in the parish."

"Only because Justin's dead," Tyler mumbled.

Amanda shook her head at him. "Like that somehow makes it better."

She looked over at us as she rose. "I'm so sorry that our party has ruined your stay. I'm sure this wasn't at all what you had in mind when you booked."

She gave Tyler one last disdainful look, then left the room.

Morgan pulled off his glasses and started cleaning them, a behavior I suspected he reverted to when he was in a stressful situation.

"Go to your room, Tyler," Morgan said. "There's no point in ruining the rest of these ladies' night."

"You're still here," Tyler said.

"I'm not the problem," Morgan replied. "I'm never the problem."

"And I always am?" Tyler asked.

"You said it." Morgan finished cleaning his glasses and slipped them back on but never even glanced in Tyler's direction. After several uncomfortable, silent seconds, Tyler jumped up and stalked out.

"I add my apologies to Amanda's," Morgan said.

"Can I ask you a personal question?" I asked.

"Yes. But I might not be willing to answer it depending on how personal it is."

"Fair enough. Why are any of you friends with him? No one appears to like him, and I get the feeling he was just as bad in high school. Why invite him to this pre-reunion get-together?"

Morgan sighed. "It would probably really dismay you to learn that Justin was twice as bad."

"Heavens," Gertie said. "Then why be friends with either of them?"

He smiled. "One of my friends from college is currently doing his residency in psychiatry. I've spent some time talking to him about us. He wrote his thesis on young adult group dynamics and interviewed a lot of different personality types for it, asking a bunch of questions about interactions with peers in high school. And although our group looks an odd mix from the outside, when you break it down by individual, it starts to make sense. At least, the way my friend explained it."

"You have to know the backstory," I said.

"Exactly. Just like a good book. The backstory matters."

"So what did your friend determine?" I asked, hoping he would take my question as general curiosity and would feel like answering.

"It would take far too long to go into the full-blown analysis, but have you ever seen *The Breakfast Club*? Teen movie about stereotypes?"

"Yes. Aunt Gertie had me watch it."

"It's more or less like that except the bond wasn't developed on one situational occasion like theirs was with detention, but instead by multiple connections leading back to a whole. Daniel and Justin had been friends since they were kids. Both athletes, good-looking, big personalities. Justin was just slightly better at everything though—a fact that Daniel's overbearing father never let his son forget. So Daniel looked up to Justin and together they ruled the school."

"Along with Brittany, no doubt," Gertie said.

"Yes," he agreed. "Brittany and Nicole's mothers are sisters, and they were born within a week of each other, so literally friends since the crib. Brittany was the popular one who likes having a following and Nicole was the quieter one who likes having a leader. Brittany was the best kind of leader because her popularity got Nicole access into the cool kids' group and all the best parties without having to earn it herself by making cheer or homecoming court and the like. Nicole was always more concerned with being included, not with being the center of attention."

He shook his head. "It's funny...the only thing Daniel ever bested Justin at was Brittany. Justin wanted her and they dated for a bit until she figured out he was hooking up with other girls on the side. Probably just as well she got his number then, because she might have ended up hitching her wagon to that star only to discover it was all flare and no substance."

"Sounds like she made the right decision," Gertie said. "A lot of young ladies ruin their lives over the good-looking bad boy."

"Brittany's a lot smarter than people think," Morgan said. "I think she knew Daniel was the best choice for a secure future, and that Justin would never grow up."

Gertie nodded. "And they still live in Houma?"

Morgan nodded. "Daniel's father owns a builders' supply company. The largest in the region. Daniel is an only child and was always slated to take over when his father retired. That was hurried along when he had a stroke that left him with some mobility and speech issues, but from what I've heard, he's still grasping the reins."

"Does Brittany work with him?" I asked, unable to reconcile her perfect hair and long polished nails with building material.

"No way. Brittany owns a gymnastics studio. She also teaches cheer classes, which fits. Two of her gymnastics students got college scholarships, which is pretty impressive."

"Definitely," I agreed. "What about Amanda? She doesn't

strike me as the cheerleader type, but I figured twins would be close."

He snorted. "Amanda made a concerted effort to do everything the opposite of her sister. Instead of cheer, she was chess club. Instead of homecoming court, she was the head of the art society. She's a brilliant woman who prefers no one realizes until it's too late."

"What do you mean?"

"She attended Berkeley on full scholarship, graduated with dual majors in accounting and law, was accepted straightaway into Berkeley's law school, again, on their dime. She's on track to make partner at one of the biggest financial legal firms in NOLA by the time she's thirty, which is practically unheard of."

"Wow," Ida Belle said. "That's impressive."

I nodded. "But if she doesn't volunteer that information then people tend to talk more openly around her, and she finds out things before they realize they gave too much away."

He smiled. "Exactly. And not only does Amanda collect information, she remembers everything, down to the last tiny detail. Poised and ready to use it against her enemy whether it's at that moment or ten years later."

"A dangerous woman to be friends with," I said. "Do she and Brittany think alike as much as they look alike?"

"Brittany is no dummy, and in high school, she always kept Amanda in her immediate circle even though they had little in common. Amanda was fine with lingering in the background being the observer."

"While Brittany wanted to be observed," Ida Belle said.

Morgan nodded. "Despite all their differences, there is no questioning their loyalty to each other. Go at one and you'll be fighting both."

"So where does Tyler come in?" Gertie asked.

"Not athletic enough to make the teams," Morgan said. "Not good-looking enough to be prom king. Not smart enough to help any of them pass classes. So he leaned heavily on making people laugh. He was the goof-off. He pulled the pranks and back-talked the teachers like others wanted to but people like Daniel and Justin had too much at risk to act a fool."

"So they goaded Tyler, who was happy to do it for them to gain admission into the group," Gertie said. "I had a Tyler every year in my classes."

"So the only one left to analyze is you," I said.

He nodded. "And one would think I'd have spent the most time on myself, but I was the easiest to explain. I was the smart kid. The geek. And mostly invisible until I started tutoring Daniel. He was a smart guy but between his father and Justin, Daniel was so used to not quite measuring up that he needed someone to help him believe in himself. He needed therapy more than a tutor, but once I convinced him he could do it, he passed with flying colors."

"And you earned a spot in the group," I said.

He nodded.

"But there's no adults that need antagonizing now," Ida Belle said. "I get inviting Justin because he was Daniel's best friend, even though I have to say he sounds very unpleasant. But why invite Tyler? His usefulness was years ago. I would think now that you're all grown, leaving him off the guest list would make things a lot nicer."

Morgan nodded, and I could tell he was seriously considering her words.

"I agree," he said finally. "I think my psychiatrist friend's habit of trying to assign a reason to all human behavior has rubbed off on me, and I'll admit it's something I did waste time mulling over after my first five minutes in Tyler's company."

"And did your mulling produce an answer?" Ida Belle asked.

"Yes, but I'm afraid that while I believe it to be accurate, it isn't very satisfying. I think the answer is guilt."

"How do you mean?"

"When you break everything down, we weren't really friends back then—not in the true meaning of things that I understand now as an adult. Except Nicole and Brittany. They're the only two who have remained close. But the rest of us were getting something out of the 'friendship' that we needed at the time. Brittany is the head of the reunion committee and she and Daniel—perhaps feeling nostalgic—suggested we get together beforehand for our own private reunion. They made the reservations and extended the invitations."

He sighed. "I guess you might have caught on that there was no love lost between Justin and Tyler. That's because Justin bullied Tyler in high school—always under the guise of 'just joking'—but honestly, it didn't appear that the dynamic had changed one bit when we arrived here. I had hoped everyone would have grown up, but apparently that's too much of a stretch for some."

I nodded. "So if Brittany and Daniel hadn't invited Tyler—who'd done their dirty work in high school and whom Justin picked on—then they would have felt guilty because they matured and perhaps realized that back then, it wasn't a relationship of equals."

"Very good," Morgan said. "Maybe you're wasted processing insurance claims."

"Maybe," I said. "Hey, you've never told us what you do for a living."

"I'm a plumber."

I blinked. "That's...nice."

He grinned. "I'm joking. I write code for a defense contractor."

He pushed his chair back and rose. "Ladies, I'm going to leave you to your evening. If I don't see you tomorrow before we leave, I hope you enjoy the rest of your stay."

He headed out and I watched him go, thinking about everything he'd said. It was interesting, the dynamics of the group—then and now—but I wasn't sure it mattered. Unless something popped up to prove things differently, Justin's death was looking like a horrible accident. It wasn't what Shadow Chaser wanted to hear, but at that point, it was the most likely answer.

"Corndog told me earlier they have after-dinner drinks and cookies in the library," Gertie said. "And to let him know if we want coffee."

Since we couldn't talk freely anywhere but my room, I wasn't thrilled with spending the rest of the night in the library, but I didn't see many choices. We needed to keep up appearances that we were on holiday and retiring to our rooms at 7:00 p.m. wasn't exactly a tourist move. If the friends were still out and about, we needed to appear as if we were getting the most out of our visit. Given that Ida Belle and Gertie were doing brilliantly playing the role of the elderly aunts, I figured we could probably head up around eight without anyone raising an eyebrow.

So we just had an hour to kill with bland, uninteresting small talk.

I hoped the drinks were stiff.

CHAPTER ELEVEN

Corndog and Petunia ended up joining us in the library. Petunia had knocked on every room door, asking if they needed anything before they retired for the night and inviting them to the library, but none of them appeared interested in taking her up on the offer. She'd come straight to the library after, so we knew we were clear to talk, but that was subject to change at any moment. To run interference, Ida Belle and Gertie headed to the entry with their drinks, intending to take some pictures. That way, they'd see if anyone was coming downstairs and could warn us to change conversation.

As soon as the door closed behind them, Corndog and Petunia gave me hopeful looks.

"I'm sorry," I said. "I can't tell you anything yet."

Corndog's shoulders slumped. "I know it's foolish to be disappointed, but I guess I was hoping for a miracle."

"It's possible he ate the wrong thing," Petunia said, clearly trying to soothe her husband. "He was really drunk. They all were. I know they said they didn't bring in anything with peanuts, but that's what they would say after something like this happened, right?"

I nodded. "Whether it was accidental or intentional, I think we can be certain no one is going to volunteer that information. It would help if I had the autopsy report and if I could see the room."

"Not much to see," Petunia said. "The sheriff took all his personal effects."

"I figured, but it helps to see everything. Have you heard from the sheriff yet?"

Corndog shook his head. "He said we'd hear from him by tomorrow morning. I don't know if that means 8:00 a.m. or 11:59, but I'm figuring the latter, given how uninterested he seemed in all of it."

"Yeah, I'd go with that one as well. I'm sorry I don't have better news, but since the sheriff isn't interested in working, do you think he'll try to pin it on you, or just let it go as some random accident among drunk people?"

"That's a good question," Corndog said. "I can't see any benefit to him pushing it as my fault, but then, he can be right contrary if you know what I mean. Still, seems like that would be a lot more paperwork."

"You can do paperwork sitting down," Petunia said drily.

"Regardless," I said, "I don't want you worrying about it. Let me get all the facts, and if it looks like he's going to make trouble for you, then I'll set you up with my attorney. What time is the group leaving tomorrow?"

"They said not to make a big buffet breakfast like this morning," Petunia said. "Told me they were planning on heading out early and getting breakfast in Houma before they check into the hotel. Their dance is tomorrow night, and they have a barbecue thing on Saturday midday."

"That fellow in charge told me on his way upstairs after

dinner that they was wanting to load up at 8:00 a.m.," Corndog said. "I have to make two trips, but I figure they should all be clear of here by nine at the latest, assuming we head out on time."

Petunia clutched her hands together. "If that fool sheriff says it's okay to go into the room, maybe it will help spark something in your mind. I'm sure you don't want to be hanging around any longer than you have to."

"Actually, I love this place. The house is beautiful and I don't have a problem with remote. Means fewer people, well, except for the whole B and B thing you have going now. And the food has been stellar."

They both smiled, and I could tell my compliments had perked them up. The best part was, I hadn't even lied. I really did love the house and the food. I just hoped I could figure out a way to salvage the situation for them because like Shadow, I hated the thought of these nice people losing the home they'd lived in for well over half their lives.

And thinking of Shadow...

"I assume you'll be talking to your nephew tonight," I said.

Petunia sighed. "That boy has already called six times. We keep telling him to either leave you alone to work or call you himself, but apparently, you scare him."

"Good. I don't want him to start texting or calling me all day. Being irritated tends to delay my progress."

Corndog chuckled. "And people are about the most irritating thing on earth."

Ida Belle and I both nodded.

Petunia smiled. "Your clothes are all done. Let me go grab them so you'll have them for the morning. I threw in a couple of my housecoats for Ida Belle and Gertie in case they need a bathroom trip in the middle of the night."

Corndog watched her go and his eyes got misty. "She's a

fine woman. More than I ever deserved. I don't know what I'll do if we lose this house. I know we can move somewhere else, but I'll be breaking my promise to her. We were supposed to grow old and die on that porch."

"I want you to die there too. No time soon, of course."

He gave me a grateful nod, and I prayed that I could find a way to make that happen.

WE HEADED UPSTAIRS AROUND EIGHT, ME TOTING A grocery bag with our clean clothes. I was glad Petunia had been able to drum up something for us to stay and get to know the other guests, but I was ready to be back in pants that fit. I was certain Ida Belle and Gertie felt the same, especially Gertie. But when I opened up the bag, I had to laugh. I assumed the two garments on the top were the 'housecoats' Petunia had referred to. They appeared to be a combination of a thin robe and old-timey dressing gown.

Both were large floral patterns and had zippers all the way up the front. Huge collars with lace on the ends looked like an itchy mess, but I supposed they weren't meant to be slept in, but rather worn outside of your bedroom so as not to offend houseguests by jaunting around in your pj's.

"That's almost as bad as this dress," Gertie said.

Ida Belle nodded. "It's definitely worse than my overalls."

I doled out the housecoats and our clean clothes and we sat around in my room for about an hour, going over everything we'd learned that day. It was a good bit of information but absolutely nothing that screamed 'Justin was murdered, and X did it.'

Of course, if things had been that obvious, I would have

been just as suspicious. I was never impressed with coincidence or easy. But this one time, it would have been nice to have something more positive to latch onto. Gertie and Ida Belle headed for their bedroom around nine and I hopped into bed with my phone, hoping that since the storm had passed, I could at least read. I was nowhere near sleepy, but there was no television in the rooms and the one in the library hadn't been able to get a decent signal anyway.

I checked my phone and sighed. One flashing bar. I was going to have to resort to carrying a rescue bag. Too many times, I'd ended up somewhere and needed things that were back at my house. No weapons, of course. They were always on my body, but a spare set of clothes, some lock-picking tools, and an e-reader probably weren't a bad idea. At least if I preloaded books, the weather couldn't strand me with nothing to do.

I checked my text messages and was surprised to see a reply from Carter. I hadn't gotten an alert but with the signal going in and out, that wasn't surprising. I tapped to open it.

Avoid Bryce. Good luck.

I smiled. It was nice having a guy who really understood you. I imagined I'd give regular men a heart attack, but I'd been fortunate to surround myself with men who didn't feel the need to be rushing in to save me all the time. Carter, Mannie, and Harrison were all well aware of my abilities and let me run with them. Of course, they had my back, as I had theirs, but that was a totally different thing than white-knighting around the helpless woman.

I knew Carter worried a lot more than he let on, because he wasn't as good at hiding it as me. I should have gotten an Academy Award for my performance after his rescue. When I was in Iran, I was 100 percent game face and that was legit.

But afterward, watching him question his entire military career had been one of the hardest things I'd ever done. Especially since the smartest thing to do was absolutely nothing. It was something I couldn't fix. The answers had to come from within Carter.

And I thought they were finally arriving.

I typed a reply and hit Send.

So far so good on Bryce. Not so much on the case. Hoping to find something tomorrow.

The text hung for a bit and finally went through, so I flipped over to my book and started to read. I dozed off at some point, but then something had me bolting up and reaching for my pistol. I'd shifted the nightstand so that my gun was in the exact location I placed it at home, so I was already standing, gun pointed at the door, before I was completely awake.

Then I heard what must have alerted me. Footsteps in the hallway outside. I hurried to slip on my pants and eased the door open. As I stepped into the hallway, Ida Belle opened their door a crack and I knew she'd heard it too. The hallway was empty, but the bathroom door was open and the light wasn't on. I motioned to Ida Belle to follow, and cringed a bit when I saw they were both wearing the horrible housecoats. I said a silent prayer that no one stuck their head out of their bedroom, because even in the dim light, the material glowed.

I crept down the hallway, trying to ascertain where the footsteps had gone. The hall bathroom was empty, as expected, and I detected no sound on the other side of any of the bedroom doors, so I continued the length of the corridor. When I reached the stairs, I heard someone moving across the entry below. I ducked back into the shadows so that they wouldn't see me if I looked up and saw Ida Belle and Gertie do the same. I waited until I could no longer hear movement below, then eased toward the railing and peered over.

The only light permeating the entry was cast from the rear, and I assumed it was a lamp on a table near the library doors, or perhaps even light coming from the library itself. It was barely enough to create a dim shadow into the space, but I saw no movement. I hurried down the stairs and just as I stepped off onto the entry floor, a boom of thunder roared through the sky and the light went completely out, as did the hallway lights upstairs.

I froze, listening for footsteps, but the storm was the only sound I heard. Then the floor above me creaked. Ida Belle and Gertie were right behind me on the stairs, so it wasn't them. I waited for the normal movement and sound of someone who had awakened and needed a bathroom visit, but everything was quiet.

Too quiet.

If someone had legitimate reasons for moving around, they wouldn't be taking such care to conceal their movement, especially in a pitch-black house that they weren't overly familiar with. At the very least, they'd fire up the flashlight on their cell phones. So what were they up to that they didn't want anyone else to know about?

A glint of moonlight streamed in through the windows, illuminating the entry enough to traverse, so I motioned to Ida Belle and Gertie to look around, then did a fork to mouth motion, indicating that if anyone inquired, they'd been hungry and were going to raid the cookie stash in the library. They nodded and headed by me, still walking quietly and without speaking, but not attempting to sneak. If someone was watching, they would not assume they were anything but two old ladies with insomnia looking for a snack.

I crept back up the stairs, and just as I stepped onto the

landing, I saw the door to Justin's room move. I eased up to the door and nudged it open an inch with my shoulder. The moonlight was sparse, but every couple seconds, a dim glow settled over the room. I didn't see anyone moving, but without light, I couldn't be certain the room was empty.

"Corndog?" I called out loud, keeping up the pretense of being a guest. "Petunia? Are you in there?"

But the only thing I heard was the wind and rain outside. I did a quick check over the rail to make sure no one was below and looking up, then shoved the door completely open with my shoulder and stepped between the police tape, careful not to touch anything as I wasn't wearing gloves. The room had a double bed with one nightstand and a wardrobe in one corner. There was no other door than the entry, so I walked for the first of the only two places someone could be hiding.

I lifted a tissue from the holder on the nightstand and used it to grab the wardrobe door. When the next burst of moonlight entered the room, I yanked the door open, ready to tackle anyone inside, but the wardrobe was empty. Before the light disappeared again, I dropped to my knees and lifted the edge of the bed skirt and peered underneath, but the space below the bed was clear.

I popped back up and frowned. Something had caused that door to move. They were solid and heavy. If it was uneven or the frame was sloped, the door could naturally inch open, but every time I'd passed the door until now, it had been in place against the broken frame. Something or someone had to have caused it. And since there was no someone that I could find, maybe it was a something. Air pressure maybe, created by someone opening an external door.

Or a window!

I hurried to the bedroom window and spotted the unlocked latches and drops of water on the inside sill and the floor below. I peered outside, but the only movement I saw was trees and the ivy surrounding the window swaying in the storm. They'd gone out the window and climbed down a trellis! For a split second, I considered going after them, then realized it was not only risky but foolish. It wasn't as if there were any place to run, so whoever had gone out that window had to come back inside the house.

I hurried out of the room, using my T-shirt over my hand to pull the door closed, and then I crept downstairs. I was aware of three doors into the house—the front door, the kitchen door, and the back door—but it was possible there were more. And whoever had planned their illegal jaunt could have unlocked any of them before they went into the room, or a window for that matter. Which gave them multiple options to reenter the house, but the one thing that they had no flexibility on was the weather.

Whoever had gone out that window in the storm would come back into the house wet.

I hurried down the stairs, listening for any sound of movement, but the only noise was the ticking of the grandfather clock. The power was still out, and the only illumination in the entry was the bits of moonlight that crept out of the clouds long enough to cast a dim glow over the space.

Then someone shrieked. Then another someone. The second one was Gertie.

It came from the direction of the kitchen, so I sprinted for the door, but when I got close, the door flew open and I barely got my hands up to keep it from smacking me in the face. I vaulted backward from the blow but before I could regain my balance, someone slammed into me, knocking me down as they bolted for the stairs. I jumped up and ran after them and out of the corner of my eye, saw the front door open as I ran past.

I tackled the fleeing figure, who let out another shriek, and we both crashed in a heap on the stairwell, but my grip on them was solid. They weren't getting away. A second later, the lights in the hallway overhead and the lamp behind me flickered back on and illuminated the face of a very scared Brittany Stout.

Who appeared to be covered in blood.

CHAPTER TWELVE

I pushed up on my knees, searching her for the source of the injury in the dim light, and heard people running from behind and above me. Brittany squinted and finally realized who I was and started yelling.

"Get off me!"

I jumped up, figuring if she could yell that loudly, she wasn't hurt. Then the big chandelier in the entry flickered on, illuminating everything as though it were daylight. Brittany popped up and I could now see that the red substance covering her definitely wasn't blood. It was way too thin. So thin, she was dripping everywhere.

Daniel rushed downstairs wearing only his boxers, and he grabbed Brittany by the shoulders, clearly distressed and probably assuming the same thing I had. Morgan and Nicole were close behind him, Morgan wearing shorts and a T-shirt and Nicole clad in her robe. Clearly, they'd all been in or preparing for bed. Amanda was the person I'd seen coming in the front door, and Tyler had come from the hallway that led to the back porch. Ida Belle and Gertie had been in the kitchen, and Gertie held a now-empty pitcher with only a couple drops of red liquid in the bottom. I had a feeling Brittany was wearing whatever that pitcher had held.

"What the hell is going on?" Daniel demanded.

Brittany pointed at me. "She attacked me!"

Daniel turned to me and glared. "Explain yourself."

"I came downstairs to get a water and heard my aunt scream. When I ran for the kitchen, Brittany came running out, almost hit me with the door, and knocked me down. I thought it was an intruder who had hurt my aunt, so I tackled her before she could get away. I had no idea who it was until the lights came back on. It was too dim to see anything but the outline of a person."

Brittany put her hands on her hips and flung her hand at Gertie. "I did not attack anyone. I was going to get water when the lights went out and then someone—obviously her—doused me with whatever this red stuff is. It startled me, and since I didn't know why it had happened or who had done it, I figured running was the smart thing to do. If this doesn't wash out of my hair, you're paying to have my hair fixed."

Everyone looked at Gertie, who gave them a sheepish look. "I'm sorry. We thought we'd try to get some pictures of ghosts but then I got thirsty and was just about to pour myself some fruit punch when the lights went out. Then we heard something moving around. I thought you were an evil spirit."

Brittany stared at her as if she'd lost her mind. "And you thought you'd protect yourself by drowning me in fruit punch?"

"I prayed on it before I threw it," Gertie said, sounding as if it was completely reasonable.

Tyler started laughing and Brittany shifted her glare to him, but it didn't even put a dent in his glee.

"It's the politically correct version of *Carrie*," he said. "Punch on the prom queen instead of blood."

He finally dropped into a chair, bent over, his shoulders shaking, and I could see his hair was damp.

"I apologize," I said. "It was obviously a huge misunderstanding. I'm happy to pay for your clothes and your hair, if it's ruined."

Brittany whirled around and stomped up the stairs, not even bothering to acknowledge what I'd said. Daniel cast a final disapproving look at the three of us and hurried after his wife. At that point, he'd spent more time chasing after his angry wife than people did running the Boston Marathon. Nicole gave us all a 'holy crap' look, then headed upstairs after her friend, calling for Brittany to wait for her as she had a good shampoo to use.

Amanda shook her head. "Anyone need a drink? I'm pouring."

"Might as well before I go mop the kitchen," I said.

Everyone followed her into the library, and Amanda hit the liquor cabinet and mixed up cocktails. Gertie took a sip and her eyes widened.

"This is really good!"

"Better than that fruit punch?" Amanda asked.

Gertie sighed. "I didn't actually get any, and it seemed rude to ask her to wring out her clothes..."

Tyler choked on his drink and started laughing all over again. Even the ever-serious Morgan couldn't hold back a smile.

"I feel horrible," I said as I did a dramatic flop into a chair. "I heard Aunt Gertie scream and then I got slammed with the door and Brittany. All I could think of was getting the person who'd hurt my aunt."

"It was rather impressive," Morgan said. "And not exactly the norm for a quiet insurance processor."

"For real!" I said and blew out a breath. "I can't believe I did it. It's like I momentarily lost all sense of self-protection. What if it *had* been an intruder? What if he'd had a weapon? Jesus, that might be the dumbest thing I've done all week. Well, besides come here, that is."

Amanda finished mixing her own drink and sat on the couch across from me, and I noticed her hair was damp and flat on her head. "Don't worry about it. Brittany will get over it. It's not like you did it with ill intent. She's a barracuda about our own grandmother. When she gets a new robe and gets the punch out of her hair, she'll be fine."

"Did I see you come in the front door when I went on my suicide mission?" I asked.

Amanda nodded. "I'm a night owl and I like to watch storms. Most people back away from them but I find them soothing."

Ida Belle raised one eyebrow. "Is that the only reason?" she asked and touched her nose.

Amanda's eyes widened. "You can smell it on me?"

Ida Belle nodded.

"Wow. You have a nose like a bloodhound," Amanda said.

Morgan frowned. "Don't tell me you're vaping again."

A flash of guilt crossed Amanda's face. "Okay," she said. "I won't tell you."

"You know how horrible it is for you," he said. "And you'd quit. Why start up again?"

"I know. I know. Come work my job for a week and let me know if you don't pick up a vice. I just need to get this big case settled and then I'll quit again. I promise."

"Hey, should we be worried that the old couple haven't come out to see who's tearing their house down?" Tyler asked.

"On the way over, Corndog told me they sleep with earplugs," I said. "I might need to get the brand because... yeah."

Morgan frowned. "I suppose it makes sense to take extra steps for a decent night's sleep when you turn your home over to strangers, but it doesn't seem without risk."

"Who the heck is going to come all the way out here to commit a crime?" Tyler asked.

"I would imagine the list is fairly short," Ida Belle said. "And given that most people around these parts sleep with a loaded firearm nearby, there would have to be a good reason to risk it. The house has some nice things in it, but nothing looks particularly valuable, except the house itself."

Amanda nodded. "I agree. The value here is in the structure, unless there's a Monet hidden in the attic."

I shrugged. "Or assuming the guests aren't the perpetrators."

Amanda gave me an appreciative look. "I hadn't considered that, but you're right. However, I still think it's probably better that Corndog sleeps through this sort of thing. With all that squinting he does, I wouldn't want him startled awake and running out with his gun."

She looked over at Tyler and narrowed her eyes. "What were you doing down here? I saw you come in from the back hallway."

He shrugged. "Same thing as you, I guess. Minus the vape."

She didn't look remotely convinced. "You were sitting on the back porch watching the rain and contemplating the next stages of your life and career?"

He grinned. "I was just contemplating breakfast and if Molly Parker's boobs got bigger since high school."

Amanda gave him a disgusted look and Morgan frowned.

"Crude, much?" Amanda asked him. "And even if Molly's boobs were as big as the parish, she still wouldn't let you put one of your dirty paws on them. Well, I'm done with my drink and since it seems the storm has moved off both inside and outside, I'm going to bed."

Morgan rose along with her and gave us a nod. "Good night, ladies."

Tyler watched them leave, then headed for the liquor cabinet and poured himself a healthy dose of straight whiskey. He knocked back half of it, refilled it, and held his glass up.

"Thanks for the show," he said. "It's not often I get to see Brittany taken down a peg or two from her ivory tower. Happy ghost hunting."

I rose as Tyler headed for the door. "I guess I better wipe up the kitchen floor. I don't want Petunia or Corndog to walk in there tomorrow morning, see all that punch, and have a heart attack."

Ida Belle, Gertie, and I headed for the kitchen and located a mop and some rags.

"Give me a minute," I whispered. "I want to make sure Corndog and Petunia are good."

I headed down the little hallway off the back of the kitchen and accessed the door to their owner's suite. It was unlocked, which was something I'd consider the downside of later, and I crossed a tiny sitting area and went for the door on the back of the room, which I assumed led to the bedroom.

I turned the knob and gently eased the door open. A night-light from the bathroom illuminated the room well enough to spot the couple in their bed, both wearing masks and I assumed, the earplugs, as they were snoring and didn't seem to have been remotely bothered by all the goings-on in the rest of the house.

Satisfied that they were fine, I headed back to the kitchen to collect Ida Belle and Gertie. I needed to tell them what I'd discovered, and I couldn't risk talking anywhere but my room. As soon as we were secured inside, I looked at Gertie.

"Why did you really throw the punch on Brittany?" I asked.

"I wanted to make sure whoever was skulking around down there was easy to identify," Gertie said. "I remembered the punch from earlier today and figured whoever was wearing it would be easy to spot."

Ida Belle shook her head. "Or you could have just turned your phone flashlight on and blinded her."

"The punch was far more exciting," Gertie said. "And she has no way of denying it was her. If I'd just blinded her we could have been the old women with bad eyesight and the power was out and blah, blah, blah."

I had to smile. "For a last-minute plan, it wasn't the worst we've seen. And the whole tackling thing helps us narrow down where everyone was, although I have to admit, I wasn't counting on half of them being downstairs wandering around. Your backup story, however, was genius. The housecoats just sealed the deal, by the way. They think you're off your rockers."

"One of us is," Ida Belle said. "Did you figure out who was moving around upstairs?"

"No. And that's the most interesting thing that has happened since we got here." I told them about someone going out the window in Justin's room.

"But why would someone go to all that trouble to hide being in the room?" Gertie asked. "Do you think someone killed Justin and left evidence behind?"

"We don't know that Justin was murdered," Ida Belle said. "And even if he was and someone had dropped a button or left fingerprints or whatever, it's still a fool's move. I get not announcing your plan to enter a crime scene, but if someone discovered you once you had, it would make more sense to just say 'My bad. I was looking for a pen I lent

Justin and was hoping I wouldn't have to deal with that idiot sheriff.'"

I nodded. "Scaling the side of a house during a storm definitely raises eyebrows. And the room was cleared of any personal items, so I assume Bryce removed them. But maybe they didn't know that. Or thought he might have missed something. Given how incompetent he is, I can see why they might."

"Maybe whoever was in the room isn't as good at making up lies on the spot as we are and they panicked," Gertie said. "Maybe they had nothing to do with killing Justin, but they lost something in his room for completely other reasons... reasons they might not want anyone to know."

I frowned. I had to admit, that was an interesting theory given that the friends had confirmed that Justin had been a serious player with the women, so the idea that someone might want to hide evidence of other shenanigans wasn't completely without merit.

"Morgan said Justin always had a thing for Brittany," I said, "but surely she wouldn't be stupid enough to carry on with him when her husband was literally right down the hall. And since she ditched him in high school for bad behavior, why make a move now when it doesn't sound like he'd changed at all, except maybe to get worse?"

Ida Belle shrugged. "There's also Nicole and Amanda. Both are very attractive women. Given Justin's less-than-stellar reputation, I don't think either would want the others to know if they'd had drunk sex with him, even though they're both single."

"Probably not," I agreed.

"So assuming you're right and someone *did* risk going out the window in the storm, who could it have been?"

"Nicole, Morgan, and Daniel all came from upstairs and were dry," Gertie said. "So it wasn't any of them."

"Amanda came in the front door," I said. "And she was damp, so she's definitely on the list, but so is Tyler. He claimed he was out back, and his hair was wet."

"So one of those two," Gertie said.

Ida Belle shook her head. "You're forgetting one. Brittany was downstairs, and since you doused her with punch, we have no way of knowing if she was wet before that. She could have planned to go out the window if she got caught and had stashed the robe downstairs just in case. Maybe her clothes were wet underneath as well."

I nodded. "Excellent point. And even if Amanda and Tyler were exactly where they claimed to be, there's a third door into the house, remember?"

"Through the kitchen," Gertie said. "She could have already been in there when Ida Belle and I walked in. Maybe hiding in the pantry when she heard us coming. We were quiet, but sound echoes down there."

"It's certainly possible," Ida Belle said. "It was too dark to see much of anything after the lights went out. She could have been standing behind the curtains for all we know. But she never called out, which is suspicious in itself. I mean, if you're not up to anything, why be so quiet about it?"

"And as Ida Belle pointed out, she could have used her phone as a flashlight," Gertie said. "I'm sure she had it on her. The robe had pockets and young people don't move without their phones."

I nodded. "She probably tried to make a run for her room when the lights went out. And the phone and not calling out aren't the only suspicious things. There's a whole mini fridge of water in the library, which is easier to access and something she would have been well aware of. Plus, it's there specifically for guests. Why go into the kitchen when guests aren't really supposed to be in there?"

"So we have three suspects, one of whom broke into Justin's room for an unknown reason and risked scaling a trellis in a rainstorm rather than get caught," Gertie said.

"We need that reason," Ida Belle said.

I nodded. "But I don't think we're going to get it. Not easily, anyway."

I RARELY SLEPT DEEPLY AND DEFINITELY NOT WHEN I WASN'T in my own house. Knowing that someone had been creeping around a potential murder scene made sleep even more impossible. So I tossed and turned and dozed a little, but ultimately, gave up around 5:00 a.m. and headed downstairs.

Because the house was completely quiet, I figured everyone was still sleeping. And since the storm had turned to a drizzle that had finally ceased sometime early that morning, this would be a great opportunity to check the window in Justin's room from outside. I headed down the hallway to the door that opened onto the back porch. It was a small area, especially compared to the front porch, which stretched the length of the house. This one was eight feet by ten feet with a roof above and lattice on each side with thick vines providing shade and privacy. Two chairs sat at the far end next to the ivy-covered lattice.

If Tyler had been sitting here, he wouldn't have seen someone scaling down the side of the house. The lack of light and the storm would have already decreased visibility to almost nil for any distance, but the vines sealed the deal. Someone could have come down the side of the house, any noise they made lost in the storm, and then entered the house through the kitchen. Or it could have been Tyler, and he could have simply come in the back door and claimed he was sitting on the porch. Or Amanda, who came in through the front.

I went down the steps and turned around to study the side of the house and as I suspected, the lattice from the porch ran all the way up the side of the house, covering a good quarter of it. Justin's window was right in the middle of the latticework, and it extended all the way to the corner of the house to my left and stopped just before the hall bathroom window on the right.

I stepped closer, carefully scanning the ground on the off chance there was a footprint, but the ground cover was thick and even if there had been prints in the small spots of dirt, the storm would have washed them away. When I reached the wall, I grabbed a slat of the lattice and gave it a tug. Most lattice was decorative and eventually rotted in our environment, but this was thick and solid and appeared to be constructed from a hard resin rather than wood. I pulled myself up a couple of feet, and while it shook with my body weight, it stayed flat against the house and didn't show any signs of instability.

I jumped back down, pulled out my phone, and took a couple shots of everything so I'd have a reference after we left. The lattice definitely made the climb down doable, but it was still dangerous, especially in a storm. One slip or one weak slat and they would have hit the ground. Given some of the sizable tree roots I spotted right below the window, a fall could have been deadly. The bottom line was that going out that window to avoid detection had been a huge risk. So was the intruder a foolish risk-taker or desperate?

I was leaning toward desperate.

I headed back inside, hoping to locate a coffeepot and get a brew going. With any luck, Corndog and Petunia would still be wearing their earplugs and I wouldn't wake them. But as soon as I reached the front entry, I could smell coffee brewing. Despite the early hour, the couple was already dressed and hard at work in the kitchen, but then I supposed one could awake with all that energy if they got in enough sleep. Living with a lack of paranoia was a blessing when it came to rest. But not so much when it came to self-preservation—at least not in my case.

"Good morning," Corndog said as I walked in. "You look like you could use a cup of coffee, if you don't mind my saying it."

"You can say whatever you like as long as I get a cup," I said and slipped onto a barstool at the kitchen counter, where Petunia was making homemade biscuits.

"Was the bed not comfortable?" Petunia asked, looking concerned.

"It's not that. I'm just not good at sleeping away from home. Heck, I'm not all that good at sleeping *at* home. But we had some events last night."

I looked back and lowered my voice. "As soon as the other guests leave, I'll fill you in, but you'll be missing a pitcher of fruit punch. I can explain that later."

Both their eyebrows went up, and I could tell they were itching for me to tell them everything now, but we couldn't risk being overheard. My caution proved out a minute later when Nicole walked in. She hesitated just for a second before easing onto the stool beside me.

"I see I'm not the only one on an early coffee journey," she said.

I nodded. "Too much excitement combined with rich food, entirely too much sugar, and more alcohol than I normally have."

"Which is also sugar, much to my dismay," she said. "I've

been lying there for an hour now, trying to force myself back to sleep, but I finally gave up. I thought I'd sneak in and get a pot going, but I see you actually beat me to it."

"Corndog and Petunia did," I said and held up my cup. "I'm just on my first. How is Brittany? Did the fruit punch come out of her hair?"

Petunia gave a start and stopped working on her dough. "What happened?"

"Aunt Gertie had a bit of a blunder," I said and sighed. "The aunts were wandering the house last night—unbeknownst to me—trying to capture a ghost on camera. They heard someone moving around when they were in the kitchen, and Brittany came in wearing a white robe right after the power went out and Aunt Gertie thought she was a ghost. Apparently, she decided blessing the fruit punch she was holding and tossing it onto her would properly expel her from the house."

Corndog and Petunia both stared at me for a couple seconds, then Corndog chuckled.

"That aunt of yours is a pistol," he said. "But don't you worry about that fruit punch. She was trying to protect my house, and I can appreciate the sentiment if not the outcome."

"Thank you," I said. "Unfortunately, I'm not certain others involved were as amused. I cleaned up the mess in the kitchen, but I'm afraid I'm on the hook for a robe and a hairdresser."

Nicole gave me a sympathetic smile. "Brittany's hair is fine. If she'd sat around like that for hours then there might have been problems given her light hair color, but she went straight into the shower. The robe is questionable, but nothing for you to worry about. It was actually mine. We're always borrowing each other's things. Have done since we were kids. I accidentally packed two and she didn't pack any, so..."

"Seems like you two would have made better sisters than her and Amanda," I said.

Nicole laughed. "We always thought so. But it would have been nice if Amanda had played the fashion game. Then we could have had three times the closet options, not just two. If you'll excuse me, I'm going to take this coffee with me upstairs and get my things together. I know Daniel wants us all out of here early. If I don't see you again, Rose, it was nice meeting you. I hope you and your aunts enjoy the rest of your vacation."

I nodded and she headed out. I could see Corndog and Petunia were practically ready to burst wondering what the real story behind the fruit punch was, but I couldn't risk telling them.

"When they clear out," I said quietly, and they both nodded.

CHAPTER THIRTEEN

I TOOK MY COFFEE AND HEADED OUT ONTO THE PORCH, figuring that would give me the best place to potentially engage my suspects in a final conversation before they left. And I was now considering them exactly that—suspects. Because whoever went out that window was hiding something. Maybe it was a crime. Maybe it was just personal and embarrassing. But whatever it was, they were willing to risk entering a crime scene to make sure it remained hidden and a life-threatening climb down the side of the house during a storm.

The entire situation was beyond sketchy.

Unfortunately, I didn't get a chance to quiz any of the others individually because they all came out within minutes of one another, some in pairs. Daniel and Brittany were first, both of them checking their watches every ten seconds, looking impatiently at the door. They'd given me the briefest of nods and a mumbled 'Good morning,' but I figured I was still on their strike list because of the whole punch fiasco.

"Your hair looks great," I said when it was clear that neither of them planned on speaking to me. "I'm really sorry about last night. My aunts have a way of getting into trouble.

It's why I try to get out of taking them places, but they're old and I love them..."

I shrugged and Brittany sniffed, but her shoulders relaxed a bit.

"It's all right," she said. "I have a grandmother who I adore but she's not without challenges, especially the older she gets."

"I'm happy to pay for the robe," I said.

"It was actually Nicole's and she said it was an old one and not to worry about it," Brittany said. "She'd planned on donating it when she did her annual closet clean. I guess we'll just consider it an early donation."

She gave me a small smile, which I returned.

"I'm not sure the donation benefited anyone," I said, "but I'll graciously accept her generosity. And yours. But I'm happy to replace it if you need one for the reunion. Oh, but you live in Houma, right?"

She gave me a nod and I could tell all was forgiven.

"Yes, but we're all staying at the reunion hotel the next two nights. I tried to encourage everyone attending to book rooms since there would be drinking. I negotiated a discounted rate."

"That's smart. Hopefully everyone will take advantage and the rest of your reunion will go off without a hitch."

Tyler and Nicole came out next, and I noticed Tyler was carrying Nicole's bag. I figured he'd probably waited at his door until she'd exited her room, then rushed forward to offer his services. His crush on Nicole was so obvious, but Nicole never gave any indication that she was aware or that they were anything other than just friends. I wondered if that was her way of turning him down gently. Given that high school was ten years ago, and it looked as if Tyler's torch was still burning, I didn't think the gentle option was getting the point across all that well.

Morgan and Amanda were right behind Tyler and Nicole, and then Corndog came out after them.

"Who wants to go first?" he asked. "I figure I'll take three at a time to make it even."

Brittany and Daniel headed down the steps and Nicole lifted her bag. "I'll go with them," she said.

Tyler watched as she headed away, the disappointment clear in his expression, but then he realized I was watching and grabbed his bag to hurry after them. "I'll just wait at the dock. Maybe I'll see some alligators."

He hurried off and Amanda came and sat down next to me. "I see my sister's hair is back in full bloom. Guess you and the aunts are off the hook."

"Thank God," I said. "I've never been so exhausted by a mini vacation in my life."

She laughed. "Are you staying all weekend?"

"No. We're actually leaving sometime today, but we're not headed home right away. I have the weekend off and there's a couple other places they wanted to check out. Apparently, there's a bar in Meditation where you have to sit cross-legged to curse?"

They both laughed.

"I know that place," Amanda said. "We used to sneak in back in high school to video them."

Morgan nodded. "It was one of the few times I was happy to have that fake ID."

"That's because it didn't work for buying beer in Houma where everyone knew our parents," Amanda said. "And the only place Justin and Tyler wanted to go was to New Orleans to stare at boobs."

Morgan blushed a bit. "Well, I'm not going to say that I never joined on the New Orleans jaunts, but the company definitely put a damper on the view."

Amanda shook her head. "I can't imagine trying to corral Justin and Tyler drunk and in NOLA. I don't know why you bothered. There's easier ways to see boobs."

He shrugged. "Mostly because Daniel asked me to and I didn't figure it was fair to leave him with it, even though they were more his friends than mine."

Amanda smiled. "You always were a good guy, Morgan. I think I'm going to head out to the dock myself. Corndog shouldn't be long, and I'm ready to hit the café and have the biggest chicken-fried steak they offer. You ready?"

"Go on ahead," Morgan said. "Petunia baked some of those chocolate cookies I loved so much and is going to pack some up for me as soon as they are cool enough to go into a bag."

She nodded and pulled out a card and handed it to me. "My cell phone's on the back. I meant what I said about our girls' night bitch sessions. You ever want to get out of the house and kick back without having to worry about men hitting on you, then come join us. Our booth is private and my girls are the best."

"I really appreciate it," I said. "I might just take you up on it."

She headed off with an overhead wave and Morgan shoved his hands in his jeans pockets and watched her go before turning back to me.

"She meant the offer," he said. "In case you were wondering. Amanda doesn't do grand gestures. If she invited you to her private girls' thing, it's because she likes you."

"I didn't take her for one who postures, but it's good to know I was right." I watched as Amanda stepped into the woods and bit my lower lip, hoping it conveyed nervous thoughts. "Are you guys going to be all right? With the death, I mean?"

Morgan's smile dissipated as he seemed to consider my

question. "I think so. Some of us more than others. To be honest, I feel worse for Corndog and Petunia than I do our group. That sheriff was a clown, and I'm worried that he can cause them trouble."

He gave me a small smile. "I guess you've figured out that some of us weren't exactly broken up over Justin's death. In fact, some might even feel he had it coming."

"Why? I mean, high school was a long time ago."

Morgan locked his eyes on mine. "Some acts are so egregious that the suffering and the desire for retribution have no expiration."

I nodded. I certainly understood that sentiment. It was one of the many reasons I was glad Kitts was dead.

"Then I guess it's a good thing his death was accidental," I said. "Otherwise, you might all find yourself suspects."

"Not all of us."

The front door opened, and Petunia came out with a freezer bag stuffed with cookies. Morgan's serious expression was replaced with a genuine smile.

"This is incredible," he said as he gave her a hug and a kiss on the cheek. "I didn't expect so many, but no way I'm turning them down. Thanks so much, Petunia."

She flushed as she passed him the bag. "I put the recipe in there as well. It will have a bit of chocolate on it but if it gets too smudged to see it, then you just give me a call and I'll help you out. Voodoo Island is a long way to go to get good cookies. I figured a smart young man like yourself might try baking some on your own."

"That's a great idea!" He turned to me and stuck his hand out. "It was a pleasure meeting you, Rose. I hope the rest of your weekend is less, uh, eventful."

"Your mouth to God's ears," I said as we shook. "It was nice meeting you too. Have fun at the reunion."

Petunia and I watched as Morgan headed off, then she smiled at me.

"Those two 'aunts' of yours are in the kitchen pouring coffee," she said. "It won't take Corndog long to get those kids across, then you can tell us both what you've discovered."

I nodded. "And I want to get a look at that room."

"If that idiot sheriff doesn't call soon, we'll just let you in and say we forgot. That's one of the beautiful things about getting older. You just do whatever the heck you want and then claim you didn't remember you weren't supposed to."

I couldn't help but grin. "I didn't know you had it in you, Petunia."

Ida Belle and Gertie were already on their second cup of coffee by the time we walked into the kitchen. They both looked over and nodded.

"Saw you on the front porch," Ida Belle said, "but we figured we'd stick inside and let you do your thing. Morgan seems to have taken a liking to you."

I shrugged. "Maybe. At least it wasn't Tyler. Good Lord, he's exhausting."

Petunia waved at a stool. "You just hop on up there and I'll whip up some eggs. Corndog carried a biscuit and sausage with him on the way out, so this way, we'll be ready to talk as soon as he gets back."

"Homemade biscuits?" I said as I sat next to Gertie. "You don't have to ask me twice."

"I can get you started on those now," Petunia said as she pulled a plate of biscuits out of the oven where she'd been keeping them warm. "And here's the sausage. It won't take me any time to scramble up those eggs."

"Don't even bother," Ida Belle said. "The biscuits and sausage are plenty and smell incredible."

I lifted a biscuit and slathered it with butter before dropping a sausage inside it, then topped the sausage with homemade strawberry jelly. I took the first bite and sighed.

"These might just be the best biscuits I've ever eaten," I said.

Gertie nodded. "And your jelly is excellent. Mine is pretty good but borders just on being too sweet. I don't suppose you'd give me your recipe?"

"Oh my," Petunia said, clearly flattered. "I surely can. It was my mother's recipe. Never modified a single teaspoon of it."

"Why would you?" Gertie asked. "It's perfect."

By the time we'd all polished off a second biscuit, we heard Corndog whistling in the entry. A few seconds later, he entered the kitchen.

"Well, we're all alone now, so you can tell us what's been going on," he said as he took a seat on a stool. "Me and Petunia's been about to burst from wanting to know."

"I don't have solid answers," I said. "But I do have a lot of weirdness."

I told them about everything we'd heard and seen over the last day and when I got to the part about someone going out Justin's window, they both stared at me in shock.

"Good Lord, why would anyone go out the window, much less in a storm?" Corndog asked. "Those trellises are strong, but it's still a dangerous thing to do, even if it wasn't raining."

I nodded. "The climb wasn't easy even though the trellis is definitely solid enough to hold someone. But unless the person who went out the window tested it beforehand, they couldn't have known that. Then you've got navigating down it in a storm and avoiding people on the front and rear porches to get back into the house. Assuming, of course, it wasn't either one of them who was our climber. The whole thing was a huge risk."

"Two people were outside?" Petunia asked.

I nodded. "Tyler claims he was sitting on the back porch, and he *did* come into the entry from the back hallway with a damp head. And Amanda was on the front porch and damp as well."

"And then there's Brittany, who could have bypassed both of them by sneaking in through the kitchen door," Ida Belle said. "We're not buying her water story. Not when there's plenty of cold bottles in the library and she knows good and well where to find them."

Corndog's eyes widened. "I hadn't even thought about that. My nephew was right. Nothing gets past you ladies, and that situation with the punch was genius. I can't believe you had the ghost-hunting cover story ready to go just like that."

"It's not our first time to invent things on the spot," Ida Belle said. "And won't be the last."

"Have you heard anything from the sheriff about accessing the room?" I asked.

He shook his head. "Not a peep, but honestly, I'm not really expecting to. That boy is about as useless as they come. He's made a career out of avoiding work and this situation falls squarely into that category."

Petunia nodded. "You should have heard him complaining when he was here the other day. He'd had to take his boat down to the launch, and had to put in fuel, and the mosquitoes were bad, and it was humid. He made it sound like that poor boy had died just to inconvenience him."

"Well, then I guess we move on to plan B, which is you two forget that you weren't supposed to allow anyone in the room," I said.

"That's not a bad plan," Corndog said. "I'm good at forgetting things."

I laughed. "It was your brilliant wife's idea. So let's get up there and you can walk me through everything that you saw, and if you heard the others' statements about the night before, I'd like to get all of that as well, but first, I want to get your account of events that night."

CHAPTER FOURTEEN

A MINUTE LATER WE WERE ALL STANDING IN FRONT OF THE door to the room Justin had occupied. It was second to the end on the opposite side of the house from our rooms.

I pointed to the bedroom at the very end of the hallway. "Who was staying in that room?"

"Morgan," Petunia said.

I nodded. The other room that shared a wall with Justin's was the shared bath. I'd already looked inside, but it was standard—toilet, vanity, and tub with shower with a small window on the back wall.

"You said when he didn't come down by noon, one of the friends sounded the alarm, right?" I asked, recalling what Corndog had told me before.

Corndog nodded. "They were banging on the door and making such a racket I heard them in the kitchen. Petunia and I came up to see what was going on. The big one was knocking and trying to open the door, but it was locked and it's solid. His wife and the smart-looking fellow were calling on their phones. We could hear a phone ringing in the room, but he never answered."

"So Daniel and Tyler broke down the door to get inside?"

"Didn't see as we had a choice," Corndog said. "By then, we was all pretty convinced something wasn't right. It wasn't like he could have gone off for doughnuts or something and even if he'd gone on walkabout, he wouldn't have left his phone. Least that's what his friends said."

I nodded. "So walk me through it step by step."

"He and the other one—the tall skinny one—managed to get the door open and they both practically fell inside. The lanky one froze as soon as he saw the guy in bed, but the rest of them rushed in and one of the girls screamed. I looked around the lanky one and wondered for a moment if we'd just torn up a perfectly good doorframe for no reason as it looked like he was still asleep, but there was the screaming, so I figured it was worse than that."

"And he was face down on the bed?"

Corndog nodded. "Face down and still fully dressed—even his tennis shoes were still on. The big one shook him, then he lost all color and put his fingers on his neck. Then he turned around and says, 'He's dead.'"

Petunia's eyes welled up with tears. "Brittany—I'm pretty sure she's the one who screamed—starts shaking him and saying it's not possible. That he can't be dead, and starts yelling for someone to do CPR. Everyone just stood there in a bunch, not knowing what to do and looking like they were all going to pass out. Then Daniel pulled Brittany away from the bed and grabbed her in a bear hug and tells her the body is cold. She practically collapsed right there."

Corndog ran one hand over his thinning hair. "It was a right mess."

"I don't suppose anyone checked the window, did they?"

"I did," Petunia said. "Well, I wasn't checking it, per se, but I was going to open it to get some air in the room. They looked like they could use some as there was the smell... But then Corndog motioned at me not to, and I realized it probably wasn't a good idea."

"I watch those detective shows," Corndog said. "They always want you to leave everything alone, but I knew why Petunia was going for the window. Didn't none of them look like they was going to be standing much longer, so I said as how we should head downstairs and call the sheriff. Wasn't nothing that could be done for the poor fellow anyway."

"But the window was latched?"

Petunia nodded.

"And you said the room key was on the floor next to the bed?"

"Yep. His arm was outstretched just above it, with his hand hanging over the side in between the bed and the nightstand. Looked like maybe he was going to put it on there but passed out and dropped it."

"And his EpiPen?"

"Right there on the stand next to the lamp. His cell phone was in his pocket."

"Was there anything else on the nightstand?"

They both shook their heads.

"Did you hear what any of them said when the sheriff interviewed them? Or I guess I should ask if he even bothered."

"He took their statements, for what it was worth," Petunia said. "I didn't see him doing much in the way of making notes, but we were all there. I remember everything that was said. My memory's always been tight as a drum."

"That's true," Corndog agreed.

"Okay, then let's start with the night before. What time did they come inside?"

"I'm not sure," Corndog said. "We came in to start cleanup

around eight. The smart one with the glasses gave us a hand carrying stuff. Cleanup took about thirty minutes, then we headed back to our suite for a shower and were probably in bed by nine. I could still hear them outside then, but after that we put in our earplugs."

"Daniel said they all drank outside until the mosquitoes moved in, then they headed for the library a little after nine," Petunia said. "They did some heavy drinking, and I know that for sure because I check the bottles of whiskey and count the beer bottles to get an idea of what's been consumed. It's the honor system for charges, but so far, people have been fair. We can't exactly afford to have an open bar—not with those kind of drinkers especially."

"And they all agreed that Justin was drunk?"

"Definitely. They said he was about to pass out, but I got the impression it still took a bit of effort to get him to call it quits. Brittany said Daniel and Tyler practically carried Justin up the stairs."

"Did they put him in bed?"

"No. They said he could walk five feet to the bed, and Tyler said no way was he undressing a grown man who still didn't know how to hold his liquor. That he could pass out on the floor in his clothes for all he cared."

"That sounds like Tyler," Ida Belle said. "Not that I blame him."

"And they're sure Justin locked his door?" I asked.

Petunia nodded. "Brittany said Daniel told him to lock the door as soon as he went inside, and they waited until they heard it click, then checked."

"That sounds a little odd," I said. "Surely they didn't think something would happen to him here."

"I thought the same thing when I heard it," Petunia said, "and apparently it was strange enough for even Sheriff Useless to ask about it. But Daniel said he wanted the door locked because he figured it would help prevent Justin from leaving the room again. I took that to mean they thought he was so drunk that once he locked the door, he might not be able to figure out how to open it again until he sobered up."

Corndog nodded. "They didn't want him falling down the stairs or worse."

"I guess that makes sense. Even if he managed the stairs without falling, they didn't want him roaming around in his condition, especially since he could have wandered outside and right into a crowd of alligators waiting for a buffet. Did they say if he had the key on him when they went back upstairs?"

"No," Petunia said. "None of them did, because that's one of the things the sheriff asked right after he found out from us that all the keys are unique and only fit their one door. They all said they'd left their keys in the lock on the inside because they didn't figure it was necessary to lock up. After all, it was only their group that was staying here at the time."

I nodded. "Did anyone try to check on Justin again that night? Or early the next morning?"

"No," Petunia said. "They all went to bed after making sure Justin was locked in, and the next morning everyone slept in. We keep watch so we know when to start a fresh pot of coffee and for me to get working on breakfast, but it was almost 10:00 a.m. before any of them came out. Daniel called Justin before breakfast, but he didn't answer. They all just figured he was sleeping it off."

"But when he still hadn't emerged two hours later and wasn't answering, they got worried," I said. "Morgan shared a wall with Justin. Did he hear anything?"

"No," Petunia said. "Bryce asked that much at least, but Morgan said he went right to sleep and didn't hear so much as a peep from the other room the rest of the night."

I knew from Ida Belle and Gertie overhearing Daniel and Brittany's argument that the walls were fairly thin, so if there had been a struggle of any kind, or raised voices, Morgan probably would have heard something. That was assuming, of course, that he wasn't lying, but at the moment, I couldn't think of a reason why he would.

"Did you see the body? The face, I mean?" I asked.

"No," Corndog said. "He was face down and once I cleared everyone out of the room, we called the sheriff. No one went back in there until the sheriff and Simpson, the medical examiner, showed up to do their thing. I didn't go in with them, though. To be honest, I didn't want to see the poor guy. I didn't even think about him having an allergic reaction until Simpson came out and asked if he was allergic to anything."

I nodded and blew out a breath. "Okay. I'd like to take a look inside, if that's okay."

"Go right ahead," Petunia said.

I pulled on latex gloves, figuring there was no sense leaving my prints in case Bryce decided to actually do his job. Then after I'd directed the others to remain in the hallway until I'd made a pass, Corndog pushed open the door and I stepped inside.

The room looked different in daylight—smaller but pleasant. It didn't look like a place a man had died, if you could ignore the smell. Death had a certain odor, and it was one I was familiar with. I went straight to the bed and scanned the sheets and pillow where Justin's face would have been, wondering why Bryce didn't take them with him, but then I remembered his laziness and answered my own question.

"This side, right?" I asked, pointing to the side next to the nightstand.

They nodded and I pulled the quilt back to get a better look at the pillows, then reached for the pillow on the far side of the bed. There was a stain of some sort in the center of it, and I wanted to get a closer look. As I pulled it closer to inspect it, I realized it was lipstick.

"Was this stain here before?" I asked.

"No," Petunia said. "If I can't get a stain out of linens, I tear them apart for cleaning rags."

"It looks like lipstick," Ida Belle said.

I nodded and pulled one finger across the stain. It spread. Not a lot, but enough to know it was reasonably fresh. I flipped the covers back a bit more but didn't see anything else and didn't want to go any lower as I knew what was there already and didn't need to see it.

I set the pillow down and took a quick picture of the lipstick stain, then put it back where I'd found it. After that, I walked the rest of the room, inch by inch, looking in the wardrobe and desk drawers and under the bed. But it was under the nightstand that I saw something twinkle. I pulled out my phone and shone the light under there and realized it was an earring.

I retrieved it and rose, showing the earring to Corndog and Petunia.

"Do you remember anyone wearing these earrings?" I asked.

"Not me," Corndog said. "But then, it's not exactly something I pay much attention to."

Petunia shook her head. "I'm afraid I didn't pay much attention either. I was too busy seeing to food and the like. I do remember that all the ladies had their hair down for dinner though, so I guess it wouldn't have been easily spotted."

"Could it have been there before they arrived?" I asked.

"No," Petunia said. "I moved the nightstand and rolled the rug up to clean the top of the baseboards and polish the floors before they came. I usually do it once a month or so."

I studied the design, a fleur-de-lis with a sapphire in the center. "Does this look custom?"

Ida Belle shrugged, as expected. Gertie leaned in and gave it a hard look but finally shook her head.

"I can't say," she said. "It could be cheap silver coating, or it could be platinum gold. And the stone might be a real sapphire or might be a fake. If it's cheap, then probably something mass produced that we might be able to find in a gift shop in NOLA. If it's real, then yeah, could be custom."

"You think that's what the person who went out the window was looking for?" Ida Belle asked.

"It's possible," I asked, then blew out a breath. "But why? Why did it matter? Why take the risk?"

"The logical answer is because she didn't want anyone to know she was in here with Justin," Gertie said. "In *bed* with Justin."

"Okay," I said. "But why not just wait until it was time to leave and then casually mention to Petunia that she'd lost the earring and if it was found, please give her a call?"

"It definitely would have been the smart thing to do," Ida Belle said. "But if it was Brittany, I can see why she wouldn't go that route."

Petunia sucked in a breath. "You think she could have been cheating on her husband?"

I stared out the window, frowning. Something was so off about all of this.

"At this point, I have no idea," I said. "All I know is someone was desperate enough to retrieve this earring that they entered a crime scene and fled through a second-story window in the middle of a thunderstorm. I'll be happy to admit that I don't think like normal girls, but it's still hard for me to fathom someone feeling a level of shame that they'd take those risks."

"Brittany owns a gymnastics studio," Ida Belle reminded her. "It wouldn't be as big a risk for her as it would for others."

"If it wasn't for the storm, I would agree with you," I said. "But taking the risk during a storm that severe reeks of desperation, not stealth."

Corndog frowned. "You don't think someone killed that boy, do you?"

I put my hands in the air. "If we assume that Justin didn't accidentally eat the wrong thing, which doesn't seem likely given he'd made it this long as a known drunk and without making that kind of mistake, then yes, the whole situation stinks. The question is whether his death was accidental or intentional."

"Some of them certainly aren't torn up over up," Ida Belle said.

I nodded. "But let's just say that one of them wanted to kill Justin and figured giving him peanuts might be a way to do it and make it look accidental. If they did so in the company of the others, they not only risked being stopped or caught, but if Justin had a reaction within minutes of digestion, someone could have easily administered his EpiPen."

"They couldn't have put peanut oil in his drink because it would have floated on top and someone would have noticed," Gertie said. "Plus, the taste would have been off, even for a drunk man, and it would have been oily on his lips. And if someone broke out candy with peanuts and offered him a bite, everyone would notice."

Ida Belle nodded. "So the only way they could decrease their risk of exposure and increase the probability of Justin dying was to dose him after he was falling-down drunk and alone in his room."

"Exactly," I said. "But how did they do it? Justin was locked inside the room, the key on the floor next to him, and the window latched."

"Could someone have gone to Justin's room after they all went to bed and gotten him to let them in?" Corndog asked.

"I suppose, but if Justin was as drunk as they're saying, then would he have even heard someone knocking? And they couldn't have knocked loudly, or they would have risked waking up the others. Maybe he could have let someone in, but it doesn't seem likely for a man who was already about to pass out and had to be carried up the stairs. And even if he had let someone in, how did they get out and manage to leave the window latched and door locked?"

Ida Belle and Gertie both frowned and I knew they were as unhappy as I was that the situation I posited was possible but there was no proof to get Corndog off the hook. I could tell that Corndog and Petunia were thinking the same thing.

"I know this is an old house but there's not enough space between these room walls for a secret passage to exist, right?" I asked.

Petunia shook her head. "I always wished we had them, especially when we were kids. It was something out of stories, of course, but apparently just being hidden on this island was enough for the pirates. They didn't need to escape, and I guess they didn't care if they saw servants, assuming they had them."

I shook my head. I hated this. It was all wrong, and everything about this room and the reunion friends made me believe it was a suspicious death, but if the ME had called it otherwise, I wasn't sure what I could do. If someone who actually cared about solving crimes were in charge, things might be different. I might be able to persuade him to take another look, but that didn't sound possible with Bryce.

"I wish I could have seen that body," I said. "Because I'm sorry, but I don't see any way to help clear you. It's absolutely possible that Justin ate something he shouldn't have later on that night. And it's also possible that one of the others slipped into his room earlier that day and left a treat laced with peanut oil on his nightstand, hoping he'd eat it before he went to sleep and be too drunk to get his EpiPen. But I can't prove it. Just like I can't prove you didn't accidentally use peanut oil because the oil was disposed of and you finished off the fish."

Petunia frowned. "We didn't eat the fish."

I stared. "The others said you and Corndog must have eaten the fish because the dish you'd wrapped it in was clean and in the drying rack the next morning."

"I promise you, it wasn't us," Corndog said. "When we cook out, we eat along with the guests, and we were both stuffed to the gills when we went to bed. Plus, I'll admit to having a shot or two of whiskey with those boys, which probably helped me along. Petunia has gotten a solid eight hours every night since I've known her. Heck, she slept through a couple hours of labor with our daughter just because it wasn't her rising time yet."

"That's a serious talent," Ida Belle said.

"He's right," Petunia said. "We didn't get up that night, or any night while they were here. And I'm afraid with our earplugs, we don't hear people moving around—which was the point of the dang things, but it seems we'd have been better off to have disrupted sleep in this case."

"Do guests normally wander around your kitchen and help themselves to food?" I asked. "I figured not since you keep drinks and snacks in the library, but missing food would indicate otherwise."

"I can't say it's normal," Petunia said, "but some do. I think sometimes they get the munchies after all the drinking or maybe they didn't eat well at supper or didn't necessarily like what I served. I don't mind, of course. As long as they're not in here cooking and messing things up, then eating some leftovers or even heating up a bowl of canned soup and helping themselves to a package of crackers has never been a problem. A couple have even cooked omelets. I could tell because some eggs were gone, and the skillet was in the drying rack."

"Can you recall anything that was missing after that night—besides the fish?"

"No. And definitely nothing with peanuts. I keep peanuts and pecans on hand for baking, but they're in the freezer and the bags haven't been opened. I checked right after..."

"What about peanut butter?"

"I always have a jar, but it was new and still sealed. We'd just had a small family reunion the week before with little kids. They tore through the peanut butter."

So another dead end.

I stared around the room, silently willing something—anything—to come to me, but I had nothing but a bunch of suspicions and no proof.

Then I heard the door downstairs open and close, and a voice called out.

"Corndog? I need a word."

Corndog and Petunia both froze.

"That's Bryce," Petunia whispered.

CHAPTER FIFTEEN

I hurried over the police tape and pulled the door shut and whispered, "Not a word about the earring. I was never in there."

I yanked off the gloves and shoved them in my pocket as Ida Belle, Gertie, and I headed for our rooms to hide. But we were too late. I heard the footsteps coming up the stairs and glanced back just as Bryce came into view. He locked in on Corndog and Petunia and then looked our way, frowning.

"Sorry, Bryce," Petunia said. "We were just about to start pulling linens and didn't hear you come in."

"Don't touch the linens in that room," he said. "I'll take them with me. You can get them back when all this is wrapped up."

"I doubt I'll want them at this point, but that's fine. Can we clean in there yet?"

"Hey, you!" he yelled just as we reached our room doors.

I knew he was talking to us. So here was the dilemma. Did we turn around and risk him recognizing us? Or did we continue into our rooms and pretend we didn't know he was talking to us? I had a feeling that if we chose option number two, he'd just come bang on our doors, so I turned.

"Are you speaking to us?" I asked as Ida Belle and Gertie turned as well.

"Yeah," he said as he finished huffing up the stairs and gave Corndog and Petunia a critical eye. "I thought you said no one else was staying here."

"They just arrived yesterday," Corndog said. "You didn't say anything about not renting the other rooms. This one is still closed off, just like you said to do."

He put his hands on his hips, clearly frustrated. "I shouldn't have to tell you not to rent any more rooms when you just had someone die here. And that goes double when, as far as I can tell, you're on the hook for it."

Corndog paled and Bryce waved at me. "I'm Sheriff Benoit and I'd like a word with you."

"Here we go," Ida Belle mumbled.

I started toward him, and he studied me as I approached. At first, his expression was one of complete annoyance, then it shifted to disbelief, and by the time I stood in front of him, outright anger.

"You," he said. "I know exactly who you are, and you've got no business in my parish."

"Really? I wasn't aware that taking a couple of vacation days was restricted to certain parishes. You'll have to point out that law to me."

He clenched his jaw. "You think I'm going to believe that you're here for a vacation? Don't even bother trying that one on me, sweetheart. I know exactly what you're up to."

"Don't ever call me sweetheart. And what is it exactly that you think I'm doing?"

"You're here to insert your nose in official police business. Well, I'm not your boy toy so it's not going to fly here." He looked me up and down and smiled. "Unless you want to give me a spin. Then maybe we can talk."

"Bryce Benoit!" Petunia said. "I can't believe you'd say such a thing and to one of our guests. You were raised better."

"No he wasn't," Corndog said.

I smiled and stared at his feet, because I'd met a million Bryces in my time, and I knew exactly where to hit them. Then I looked back up at him.

"Size nine. Carter's an eleven, so I'm going to pass."

Ida Belle snorted and Gertie started laughing so hard she choked. Bryce's face turned beet red.

"I ought to arrest you right now," he said.

"For taking a vacation or pointing out your, um, shoe size?"

"We both know you're not on vacation."

"Well, good luck proving that. The Department of Defense tried and couldn't manage it, so I have my doubts that you can."

"Why is it not a surprise that you're in trouble with the DOD?"

"Oh, I'm not in trouble with them. I'm helping coordinate a lawsuit *against* them, but my attorney and I still have some bandwidth if you'd like to be added to the list. He loves taking down people who abuse power."

His eyes widened and I knew he had no idea what to make of my cryptic statement. But given my past, he also knew I might be telling the truth.

"If you're done with the threatening and gross soliciting part of this conversation," I said, "I'd like to go brush my teeth and head out for a hike. I came here to relax, and you're upsetting my chi."

"You came to relax where a man just died?"

I shrugged. "I didn't know him. Didn't know anything about his death until I got here. He died from an allergic reaction, right? Since the three of us aren't allergic to anything, we're probably safe."

"I'm allergic to buttholes," Gertie said. "And I'm getting itchy."

"Get out of my sight," Bryce said. "But if I find out you have anything to do with my case, then I'll have you sitting in a jail cell with so many charges your attorney will never get you out."

I laughed and his entire body tensed. "Sure you will."

I turned around and headed for my room at a leisurely pace, which I knew would only serve to hack him off even more. I heard stomping and glanced over as I opened the door to my room to see him headed back down the stairs carrying a wad of linens and nary an evidence bag in sight. Corndog looked back at me and gave me a thumbs-up, and Petunia grinned before they both hurried after him.

"I'm sorry they have to deal with him," Gertie said as we headed into my room. "He really does make me itchy."

"He definitely hasn't changed any," Ida Belle said.

"Sure he has," Gertie said. "He's gotten worse. What the heck was he thinking, coming in here and threatening Corndog and Petunia? They are some nice people, and I don't care if Corndog's memory and eyesight aren't what they used to be, I still don't think he used the wrong oil."

"I'm not convinced either," I agreed. "But there's what we think and what we can prove."

Ida Belle nodded. "The interesting thing is that Petunia had no peanuts or peanut-based items open and available in her kitchen. That means Justin either brought something in himself or got something with peanuts from one of the others."

"I'm betting on one of the others," Gertie said. "If he'd

brought something in himself, wouldn't they have found a food wrapper somewhere in his room?"

Ida Belle shook her head. "Bryce didn't find the earring or notice the lipstick stain on the pillow, so even if he found a wrapper would he have bagged it as evidence or simply tossed it?"

"He's stupid enough to have tossed it," Gertie said. "I wish we could see the evidence and the ME's report. If we knew what food the peanuts were in it might help narrow things down."

I nodded, trying to come up with a way to get the report that didn't involve breaking and entering, but I couldn't think of a single thing. Justin *had* been a resident of another state, but I didn't know anyone in Miami who could push the issue.

Figuring it wouldn't hurt to ask someone who might have some ideas, I pulled out my phone and dialed Detective Casey, a NOLA homicide detective who had helped us out a few times and was someone I trusted to keep things to herself. Especially *my* things.

"It's my day off, Redding," she said when she answered. "I'm having a massage for the first time in two years and getting my hair done for the first time in three. So help me God, if you cause any trouble in New Orleans, I'm canceling our friends card."

"We're not even in Orleans Parish, so your hair and muscles are safe."

"Thank God because I'm going gray. Gray! I'm only forty-one. I'm not supposed to go gray for another twenty years or better. I blame you for that as well. Partially, anyway. The captain gets a chunk and a few are probably on my daughter. So what legally questionable pursuit are you up to now?"

"Nothing legally questionable. Well, not yet, anyway, but I've got a situation and wanted a second opinion on options."

I gave her a rundown on the case and she groaned.

"What is it with you? Are you offering discounted rates for cases run by incompetent cops?"

"I take that to mean you know Sheriff Benoit?"

"I'm not calling that idiot 'sheriff' or anything else remotely resembling a law enforcement title. He's a joke. Worse than a joke. Jesus, Redding. Can't you give me something better to work with? How about a nice financial crime in the city? Why do you always have to have impossible crimes with crap cops and sympathetic collateral damage?"

"Just a talent, I suppose. What I would like to see is the ME's report, but I can't figure out an angle for acquiring it that doesn't fall under illegal activities. And Bryce is just itching to put me in jail."

"He just met you five minutes ago. That's a record, even for you."

"It's not about me. He grew up in Sinful in Carter's shadow."

"Bryce grew up under the shadow of cockroaches."

Gertie snorted and I had to laugh.

"Miami would be the only jurisdiction that could access the report given that he was a resident," she said. "But it doesn't sound like they'd have a good reason to."

"Not really. The death has been put down to natural causes, so unless he had people in Miami gunning for him, who came to Voodoo Island unnoticed and accessed a locked room to kill him, I don't suppose they would."

"Impossible and undetectable crimes—that's your specialty. Don't get me wrong, if you say something's up with the whole thing, then I believe you, but I'm afraid they don't just let us pull background reports and files from other agencies without good reason. And trust me, the narcs in Internal Affairs check everything. Bunch of haters who couldn't make detective, most of them."

She blew out a breath. "I'm afraid I don't have a good answer for you. I don't know anyone in Miami either, and even if I did, they'd be sticking their neck out and there's not anything in it for them. This Justin doesn't sound like a great guy, so my guess is Miami isn't going to miss him. There certainly no incentive for them to get crossways with another police force or with their own IA."

"What about this ME...Simpson? Do you know anything about him?"

"Oh yeah. We call him Dr. Who. As in 'who gave him a medical license?' You're really batting zero on this one."

"So you're saying there's a good chance he made an incorrect call with accidental death."

"Let me put it this way—Bungling Bryce and Dr. Who wouldn't know a homicide unless they committed it themselves."

I sighed. I'd figured as much.

"Now, that doesn't mean this is murder," Casey said. "But if we're talking your instincts versus their track records, I sure as hell wouldn't accept accidental as the gospel."

"Well, it seems that legally, I have no other option but to accept their take."

"Uh-huh. *Legally*, that's correct. I'm sorry I can't help with this one, but I don't see a way to insert myself that the captain can pitch a good story for. Even though I know he likes Bryce and Dr. Who as much as I do. If you figure out a way to tie it to NOLA, let me know."

As I slipped the phone back in my pocket, I heard the downstairs door slam.

"Sounds like Bryce left," Ida Belle said.

I nodded. "We better head down and see what kind of trouble he brought with him."

Corndog and Petunia were standing in the kitchen and they both looked pale.

"What's wrong?" I asked.

Corndog dropped onto one of the stools. "He said he's going to charge me with manslaughter."

My heart dropped, and Gertie sucked in a breath. It was even worse than I'd imagined.

Petunia shook her head, tears of anger and fear already forming. "Why would he do that? Even if Corndog made a mistake—which I don't believe for a minute—how can he charge him with killing that boy?"

I shook my head. "It honestly doesn't make sense to me. I don't know what he gets out of it. You said there's no bad blood between you, right?"

"We don't like him," Petunia said. "No one with a lick of sense does, but we haven't ever had bad doings with him. Certainly nothing that would make him want to charge Corndog with a crime."

I blew out a breath. "Bryce can't actually charge you with anything. The DA has to do that."

"But he's the one whispering in the DA's ear, isn't he?" Corndog asked.

"Yes. But I have my doubts the DA would want to pursue it. It wouldn't look good, and most DAs are all about their image. The majority are looking to make a go at a political career, and launching legal attacks on senior citizens is bad for voting business."

"What if they offer me a plea to avoid trial?" Corndog asked. "That's what they do in the TV shows. Not that I'd agree, mind you. I know darned good and well I didn't make a mistake. I'd have to sign a statement saying I did it, wouldn't I? That's the same as lying under oath."

I could tell he was getting worked up and tried to calm him down.

"It's more likely the entire thing will be dropped because no one can prove what actually happened. They can't prove you used peanut oil any more than we can prove Justin didn't eat something after dinner that had peanuts in it. There's enough reasonable doubt here to fill the Gulf."

"Then why bother pushing this to the DA at all?" Petunia asked. "Why try to cause us trouble when he knows nothing is likely to come of it in the end?"

"Except costing us a bunch of money for an attorney," Corndog said. "And the rumors will kill our business. No one will want to stay someplace where the owners kill their guests."

Petunia gave him a bleak look, and I clenched my jaw in frustration. He was absolutely right. Even without proof, the court of public opinion could ruin them. I wasn't worried about Corndog going to prison or even facing a conviction. Alexander would never let that happen. But I couldn't do a thing about gossip.

And gossip was more lethal and more corrupt than the legal system.

As soon as we were in Ida Belle's SUV and on our way home, we went over our options. It was a brief discussion because there weren't a lot of them. Either we turned the mess over to Alexander and let him deal with the DA while the gossip chips fell where they may, or we pushed the homicide theory with zero support from the ME, no proof, and a handful of suspects by reason of opportunity but with no solid motive.

"If we want to pursue this, I think we have to work it backward," I said finally. "Usually we have a murder and we look for motive and opportunity. In this case we have opportunity but no clear indication of murder and no motive. We're out of luck on the murder verdict because Simpson doesn't sound any more competent than Bryce. So that leaves motive to pursue."

Ida Belle nodded. "You want to figure out who had a good enough reason to kill Justin and then maybe you can back into the how and when."

"Exactly. If we can get enough, Alexander might be able to push the state police to step in, and then we'd have a real investigation. And hopefully, a qualified autopsy."

"If the parish is stuck with the cost of burial, they'll cremate him," Gertie said. "For that matter, if his friends decide to take that on, they will probably make the same decision. Younger generations aren't as hung up on burial traditions as older folk."

"And it's a lot cheaper," Ida Belle said. "I'm going to be cremated. Already got it arranged. If I'm not sleeping on silk sheets with a ten-thousand-dollar piece of wood around me while I'm alive, I'll be darned if I'm going to when I'm dead."

I nodded. "I think the first place we have to start is that earring. If Bryce had discovered it, then he would have blundered into the middle of the group and asked them who it belonged to. He doesn't strike me as the type who knows when to keep an ace in the hole."

"Definitely not," Ida Belle said. "The person who lost it must have been worried that it had come off in the room and it was still there since Bryce never mentioned it. But if Petunia found it while cleaning and turned it over to Bryce, then he might ask questions they didn't want to answer."

"So what's our first move?" Gertie asked.

I stared out the window for several seconds then huffed.

"We head home and pack a bag. We have a reunion to crash."

CHAPTER SIXTEEN

MERLIN GAVE ME A DIRTY LOOK WHEN I WALKED INSIDE, and I waved a hand at him.

"Don't give me that crap. I know Carter stayed here last night and I can smell your tuna, so you've already had breakfast."

He glared at me and stalked off, swishing his tail. I'd probably pay for my admonishment, but not today. Because as soon as I had a shower and put a bag together, Merlin and his attitude were Carter's problem again.

I was freshly showered and had just stepped into the living room with my bag, ready for Ida Belle to pick me up, when the front door opened and Carter walked in. He took one look at my bag and frowned.

"Going somewhere?" he asked.

I nodded. "I was going to stop by the sheriff's department on our way out. We're headed to Houma to do some more looking into things."

I brought him up to date on what we'd found.

"You think he was murdered?" he asked.

"Honestly, yeah. But I can't prove it."

"But it could have been a mistake by the owners, or his friends, or the dead guy himself."

I nodded. "It could have been, but I don't think it was—a mistake, I mean. There's too much undercurrent, and my spidey sense is on alert."

"Crap."

Carter knew exactly what my spidey sense meant, and it was rarely wrong.

"I'm afraid I ran into Bryce this morning. He showed up at the house, let himself in, and came upstairs before I could clear out of his line of sight."

Carter sighed. "I know. I've already had a phone call from him informing me that he didn't allow people to get away with things in his parish like I did, especially since he wasn't getting any 'favors' in return. And that I'd better get a leash on you, or you'd wind up warming a cot in his jail."

"A leash?" I asked, feeling my blood pressure rise.

Carter shrugged. "That's probably the only way he could get a woman to stick around, although I have doubts he's capable of leashing a puppy. Bryce always spent too much time running his mouth, but that's all he's good for. Mind you, he would have never said any of that to my face."

"Of course not. So what did you tell him?"

"I told him that men who put leashes on women are called rapists and that last time I checked, vacationing wasn't illegal in *any* parish, but he should let me know if the laws have changed."

I snorted. "I told him the same thing. But I don't get it. He had to know he wasn't going to get anywhere with you. Why call?"

"Probably to remind me of all his money he has and how his buddy is considering a run for sheriff against me."

"Seriously? He's threatening you with backing someone else for sheriff because I stayed overnight in his parish?"

"He's threatening me because he knows good and well you weren't there to vacation, and he's afraid you'll make him look stupid even though he's doing a fine job on his own. Obviously, he can't arrest you for anything if you don't do anything, but I know how you work. So watch your back."

I nodded. "Always."

He pulled me into his arms and gave me a kiss. "I guess you need me to take care of that demon cat again. You're lucky I love you."

He gave me another kiss, then headed out. I pulled out my laptop and went to work.

Ida Belle and Gertie arrived ten minutes later, both looking refreshed and Gertie's hair back to normal. She'd exchanged her taped-up glasses for a pair that didn't need tape to hold them together, and since she'd already stated the broken ones had been her last pair of the current prescription, I had to wonder exactly how many years ago this pair was viable. But there was no way I would ask.

"I wasn't sure what to pack," Ida Belle said. "Equipment wise, I mean. We've got clothes to run in because we always seem to end up doing it, and we always have some medical supplies and our breaking-and-entering stuff. Gloves and firearms are a given, but I wasn't sure what you had in mind."

"I don't know that I had anything in mind except lurking around and trying to pin down a motive. Since cell service is better now and we'll have Wi-Fi at the hotel, we can troll the internet to see what else we come up with. I wish I could get more time speaking to each of them—and alone, preferably. I think I have a better chance on getting the dirt on people that way."

"I think we should break into the ME's office and commit a heist," Gertie said.

Ida Belle stared. "You want to steal a body?"

"No!" Gertie said, then frowned. "Unless it would help. I was just thinking if we had the autopsy report and could see the body, that might make a difference."

"I would love to have that report and get a look at the body," I said, "but no way are we breaking into the ME's office. Bryce has already called Carter about my presence in *his* parish."

I told them about the phone call, and they both looked disgusted.

"I hope they get him out of office next round," Gertie said. "Those people deserve better."

"They deserve what they voted for," Ida Belle said. "If they didn't know better before, then they certainly do now. If he's reelected then that's on them."

I nodded. "What we need is a way to accidentally bump into the friends. We already have our cover about going to the bar in Meditation, so that's one reason to be nearby. And I told them I was off this weekend so we might poke around some other places."

"Houma is full of antiques shops," Gertie said.

"Perfect," I said. "I've already done some legwork on the hotel and there's only one hosting a class reunion. I booked us a suite."

"I wonder if they're going to think it's weird if they see us in the same hotel," Ida Belle said.

I shrugged. "It's a risk we have to take. If we book somewhere else, there's no chance of 'accidentally' running into them."

Gertie leaned over and looked at my laptop. "That place offers the best senior discount and free breakfast. And it's a national chain so you can always say you used points for the rest. After all, none of us is supposed to be well off."

"That works," I said.

Gertie frowned. "The dance... Brittany said it was a masquerade ball, right?"

"Yeah, Mardi Gras theme, which was apparently what their prom was," I said, then I realized where she was going with that and shook my head. "Oh no, we are not going to that prom."

"Well, *we* probably couldn't," she said. "But there's no reason you can't. You'd be wearing a mask."

"It's a small school," I said. "I'm pretty sure they'd know I wasn't a classmate as soon as they asked any one of ten thousand questions I can't answer."

"There's got to be a female Morgan that graduated with them," Gertie said. "Some poor girl who ran to university five seconds after graduation and never wants to see them again as long as she lives."

Ida Belle pursed her lips. "I hate to agree with her, but it's definitely a possibility. The brightest students tend to flee small towns for bigger opportunities."

Gertie nodded. "And we all know the ugly duckling becomes the swan. So we find that person, make sure they're not attending, dig up some basic information online, and then you show up last minute as a surprise."

I threw my hands in the air. "Do you know how many things could go wrong with that plan? What if her best friend from high school is there? Or her science professor who wrote her an admission letter for MIT? What if Morgan dated her? And they make you wear name tags at reunions, don't they? I'm sure that goes double for a masquerade."

Gertie waved a hand in dismissal. "Minor details. I'm not saying you should make a spectacle of yourself. Just lose the tag after you get inside and wander around, listening to conversations."

"And what if one of the group approaches me?" I asked. "They'd recognize my voice."

Ida Belle raised one eyebrow.

"Okay, fine, I know how to disguise my voice, but still."

"Are you trying to tell me that going undercover at a high school reunion is more difficult than being undercover on a CIA mission?" Ida Belle asked.

"In some ways, yes. On missions, I was a stranger playing the role of someone they'd never met. Playing an existing person with a past in a small town is a completely different thing. Plus, I'm not allowed to kill any of them."

"Okay, I'll give you that," Ida Belle said. "But it couldn't hurt to try, right? If you think you're going to be compromised, you duck out, change clothes, and no harm, no foul."

I frowned. I couldn't find fault with the idea, other than the million ways it could go wrong. And since news of Justin's death would have circulated among all the attendees by tonight, it might give me a chance to overhear stories 'out of school' so to speak.

"I don't have anything to wear," I said, issuing my final weak protest.

"Call Ronald," Gertie said, which was exactly what I'd expected her to say.

I picked up my phone and sent Ronald a text.

Dress emergency. Need your help.

Less than twenty seconds later, my front door flew open and Ronald burst inside, huffing as if he'd just run a mile.

Or flown.

He was wearing his Fashionista superhero leotard, complete with cape and mask. Ida Belle let out a strangled cry and immediately fled to the kitchen, mumbling something about dehydration. Gertie, as expected, took in the entire disaster like a kid at the circus.

"That's fantastic!" she said. "Fortune told me about it, of course, but it's so much more in person. I didn't know about the mask."

"That's new," he said. "I was thinking the whole thing was lacking something."

"Non-clingy material?" I suggested. "A cape that drapes over the entire front?"

"You can't do fashionista exercises in a huge cape."

"What are fashionista exercises?" Gertie asked.

"First, you bend from the knees to get something off a lower shelf. I don't know why some stores still insist on keeping things below waist level, but you can't just go sticking your rear out at people, so you have to practice. Then there's the high-heeled tiptoe to get things off the high shelf. After that is balancing of shopping bag weight so that you don't lean to one side when you walk and cause foot or knee issues. And finally, you walk, in heels, with the bags, without breaking a sweat. The whole routine wipes me out for the rest of the day."

"Sounds hard," I said.

"Sounds impossible in Louisiana in the summer," Gertie said. "That sweating part anyway."

"The secret is to roll clear deodorant across your forehead."

"Doesn't that clog your pores?" I asked. Ronald was forever harping on me about my pores.

"You don't leave it on there. You use a good cleanser and do a deep moisturizing and a mud mask after."

"Sounds like more work than the walking thing."

He closed his eyes and looked up at the ceiling, probably praying for my skin.

"So what's this dress emergency?" he asked when he looked back down. "I see you're in your current discount wear."

"I have a thing... I *might* have a thing."

"Girl, you're going to have to be more specific than that. Is it a thing you're attending or a thing that needs to fit into the dress? Because I can handle either, but I need more information."

"Both. I need to fit a gun in there, but I can strap it to my leg, so it can't be anything with a slit up to my navel. And it has to be a cocktail dress at least because it's a class reunion dance with a Mardi Gras masquerade theme. Since I'm undercover I need something that fits me but doesn't 'scream hey look at me.' Bonus points if you have a mask that matches."

He frowned. "I was with you until the 'hey look at me' part."

I nodded and waved a hand at his outfit. "I get that."

"But I might have something... No, I think I donated it, or wore it at a friend's garage sale. Wait! I still have it. I shoved it in the back of my guest room closet and it didn't make the donation pile."

I perked up a bit. If he'd worn it for a garage sale, it might be suitable for public. It might not even scream at people to pay attention.

"Let me go grab it," he said. "It's a straight cut, so you won't have to worry about the whole clingy curves calling attention thing, but you'll have to handle shoes. You'd run right out of mine, and you always end up running."

Gertie nodded.

He hurried off, and Ida Belle sidled back into the room after the door closed.

"Coward," Gertie said and grinned at her.

"You can call me whatever you like as long as I don't have to see Ronald in tights. I'm surprised Carter didn't resign and move after catching sight of that spectacle." She looked over at me. "I get why Gertie isn't disturbed, but you didn't so much as blink."

I shrugged. "I have to rescue Gertie and Jeb from their sexy-time disasters, remember?"

Ida Belle cringed and held up one hand. "Say no more."

My door popped open, and Ronald swept in with the dress. I had to admit, it wasn't horrible. In fact, compared to Ronald's usual fare it was downright boring. I could see why he'd relegated it to garage sale wear.

The dress was sleeveless and as advertised, a straight cut that would probably hit a couple inches above my knees. The fabric was a shiny purple but wasn't stretchy or clingy. Over the straps and around the top were purple, green, and gold sequins, but just enough to pull in all the Mardi Gras colors and not enough to blind people under good light.

"This is nice," I said. As far as dresses went, anyway.

Ronald sighed. "Of course you like it. It's all yours. I'll consider it my contribution to taking down whatever criminal you're currently pursuing."

"How do you know I'm pursuing a criminal?"

"Because there's nothing else that would get you in a dress."

"I wore a dress to Good Friday dinner."

"Oh Lord!" Ronald said and put his hands on his chest. "Don't even mention that. I'm still having nightmares. I left the café the other day without even ordering because Pastor Don came in. I see him and have this overwhelming urge to flee."

I grinned. Ronald had led a very drunk Pastor Don on a merry chase at the Sinful Good Friday dinner. General public opinion fell into two camps—entertained or annoyed. Pastor Don had been delighted. Ronald had been terrorized.

"I better try this on, just to make sure," I said.

"Take this as well," he said and pulled an auburn wig from his purse.

"I wasn't planning on wearing a wig."

"A fancy dress means you're attending an event with women—usually—and you're undercover. If any of those women have seen your perfect locks without a single split end, despite how horribly you treat your hair, they will recognize you by the strands alone."

I wasn't sure about split end profiling, but I figured Ronald knew women better than I did. I took the wig and dress and headed to my office and tried everything on. I didn't have a mirror to check the look, but the fit was perfect, meaning neither my chest nor my nine would be exposed, and it wasn't so short that it would attract unnecessary attention, but the length allowed for running and a decent hook kick if needed. I pulled the wig on and headed out.

When I walked back into the living room, Ronald sighed and shook his head.

"Of course you look fabulous in it," he said. "I swear you could make a potato sack look good. Here, give the mask a whirl."

He handed me a glittery purple Venetian mask with gold, green, and purple feathers. I slipped it on, and he nodded.

"It's perfect but the eyes might still give you away. Not a lot of people have that shade of turquoise."

"I have colored contacts for undercover."

"Of course you do. I brought this just in case." He passed me a small gold bag with a long chain.

I took the bag and gave it a look. "Can't fit my nine in it, but this chain is pretty strong. I could probably strangle someone with it."

He closed his eyes and shook his head. Ida Belle, who'd

forced herself to stick around for the unveiling, gave it a tug and nodded.

"That wig is real hair, and nice hair," he said. "So don't do anything to it you wouldn't do to your own. You know what, scratch that. Treat the hair like it's a Fabergé egg you were hired to protect."

"Thanks, Ronald," I said. "Seriously, this is perfect. I owe you."

"Hmmmm, I was rather hoping not to need the services you provide."

"Everyone is, and yet..."

I hurried to my office to change back into my street clothes, then came out and waited an agonizing thirty seconds while Ronald hung the dress back on the hanger and smoothed it down, then gasped when I shoved the whole thing into my overnight bag, followed by the wig. He didn't even say another word—just walked out with one hand held over his mouth.

"Let's get this investigation rolling," Gertie said.

"I had a thought when I was changing," I said.

"A sexy thought?" Gertie asked.

Ida Belle threw her hands up. "Why in the world would she be having sexy thoughts in the middle of an investigation?"

"Because she's half naked?"

"She's completely naked every night when she showers—you know what, do *not* respond to that." She looked at me. "What was your thought?"

"Remember how on Voodoo Island, members of the group kept ducking outside to sit in the rain, vape in secret, or whatever else they were up to out there? Well, I was thinking that people might do the same at the dance tonight. And if two people are ducking out together to have a chat, then they probably wouldn't do that in the lobby where they could easily be overheard."

"And since a lot of them probably still live in the area or are staying with family, then they won't have rooms to go to for private conversations," Ida Belle said. "I'm following you so far, but I don't think an outside smoking area will provide enough cover for us to hide out there all night."

"Especially if we're crouching," Gertie said. "I'm good for four or five seconds in a crouch. The other day I crouched too long checking a casserole, and it took me twenty minutes to get upright again. And here I went and installed those ADA-height toilets thinking they'd be easier. Well, not when you're stuck in a crouch."

"No crouching required," I said. "I was thinking you could park the SUV behind the hotel and use the parabolic microphone. There's smoking and nonsmoking patios on the back and the exit to them is just outside the doors to the conference room, so more people will probably use the back than loiter around the front."

"That's good thinking," Ida Belle said. "Let's load up then. Are we going to the hotel first?"

"No. Let's head to the cross-legged bar first."

Gertie clapped her hands. "I didn't know we were really going!"

"I figure we need to at least duck in and take some pictures," I said. "After all, I told the group we wanted to check it out. Having pictures helps with our cover. And since the bar is on a turnoff before you get to Houma from Voodoo Island, it makes sense we'd stop on our way into town. Then we have pics in case someone spots us checking into the hotel."

"But it will be pictures from the middle of the day," Gertie said.

"Yeah, we're old people," Ida Belle said. "We need to get

things done in daylight and be back at the hotel and ready for bed before dark."

"I am *not* old."

"We're undercover," I reminded her. "I'm playing an insurance processor who is down on men, plans on becoming a cat lady, and doesn't like to leave her apartment."

Gertie pointed at Merlin, then held her hands up. "You're batting .500."

"Fine. How about this—if I have to play dumb, you can play old."

I grabbed the case with the microphone and put it and my bag in the SUV, then collected my laptop. Merlin was in the living room glaring at me when I went to leave, so I gave him a pat and a promise that Carter would make sure his dinner wasn't late.

He didn't look convinced.

CHAPTER SEVENTEEN

I HAD MY LAPTOP OPEN BEFORE IDA BELLE HAD EVEN BACKED out of the driveway. I hit social media first and started with Brittany, figuring she'd be the most likely to keep a continuous account of her life online. She was easy to find and sure enough, made multiple posts a day, often with selfies and verbiage that sounded as if she was trying to cheerlead her followers into living their best life. I could see why Amanda had gone the opposite route. Brittany seemed nice enough, but I couldn't be friends with her for a day without wanting to tape her mouth shut.

Her last post was after their arrival on Voodoo Island, but only contained a picture of her and Daniel standing in front of the house and a short post about how excited they were to stay in this famous historical property. She'd posted nothing at all after Justin had died, but then, that probably stood to reason.

The post before was about their upcoming high school reunion and featured a photo of the group from back then. I clicked on it and scanned the faces, easily recognizing the younger versions of all of them. Except two, and I had to enlarge the photo and take a second look. Daniel and Justin didn't look exactly alike, but Morgan had been right when he'd said they could have been brothers.

"Look at this," I said to Gertie and pointed to the two men.

"Wow," she said. "They really do look alike."

"Driving here," Ida Belle reminded us. "Who looks alike?"

"Daniel and Justin," I said. "It's easy to tell the difference when you're actually looking, but I can see why people might have thought they were related."

"Back then people might have," Ida Belle said. "But after years of Justin drinking, I bet that's not the case anymore."

She pulled up to a stop sign and I showed her the picture.

"There's something else," she said, and pointed to a young, lanky Tyler. "He's wearing an earring."

"Good eye," I said.

"He wasn't wearing an earring on the island," Gertie said.

"Maybe because he lost it in Justin's room," Ida Belle said. "It wasn't a girlie sort of earring. A guy could easily wear it and get away with it, especially being from Louisiana."

I nodded. "Brittany didn't post anything after the arrival at Voodoo Island, so let me see if I can find a profile for Justin."

I searched his name and Miami and his profile popped up at the top of the list. I clicked and whistled. "You weren't wrong, Ida Belle. He looks a good ten years older than the others."

"More like fifteen or twenty," Gertie said. "He could have passed for Daniel's father."

"That's what alcohol and living hard will get you," Ida Belle said. "Anything interesting?"

I scrolled down the page. "No. Just selfies of Justin with women—always different women—Justin in bars, Justin in boats, Justin in a Ferrari. I wonder if it's his."

"Is his job listed?" Ida Belle asked. "I don't think anyone ever said what it was."

I checked the profile. "Construction sales. I guess he works with builders?"

Ida Belle nodded. "If he was any good, he might have made a lot of money."

"There's a lot of money," I said, "and there's driving a Ferrari and living in Miami. Let me see if I can run down an address."

I did a quick check and got a pretty long list. "Looks like he moved living quarters every six months for the past couple years."

I pulled up the last known address and frowned. Surely this couldn't be right. The place in the picture was a building with bars on the windows, tall weeds for a lawn, and looked as though it hadn't seen a lick of paint in decades.

Gertie whistled. "Apparently the mighty have fallen. I wouldn't even go in that building without a SWAT team for backup."

"He's definitely not parking a Ferrari there," I said. "But this shows him moving in four months ago and the picture with the Ferrari was just two weeks ago."

"Probably rented for a day or two," Gertie said. "I see videos all the time about it. Guys rent exotic cars down there to pick up hot girls. But the girls are getting wise to the rentals. At least the locals are. I suppose the tourists are practically a buffet for men like Justin though. They wouldn't know any better."

"I wonder if the others knew about this," I said.

"Doubt it," Ida Belle said. "Why would he let anyone know? He was the big man on campus. People like Justin never stop living that high school glory because they fail to attain any as adults. But being the big man in Houma, Louisiana, in no way qualifies you to matter at all in a place like Miami. Especially if you're broke."

I nodded. "Let's do Tyler next. Here's his page—pictures of him on a boat, at a football game, at a concert. Never with a woman. Looks like the bro squad. Oh! He's wearing an earring in this one, though, and that was only a couple weeks ago. But it's not the one we found. No mention at all of the class reunion. Okay, let's move on to his teen crush Nicole."

"I'd say that one has progressed long beyond teen," Gertie said.

"You think she knows?" I asked.

"Of course she knows," Ida Belle said. "Women always know when a man's interested. Heck, even I know and you're aware of how many girl genes I'm lacking. But she's not about to let on that she knows."

"Why not?" I asked.

"Because if he knew that she knew, then he would push for a response," Gertie said. "And then she'd have to tell him she doesn't share the same feelings. Nicole strikes me as the type of person who's always putting other people's feelings ahead of her own. Look how she follows after Brittany to make sure she's all right every time she has a meltdown."

"True," I said. "But I'd rather just confront the guy, even if it hurt his feelings, so that he'd move on."

"She probably thought he had," Ida Belle said. "Remember, most of them have only interacted rarely since high school, if at all. Tyler's in Baton Rouge and Nicole is in NOLA. I suppose she might run into him occasionally in Houma if she's home for a visit, but there would be no reason for her to think he'd continued to hold a torch."

"Until she got locked in a house with him for days," I said. "He brought her favorite chocolates."

"What?" Ida Belle asked.

"Nicole is type 1 and told me she only breaks out the insulin for her favorite chocolates and the occasional glass of wine. The chocolatier is in Baton Rouge and she said Tyler brought her a box of the chocolates."

"Then she most definitely knows he's still hung up on her," Gertie said. "Men don't remember things like a woman's favorite chocolate unless they're into them. But no way she would have addressed it with all of them closed up together. It would have made the whole situation uncomfortable."

"Pretty sure Justin's dying did that," Ida Belle said. "What's on Nicole's socials?"

"Mostly just shots of homes she's been the designer for, and posts from homeowners, smiling in new kitchens and bathrooms, thanking her for all her help. The only personal posts I see are pics of her and Brittany in the French Quarter. But nothing remotely scandalous. Just dinner, beignets, Jackson Square looking at the art... If this is an indication of her real life, she's as insulated as Rose is supposed to be."

Ida Belle nodded. "I figured as much when she didn't put in her two cents on Amanda's girls' night. She's in the same city, but apparently doesn't go."

"Look at Morgan next," Gertie said. "I have a feeling that one might be as lacking in personal touch as Nicole's."

I put in his name and scanned the list but didn't see a profile that fit. I tried a couple other social media sites with the same result.

"Looks like no social media at all," I said.

Ida Belle shrugged. "That's not really surprising."

"He's watching it, though," Gertie said. "Or he wouldn't have known what fantasy books were trending. Probably private accounts, and he might not be using his real name."

I frowned. "True. Let me try to run down an address."

I did a search for his name and Baton Rouge and found a

listing for a previous address. "Looks like he moved from that place six months ago. Nothing else since."

"He said he wrote code for a defense contractor," Ida Belle said. "Maybe his new place is in their name. Some of that work requires a high-level security clearance. Might also be why he's clearly looking at social media but not on it himself."

"That's true," I said. "My condo in DC was buried in corporate filings which eventually led back to the government but never to me. But I was an assassin. You have to be in pretty deep to be covered up that well."

"Could also be an inheritance thing," Ida Belle said. "He might have had an old aunt who passed and left him her house and he's never changed the deed. A lot of people don't bother if they're going to live there. And even if they do, it sometimes takes a while to process, much less make the internet rounds."

"Oh well, off to Daniel then," I said. "Looks like what I'd expect to see. Daniel and Brittany in what I assume is their backyard pool. Daniel and Brittany at dinner. The last one was him and Brittany on the boat with Corndog. No mention of the class reunion though, but then, he doesn't post much. Maybe once every couple months or so."

"So last but not least is Amanda," Gertie said.

I located her easily and scanned her feed. "It's mostly just pics of her and her girlfriends doing things around New Orleans. Nothing remotely scandalous, not even their outfits."

Gertie snorted. "They're all dressed like you. Except at night. Apparently, they upgrade to jeans and heels."

"Amanda can't afford any questions in her public-facing image," Ida Belle said. "Not if she wants to make partner."

"She's finance, not criminal, and I don't see her for political aspirations," I said.

"Doesn't matter," Ida Belle said. "The rules are still different for women. Impropriety on her part, broadcast online, could cost her the promotion. It's sexist and unfair, but a lot of professions are still like that, especially those that work with the public and on referrals. All it takes is one partner at that firm interested in politics and the whole ship has to toe the line."

I closed my laptop and stared out the window. "That didn't yield much."

"What did you expect?" Ida Belle asked. "That someone had posted a rant about hating Justin and wanting him dead?"

"It might have been nice."

"You wouldn't have believed it. You hate it when it's easy."

"True. But I'd like more to go on than we have. We don't even know that it was murder. In fact, everything points to it being an accident, but that puts Corndog squarely on the hook unless we can prove Justin ate something besides the fish."

"We have your intuition," Gertie said. "That's all I need."

Ida Belle nodded.

"I appreciate the vote of confidence, but we're going to need more than my opinion on the matter to protect Corndog and Petunia."

"You'll figure it out," Gertie said. "You always do. *You're* the one who should be wearing a superhero costume."

"Ha. I can be the Fantastic Frustrated, since that's the way I seem to feel most when we're investigating."

Ida Belle turned off the highway onto a shell road. "You're going to need to be Man of Steel for this road."

We bumped along for a bit and finally pulled into a clearing that served as a parking lot. The bar was located on pilings right on a bayou, and the whole setup reminded me of the Swamp Bar. A weathered sign on the front of the building read Namaste Bar and I had to laugh. You really couldn't make this stuff up. I said a quick prayer that our bar track record was different here than in Sinful and climbed out of the SUV.

Despite it being the middle of the day, the bar was half full. We headed for the counter, figuring barstools would give us an elevated view of the place, and were about five steps inside when Ida Belle grabbed my arm.

"Far end of the bar," she whispered.

I glanced over and was surprised to see Morgan and Amanda sitting at the bar. They looked relaxed and had po'boys and mugs of beer in front of them.

Gertie clued in on them as well and smiled. "Looks like our opportunity for questioning starts now."

CHAPTER EIGHTEEN

I SILENTLY DEBATED WHETHER OR NOT WE SHOULD DUCK out before Morgan and Amanda saw us. After all, how many times could you run into the same people before it was outside of coincidence territory? But then, on the other hand, I'd told them we planned to visit this bar today, and I had the 'old people have to do things early' notion firmly in my court.

"The only three seats available in a group are next to them," Ida Belle said. "I say we take them and see what we can get. They might be willing to cough up more without the others around."

I nodded.

We wove through the tables and headed around the bar for the back corner. When we were halfway there, Amanda looked over and caught sight of us. She looked a tiny bit surprised at first, then she nudged Morgan and they both looked over at us, smiling.

"I see you made it," Morgan said as I slid onto a stool next to him with Ida Belle and Gertie taking the next two stools.

"I hope the drive was worth it," I said. "Might need new shocks on my car."

Amanda laughed. "We've seen a couple of people dipping already. It's not nearly as active during the day, but we've got the reunion dance tonight and the whole family barbecue thing tomorrow, so this seemed like the best opportunity."

"The rest of your group didn't want to come?"

Amanda raised her eyebrows. "We kind of didn't tell them. After breakfast, Morgan and I were talking outside and he mentioned the bar, saying he hoped you guys found it fun. God knows, this reunion has been a shi—crap show. Whew—almost had to hit the floor on that one. Anyway, we thought we'd duck in and see if we could actually relive something fun from high school. The dance is going to be rough... The news will have made it around by then."

I nodded. "Well, sounds like he always wanted to be the center of attention, so maybe it's befitting."

"Rose!" Gertie said. "Good Lord."

"What? They said he was a butthole. Is 'butthole' cursing? Do I need to dip?"

"You *need* to get out of your apartment more because clearly your manners have all but disappeared," Gertie said.

Amanda, who'd been staring in silence during our exchange, started laughing. Morgan only hesitated a second before joining in.

"Oh my God," Amanda said, wiping her eyes with a napkin. "That might be the most accurate statement about Justin that anyone has made since we've been back home."

"And the tackiest," Gertie said, still in her role of disapproving aunt.

Amanda shook her head. "Tyler is still firmly in first on the issuance of tacky statements. Well, I suppose second really, because Justin was in first until he died."

"As Rose so eloquently pointed out," Morgan said, "Justin always had to be in the spotlight."

They lifted the beer mugs and clinked them, then laughed some more. A bartender looked over at us and I pointed to their mugs and held up three fingers.

"So what else is on your agenda for the weekend?" Morgan asked.

I shrugged and inclined my head toward my 'aunts.'

"There's some antiques shops we want to check out," Gertie said. "And definitely the flea market."

Ida Belle rolled her eyes. "I want to go to the boat store."

"You have several boat stores in New Orleans," Gertie said.

"And you have a million antiques shops and the French Market. I know all the boat store people in New Orleans. I want to talk to someone new. Someone whose fish stories I haven't heard."

"We can drop her off, then hit the antiques shops," Gertie told me.

I looked back at Amanda and Morgan and smiled. "There you go. The rest of my weekend I'm the antiques shop, flea market, boat store Uber."

"You're also the one with hotel points," Gertie said. "I hope they give us a free upgrade."

Morgan and Amanda both grinned, then Morgan sobered. "How were Corndog and Petunia when you left? I've been worried about them. That sheriff appeared to be lacking in every way."

"Please," Amanda said. "That guy was ridiculous. Barely asked questions, and I swear if you hadn't asked him about a forensics team and the ME, he would have just dragged the body down the stairs in Petunia's quilt and heaved it into the bayou."

I shook my head. "I wish I could say I didn't believe it, but he showed up right before we left. We headed back to our room as soon as he came in to try to give them some privacy, but I'm afraid we overheard him. You know how the house echoes."

Their eyes widened.

"What happened?" Morgan asked.

"He told Corndog he's going to be charged with manslaughter."

"What?" Amanda said, looking shocked. "That's outrageous. Where's the proof? Unless the DA is as lazy and corrupt as the sheriff, that can't possibly go anywhere. I'm an attorney, by the way. Not criminal but jeez, even our receptionist knows better than that."

I nodded, deciding to play my 'overhearing' to my advantage. "I'm certainly no lawyer, but it sounded like a reach to me too. Then I heard Corndog and Petunia talking when I brought our bags down—after that sheriff left—and they're worried about the money to pay for an attorney. And even if they could come up with it, they're afraid the publicity will ruin their business. I got the impression that the bookings are the only thing keeping them in their house."

Amanda shook her head, clearly angry. "If I was a criminal attorney, I'd defend them for free. What a load of crap, and just what you'd expect from this small-town nonsense, which is why I got out as soon as I could."

"The autopsy would show what was in Justin's stomach," Morgan said. "If he ate anything besides what Corndog served, then wouldn't that be reasonable doubt?"

"Sure," Amanda said. "But that ME declared it anaphylaxis. Unless it's deemed a suspicious death, there probably won't even be an autopsy. Not if that's the way that idiot is running investigations. And it's not like there's any family of Justin's around to push for it."

I sighed. "So no autopsy if it's not suspicious, but no way to determine if it's suspicious without an autopsy. That doesn't seem right."

"It's not right," Amanda said. "But far too often, it's an unfortunate reality. Especially with sheriffs. They're essentially politicians, and too many of them aren't in it for the job they're elected to."

I frowned. "But doesn't the ME decide if it's homicide? Or do the TV shows have it wrong?"

"The ME would make the call," Amanda said. "But in this case, he struck me as not only incompetent but also as kowtowing to the sheriff."

"Jesus, that sucks," I said.

"The whole thing is just wrong," Gertie said. "They're such a nice couple."

"I wish there was something we could do," I said. "I don't suppose there's a way to get a second opinion from another ME, is there?"

Amanda sighed. "It's not like getting a second opinion for your foot surgery or the like. Unless there's a compelling reason, no one is going to step on toes, even incompetent toes. But I have to admit that if I had that compelling reason, I might start calling around and see who could push buttons. I'd hate for Corndog and Petunia to lose their home. Especially over Justin."

"It seems he makes just as much trouble in death as he did while he was living," Morgan said. "If he was going to eat the wrong thing, he could have at least waited until we were at the hotel."

"Unless he didn't mean to eat the wrong thing," Amanda said.

"Do you think Corndog had a mix-up?" I asked.

"I don't know," Amanda said. "But if he *did* use the wrong oil, then I'm absolutely certain it was a mistake. There's no reason to ruin the man's life over it. It's simply a tragedy and you move on. At least there was no wife and kids to worry about supporting. Or an elderly parent and the like."

"So no one loses from his death, except Corndog and Petunia," I said. "People who didn't even know him before that night. Seems really unfair."

Morgan nodded. "Especially when some would say Justin had it coming."

Amanda's eyes widened. "I'm surprised to hear something like that coming from your mouth."

He shrugged. "He wasn't a good person, even in high school, and he's only gotten worse. He hit on you, Nicole, and even Brittany the second he caught sight of you all, and continued until Daniel told him to knock it off. Then he transferred his energy to bullying Tyler again, which is exactly why Tyler has been so callous about his death—not that I'm condoning it, mind you, because we should all try to be better humans regardless of what others fling at us."

"A worthy sentiment," Ida Belle said, "but not always an achievable one."

Morgan nodded and sighed. "The reality is, the whole first night was just like we were back in high school, which is the point of a reunion, I suppose, but no one wanted to relive the worst of Justin, and that's exactly what we got."

"Yeah," Amanda agreed. "He was really pushing buttons, wasn't he? I saw him and Daniel arguing, and Daniel was always the one who could take him the most."

"I would think hitting on someone's wife would do that," I said.

Amanda frowned. "Perhaps so."

But I could tell by her expression that she thought the arguments were about more than Justin hitting on her sister.

My cell phone signaled an incoming call, and I saw Corndog's number in the display.

"I need to take this outside where I can hear," I said and hurried out of the bar.

I barely caught the call before it disconnected, and Corndog was beside himself.

"There's a man who booked a room for the night," he said. "I just got back from picking him up at the dock. He walked all over the house, strange-like, you know. Even asked if he could look in the attic, which I refused. Then he says he'd like to make an offer for the place and comes out with a figure that's half what this place is worth."

"What!?"

There was absolutely, positively no way this was a coincidence.

"He gives me a business card and says he can make an all-cash offer and we can close in a couple weeks. That he's heard about the trouble we had here but since he's wanting the place for his personal residence, that 'unpleasantness,' as he called it, won't affect him. He says with the money he'll pay that we can find another place—something smaller and easier to maintain and that way, I can still take care of my wife. I swear, if I were forty years younger, I would have punched him right in the mouth, just like you did that gator."

"I probably would have helped."

"I'm not selling my house. And even if that's what it comes down to, there's no way I'd sell it to the likes of him."

"Is he still there?"

"No. He asked me to take him back over. Tried to pay for the night he booked, but I refused to take it."

"Take a picture of his business card and send it to me. And this goes without saying, but don't you dare do or sign anything without talking to me first. I'm going to get my attorney involved. This has gotten completely out of hand."

"So does that mean you're not looking into it anymore?"

"Not at all. In fact, I'm on the case right now. We're in Houma inserting ourselves into the friends' circle, looking for clues. I'll let you know if I come up with something. But regardless, I'm going to fix this."

"I believe you will."

I disconnected and huffed. I'd gone and made promises. Jesus, I was getting bad about that crap. Now I had to figure out a way to make this all right. And dumping it on Alexander wasn't going to solve everything. It would keep the DA from bringing charges—something I still wasn't convinced he'd do anyway—but it wouldn't fix the reputation end of things. And solving this for Corndog and Petunia meant saving their business as well.

And now I had this fool trying to scam them into selling their home at a huge discount. There was no way the timing was incidental. And since I hadn't seen a single post by the friends about Justin's death, I had to assume they'd all agreed to keep it off social media. Lord knows, Petunia and Corndog hadn't been spreading it around, so that meant the tales out of school had to have come from Bryce or Simpson.

My cell phone signaled, and I saw that Corndog had sent a pic of the business card. As soon as we were out of the bar, I'd dig into that. But at the moment, I had to decide whether I used this new bit of information to prompt Morgan and Amanda into further outrage and potentially revealing more or keep it to myself. And if I *did* use it, how did I present it as someone who was supposed to have only just met the couple the day before?

I rolled around scenarios for a few seconds, settled on the best one, then called Corndog back.

"If anyone from that group calls and asks you about an earring, tell them the person who lost it contacted you."

"Huh? You're going to tell them about the earring?"

"No. I'm just going to tell them you found an earring in case any of them lost one to see how they react."

"Oh! That's smart."

"Tell Petunia, if anyone calls asking about it, you found the owner already. Make sure she knows to assure them the earring belonged to someone else."

"You really think the person who dropped it will call about it?"

"No. But there's always a chance. I like to cover all bases."

I disconnected and headed back inside.

"Is everything all right, dear?" Gertie asked as I settled back on my stool.

"Yes, I thought it might be my landlord as he's supposed to fix my sink this weekend, but it was actually Petunia."

"Petunia?" Gertie asked. "Why would she call you? Was there a problem with your credit card? I told you we were happy to pay."

"Nothing like that. I left my earbuds in my room is all."

"Do we need to go back and get them?" Ida Belle asked.

"Not necessarily. She said if we don't have time to meet Corndog at the dock before we head back to NOLA that she'll drop them in the mail for me." I looked over at Morgan and Amanda. "Oh, and she said they found an earring. I thought I'd tell you in case any of your lot lost one."

Morgan shrugged. "Not my arena."

Amanda pursed her lips. "I haven't but I'll ask the others. What did it look like? And where did they find it?"

I frowned. "Sorry, they didn't say and I didn't think to ask since none of us were wearing any. I was kind of distracted by the heated conversation in the background."

"In the parking lot?" Gertie asked.

"No. At Corndog and Petunia's. When I was talking to Petunia, I heard Corndog and another man talking. Corndog sounded angry, which isn't the norm, so I asked if they were okay. She said it was nothing—that some fool had booked a room, but when he got there, he started trying to convince them to sell their house for half of what it was worth. Corndog was 'setting him on his ear,' as she put it."

Morgan shot a concerned glance at Amanda, who frowned.

"The vultures have moved in quickly," Amanda said. "That's not good."

I shook my head. "Man, I wish there was something someone could do. You're sure none of you had something with peanuts in it that Justin could have got a hold of? Just someone saying that was the case might be enough to make all of this go away."

Morgan stared ahead, a grave look on his face, and shook his head. "Tyler had a convenience store bag with snacks, and his favorite candy bar was Snickers. I know he claimed he didn't bring any, but I'm sure he'd never admit otherwise given the circumstances. I suppose if he's not willing to fess up one of us could lie—at least it would muddy the waters enough to get Corndog off the hook. I could do it."

"No," Amanda said. "That would just put you on the hook with Sheriff Stupid, and you've got security clearances to consider. It could cost you your job."

"But it could cost Corndog and Petunia their home." He blew out a breath and ran one hand over his head. "This whole thing is a disaster. I wish Brittany had never put this pre-reunion together. Justin is still ruining lives."

He slid off his stool, mumbling something about the men's room, and walked off. Amanda watched him go, a pensive look on her face.

"He's very buttoned up, our Morgan," Amanda said, and I could hear the concern in her voice. "But he's always trying to make things right in the world. He's worried about that couple, because that's the kind of person he is. It's the kind of person he's always been. Kind, caring, and so morally upright."

She pinned her gaze on me. "Tyler wasn't the only person Justin bullied. He went at Morgan hard for a while in high school before Daniel found out and put a stop to it. Morgan wouldn't defend himself. Not back then. That's probably why he can't stand the thought of Justin costing the couple their home and wants to help."

I nodded. "So Daniel didn't stop Justin from picking on Tyler as well?"

"Sometimes he did," Amanda said. "When Justin took things too far. But for the most part, Tyler is hard to offend and could hold his own. The only way that Justin could really get to him with was through Nicole."

"Nicole? Her and Justin were a thing?"

"No way. Nicole's too smart to go down that dead-end road. But Justin was always trying his luck with her. He kept bragging that they hooked up at a party before graduation, but no one believed him. He just did it to get Tyler riled up. In case you hadn't noticed, Tyler has a thing for Nicole. Always has. Apparently ten years of being apart hasn't changed his feelings any that I can see. I don't know whether that's romantic or sad."

"Romantic if there's a happily ever after in it," Gertie said. "If not, then sad."

Amanda nodded. "Sad then. Because Nicole has only ever loved one person and I don't think that's going to change."

"Then why isn't she with him?" I asked.

"Because he's living that happily ever after with his wife, the only woman *he's* ever loved. But Nicole, poor thing, never moved on. So this is definitely a tragedy and not a romance. At least where Nicole is concerned."

"Oh, wow. Do that man and his wife know?"

"Doubtful. I don't think anyone knows. Nicole's very good at hiding things. I'm just better at seeing them."

"Maybe you *should* consider that move to criminal law." I said.

"Too depressing." She left some money on the counter and jumped off her stool. "I'm going to grab Morgan and head out. We need to get ready for tonight. Brittany wants to meet to cover what information about Justin we should share and I think she wants us to all say something tonight. I'm hoping she nixes the idea but if not, I'm going to tap the kind and proper Morgan to help me out."

I nodded. "Good luck."

"Thanks. Enjoy the bar."

I watched as Amanda intercepted Morgan on his way back to the stools. She leaned over and said something. He didn't look happy, but he nodded, then lifted a hand to wave at us. We all waved back and they headed out.

"What the heck is going on with Corndog and Petunia and this house buyer?" Gertie asked. "Please tell me you were making that up."

"Only the part about the earbuds, and it was Corndog I talked to, but the guy and the offer is no joke."

Ida Belle shook her head. "I smell Bryce all over this."

"So do I," I said. "But the only thing we know for sure is that Bryce didn't kill Justin."

"So this guy is an opportunist, scavenging off the bad luck of seniors," Gertie said. "Not surprising if he's a friend of Bryce's. What a piece of—"

And she said the word.

CHAPTER NINETEEN

IT WAS LIKE A SCENE IN THE MOVIES, WHEN EVERYTHING goes quiet and the music shuts off, because that's exactly what happened. Someone killed the music and everyone in the bar turned and stared.

"Well..." Ida Belle looked at Gertie and waved at the floor.

"Good Lord, I'll never get up from there," she said and looked at the other patrons. "You're really going to make an old lady get on the floor? When was the last time it was mopped?"

"It's not just the law, it's the curse," a man said. "You get on that floor or everything in this town goes to heck. Last time someone refused, a hurricane rolled in a week later and darn near took out this bar. So get to it, granny. Your friends can help you up."

"I'm not shooting our way out of this one," I said. "I've only got fifteen rounds and my hand hurts from twisting around in your bra. So I suggest you get to dipping."

"She probably can't even cross her legs," Ida Belle said.

"I can too!" Gertie argued.

Ida Belle motioned to the floor again and Gertie sighed and climbed off her stool.

She started to bend, then her knees apparently said to heck with it all and she plopped onto the floor, probably giving herself a decent butt bruise. She pulled her legs in, but as Ida Belle had predicted, they weren't interested in crossing.

"All the way," the man said. "You have to get the legs up."

"I'm pretty sure they'll break and bend them if you don't," I said, glancing around at the stern faces.

Gertie grabbed one leg and pulled it in, then grabbed the other and after much huffing, managed to get one ankle over the other.

"Good enough," the man said and turned back to his friends at the bar. The music fired up again, and the crisis was over.

Except for getting Gertie off the floor.

She pushed her legs apart, but I could tell by the way she moved that the twisting had really angered her left knee. Even more concerning, she probably had something from Nora in her purse. God only knew what kind of horror that might bring.

Ida Belle extended her hand and Gertie glared at her.

"Now you want to help?" she asked. "I can manage."

She twisted to the side and grabbed the barstool, then got onto her knees. I saw her cringe when her left knee touched the floor and knew I'd called that one correctly. She pulled herself up to a standing position, still leaning heavily on the stool, and I could tell the majority of her weight was on her right leg. Then she gave Ida Belle a triumphant look.

"Told you so!" she said and let go of the stool.

And Gertied.

The instant her hand came off the back of the stool, her weight involuntarily shifted onto her left leg to maintain her balance, but her left knee wasn't having any of it. She let out a yelp as she pitched forward, slamming right into the back of the man who'd made her sit.

The man, who had just picked up a full mug of beer, stumbled forward, cracking the man in front of him right in the nose with it, which sent the beer flying right into the face of a woman walking toward the bar. Beer Mug man and Broken Nose man both cussed, then flopped onto the ground and scrambled to get their legs crossed.

The woman who'd gotten a beer bath stumbled backward, temporarily blinded, and sat on a plate of boiled shrimp on the table behind her. She came up as quickly as she went down, cursing like a sailor, and I could see shrimp lodged in her butt. But before anyone could warn her, she plopped onto the floor and let out another round of cursing that put sailors to shame, then bolted up onto her knees and started swiping her butt to remove the lodged shrimp.

A man seated at the table decided to take the opportunity to 'help' and at the first swipe of his hand on her rear, she punched him dead in the face. He cussed as his chair went flying backward and crashed into a guy just gearing up to throw a dart. The dart flew out of his hand and landed right in the middle of the back of a huge man with motorcycle gang tattoos who was playing pool.

The dart guy cursed and dropped down to the floor, and the motorcycle gang dude spun around, cursing about everything under the sun and looking for someone to kill. In his spin, he clocked two men and a woman with his pool cue.

By now, half the bar was down on the floor and the three of us just stood in wonder of it all.

"I didn't even get video of this," Ida Belle said.

The bartender tapped a camera over the bar. "Twenty bucks and I'll put it on a USB for you."

I pulled fifty out of my wallet along with a business card. "That's for the beer and the video. Can you mail it to that address? I think we should probably leave before everyone gets up."

"Good call," he said and pocketed the money and card.

Ida Belle and I each grabbed one of Gertie's arms, to make sure she didn't set off Stop, Drop, and Leg Cross War II on the way out, and practically ran out the door. We shoved her up and into the SUV and Ida Belle tore out of the parking lot and down the bumpy road so fast I couldn't even get my seat belt on. When one dip finally had us all hitting our heads on the roof of the vehicle, she slowed.

That's when Gertie started laughing.

Ida Belle glared at her in the rearview mirror, and I knew that if the road had a shoulder and we hadn't been on a getaway run, she might have pulled over and made her walk back, sore knee and all. Since everyone was in one piece and the only real casualties had been some beer, shrimp, and that woman's dress, I figured we'd come out better than usual.

"Wasn't that a hoot?" Gertie said. "Stop glaring at me like you didn't enjoy it. You're the one who was sad about not having video."

"I wanted video because it's a spectacle that bears rewatching when I'm not in fear of being pummeled by the locals," Ida Belle said.

I nodded. "It was like a human pinball machine. Fascinating really. Because I don't think any of them really care much about the law. Apparently, it's superstition that has them adhering to the rules. These small-town things never cease to amaze me."

"Given the situation Corndog and Petunia are in, I don't know that we can rule out curses," Gertie said.

"That's not a curse," Ida Belle said. "I'd bet money that's a sorry excuse for a sheriff using a bad situation to benefit a friend."

"Curses aside," I interrupted, "because a curse didn't kill Justin, let's discuss our conversation with Amanda and Morgan. Talk about a doozy."

Gertie frowned. "Was it? I mean, there was some stuff we already knew and that sad part about Nicole. Did I miss something?"

"Apparently so," Ida Belle said. "Starting with the fact that Justin bullied Tyler and Morgan in high school and was apparently hard at it again at the B and B."

I nodded. "Then there was the whole Nicole and Justin thing, with Justin claiming he hooked up with her to get more digs in at Tyler."

"And Tyler wears an earring," Ida Belle said, "but he didn't have one on while we were there. I think the first thing we should do is comb his social media and see if we can spot him wearing that earring."

"So Tyler is in love with Nicole, who is in love with a married man, who is in love with his wife," Gertie said. "The whole thing sounds like a bad soap opera. Do you think Amanda's right on all of that?"

"Yes," I said. "Morgan told me that Amanda noticed everything and stored it away. Whether she uses her powers for good or evil apparently depends on the situation."

"So why spill Nicole's secret to us?" Gertie asked.

I frowned. "I don't know. Maybe because we're strangers and there's not really anything we could do with the information, at least not as far as she knows."

"It seemed like it bothered Amanda a little, which is odd," Gertie pointed out. "Amanda and Nicole appear to only be friends because of Brittany and being cousins. And Amanda doesn't strike me as the emotional, overly sympathetic type when it comes to romance tomfoolery. So why would it bother Amanda if Nicole is wasting her life pining for a married man?"

I smiled as it hit me. "Because that man is married to her sister."

"What?!"

"No way!"

They both yelled at once.

"You think Nicole is carrying a torch for Daniel?" Ida Belle asked.

"It makes sense," I said. "Amanda was completely certain in her statement that the man had only ever loved his wife and they were living their happily ever after. And I took her statement to mean Nicole had loved this man since she was old enough for man-woman romance. That's high school. If Nicole had her heart broken *after* high school, Amanda probably wouldn't have known the details of it because they're not close."

"Brittany could have told her," Gertie said.

"She strikes me as too proper to share her best friend's personal heartache, even with her twin," I said. "Besides, Amanda has to know who the married man is and that his life is happy. Why would she know that person so well if it was someone Nicole met after high school?"

"Good Lord," Ida Belle said. "Do you think Brittany knows?"

"Amanda doesn't seem to think so," I said. "She doesn't seem to think either of them know."

"But you think they do?" Gertie asked.

"I think Daniel might," I said. "That's probably why most of Brittany and Nicole's visits are girls only and seem to be more in New Orleans than in Houma. I mean, it's possible he's giving the besties time to themselves, but it's also possible he'd rather it not be just the three of them."

"Because he knows Nicole has always had feelings for him," Ida Belle said. "And being around her is uncomfortable."

"Good Lord, that's a mess," Gertie said.

I nodded. "What did you guys think about Morgan offering to say he brought in something with peanuts?"

"Sounds like he was being nice to me," Gertie said. "Amanda said he was always the nice one."

"Or he's feeling guilty," Ida Belle said.

"Guilty about what?" Gertie asked.

"Killing Justin?" Ida Belle said. "Amanda said Justin bullied Tyler *and* Morgan and we have no reason to doubt her statement, especially given everything else we know about the three of them."

I nodded. "And Amanda also said, 'Morgan wouldn't defend himself. Not back then.'"

Gertie's eyes widened. "You think she meant he defended himself now. Wow. That was one I didn't see coming. So the guilt is because Corndog is on the hook for what he did."

"It's possible."

"But Morgan came from upstairs when the person broke into Justin's room and went out the window," Gertie said. "And he doesn't wear an earring."

"We don't know that the killer and the earring wearer are the same person," I said. "Maybe it was like we originally thought and one of the girls hooked up with Justin and didn't want anyone to know. The peanut consumption could have happened after that interlude. Morgan could have left something laced with peanut oil in Justin's room for him to find later that night."

Gertie sighed. "Which means everyone is back on the suspect list. So if we go with the killer and the acrobat being two different people, who was the woman with the lipstick?"

"My money's on Brittany," Ida Belle said. "She used to have

a thing with Justin in high school and she teaches gymnastics. She could have easily made that climb down."

I nodded. "It would definitely explain why she was willing to take the risk to recover the earring even if it meant scaling the house in a storm."

"Good Lord," Gertie said. "What about Amanda? She was outside too."

I frowned. "I can't see it, but I also think Amanda is gifted at making people see what she wants them to see. Still, neither Amanda nor Nicole for that matter have anything to lose by hooking up with Justin. They'd just take grief from their friends over it. But you're right. We can't take her off the table."

Ida Belle frowned. "You think Amanda is hiding things?"

"They all are. The question is whether or not it's relevant to Justin's death. Let's head to the hotel and get checked in. We can work on the internet searches until it's time to get into position for the dance. And I want to check out this 'buyer' who blindsided Corndog and Petunia. I'm sure he's connected to Bryce, but it would be nice to have proof before I take all of this to Alexander."

I stared out the car window as Ida Belle drove, all the things I knew running through my mind. And it was a lot. Unfortunately, the list of things I didn't know was longer. But I had a feeling that this case was about to break loose.

WE MANAGED TO GET CHECKED IN AND UP TO OUR SUITE without anyone in the group spotting us, which was good. The more time between "run-ins" the better, and we'd just had one with two members. I knew the friends had all seen Ida Belle's SUV at the dock, so I had her park in the employee lot behind the hotel in a spot that gave them a direct shot at the smoking porch with the parabolic microphone but that was far enough away that hopefully, none of them would lock in on it.

On our way to the hotel, Gertie had looked at the hotel amenities and pointed out the limited room service options, so we'd picked up lunch on the way and were now at the table in our suite enjoying a stellar round of fried shrimp, jalapeño hush puppies, and coleslaw. The batter on the shrimp was thin and flaky and they'd been expertly fried. The hush puppies were the stuff legends were made from, and the servings had been generous. We had plenty for leftovers and since the suite came complete with a mini fridge and a microwave, we were all set for a post-investigative snack later that night. And we hadn't even dug into the pint of banana pudding yet.

Gertie leaned back in her chair and groaned. "Good Lord, that was some fine eating. I'm glad I don't have to wear a dress or heels tonight."

"You can't walk in heels on a normal basis," Ida Belle said. "With that gimpy knee, you wouldn't make it one step in a pair now."

Gertie waved a hand in dismissal. "I have some of Nora's latest concoction. My knee will be fine by tonight."

Ida Belle stared at her in dismay.

"You and Ida Belle will use the side exit after dark and head to the SUV," I said. "It's not a long walk and you'll be sitting the rest of the night, so you should be good. Worst case, Ida Belle can pull around to the exit and drop you off when you're done."

Gertie shrugged. "Sure. Like I said, it's no big deal."

"It's no big deal because you won't be moving," Ida Belle said. "We're making sure you're clear on that part. So no need to take whatever Nora has cooked up."

"You say I won't be moving, but how many times has that actually worked out?" Gertie asked.

I shook my head. There was no use arguing. She was going to take whatever it was regardless of our plans, and I had research to do. I pulled out my laptop and Ida Belle and Gertie retrieved their iPads, then we divvied up the group and started the long, boring process of looking for earrings. I'd taken Brittany, since I considered her the most likely suspect in that regard, Ida Belle took Amanda, and Gertie took Tyler.

We'd been scrolling for an hour when Ida Belle placed her iPad on the table and leaned back and stretched her arms over her head.

"If I never see another earlobe in my life, it will be too soon," she said.

Gertie nodded. "They're supposed to be sexy, I think, but if they ever were for me, they're certainly not now. For all we know, the earring belonged to Justin."

"His ears weren't pierced," Ida Belle said.

"Some people have piercings where only sexy-time people can see them. Once, on Bourbon Street, I saw a guy get a piercing right through his—"

"No!" Ida Belle said and held up her hand.

"Just flopped it all out there on the table, right in front of the picture window," Gertie said.

Ida Belle stared at her in dismay. "What part of 'no' did you not understand? I don't want to hear about some man's business being pierced in public."

Gertie rolled her eyes. "Anyway, he passed out on the spot. But I talked to the piercing guy afterward, and he said the earring is great for women during sexy time."

"For the love of all that is holy!" Ida Belle cried out. "We get it. The earring might have belonged to Justin. And maybe it got caught in a hole in his underwear and he yanked it out.

Or maybe it was chafing. Or he lost it during...a business meeting."

Gertie snorted. "Is that what we're calling it these days?"

I couldn't help smiling at their exchange, but Gertie had also made a valid point. Maybe the earring had belonged to Justin. And if he was wearing it in places he couldn't post online, then we wouldn't be able to track it down.

"Did Amanda look flustered at all when you mentioned Petunia finding an earring?" Ida Belle asked.

I ran the scene back through my mind and shook my head. "No. But then, she never does. The only time I've ever seen her venture outside of calm and collected was when she was drunk, and even then, she was still very aware of what she said."

"Attorney," Ida Belle said. "Full scholarship to Berkeley and about to be made partner at a top firm before she's thirty. You realize if she did it, we'll probably never be able to prove it. Out of all of them, she's the one best equipped to pull off a murder and get away with it."

I held in a sigh because my personal feelings weren't relevant to the case. But if I was being honest, I didn't want it to be Amanda because I liked her. I appreciated clever, intelligent, and direct. But I also agreed that all those talents, combined with years of studying case law, gave her the ability to commit the perfect crime.

"Back to it," Ida Belle said and picked up her iPad. "That earring isn't going to find itself."

I nodded and moved to the next post, which was a video of Brittany and Nicole teaching two young girls—probably around ten—how to do flips on a trampoline. The two women demonstrated, then the girls took turns trying. It only took a few attempts for the girls to nail it.

The description read *Helping my neighbors' girls prepare for cheerleader tryouts. I'm betting they make it.*

I froze the video on the ears and zoomed in, but they weren't wearing earrings. On to the next one. It was a picture of Brittany and Daniel, having dinner at a restaurant on a bayou at sunset. It was pretty and they were dressed up. I checked the description.

Nine years of marital bliss. Over a decade of love.

Corny, but I had to admit, they did look happy. If Brittany had 'settled' for Daniel, then she was committed to making it work. Or at least making it look as though it worked on social media. But that was the entire problem with social media, wasn't it? You didn't see people's real lives. You only saw the parts that made them look good. The things they wanted you to see.

I scrolled through a few more landscape and decorating pictures, some pictures of Brittany's students performing, and then I paused on a picture of Brittany at an awards banquet. She was being honored as businesswoman of the year, but it wasn't the award that caught my attention, or even what she was wearing. It was the form of the award.

Fleur-de-lis earrings with a single sapphire in the center.

Bingo.

CHAPTER TWENTY

"I found them," I said, and showed Ida Belle and Gertie the image.

"An award gift," Ida Belle said. "That means they're probably real and possibly even a custom job."

Gertie nodded. "Even if they were mass produced, would her friends rush out and buy a pair of earrings like she received for an award? That's not exactly tacky but it's tacky adjacent."

"Yeah, I don't see any of them doing that. So Brittany is our earring loser."

"Thank God, we found her," Ida Belle said. "I was afraid Gertie was going to track down those young people and start asking them if Justin's business meeting equipment was accessorized."

Gertie didn't protest, which was a bit concerning, but thankfully, not something I needed to worry about anymore. My focus now was trying to get enough on Brittany to force an investigation. A real investigation. Not a Bryce farce.

"So we have motive for going after the earring," I said. "The ability to make that climb, and Brittany was downstairs and wet. I think we have one part of this mystery solved."

Ida Belle shook her head. "I didn't want to believe it was her. I hate that she was cheating on Daniel. He seems like a nice young man and Justin sounded like anything but."

"There's no accounting for animal attraction," Gertie said. "Look at me and Jeb. You glance at him and think 'just a shriveled old man,' but boy is he a dynamo—"

"No." Ida Belle reached over and grabbed a Bible off the dresser. "Do I have to perform an exorcism to get you to stop?"

"You know that hotel Bible isn't enough to take me," Gertie said. "So what now?"

"We connect the Bryce dots on the guy wanting to buy Corndog and Petunia's house," I said.

I pulled up the business card Corndog had sent me for the prospective 'buyer' and did a search on the name. I got a hit on social media and clicked over to see what he had going on in his feed. It didn't take two clicks of the mouse to find a picture of the buyer and Bryce at a fishing tournament.

Ida Belle gave the picture a disgusted look. "Well, we figured that was the case, but I guess it helps to have proof."

I blew out a breath. Yes, it was proof that the buyer had gotten his intel from Bryce, but could I prove Bryce was threatening Corndog with charges in an attempt to force them into a fire sale? I didn't believe for a minute that the DA was going to go for his plan, but when rumors of Corndog accidentally killing a guest circulated, they'd probably lose enough business to put the house on the chopping block anyway. Bryce's friend might not want it at a fair price, but if they were forced to sell later, even at a higher price, that still meant they'd be homeless.

And that sucked huge.

But for the life of me, I couldn't figure out a way around the rumors that were bound to fly. The only permanent fix I could see was proving that someone else killed Justin—accidentally or intentionally—or that Justin made the mistake himself. Talk about an impossible situation.

"I really wish I could see the ME's report," I said. "Even if he didn't do an autopsy, the details might help."

"We could break in—"

I shook my head. "Bryce knows we're in the area. He'll be expecting me to make that sort of move."

Gertie put her hand in the air and gave me a 'so what' look. "You just sneaked into Iran and freed Carter from a compound occupied by terrorists, and not even the DOD can prove you were there. Am I supposed to believe that you can't evade Bryce Benoit?"

"She has a point," Ida Belle said.

"You think I should break into the ME's office?" I asked her.

She shrugged. "It's not usually my first suggestion, but desperate times, you know?"

I frowned. "Let me think on it. It would have to be late, anyway. Midnight or after, so it wouldn't interfere with our plans for tonight. But just in case I lose all common sense and get desperate, I think we should do some reconnaissance."

I looked up the ME's office and found the location in a single structure in the middle of town.

"Looks like it's located in a medical district, of sorts," I said. "A hospital and a bunch of labs and clinics branch out over a couple of blocks, with a few eateries thrown in."

I shut my laptop.

"Let's go take a look," I said. "I can only get so much from satellite, and if I'm going to do this, I need to know where every security camera is, and we need to find a meetup place and plan alternate escape routes."

"If it's a medical district, there's going to be cameras everywhere," Ida Belle said. "Too many break-ins by drug seekers for them not to be covered."

I nodded. "I know. But they can't be any worse than terrorists, right?"

Gertie clapped her hands. "We haven't done any breaking and entering in a while."

"We broke into the Catholic church to put those chicken poop candies from the Easter debacle into Celia's stash just a couple weeks ago," Ida Belle said.

"Technically, we didn't 'break,'" Gertie said. "Father Michael let us in, so we just entered, which isn't illegal when you're invited. And since the candies were perfectly okay other than having been inside plastic eggs that chickens sat on, I don't see where any charges can be applied on that one either."

"So unless you can go to jail for it, it doesn't count," I said and popped up. "Got it."

Gertie attempted to jump up as well, but her knee gave out on her and she promptly fell back onto the chair.

Ida Belle shook her head. "We are not carrying you out to the vehicle."

"You go get the car," I said. "I'll meet you at the side entrance with Gertie."

Ida Belle headed out, still shaking her head.

"You can't carry me out of here," Gertie said. "Not that I don't think you could manage it, but because it will attract attention. We're supposed to be undercover."

"Now you're worried about being undercover?"

Gertie crossed her arms. "I don't want Corndog and Petunia to lose their house, and if it means I have to sit here by myself in this room for that to happen, then that's what I'll do. I'll complain about it every chance I get for the next year or so, but you'll live."

I grinned and headed for the closet. "Don't worry, I have an idea."

I pulled the wooden closet rod out and cracked it across my knee.

"Give me the rest of that adhesive bandage that you put on your knee," I said.

I wrapped the splintered section of the closet rod with the bandage, then presented it to Gertie.

"There you go—a cane."

Gertie's confused expression cleared and she smiled. "Perfect."

"I don't know about perfect, but it will do until we can stop at the pharmacy and get you a real one."

I helped Gertie up from the chair, made sure she was steady with the cane, then grabbed her other arm and we headed out. It wasn't the fastest I'd ever walked, but we still managed to get there without incident. Ida Belle was already parked next to the curb when we arrived.

"Nice," Ida Belle said when she spotted the makeshift cane.

"I figure we can pick up the real deal on the way back," I said. "We should probably keep one in the SUV with the other supplies."

"I keep saying we should get a walker or one of those portable wheelchairs," Ida Belle said.

"Sure, it's funny when you've got two good knees," Gertie said. "But neither of you had to get down on that floor."

"I could have done it," I said.

"You don't count," Gertie said. "Your knees are young."

Ida Belle raised one eyebrow. "So you're saying your knees are old?"

"Forget it," Gertie groused, and Ida Belle and I laughed.

It was a short drive to the medical district, and I started making note of cameras, streetlights, and parking. When we turned onto the street with the ME's office, I grabbed Ida Belle's arm.

"Parking lot! Now!" I yelled.

Ida Belle made a quick turn into a parking lot and pulled to the back before stopping.

"What the heck was that?"

"Bryce was coming out of the ME's office," I said.

"Crap," Ida Belle said. "I didn't even see him."

"His car was at the curb. Inch forward so we can see if he's gone."

She moved to the entrance and I scanned the street. No sign of the sheriff's car.

"Looks like we're in the clear," I said. "Do a slow pass. I want to video the street to review later on."

She pulled out of the parking lot and crept down the street while I filmed both sides. The ME's office was in the middle of the street and in keeping with older construction, the building walls were shared with no walkways between.

"There must be an alley," Gertie said. "They're not hauling dead bodies out here in the middle of the road."

Ida Belle turned right at the end of the street, and I yanked a ball cap out of her glove box.

"Pick me up at the other end," I said and jumped out while she was still moving.

I hurried for the back of the buildings, then kept close to the side, figuring the scattered landscaping and trash cans would give me a bit of cover. I kept my head down and the hat pulled low as I went, making sure none of the cameras got a clear shot of me. Not that I expected Bryce to check them—that might mean doing some actual police work—but anything was possible.

When I reached the ME's building, I spotted the camera in the corner and smiled as it rotated. A simple setup and an easy one to avoid. You simply positioned yourself outside of the range and moved when it did until you reached the back door. Alarm systems were a different beast, but I hadn't seen any signs indicating there was one. That seemed odd given that the ME's office handed out homicide edicts, but then they didn't carry opioids, and that was probably the main thrust of break-ins in this area. There probably weren't many people looking to read an autopsy report and even fewer looking to steal a body. Satisfied, I headed for the other end of the street and jumped into the SUV as Ida Belle slowed.

"A toddler could work around the camera," I said. "And I didn't see any indication of a security system, so not sure on that count. But even if there is one, it's probably crap. Most of them are."

"Says the woman whose home is geared up like a terrorist compound," Ida Belle said. "But that's good for us."

I nodded. "There's a pharmacy on the next block. We can pick up a cane for Gertie while we're there. And restock the first aid kit."

Ida Belle pulled up to the curb in front of the pharmacy and I hopped out. "I can get everything. Do you need anything besides our supplies?"

"A couple of sodas, maybe?" Gertie said. "The hotel wants four dollars a can."

"Yikes," I said. "Okay, be right back."

I hurried inside, grabbed a basket, and collected sodas, bandages, and more adhesive tape. Then I tossed in some chips and a large bag of M&M's as well since I figured we'd eat the banana pudding before the dance, and I always had the munchies after an undercover job. This covered salty and sweet, so I was set.

I had just picked out a hot pink cane when I heard a voice behind me.

"I know what you're up to."

I turned around and gave Bryce a big smile as I held up the cane. "Buying medical supplies? Is that against the law?"

"Stop pretending you're here for any other reason than trying to pin that guy's death on someone other than Corndog."

"I will as soon as you stop pretending you're not trying to railroad Corndog for that death so that your buddy can steal their house."

His eyes widened, and I could tell he was a bit panicked that I'd caught onto him and his friend's maneuvering so quickly.

"Word gets around on things like this," he said. "Small towns. You know how they operate. If someone wants to make an offer on their house, that's not against the law."

"It is if they're colluding with you to force them into a sale."

"Who's colluding? The guy died from eating peanut oil. Corndog made a mistake. That's the simple truth of it, whether you want to believe it or not. So why don't you stop pretending you're vacationing or need medical supplies right down the road from the ME's office, and head back to Sinful, where your boyfriend covers for you."

"So let me get this straight. You think I stopped in a pharmacy to buy a cane and bandages because there's a portal into the ME's office here? It so happens that we are on vacation and hit that silly bar with the cursing laws this afternoon. Gertie slipped, had to sit, and torqued her knee. Since she plans on antiques shopping tomorrow, I'm trying to fix her up."

He rolled his eyes. "Does anyone really buy those stories of yours?"

"Okay, then tell me how shopping here gets me anything to do with your case. I'll wait."

He stiffened and I knew I'd struck a nerve. Because the reality was, there wasn't anything to be gained by my being in the pharmacy, buying these items, except for the reason I'd stated.

"Tell you what," I said. "If I'm doing something illegal, go ahead and arrest me. Oh, wait. You're not 'real' police. You paid for that badge like you bought it off eBay."

His jaw clenched. "I have jurisdiction over the entire parish. I can arrest you if I want to."

"Then do it or let me finish my shopping. I assume the Houma PD isn't going to be very happy about you harassing visitors over trumped-up misdemeanors and conspiracy theories. But hey, roll the dice."

His face turned red, and he whirled around and stomped off. I shook my head. The man was exhausting. No wonder his parents had moved away as soon as they were legally able. They'd created an incompetent, obnoxious monster and wanted to be rid of him. Or given that he'd likely been molded after them, maybe they considered him too much competition.

"Have a great day, Bryce!" I called after him.

He didn't even pause.

By 7:00 p.m. I was in my dress and a pair of silver heels I owned from a previous shopping trip with Ronald for a past adventure. The wig had been brushed to perfection and I had to admit, worked well with the dress and my tan. Gertie had 'tarted me up'—whatever that meant—with her makeup, even though most of my face would be hidden behind the mask.

I'd cruised the online yearbook until I found a student that

I didn't figure would attend. She was pictured exactly once—no clubs, no groups, no sports, and apparently, no friends because she didn't attend a single school social event either—and the one photo pictured a sad, frumpy-looking girl who wouldn't even look directly into the camera. I'd managed to track her down to MIT for college and found that she was now a data analyst for a corporation in Japan. She had zero social media and no family left in Houma that I could find.

On the surface, she appeared to be the perfect duckling-to-swan cover.

I put the mask in place and headed out a little after seven. People were allowed to check in starting at six thirty, but I wanted to slip in a little after the crowd. The fewer eyes on me in direct overhead light, the better. But I wanted to get there in time for the opening greeting because I figured someone would talk about Justin's death. If people were going to dish the dirt on him, it was going to be then.

Ida Belle and Gertie would slip out then, too, and get in position in the SUV and set up the microphone. Hopefully, they wouldn't run into any of the group. I'd originally planned for them to get into place in the dark, but when I found the info for the reunion online and saw that the greeting was at 7:15, I figured I needed to get them into place earlier because people who hadn't heard the news already might slip outside to talk right after the announcement, especially if the music started and it was hard to hear inside.

Once Ida Belle and Gertie were in the vehicle, the window tint provided them complete coverage. If they found they were blocked by large vehicles, they could move right in front of the smoking area, and no one would know they were sitting there. But I was hoping they'd be able to keep their distance since the friends might recognize the SUV.

I eased into the lobby from the hallway and peered around

the corner toward the meeting room. Two women sat at the table handing out tags, and I breathed a sigh of relief that Brittany wasn't one of them. So far, so good. I waited until they finished with a large group, then hurried over when the table was empty.

"Janice Millner," I said.

Game on.

CHAPTER TWENTY-ONE

THE TWO WOMEN LOOKED UP AT ME AND BLINKED.

Finally, one of them found her voice. "Janice. Wow. You look great. So different. We didn't know you were coming."

"Neither did I. But a last-minute business thing had me in NOLA for a few days, and I figured why not pop over and see what everyone's accomplished since high school."

"Right, of course. You didn't RSVP so we didn't print you a tag, but I brought some extras just in case...hold on."

She wrote Janice's name on a card and slipped it into a plastic sleeve, then handed it to me.

"The tag's magnetic," she said. "We don't want to ruin dresses."

"Is that bag Chanel?" the other girl asked.

I smiled. "No idea. My boyfriend bought it for me. I just liked the color. Thanks, girls. We'll catch up later."

I took the tag and hurried off, leaving the two of them gaping behind me. As soon as I got inside the conference room, I inched around the wall to the darkest spot, grabbing a punch off a table as I went. Then I slipped the name tag into my purse. Based on the lobby girl's reactions, I figured more people might ask questions if I had it on than not wearing one at all but dressed the part.

Being Janice might not have been the perfect option, but at least I was in and the dress wasn't short, clingy, or cut too low. That would have attracted attention from men—probably mostly married men—which would have attracted attention from wives. I needed to blend.

I found a group of women standing next to a group of men. The women weren't wearing tags, so I presumed they were married to students—likely the group of men next to them—but weren't graduates of that class themselves. Perfect. I'd just sidle up beside them and wait for the opening speech.

One of the women looked over at me as I approached and gave me a friendly nod. "Are you a class wife?"

"No. Actually, I'm a classmate, but I'm afraid I wasn't a very involved one. I was a painfully shy teen and a bookworm."

The woman nodded. "Sorry. I just figured since you didn't have a tag..."

"It's in my purse. The darn thing keeps falling off and who wants to bend all night in Lycra, right?"

Thank God for Ronald and his vocabulary.

She laughed. "I finally taped my husband's—he's Bill Church—do you remember him?"

I shrugged. "A little. I didn't mingle much back then. I just happened to be in NOLA for business and popped in on a whim. I live in Japan. My name's Janice, by the way."

"Oh wow. That's a flight. You'll probably win the prize for longest commute to the reunion."

"Prize? They're doing prizes?"

"Yes. Around ten o'clock, I think, so those of us with babysitters can see the ceremony without having to hang around until midnight."

I nodded and made a mental note to be long gone before ten.

"Attention."

Brittany's voice sounded over the PA system and the crowd stopped talking and looked toward the platform at the front of the room.

"Hello, classmates, and welcome to our ten-year reunion. Can you believe it's been that long?"

She launched into some facts and statistics about the class, and I saw a lot of smiling and eye-rolling, and then she introduced Daniel.

"And here's your class president, and my husband, Daniel Stout!"

There was a round of applause and some healthy cheering when Daniel took the stage, and I could tell that most people liked him. Or had liked him. From everything I'd heard, that made sense. It sounded as if Daniel had always been a stand-up guy.

I inched past the group of wives to stand between their husbands and a group of men and woman all wearing name tags. If anyone was going to talk smack about Justin, it was going to be his classmates, not their spouses.

"Thank you all for coming," he said. "It's good to see so many familiar faces. As you know, Brittany and I still live here, but most of you do not. It's nice to have an excuse to force you all back into town, even if we all had to lose a bit of hair and muscle to get it."

Everyone laughed and some men nodded.

Daniel sobered. "I'm afraid that my next announcement isn't going to be a pleasant one. Our prom king and football team captain, Justin Barbet, passed away earlier this week from anaphylactic shock."

There were a lot of gasps and wide eyes, and I figured at

least 90 percent of the room hadn't heard about Justin's death yet.

"Some of the old crew spent that night reminiscing about old times, so I want everyone to know that before his death, Justin was happy, engaged, and as entertaining as he always was. Some people never change, and Justin was one of them. Now he'll be eternally immortalized as the guy we knew from high school. Let's have a moment of silence for our lost friend."

Everyone bowed their heads, and the room went deathly quiet. Daniel held them that way for about ten seconds before coming back on the microphone.

"Now, everyone enjoy the dance. Enjoy each other. It's what Justin would have wanted. And I am going to kick things off by dancing with my beautiful wife."

"Ha," one of the guys near me laughed. "Justin 'kicked things off' with his beautiful wife back in high school."

One of the other guys nodded. "I never understood how they were friends. Daniel was always cool, and Justin was always a jerk. I bet I can count on one hand the people here who are still mourning his death, and it hasn't even been a minute since we found out."

"Michael," the woman next to him admonished. "You shouldn't talk bad about the man when he just died."

"You didn't go to school here and didn't know him. Trust me, if you had, you would feel the same way I do. The only people he treated worse than boys were girls."

The other women in the group, all wearing name tags, nodded, and the one who'd spoken out looked slightly embarrassed.

"I'm sorry. I didn't realize."

"Why would you have?" one of the women with a tag said. "But Michael is right. Justin was a horrible teen and I've heard he didn't improve any as an adult. Daniel was right to say he was immortalized as the boy from high school because apparently, he never grew past it."

"Like father, like son," another man said. "His old man screwed over so many people he'll never see outside Angola walls again. Now, who wants to go fishing tomorrow?"

I eased away as they made an obvious shift in subject and slipped in beside other groups and couples, hearing much of the same thing repeated. No one seemed broken up over Justin's death. Many stated they were surprised he'd made it this long given his drinking habits. Some claimed he was already an alcoholic in high school, and others said running with the fast scene in Miami likely meant he'd moved on to stronger things than drink. It was no wonder he'd eaten the wrong thing. It was bound to happen at some point.

All of which fit with what we'd already learned, but the ramping up of the addiction was a good point. If Justin had moved on to stronger stuff, then he might have made a mistake with food. If there was an autopsy, they would test for illegal drugs—the common ones anyway—and if anything stronger than booze was found, it would bulk up Corndog's defense.

I sighed. All roads led back to that nonexistent autopsy. And all because Bryce had no intention of doing his job, especially when his buddy could potentially capitalize on Corndog and Petunia's misfortune. Surely there was something I could do to make that happen, but I had no idea what.

And since there was nothing to be done about it at this moment, and I was already in a dress, I figured I'd better move on to the next round of gossip. This group comprised only women, who barely gave me a glance as I sat at the table next to them with my plate of finger foods and pretended to be reading texts while I listened in on their conversation.

"Well, I bet Amanda didn't shed any tears over him."

"I can't picture Amanda shedding a tear over anything, but yeah, Justin basically stalked and harassed her all of high school."

"That's only because he couldn't have Brittany."

"Oh, he had Brittany. She just wised up and traded him in for a better model."

"The right choice isn't always the exciting one though. Justin was hot."

"Sure, and the biggest whore in the parish. He literally showed up at my house one night expecting a booty call after he dropped Brittany off from a date. The guy was a total loser."

"If you were wanting him for a boyfriend, for sure, but if you were just looking for a good romp, he wasn't a bad option. At least he was always *up* for everything."

They all laughed.

"Justin gave Nicole a fair amount of grief too."

"Well, if Tyler hadn't been such a wimp, he would have done something about it and maybe won the fair maiden's hand and all that white knight crap. That guy's been carrying a torch longer than cave dwellers."

"I think it's kind of sweet, but also pathetic. I mean, ten years and the guy still hasn't made a move, yet he's still following her around like a pet. I know Nicole's not here with anyone, but does she have a regular?"

"Not that I know of. I never see anything on her socials anyway. My mom said local gossip was Nicole got hot and heavy with someone in Europe when she went to visit her aunt the summer after graduation and that she refused to come home. That's why she started college a year later. Maybe she's still pining over her foreign fling."

"Justin claimed he hooked up with Nicole back in the day,

but I think he was lying. It was just another way to get at Tyler."

"I never understood why he hated Tyler so much. I thought they were supposed to be friends, of sorts. Justin had always given him grief, but it seemed like one day he simply ratcheted it up by a thousand percent. I always thought it would have made more sense if Justin had hated on Daniel, especially after Brittany took up with him."

"You didn't know? Tyler's dad was the one who turned in Justin's dad for one of his scams. He's some finance guru and smelled something stinky in a client's books. Since the client was out of state, it was a federal thing. Tyler's dad had a friend at the FBI and dumped it all in their lap, figuring if he found one instance there were others. Took them a couple years to build up this massive case, so we were all graduated and gone before it went to trial. Dude got like eighty years or something."

"Wow. I had no idea. Jeez, that makes more sense now. I mean, in a Justin-was-a-douche sort of way. Not like Tyler or his dad did anything wrong, but it's just like Justin to blame everyone but the actual guilty party."

"His dad screwed a bunch of people out of their life savings. Some had to close their businesses. It was massive. He deserves every one of those years plus more as far as I'm concerned."

"So the only one of Brittany's Band that we haven't talked about is Morgan. I have to say, he got cute."

"But he's still just as quiet. I bet he has some über-smart girlfriend who's just as introverted as he is. She's probably back at their house writing code that will cure cancer or something."

"Idiot. You can't cure cancer with code."

"Fine, then she's going to figure out world peace. Whatever. Are you guys ready to dance, because I've got to work off a boatload of calories to have more drinks. And those chocolate-covered strawberries are teasing me."

"Let's go find our men."

They all rose as if connected and headed off in search of their dance partners, and I saved the notes I'd made on my phone while they were talking. What a gold mine. I now had motive for all three of our downstairs suspects to have a grudge against Justin. Granted, it sounded as if most everyone who'd ever known him had a reason for a grudge, but the one that really stood out was Tyler. I needed to find out more about the trial that put Justin's father away.

I walked around for another hour, careful to avoid 'Brittany's Band,' but the more time that passed, there was more drinking and less talking and people didn't seem to be dwelling on Justin's death, which pretty much said everything I needed to know about him. Unfortunately, the drinking and passage of time also meant my suspects had split up and it was getting harder to avoid them.

I was just wondering if I should cut out when I felt someone's gaze on me. I rose and lifted my phone for cover and scanned the room. Across the dance floor from me, I spotted Morgan, talking to one of the women who'd given me the name tag who was looking my way. Then she lifted her arm and pointed at me. Morgan looked and nodded and headed my direction.

Crap!

Of course he wanted to talk to the person who was likely his female counterpart. They had been co-valedictorians, both with perfect GPAs. Morgan had taken a picture with the award. Janice had apparently opted out and only her name and a picture of the plaque had been featured in the yearbook.

I was certain my disguise was great, but masks were easy to

remove and if he asked to step outside to catch up, as I assumed was common at this kind of thing, I was pretty sure he would expect the mask to come off. And even if he was so drunk he didn't recognize me, and even though I was excellent at changing my voice, the hyper-observant Morgan still had a really good chance of figuring out who I was. I'd been avoiding him and Amanda, in particular, for just that reason.

I whirled around and shot out of the ballroom at a clip, dodging people as I went. I glanced back when I reached the door and saw that he was already halfway across the room and closing in fast. I slowed only long enough to yank off my shoes, then ran for the lobby. I was sure it would look strange if he saw me sprinting across the parking lot, but at that point, I didn't care. Maybe Janice had been odd enough that he wouldn't give it much thought. But as soon as I hit the lobby, I spotted Amanda standing right in front of the entry doors with a group of people. And there was no way out but straight through them.

Aside from the front desk clerk, who was hidden from the glass doors by fake plants, the lobby was empty. Perfect.

I sprinted across the lobby and vaulted onto the desk, then dropped my shoes next to the clerk, who didn't so much as blink.

"I'll be back for those later," I said, as I leaped for the second-floor balcony.

I grabbed the rail and pulled myself up, then flipped over and bolted into the hallway. I paused only long enough to drag in a breath before peering down. Morgan came hurrying out of the hallway and stopped in the middle of the lobby, frowning as he checked every direction. I ducked back around the corner of the wall and waited as his gaze went up.

"Did you see a woman wearing a purple dress come through here?" I heard him ask.

"Yeah," the clerk said, sounding completely bored. "About a hundred of them. It's a theme color of your party."

"I meant just now, did a woman come through here?"

"Sorry, I was doing paperwork. But people have been through here all night."

"Okay. Thanks."

I peered out again and saw him give the lobby one more glance, then he must have spotted Amanda outside, so he headed for the doors.

"You're in the clear," the desk clerk said. "And I saw absolutely nothing—but nothing was impressive. Would have been more impressive in the heels though."

I leaned over the railing and gave him a smile. "You ever think of joining the CIA? You have the nerves for it."

"Honey, not if they're going to put me in a straight cut. I'm already curveless enough. And that's not nerves. That's numb. That move of yours didn't budge the needle compared to what I found going on in housekeeping when I came on shift. And last month we had a heavy metal band's bus break down right outside of town. The hotel insisted on paying for therapy. What does that tell you?"

"Hmmmm."

"Do you want me to toss these shoes up? God, they're gorgeous. I might reconsider a straight cut if I got a pair of these."

He gave them a wistful look and I motioned for them.

"I owe you," I said as I caught the shoes.

He put one hand up, already looking back down at his paperwork. I peered out to see if Amanda and company were still outside. They were, but it looked as if the party was breaking up. Amanda gave the other people a wave and she and Morgan headed across the parking lot toward the diner across the street. I figured Brittany and Daniel were there for the duration of the party given that she was in charge, so that left Nicole and Tyler unaccounted for, but the odds were decent that Ida Belle and Gertie could get back to the room without being seen. And even though we had a perfectly good reason for being there, I was afraid a few more run-ins might have the extremely perceptive Amanda taking a harder look.

I pulled out my phone and called Ida Belle, anxious to compare notes. She answered on the first ring.

"It's gone dead here," she said. "Haven't seen anyone in almost thirty minutes. I don't think there's a lot of smokers in that generation, and all the people coming outside to gossip about Justin did it right after the thing started."

"Yeah, I think they got it over with and now they're mostly concentrating on drinking."

"Can we come back?" Gertie asked. "My butt is numb and I have to pee."

"I'm getting a little stiff myself," Ida Belle said.

"Yeah, I've called it as well. Pull around to the side and use that door."

"You sure?" Ida Belle asked.

"Yeah. It's closer to the elevator. Amanda and Morgan just headed across the street to that diner, and my guess is Brittany and Daniel are at the event for the duration, so odds of you being seen are low. I'll meet you upstairs."

"Awesome!" Gertie said. "I hear leftovers calling me."

I yanked off the mask and headed for the stairs, not in a rush since none of the friends were likely to be walking the stairwell, especially the ones in heels. When I reached our room, I hurried to make some notes on my laptop. Then I pulled the food containers out of the mini fridge and did an assessment. We probably had enough to cover us all for dinner, but worst case, I'd spotted a menu for Chinese delivery in the desk drawer, so at least we had a backup plan in case we were all hungry. By the time I finished, ten minutes had passed since my phone call but they hadn't yet appeared.

My phone rang and I saw Gertie's number in the display.

"Houston, we have a problem," she said.

"What kind of problem?"

"We've fallen and we can't get up."

"Who's fallen? Where? And why can't you get up?"

"Ida Belle and I have fallen. And just so you don't go jumping to conclusions, she fell first. I fell trying to help her up and twisted my knee again."

"Where are you?"

"In the side parking lot. Back row. You might want to come get us in case a fire starts."

"Why would a fire start?"

"Hey, stuff happens, but we're both laid out in the fire lane, so it would be a problem."

I pulled on my tennis shoes and hurried down the stairs, then burst out the side door and scanned the parking lot. I spotted Ida Belle's SUV and ran over. Sure enough, they were both sitting on the pavement as if they were preparing for a picnic, but without a blanket or food.

"What happened?" I asked. "Are you okay?"

"It was the strangest thing," Ida Belle said. "I stepped out of the SUV and as soon as my feet hit the ground, my legs just collapsed. I can't even feel them. My knee's already swelling, and I can't feel a darn thing. Look!"

She pulled up her pants and pressed her finger against a knot and didn't so much as flinch. I started to panic. I'd seen something like it before, but usually when someone had been shot and they were paralyzed. Sometimes temporarily. Sometimes permanently.

"How can I not feel that?" Ida Belle said.

Gertie was uncharacteristically quiet, and when I looked

over at her, she widened her eyes and shrugged. "Maybe it's a pinched nerve from all that sitting."

"I sit all the time," Ida Belle said. "Why the heck would a couple hours pinch a nerve? And I've never heard of a pinched nerve eliminating pain. It usually *causes* pain."

I gave Gertie a hard look. "I don't suppose you shared Nora's stash with Ida Belle, did you?"

"No!" Gertie insisted. "I swear I didn't offer a thing."

"And I wouldn't have taken it if she did," Ida Belle said. "The only thing I've had is a bottle of water, and only half at that. Didn't know how long I'd be out here."

I narrowed my eyes at Gertie. Something wasn't right, and whatever it was, Gertie was right in the thick of it.

"You spiked your water with Nora's latest brew, didn't you?" I asked her. "And then you got the bottles mixed up and Ida Belle drank it."

Ida Belle whipped her head around to stare at Gertie, who turned to stare at the fence, answering my question.

Ida Belle threw her hands in the air. "Are you trying to kill me? What if my heart had stopped instead of my legs? And what the heck am I supposed to do now? I can't sit here all night, and Fortune can't carry us to the room."

"I think you should go to the hospital," I said.

"Over my dead body," Ida Belle said, and I was quite certain she meant exactly that.

She glared at Gertie. "You just wait until I can move my legs again. I'm going to put one right up—"

"Give me a minute," I said and ran back into the hotel.

I hurried to the lobby, which was thankfully clear, and up to the desk clerk. "I have a medical emergency," I said. "My two old aunts have fallen in the parking lot, and I can't get them up."

"Do you want me to call 911?" he asked without so much as a raised eyebrow.

"No. I just need to get them to my room and they'll be fine. I don't suppose you have a wheelchair, do you?"

"This isn't a hospital, honey."

"What about your office chair?"

He frowned. "What about it?"

"Can I borrow it? And the other one? And you? That way I could get both of them out of the fire lane at the same time... just in case you had a fire."

"It wouldn't be the first time all that happened. What the hell. I'm due for a break anyway." He looked over at another clerk who'd walked up as I was explaining the situation. "Handle this while I go play orderly, will you?"

Clerk Two's eyes widened. "If they've fallen in the fire lane—"

"Do I need to remind you?" Clerk One interrupted.

Clerk Two shook his head. "Make it happen. We didn't see anything. We don't know anything."

Clerk One dragged the chairs from behind the desk. "Lead the way."

Gertie cheered when she saw the office chairs. Ida Belle just sighed. I was able to get Gertie into one by myself because she still had one good leg, but it took both me and the clerk to get Ida Belle in the other. Much to her dismay.

"The service elevator is down the next hall," he said as we pushed. "It will be easier to get the chairs into than the guest one."

"Good. Maybe fewer people will see my humiliation," Ida Belle muttered and cut her eyes at Gertie.

A couple of people approached us in the hallway, so I moved behind the clerk to allow them by. They gave us curious looks, but no one appeared interested in asking questions, which was always the best course of action when viewing something odd in Louisiana. We were almost to the hallway when the clerk suddenly whirled around, almost knocking me over, and took off running in the opposite direction.

I had absolutely no idea what was up, but a general rule to follow is if someone who has no reason to run is running, you should run too. So I whirled around and took off after him. He skidded on the floor to get the chair around the corner and into a hallway we'd passed, and for a second I thought he and Ida Belle both were going to go sprawling. But he managed to collect himself and I followed him around the corner, glancing back as I went.

And that's when I saw Morgan coming down the hall.

Good. God.

CHAPTER TWENTY-TWO

I WAS STILL WEARING MY PARTY DRESS, BUT I'D DITCHED THE wig, so there was no hiding my identity and no explanation good enough for me to be dressed for their event. I tore out after the clerk, practically running him over in an effort to find someplace to hide. Ida Belle and Gertie hadn't uttered a peep. Clearly even though they had no idea why we were all running, they figured it was necessary, so they simply maintained a white-knuckle grip on the chairs and leaned around turns to help balance.

At the end of the short hallway was a set of double doors and the clerk burst through them, not even slowing. I saw the word *Laundry* on the door as I flew inside after him. I'd barely had time to breathe again when I heard a voice coming down the hall.

"Excuse me, sir?"

Crap! He was following us.

"Hide!" the clerk ordered.

Which was easier said than done.

The laundry room didn't offer much in the way of hiding places. In fact, with washers and dryers lined up on one side and shelves on another, it didn't offer much in the way of room at all, much less a cloak of invisibility. The clerk shoved Ida Belle's chair next to a commercial dryer and grabbed a sheet off the top of it and threw it completely over her. Gertie pushed herself out of the chair and dived headfirst into the open dryer, pulling the door shut behind her.

And the dryer came on.

I was already mid-dive into a huge laundry cart full of damp towels and by the time I landed, I heard the doors open. I yanked the towels over my head and cringed as loud knocking from the dryer echoed through the room.

"Is everything okay?" Morgan asked.

"Yes, of course," the clerk answered. "There was a bleach spill. Got to get these towels in the wash quickly or I'll have to pay for them. Is there something I can help you with?"

"There was a woman with you..."

"Head of housekeeping. Her shift was over, so she headed out the back door."

"But she was wearing a purple dress."

I heard the clerk sigh. "Management has spoken to her about overdressing time and time again, but she's simply a wizard at cleaning, so he's finally given up. If she wants to dress up to scrub toilets then that's her budget's problem. Did you need more linens?"

"No," Morgan said, sounding completely and utterly confused. "Thanks."

I heard the door open and a second later, the clerk called, "Clear."

I popped up out of the laundry cart and rushed over to the dryer as the clerk yanked it open. Gertie was upside down inside, so I spun the drum around until she was upright. Sort of. She groaned, and the clerk and I both reached in to grab an arm. As soon as our hands made contact with her shirt, sparks flew.

The clerk jumped back and Gertie let out a yelp. Even I had to admit that it had surprised me a bit and kind of smarted.

"This is exactly why I keep begging for fabric softener," the clerk grumbled, making me wonder exactly how many times this had happened.

We reached in again, knowing to prepare for the static light show, and eased her out of the dryer and back onto the chair. Ida Belle had pulled the sheet off her head, and I could tell it was killing her not to be able to help.

"Are you all right?" I asked.

Gertie looked like...well, like she'd been rolling around in a dryer. Her hair stood on end as if she'd stuck scissors in a light socket, and her skin was all red and splotchy from the heat. Giant beads of sweat rolled down her forehead.

"I feel like I've been in a sauna with a dinosaur shaking me like a James Bond martini," she said.

"That's very specific," the clerk said. "But at least I don't have to call the medical examiner this time."

We all stared at the completely nonplussed clerk.

"Why did you run?" I asked, curiosity overwhelming me.

He raised one eyebrow. "You vaulted onto my desk and scaled the second-floor balcony to get away from that guy earlier. I didn't figure you were interested in seeing him now."

"Ah, yeah. Old boyfriend." I tossed out the first story I could come up with.

He snorted. "Girl, that man was *not* dating you. But I don't want to know. I don't know anything. Can we please get to your room before 911 is back on my potential call list for the night? Don't worry—your 'old boyfriend' has a room on a different floor and the service elevator is just around the corner."

We managed to get back to our room without further incident, if you didn't count that anytime someone's hand got close to Gertie, it set off an electrical storm. The clerk helped me get Ida Belle into a chair at the table. Then we hefted 'shaken not stirred' Gertie into a chair beside her. When the infirm were securely seated, the clerk grabbed the backs of both chairs and started to head out.

"Wait!" I said and opened the closet.

He started to protest, assuming I was getting him a tip, but then his eyes widened in the first show of emotion I'd seen when I handed him the silver heels. He stared at the shoes, then whipped his gaze up to mine, studying my face, and I could see him trying to make sense of my balcony escape and the two seniors he'd just pushed in office chairs.

"You're giving me these?" he asked.

"You earned them. And it looks like they'll fit."

"These are eight hundred dollars."

I shrugged and pulled a card from my bag and handed it to him. "If you ever change your mind about your line of work, let me know. Your kind of calm is hard to come by. I know people who might be interested."

He took the card and read it, and his eyebrows went up. "My aunt always said I'd make a good priest or a serial killer. I'm never quite sure how to take that."

"Those aren't the only two options."

His lips quivered and a smile finally broke through. "Thanks for these. They're incredible."

I nodded and he headed out.

Gertie opened her purse and pulled out a small bottle. "I don't understand what happened. Nora wrote the dosing instructions right on the bottle, see? One tablespoon per eight ounces of water."

Ida Belle grabbed the bottle to read, then closed her eyes, and I figured she was praying, but I wasn't sure if it was for the strength to not commit a crime or for Gertie's eternal soul because she was about to meet her maker.

"It says a teaspoon!" she yelled. "Not tablespoon. Your bad vision is going to kill us all one day. How long is this going to last?"

"Nora said it was only good for about three hours, then you have to re-dose. There's three teaspoons in a tablespoon, so nine hours? I never liked math."

"But you only drank half," I reminded her. "So maybe four hours or so, and some time has already passed, although you probably sipped, so anyway...you should still be up and around by tomorrow."

"Great. I guess you can just prop me up bottoms-down on the toilet to sleep."

"Maybe you shouldn't drink anything else," Gertie said. "So I guess this means breaking into the ME's office is off the table since our getaway driver is incapacitated. Or I could drive."

I said a quick prayer of thanks that I'd put Ida Belle's pistol out of her reach because there was no mistaking her glare.

Gertie pretended not to notice. "Can you pass me my cane? I wasn't joking about having to pee earlier. I almost had an accident in that dryer."

"Don't worry," I told Ida Belle as Gertie hobbled off. "We'll figure out this leg thing. Let me ditch these clothes and stuff, and then we can talk business."

I shed the dress and my nine and pulled on my shorts and tank, scrubbed off the makeup, and brushed my hair back into its usual ponytail. Then I popped our leftovers in the microwave and started loading them onto the table about the time Gertie returned.

"So now that we're not running or hiding or doing laundry, did you get anything?" I asked.

"Oh yeah," Ida Belle said. "I've got the USB in my pocket. What about you?"

I nodded and relayed the conversations I'd overheard as I served the food. They looked stunned at my reveal about Tyler's dad being the one who'd blown the whistle on Justin's father and had a good chuckle at my leap to the second-floor balcony.

"At least all that running makes sense now," Ida Belle said.

"I think the clerk is a little in love with you," Gertie said.

"He's just in love with those shoes," I said. "We should send Shadow over here to take lessons. That guy has no pulse."

Ida Belle nodded. "Everything you heard at the dance adds weight to our suspicions. Unfortunately, it adds weight to all of them. I think you're going to find this recording very interesting, especially in light of everything else."

She pulled the USB out of her pocket and passed it to me. "I think this might give you some more perspective, especially about Amanda."

I popped the USB into my laptop and queued up the audio, then sat back to listen. Ida Belle pulled out her phone with pictures she'd taken of the individuals while they were speaking. The first groups were random classmates and most of them said more of what I'd already heard about Justin back in high school. No one seemed broken up or surprised about his death. More than a few had suggested karma had finally caught up with him.

"Amanda and Brittany came out next," Ida Belle said and showed me some pics. Brittany looked upset and worried, and Amanda looked stern and worried.

"I can't believe Daniel was able to pull off that speech," Brittany said. "Talking like Justin was such a great friend."

"That's what he needed to do," Amanda said. "Anything else would have looked odd. Given the way this went down, you can't afford for anyone to know what happened. I don't know what that idiot sheriff is trying to accomplish, but the last thing you want to do is be on his radar. He's already trying to use Justin's death to screw Corndog and Petunia. As far as your unfinished business with Justin goes, it never happened."

"We can't just pretend it didn't happen when a chunk of material is gone, and the receivable is still there glaring at Daniel every time he opens the books. We should have sued him before this. I asked you about it, time and time again."

"And I told you that it does no good to sue someone if they don't have anything. Justin conned Daniel, just like his father conned all those people. That's the bottom line. I don't even know why you invited him here."

"Because Daniel foolishly thought by forcing him into some high school replay, he'd be able to convince him to do the right thing."

"Are you even listening to me? Even if Justin wanted to do the right thing—which has never happened a single day in his life—he couldn't. I'm the absolute best at my job and if there was even one thin dime to be gained, I would have gone for it. He was never going to pay you. It was always just another lie."

"What if he had life insurance? Wouldn't Daniel be a creditor?"

"I'll check, but if you think someone like Justin paid for a life insurance policy, you're smoking better weed than what Ricky used to grow in his mom's old greenhouse. Number one, who would he have been covering? He only cared about himself. Number two, Justin never planned on dying. His death is just going to be another bill of his that others have to pay."

"Then I guess it's a good thing he's dead. At least he can't ruin any more lives. Because when Daniel's father finds out, it's going to be hell on Daniel."

"What's he going to do, fire his only child from the business he's going to inherit?"

"He's threatened him before when he's made a mistake—and one much less than a hundred grand. He keeps saying he'll leave the business to his cousin's son."

"That douchebag who was quarterback at LSU?"

"That's the one. He throws that guy in Daniel's face every chance he gets. He's still angry that Daniel didn't play college ball."

"Daniel wasn't good enough to play college ball. Hell, he was Justin's backup in high school. What's there to be mad about?"

"That he wasn't good enough. As far as his father is concerned, that was Daniel's failure to train hard and apply himself."

"Bullshit. Training can't make you taller, and quarterbacks these days need to be taller to see over those giants rushing at them. Justin didn't get any offers for college ball either. The best in Houma doesn't hold a candle to the rest of the country's stage."

"You think I don't know all that? Daniel has pushed himself to the edge of his capabilities every day of his life, but if you ask his father, Daniel isn't worth the oxygen he's consuming."

"His father is a douche. We've always known that."

"But that business is all Daniel knows. And if he loses his job, we'd have to move. Even if he could find another supply company hiring, they're tiny in comparison and it would be a huge pay cut. We couldn't survive on half or even less of his current salary. We'd have to move to a bigger city in order for him to get decent pay. That means closing my studio and selling my house. It means my whole life would be over."

"Hopefully, it doesn't come to that, but things will be a whole lot worse if Sheriff Stupid finds out about Justin screwing over Daniel. I'm going to tell you like I told Tyler—*stop* saying anything about Justin. Don't even mention his name, and you sure as hell don't talk about anything he did wrong."

"But—"

"Not a word. And whatever it is you're still not saying—and I know you're hiding something—I don't want to know what it is. For once in our lives, take my advice. My very educated, *professional* advice. Not. Another. Word."

I stopped the audio and looked at Ida Belle and Gertie. "Holy crap! Here I was thinking when Amanda mentioned Brittany's unfinished business with Justin it was going to be romantic business. I didn't even see a business scam in there."

Ida Belle nodded. "It was definitely a twist we didn't see coming, but boy does it change the way I see things."

"Agreed," Gertie said. "Brittany just moved to the top of my suspect list. She could have easily used Justin's lecherous behavior to get close enough to poison him. Maybe that's what Amanda suspects but doesn't want to know."

"Definitely a possibility," I said. "But that doesn't necessarily explain the lipstick on the pillow. She didn't need to get in bed with him to slip him doctored food. It doesn't sound like she could even stomach the thought, much less pull it off. And then there's the other side of the coin—what was there to gain? If they couldn't get the money he scammed out of Daniel because he didn't have it, then what good did killing him do?"

"You're right," Ida Belle said. "It's damning, but still not an exact fit. Maybe Brittany didn't believe Amanda and thought there had to be assets or insurance hiding somewhere. Or maybe she finally realized they were never going to get the money and figured revenge was as close as she could get to settling the score. It's not perfect, but it *is* motive."

"Enough to force an autopsy?" Gertie asked.

"Not as long as Bryce is calling the shots," I said. "Corndog and Petunia have zero reason to murder someone, so an accidental death is the only way to pin it on them, but that's all he needs to tie this up in a pretty bow and pave the way for his friend to buy their house. If this becomes a homicide, all the focus and blame shifts away from them due to lack of motive. Then they become the victims, which is the last thing Bryce wants, because then they're likely to get *more* business, not less."

"True," Ida Belle agreed. "So how do we force his hand?"

"I wish I knew. I'll try calling Casey tomorrow and see if she has any ideas on that one."

"You're going to want to hurry," Ida Belle said. "Hit Play. After Amanda issued her go silent rule, she and Brittany went back inside. Then Daniel and Morgan came out."

I hit Play on the recording again.

"Have you heard anything about what they'll do with him?" Morgan asked. "Given that he has no family to handle things, I mean?"

"The sheriff said the parish would take care of it if no one steps forward," Daniel said.

"So let me guess, you stepped forward."

"What was I supposed to do? Let the parish put him in a box and an unmarked grave?"

"That's not what they would do."

"Yeah, but it still didn't seem right. I told him I'd pay for cremation. Then I can scatter his ashes somewhere—the football field, his favorite fishing spot—somewhere like that."

"You're not going to ask for an autopsy?"

"I don't think I can. And even if I could, why would I? We all know what happened."

"I think that sheriff is using Justin's death to try to con that couple into selling their house for half its value. He told Corndog he was pushing for manslaughter charges."

"Jesus. How did you find that out?"

"Amanda and I ran into Rose and her aunts at Namaste Bar earlier today. They overheard the sheriff at the house while they were getting ready to leave saying that he was taking it to the DA."

"I didn't like that guy at all. What the heck is he thinking, going after an old man like that? Can he even do that? What did Amanda say?"

"She said it would be up to the DA to make the call after looking at the evidence but said it's doubtful he'd pursue because it's not a good look for a DA to go around pressing charges against seniors for a mistake. Especially if he has any political leanings."

"They all have political leanings."

"Agreed. So I figured nothing would come of it, but then Petunia called Rose while we were at the bar about leaving her earbuds behind and Rose heard Corndog arguing with someone in the background and asked what was going on."

"Was it the sheriff again?"

"No. Some guy was there trying to scam them into selling their house—at a huge discount—since their business was about to be in the toilet and they would need the money. It sounds like even if there's no charges, it's going to ruin them. You know how the gossip mill is. And there's no way that guy just showed up, knowing all of that, without it coming from the sheriff or one of us, and I know it wasn't us. So... That's why I was wondering about an autopsy."

"Good Lord. This is all horrible. But how would an autopsy help? We all know he died from consuming peanuts somehow."

"If there's something in his stomach besides that fish, that's enough reasonable doubt to clear Corndog. You know how drunk Justin was. He could have gotten a hold of something and eaten it after he went to bed. Hell, he could have had a bag of peanuts from the plane for all we know. He never said no to anything free."

"Look, it sucks, for sure, but I still don't know what *we* can do about it. When it comes down to it, we're nobody where Justin is concerned. Crap. That's Brittany calling me. I better get inside and see if something is going on."

"Daniel left after that," Ida Belle said, and I paused the audio. "He looked very uncomfortable with the entire conversation and practically bolted away. I took some pictures while they were talking. That third one is when Morgan mentioned Corndog and Petunia losing their house."

She passed me her phone and I scrolled through the pictures. When I reached the third one, I immediately saw the shift in Daniel's face. He'd looked depressed when they'd first come outside, and I assumed that had to do with figuring out how to tell his father that he'd been scammed by his supposed friend. But then it shifted to fear, which I found interesting. What was he afraid of? Daniel struck me as a nice enough guy, but Corndog and Petunia were basically strangers to him. Unless he knew or suspected that someone had deliberately slipped Justin peanuts, why would he look so scared?

Was he worried his wife had settled the score?

The next picture was of Morgan looking at Daniel as he

walked away, his expression thoughtful. Did Morgan know what had really happened? Or at least suspect? He didn't seem to miss much, and he'd obviously learned a lot from his psychiatrist friend. Was that why he'd offered to say he'd accidentally given Justin something with peanuts? Because he knew one of his friends had deliberately done it and he was attempting to cover for them while trying to shift the blame off Corndog and Petunia?

In his own words, Morgan always 'put things back together.'

I hoped that wasn't what was going on now because in high school, the things he did to make up for the others' shortcomings might have gotten him punished or at worst, detention. But if he was covering for someone now, it might be accessory to murder.

"I wonder if anyone called Petunia about the earring," Gertie said, breaking into my thoughts.

I checked my watch. It was almost eleven. "I'm going to guess no because I figure I would have heard from them otherwise, but I'll double-check in the morning."

"Brittany would be a fool to call about that earring," Ida Belle said. "And she might not be as sharp as her sister, but she doesn't strike me as foolish."

"But wouldn't she worry that Petunia will give it to Bryce?" Gertie asked. "Assuming she's certain she lost it in Justin's bedroom."

"She might not be certain," I said. "She didn't risk going back for it a second time."

"After everything that happened the first time, no one would have taken that risk," Ida Belle said. "Maybe she had time to think on it and decided it was easier to claim ignorance about the whole thing. She could say she lost the earring somewhere and Justin must have found it and pocketed it, planning on giving it to her later, but he dropped it along with the key."

I nodded. "The lipstick might prove she was in the room, but Bryce didn't even notice it. He definitely won't test it. It doesn't fit his narrative. Amanda knows she's hiding something and I'm certain she's right. If anyone can read Brittany, it's her twin. I just wish Amanda hadn't told Brittany to keep whatever she's hiding to herself."

"Do you think Brittany would have admitted to sleeping with Justin?" Gertie asked. "Or killing him? Or both?"

"I wish I knew. Was that all of the recording?"

"No," Ida Belle said. "There's one more. Tyler came out while Morgan was still there, but I couldn't really make heads or tails of their conversation."

I pressed Play and after several seconds of silence the conversation began.

"What's up?" Tyler asked.

"Just talking to Daniel about how that sheriff is going to screw over the old couple," Morgan said.

"What are you talking about?"

Morgan explained the situation to Tyler as he had to Daniel.

"Man, that's seriously screwed up," Tyler said when he'd finished.

"I agree. And all it would take to fix it is if one of us admitted to bringing something with peanuts onto the island."

"Why would that matter?"

"Because if Corndog didn't make a mistake with the oil—and I'm not convinced he did—then that means Justin got those peanuts somewhere else. If we can force an autopsy and they find something in his stomach other than the fish, then Corndog is good."

"You're not suggesting *I* be the person who makes that claim, are you?"

"You're the only one who brought a bag of snacks onto the island."

"That you're aware of. Other people might have had snacks in their luggage."

"True. But the others' favorite candy bar isn't Snickers. And Justin didn't try to set up anyone else for an assault charge."

"That woman retracted her statement, and you know good and well I never assaulted her. I'm certain Justin offered her money, then didn't pay, which is why she changed her story. You're not suggesting I intentionally gave the guy peanuts hoping he'd be too drunk to save himself, are you?"

"I don't recall suggesting anything. Just pointing out facts."

There were several seconds of silence before I heard Tyler issue a statement that would have had him sitting cross-legged in Namaste Bar for a month at least.

"I took video this time," Ida Belle said and passed me her phone.

I watched as they talked and saw Tyler's increasing agitation as Morgan spoke. Finally, he jumped up from the bench and issued his directive complete with hand signals and stomped back into the hotel. Morgan watched him as he went and stared at the door after it closed, frowning. After ten seconds had passed, he rose and headed into the hotel.

"Wow," I said, leaning back in my chair. "So it sounds like some woman accused Tyler of assault and Tyler suspected Justin of hiring her to do it. But then she backed off her story."

"Maybe Justin was looking for revenge for his father's conviction," Gertie said. "I know it was Tyler's father who sent him up, but Tyler is the one Justin had access to."

Ida Belle nodded. "Based on everything we've heard about Justin, I have to say it wouldn't surprise me."

"I agree," I said. "And it definitely puts the spotlight on Tyler. Maybe we're barking up the wrong tree with Brittany. Morgan seems to have Tyler in his sights, and I don't think he misses much."

Ida Belle nodded. "But unless Tyler cops to having something with peanuts, we still don't have enough to force an autopsy. Unless Morgan makes an accusation. Do you think he'll take it that far?"

I frowned. "Hard to say. He seems the type that wants things to be fair and moral, but if he doesn't know for certain that Tyler is the one who pushed something with peanuts—even if it was accidental—then I'm not sure he'd put it out there."

"You think that's why Amanda was telling Tyler to stop talking?" Gertie asked. "You think he called her for legal advice when the assault accusation happened?"

"I'd bet on it," I said. Then I had another thought and pulled my laptop over and did a quick search. "Tyler brought Nicole her favorite chocolates from that chocolatier in Baton Rouge. Let me look at something. Hmmm."

I spun the laptop around to show them. "Nicole's favorites don't have peanuts, but look at their bestseller."

"Peanut butter chocolate," Ida Belle said. "Definitely would have been easy enough for Tyler to buy a few and slip some into Justin's room. Look how they're sold—individually wrapped and sold and then packaged in those fancy velvet bags."

I nodded. "It would have been easy to grab a couple peanut butter ones and take them out before he gave the bag to Nicole."

"Absolutely," Ida Belle agreed. "And it might be that Tyler wasn't trying to kill him. Justin *did* have an EpiPen. Maybe he just wanted to make him sick and miserable and because Justin was so drunk, things went sideways."

"Certainly plausible," I agreed. "But completely unprovable."

Gertie sighed. "So we're all the wiser on everyone, with a couple of big surprises, and some even better theories, but we're no closer to forcing an autopsy. I vote for breaking out the banana pudding and everything you two don't eat, I'm going to eat myself in one sitting. Then I'm going to bed. It doesn't look like there's anything else we can do tonight."

Ida Belle huffed. "I guess I'm going to sit here in this chair all night."

I shook my head. "You're going to eat a big serving of banana pudding, then I'm going to help you to bed. Can you feel anything yet?"

Ida Belle poked her leg and brightened. "I felt that. And I can move them a little. Maybe I'll be okay by morning. Then I can kick Gertie out of bed. And I mean really kick her."

"Seems fair."

Gertie didn't even argue.

CHAPTER TWENTY-THREE

ALTHOUGH IT COST HER IMMEASURABLE DIGNITY, AND I HAD no doubt that kick for Gertie was coming, we managed to get Ida Belle in for a bathroom visit and changed into sleeping clothes before putting her to bed. She was able to balance some on her legs, which definitely helped, but she didn't have the strength yet to walk or stand on her own. I was pleased she'd made that much improvement in a matter of hours, so the next morning looked good. If she wasn't back to normal, I was going to make her go to the ER, an argument I was really hoping not to have.

Ida Belle and Gertie had a connected room with double beds, and I had the one with a queen, so after I picked up some of the dinner stuff, I grabbed my laptop and headed for my room. It was late, but I wanted to give Carter a call and see if he had any thoughts on my case. I hoped he hadn't dozed off already. He picked up on the first ring, which answered my dozing question, and I could hear the TV in the background.

"Can't sleep?" I asked.

"I'm watching an old movie, but I'm getting there."

"If you moved to your bed, you might get there easier. Your furniture isn't good for sleeping."

"I know. That's why I'm in your recliner. One day, you're going to come home from one of your jaunts and this recliner is going to be gone."

"You know they made more than one, right?"

"Hmmm... I was thinking if I moved in with you, I'd have a place to tie off my boat *and* a new chair."

"Then you'd be wrong, because it would still be my chair."

He laughed. "How's the case going? You dig up any dirt today?"

"Today was all about mudslinging. Thick, slimy, bottom-of-the-bayou mudslinging."

I filled him in on everything we'd discovered.

"If Alexander is representing Corndog, can he require an autopsy?" I asked when I was finished.

"To be honest, the DA would be a fool to pursue charges on this. Which means no charges for Corndog but also no proof of a potential crime."

"I figured Bryce was lying about the charges, trying to let his buddy convince them to sell the house at a huge discount, which ought to be illegal."

"Well, it's fraud, so it *is* illegal. And a case could be made for coercion and corruption as well."

"So how do I take him down for it?"

"You don't. If you see the DA with those claims, Bryce will just say it was an ongoing investigation that was ultimately deemed an accidental death from an unknown source and there will be no charges filed."

"So he'll be able to weasel out of everything."

"It's the only skill he has and the only thing he puts effort into."

"But in the meantime, Corndog and Petunia's reputation

goes to crap even if there are no charges. People won't stay at a B and B where the owners are killing the guests. And without proof of how it actually happened, you know what the Louisiana gossip mills will do to them."

"Unfortunately, I do. And I agree that you've got plenty of motive and opportunity among the friends given that anyone could have slipped something into his room figuring he'd eat it without checking. Quite frankly, given the guy's history with substance abuse, I'm a little surprised something like this hasn't happened already."

"Maybe it has and someone was there to inject him or call 911."

"That's true enough. I know this isn't what you want to hear, but you've done everything you can. Unless you can locate a family member who is willing to raise a stink about an autopsy—which sounds highly unlikely for a lot of reasons—I don't think you have any options left."

"I know, but I'm still going to be angry and stew on it."

"You wouldn't be you if you didn't. It's hard, Fortune. It's hard to do what we do when you care and you know the system is letting someone slip through the cracks. But the alternatives are worse."

I sighed. I knew exactly what he was saying. I could not care at all, which would make me a horrible person assuming I could even manage it. Or I could stop this line of work, which wasn't an option.

"You coming back tomorrow?" he asked.

"Why? You miss me?"

"Always."

"Unless I come up with something while I'm sleeping, probably so. Might be later in the day though. Ida Belle is kind of paralyzed from the waist down at the moment, and you know she's not going to let me drive her vehicle."

"Paralyzed?"

"Trust me, you do *not* want to know. And I wouldn't pass that one on to Walter either. Not unless I'm forced to take her to the ER tomorrow."

"Oh, no way I'm talking. I smell Gertie all over this one. I'll see you tomorrow."

I hung up and decided I should probably close my laptop and attempt sleep when my PI email signaled an incoming message. Figuring it was probably an insurance job, I clicked over, but my pulse quickened when I saw the 're.'

Justin Barbet Autopsy

I clicked on the email but there was no message. Just an attached file. I clicked on the file to open it and stared in shock as Justin's autopsy report flashed onto my screen. An autopsy *had* been done. Which begged the question—why was Bryce hiding that fact?

And who had sent me the email?

I copied the sender's email address and started a trace, but it bounced off a server in India. My PI email was no mystery. It was on my business cards and my website, but only a handful of people knew I was here investigating Justin's death. One of them had to have sent me the file.

It wasn't Carter. He wouldn't have taken the risk, especially with Bryce already aware that I was involved. But the only other person who knew I wanted an autopsy and could have managed access was Detective Casey. She'd gotten me files before that I wasn't supposed to have, so maybe she'd figured out a way to do it again.

But the real stunner here was that there had been an autopsy.

I was dying to dig into the report, but knew if I did so without telling Ida Belle and Gertie, I might be second on the kicking list in the morning. So I jumped out of bed and hurried into their room, flipping on the light as I entered.

"Wake up," I said.

Ida Belle bolted upright and twisted for the nightstand, probably going for her gun. That's what I would have done. But her legs still weren't back to normal, so she got as far as her side and then lost her balance and flipped onto the floor.

"This is your fault, Gertie!" she yelled.

Gertie hobbled over to look at her. "How is this my fault? Fortune came in yelling and flicking on lights."

"I didn't yell," I said. "But I should have. You're not going to believe what I have."

"A forklift, I hope," Ida Belle said.

I bent over and stuck my arms under Ida Belle's armpits and hoisted her back up and onto the bed. Gertie whistled.

"That was impressive," she said. "Ida Belle is no lightweight."

Ida Belle glared at her. "You do know my legs are going to go back to normal, right?"

I waved one hand in the air. "Later. I have Justin's autopsy."

They both stared, jaws dropped, eyes wide.

"No way!"

"What the heck—"

"How?"

"I thought they didn't do one."

I nodded. "Yes, way. Someone sent it anonymously, and I can only think of one reason Bryce would lie about it."

Ida Belle's face flushed with anger. "He wanted to scare Corndog and Petunia into selling their house to his buddy. That's a whole new form of low."

"So it wasn't the fish that killed him?"

"I haven't read it yet. I just tried to trace the sender and couldn't, then came in here and here we are."

Gertie plopped down on the bed next to Ida Belle and waved her hands at me. "What the heck are you waiting for?"

I sat down next to Ida Belle, who was propped against the headboard, and opened the file.

"All the signs of anaphylactic shock," I said as I scanned the document. "And here we go. Stomach contents—fish, potatoes, bananas, and whoa, what have we here—chocolate."

"Nothing with chocolate was served at dinner," Ida Belle said.

"But we already know he could have gotten it from one of the others," Gertie said. "No peanuts?"

I shook my head. "But the presence of chocolate proves that he ingested something other than what Corndog served. So unless they can prove the peanut oil was on the fish, Bryce can't pin this on Corndog."

"So his buddy was trying to rush in and get a quick deal on the house before Bryce was forced to let the truth out," Gertie said. "What a scumbag."

I nodded and scrolled down to the pictures of his face. "Look at this. It's petechial hemorrhaging. Common with asphyxiation."

"So he might have really died accidentally," Ida Belle said. "I mean, assuming he got a hold of the chocolates on his own or your theory about Tyler wanting to make him sick is accurate."

"That's what it looks like..."

"But it still doesn't feel right," Ida Belle said.

I shook my head as I continued to look at the autopsy photos. The whole time we'd been investigating, I hadn't been able to shake the feeling that there was more to it than an accident. And even reading the autopsy hadn't changed that.

When I reached the picture of his back, I knew why.

"He was murdered," I said and pointed to the photo.

"It's a bruise," Gertie said.

I nodded, excited. "If you dosed someone with a peanut allergy and wanted to ensure they died, what would you do?"

"Smother them with a pillow when they went into shock," Ida Belle said.

"Bingo. The more they resisted, the more petechial hemorrhaging, and I'd bet anything that big bruise in the middle of his back was a knee."

Ida Belle stared at it again. "Can you tell anything about the size of the person by the bruise?"

"Not really," I said. "All of them have similar enough knee size except Daniel, and it's impossible to judge weight from this."

Gertie stared at the image and shook her head. "So he passed out face down in bed and someone put a pillow over his head and knelt on him to keep him there when he went into shock... If there was a struggle, that might have been when lipstick got on the pillow."

"Maybe," I said. "Or the lipstick wearer and the killer could still be two different people."

Ida Belle frowned. "You realize what the problem is here, right?"

"We don't know if Tyler wears lipstick?" Gertie asked.

"No," Ida Belle said. "If someone murdered Justin, then how did they get out of the room and lock the door behind them?"

I blew out a breath. "Exactly."

"The window?" Gertie suggested.

I shook my head. "The window was latched. Petunia said so. And the key was next to the nightstand. The door was definitely locked because Corndog checked it himself and Daniel and Tyler had to break it down. Corndog said each key was individual and there is no master or duplicates."

"Even if there were, how would any of the friends have gotten their hands on them?" Ida Belle asked. "And I don't know that you could pick a lock to close it, much less those ancient locks."

"I have to say, it's something I've never had a reason to try," I said. "It doesn't seem likely under any circumstances, but especially for our suspects. They're not exactly art thieves or locksmiths."

"Or spies," Ida Belle said.

Gertie huffed. "We've just traded one set of unanswered questions for another."

I nodded. "And the biggest question here is why this death wasn't ruled a homicide. I don't care how crappy that ME is, there's no way he didn't see this bruise on his back and know exactly what it meant. This should have been ruled a suspicious death."

"No one—not even Bryce—does that kind of favor just so his buddy can buy a house for cheap," Gertie said. "What's really going on here?"

"My best guess—Bryce paves the way for the cheap purchase, then they flip it for double and split the profit, and the ME gets a cut. No way this works without him in on it."

"What do we do now?" Ida Belle asked. "We have the proof but can't use it. Not really."

"I'll figure something out. But no way in hell Bryce is getting away with this."

I BRIEFLY THOUGHT ABOUT CALLING CARTER, BUT QUICKLY decided putting him in the position of knowing that I'd received confidential information wouldn't do him any favors. And there was nothing he could do about any of it without admitting that he'd seen the documents. So I needed to come up with a plan, and part of that plan was to get enough rest to think straight.

I tried to sleep, but mostly flopped around, dreaming about locked doors, earrings, pillows, catfish, and chocolates. In the movies, all of that would mean something, and I would have awakened refreshed and with the answers to everything. Instead, I woke tired, with a headache, and more confused than ever.

But there was one thing I did know and had the proof for —Justin was murdered. The problem was I wasn't supposed to have the proof and the only person who could utilize the proof to pursue a murderer was burying it for his own gain. Since Justin's body would go for cremation as soon as the crematory got hold of someone's credit card, I had to do something fast. The autopsy was great, but there was more that could be checked. Just not without a body.

I finally gave up around 5:00 a.m. and put on a pot of coffee. I sat at the table drinking it and staring out into the parking lot, trying to figure out a plan to take Bryce down and get Corndog and Petunia completely cleared. It took me two cups until a thought crept in. It wasn't the greatest idea, and it was also illegal, but at that point, I no longer cared. I was ready to roll the dice to make this right.

I opened my laptop and did a quick search, then made note of my research in my phone and headed for the shower. Ida Belle was sitting at the table drinking coffee when I finished dressing, and I felt a surge of relief seeing her sitting there.

"The legs are back to normal?" I asked.

"Good as new. In fact, my right knee had been giving me a little trouble and now it doesn't. But don't you dare tell Gertie that. I'll never be able to drink out of an open container again. She'll be trying to share her discoveries with me."

"I notice she didn't have any after your legs went numb."

"So did I. And I won't be letting her forget it. Did you figure out the Bryce situation?"

"I have a plan. Well, it's more of a really bad idea, but I think I'm going to run with it."

"Sounds good to me. I'll go hop in the shower."

Thirty minutes later, we were dressed and ready to head out.

"Let's stop and grab some breakfast at the diner across the street," I said.

"Lord, you must have read my mind," Gertie said. "I'm all for the PI stuff but not on an empty stomach. And coffee does not count as food."

"Are we checking out?" Ida Belle asked.

"Not yet," I said. "According to people at the dance last night, there's a barbecue and tag football game today at the high school—one of those bring-the-family deals. I got a look at the sign-up list, and it looked like all the friends are going to be there."

"Maybe they'll all be at the hotel another night," Ida Belle said.

I nodded. "That's what I figured. So if they're staying, we're staying."

"We can't do any investigating at the barbecue," Gertie said.

"No, but they'll come back to the hotel at some point. I'd love another chance to chat with some of them. It seems like Corndog and Petunia's plight is weighing on Morgan. I think he knows something, or at minimum, suspects."

"You think that's why he was pushing Daniel about the autopsy last night?" Gertie asked.

"Fat lot of good it will do him," Ida Belle said. "If Brittany is the one who killed Justin, no way Daniel is going to pursue this any further."

"But there *was* an autopsy," Gertie said.

"Neither Daniel nor Morgan knows that," I said. "So someone thinks they've gotten away with it. They don't know Bryce is hijacking their murder for his own con."

"If anyone has figured out what happened, it's Amanda or Morgan," Ida Belle said.

"Unless it was Amanda who did it," Gertie said. "She was outside. Maybe she's telling everyone to shut up because she's afraid if motive crops up then there might be an investigation and they'd take a harder look at her. Control makes the best killers. You just don't hear about them because they got away with it."

"At this point, anything is possible," I said. "But we still have the locked door problem. It's possible that Justin managed to let someone into the room, but there's still no way they could have gotten out and locked the door from the inside unless they can walk through walls."

"Could they have locked it from the outside, then slid the key under the door?" Gertie asked.

I shook my head. "No way to get it in between the nightstand and the bed from the door. It would have had to do a ninety-degree turn around the nightstand and jumped onto the rug that's under the bedroom furniture."

"Crap," Gertie said.

"There has to be something we're missing," Ida Belle said.

"I'm working on it," I said. "Let's grab breakfast, and I'll tell you my plan on the autopsy."

And hopefully, everything else would start to make sense soon.

CHAPTER TWENTY-FOUR

Ida Belle pulled up to the curb in front of a tidy cottage tucked at the end of a street in an older neighborhood and looked over at me. "Are you sure you want to do this?"

"No. But I can't come up with anything better."

"I think it's a great idea," Gertie said.

"Of course you do," Ida Belle said. "You're not the one who'll go to jail for it."

"Fortune just pulled a rescue mission in a terrorist compound in Iran," Gertie said. "How bad can jail in Houma be?"

"I'm not planning on going to jail," I said. "I'm planning on scaring him so bad he does the right thing."

"I'm all for it," Ida Belle said, "but I wouldn't be doing my job as backup if I didn't ask."

I grinned. "Well, Backup, let's go threaten a medical examiner."

We headed up the sidewalk and I knocked on the front door. Then I heard someone moving quietly inside, their footsteps stopping in front of the door. Most people wouldn't have heard anything at all, but most people also weren't former CIA assassins. I waited a couple seconds, but when no other movement was forthcoming, I assumed he'd looked out the peephole and known who I was, so therefore wasn't about to answer the door.

"I know you're standing on the other side of the door," I said. "And I know you lied about Justin Barbet's death because I've seen the autopsy. So you can either open this door and we can have a discussion like regular people, or I'll take what I know to a federal prosecutor. Your choice."

The door slowly opened and the medical examiner peered out, his eyes wide.

Five foot six. A hundred forty pounds. So little muscle tone that I wasn't sure how he was standing without aid. Skin even whiter than Shadow Chaser's—something I hadn't thought was possible. Absolutely, positively no threat to anyone, anywhere, at any time, unless he was lying about an autopsy that left them on the hook for a death.

"I have to assume you know who I am," I said.

"Bryce said you're a meddling PI and that I wasn't to speak to you."

I raised an eyebrow. "I suppose he left out the part where I'm a former CIA agent."

I didn't think it was possible for him to get any whiter, but he still managed.

"He didn't mention it," he finally croaked.

"Of course he didn't. Look, I don't know what he's promised you but trust me, it can't be worse than going to prison for helping railroad a guy for manslaughter. I will buy Corndog and Petunia's house for market price before I let Bryce and his disgusting friend get their hands on it."

He blushed and I knew that he was well aware of what was going on.

"How much did he promise you?" I asked.

"Nothing. I swear."

"Then why would you do this to an old man and his wife? Why would you help kick them out of their home?"

"Because he said he'd fire me. This is probably the last place in Louisiana I can get a job. Trust me, I don't like Bryce any more than anyone else does, but I have bills like everyone else."

"But not a backbone. You know good and well Justin consumed food other than the fish, and you also know that mark on his back was a knee. This is murder. You're deliberately hiding a murder so that Bryce can fleece seniors out of their home. No one on the planet will employ you when I blast that all over the country. So pick your poison."

Sweat rolled down his forehead, and I wondered for a moment if we were going to have another death on our hands in his doorway. Finally, he swallowed and shook his head.

"To hell with Bryce," he said. "He's a horrible person. He planted drugs on the mayor's son to get me this job and takes 25 percent of my pay for it. But I'm done. I don't care if I have to be the receipt checker at Walmart. My hair has been falling out in handfuls, and I haven't slept in three days. I'll say I was sick and made a mistake and change it to a suspicious death. In fact, I'll go down to the office and do it right now. Just please don't kill me."

"I'm not in the habit of killing people unless it's government orders or to defend myself or others," I said.

"But it happens," Gertie said.

Simpson visibly swallowed. "You know what, I don't even need to change my shoes. These Crocs will be fine. I'll just grab my car keys."

I smiled. "Cool. We'll follow you to the office. We won't come in, of course, but if things don't go as we discussed, I'll find you. *Anywhere*."

He paled again and slammed the door. We headed back to

the SUV and before we'd even climbed inside, his garage door opened, and his car backed out of the drive and took off. We followed him to the ME's office and pulled over to the curb until he went inside.

"You want to wait for him to come out?" Ida Belle asked.

I shook my head. "He's more scared of me than Bryce, and he looked to already be at heart attack level over this when we showed up. He can't handle playing this out. He doesn't have the backbone and likely has an ethic or two more than Bryce."

"So are we headed back to the hotel?" Gertie asked.

I shrugged. "The friends are at the barbecue until probably midafternoon, so no point in going back there unless you want to sleep. I figured we could hit a couple of those antiques shops and maybe buy a few things, or at least take some pictures. It helps with the whole undercover thing."

Gertie clapped her hands and bounced on the seat. Ida Belle sighed but started the SUV and headed off for the shops. I sent Carter a text that we'd gotten onto a line of inquiry and might be staying another night. I'd let him know later and to fill in all related parties. I got back a thumbs-up and figured we were covered in Sinful until further notice.

Then I rang Corndog.

"Has that guy contacted you again?" I asked.

"No. But the sheriff called and told us we still can't rent the room and that he's thinking about closing us down until his investigation is complete. He's trying to ruin us."

"He is," I agreed. "But all of that is about to change. You can't repeat any of this, but I found out that there was an autopsy, and Justin's death was suspicious."

"So it was murder?"

"Yes. So as soon as the ME revises his report, it will force an investigation. There is absolutely no way to pin this on you at that point. You have no motive for wanting a stranger dead, but his friends are full of them. And you didn't serve chocolate, which was in his stomach contents. This might take some time to work its way out, but you're going to be fine."

"Oh Lord, that's a relief," he said, and I could hear Petunia laugh-crying in the background. "I've got about a million questions, but they can all wait until you're allowed to talk. I hate to think that one of those young people is a murderer though. They all seemed nice—well, except the one who died. I know you're not supposed to speak ill of the dead, but he seemed a bit of a butthead."

"I think he was a lot worse than that, but you can't just go around killing people, much to my dismay at times."

Corndog chuckled.

"This will get handled," I said. "Either Bryce will have to step up and do his job or I'll figure out a way to get the state police involved. Regardless, it's no longer on you and that's what we needed."

"I don't know how we'll ever thank you. Our nephew said you were absolute hell and if anyone could figure this out it would be you. I thought he was going on at first, but then you punched that gator and I knew if you couldn't fix it, no one could. I owe you."

"You don't owe me anything. I'm happy to help. But maybe Carter and I could sneak away for a couple days and stay at your house. I think he would really enjoy it."

"We'd love to have you. Just name the date."

I disconnected and smiled. That was the best part of the job. When the good guys won.

The only thing that would have been better was seeing the look on Bryce's face when he realized Simpson was no longer under his thumb.

We spent several hours out around Houma, first cruising some shops where Gertie picked up a couple of knick-knacks and Ida Belle managed to find an antique reel that she wanted for her bookshelves. I balked at more stuff to dust, so I managed to get away with no shopping bags. But carrying them into the hotel was a good cover, and I was glad I'd suggested it because we ran into Morgan and Amanda in the lobby.

Morgan gave us a big smile. "Fancy meeting you here. I see you've gotten your shopping in."

"Only a couple hours," Gertie said. "But my feet need a rest."

"Your wallet needs a rest," Ida Belle said.

"Rose covered the hotel with points, remember? That gives me extra cash to spend."

"Maybe you should spend it on better walking shoes or a cane."

Amanda and Morgan both grinned and I could tell they enjoyed my 'aunts' antics. If they only knew.

"How was your dance last night?" I asked.

"Unfortunately, as bad as high school," Amanda said. "I swear, if it wasn't for Brittany, I wouldn't have come. It's like some of these people never progressed beyond senior year."

Morgan nodded. "Sad but fairly accurate. I think that's what happens when you stay in a small town and never branch out. Brittany and Daniel aren't so bad, though."

"Not *as* bad, but they still have their moments. Anyway, we just came in from the barbecue, which was even more exhausting because everyone had their kids. Good Lord, our class loves to have a bunch of babies. I think I'm skipping the dinner tonight. It's a pizza party, and if I have to pretend that one more tiny, shriveled human is the second coming of

Christ, I'm going to need a vacation to recover from my class reunion."

I laughed. "I completely understand. I tend to stay away from children if possible and babies outright terrify me."

Morgan laughed. "You really should go to Amanda's girls' night, Rose. You two have a lot in common. Anyway, we're about to hit the pool and order drinks all afternoon. If you guys feel like a dip, maybe we'll see you out there."

"Oh!" Gertie perked up. "Is there a hot tub?"

"There is," Amanda said. "Which would probably be good for those feet of yours."

"Better than more shopping for sure," Ida Belle said. "Wouldn't mind sticking my own feet in, but I'm not putting on no bathing suit. Haven't owned one in forty years and I'm darned well not going to start again now."

"I think you'll be fine rolling up your pants and sticking your feet in," I said and gave Morgan and Amanda a smile. "Maybe we'll see you out there. I could definitely use a drink and a pool lounger."

Amanda gave me a knowing nod. "I'll bet."

They headed off for the pool and Ida Belle frowned.

"If Amanda committed a murder or knows who did," she said, "she's awfully relaxed about it."

I shrugged. "The good ones always are."

"Are we going to the pool?" Gertie asked, looking hopeful. "I brought my suit. I used it to wrap some dynamite sticks. You have to plan for everything."

Ida Belle's expression was priceless.

"I didn't bring a suit, but I have shorts and a tank and wouldn't mind stirring up some more conversation," I said.

"You think we'll hear from the ME?" Ida Belle asked as we headed for our room to change.

"Doubt it. He's probably checking his passport and

packing his valuables to move. But now that it's going to be a homicide investigation, Bryce will be by to question the friends. Maybe we'll get lucky and he'll do it while they're at the pool. He'll want to catch them before they leave town."

Ida Belle snorted. "Bryce working on the weekend?"

I shrugged. "He might if he's afraid the state police will swoop in and take over. They might notice the gaps in his 'work.'"

"We can only hope."

TWENTY MINUTES LATER, I WAS PROPPED ON A POOL lounger next to Amanda and Morgan, drinking a cold beer. Gertie had staked her spot in the hot tub and seemed determined to remain there the rest of our stay. Ida Belle sat on the edge, her feet dangling in front of one of the jets. She occasionally gave an involuntary jump, claiming it tickled.

As soon as we got through the regular pleasantries and I'd gotten my drink, Morgan asked if I'd heard anything else from Corndog and Petunia. He tried to sound casual, but I easily picked up on the edge in his voice.

I shook my head. "But then, I don't expect I will. I don't know them really. We just overheard some things we weren't supposed to hear. I can't help but worry about them though. They were really nice, and that sheriff seemed like he was out to get them."

They both nodded.

"The sheriff is an ass," Amanda said. "My firm only deals with financial cases and even we've heard the stories."

"I wish there was something we could do," Morgan said. "I still think if one of us claimed to have brought in something with peanut butter, it would be enough to muddy the water."

"Sure," Amanda agreed, "but the only two who have the backbone to pull it off are you and me, and we're the only two with careers on the line if we get wound up in it with that idiot. I feel horribly for Corndog and Petunia, but I'm not sacrificing my career for them. Lying to cops about a death is a really bad look for an attorney, even one who's not practicing criminal law. Besides, it's not a surefire path to anything."

Morgan frowned. "It's not?"

Amanda shook her head. "Think about it—if one of us says we brought in a candy bar with peanut butter in it and we think that Justin might have eaten it, all it will accomplish is an autopsy. Then when they don't find any of said candy bar in the stomach, we're right back to square one but with our names on a suspect list."

Morgan's shoulders slumped. "I hadn't thought it through that far, but I guess you're right. I just have trouble believing Corndog made a mistake. I know he forgets things and I suspect he needs glasses, but his mother had a peanut allergy. I just can't fathom him fouling up that big on something so important."

Amanda shook her head. "But if his memory isn't what it used to be, it only took a few seconds of lapse to pull the wrong container of oil off the shelf."

"Yeah, I guess you're right."

He let out a sigh and I could see how troubled he was. In contrast, Amanda's expression was completely blank and her tone neutral. I was absolutely certain she knew or suspected something, but she was giving zero indication. She'd have been hell as a criminal attorney. Or a CIA agent.

I was trying to figure out a way to prompt more out of them when the rest of the group turned up. Brittany and Daniel came out first and sat in chairs on the other side of Morgan and Amanda, and Nicole dropped into a chair next to me. Tyler, her ever-present shadow, dragged another chair over and positioned it next to Nicole.

"Let me move," I said. "I don't want to get in the middle of your reunion stuff."

Nicole waved a hand at me. "Stay where you are. We've reunioned enough for the next ten years. I take it you're still on a parish tour with the aunts?"

I waved a hand at the hot tub. "We're currently letting feet recover from all the shopping earlier. Aunt Gertie bought bags full of stuff that she'll have to dust. That's Aunt Ida Belle's official description."

Nicole smiled. "Seniors are a law unto themselves, aren't they?"

"Mine certainly are."

Daniel had given me a curt nod when they approached but Brittany had remained silent, absorbed with something on her telephone. Then she dropped the phone and gave the pool a wistful look.

"You going in?" Nicole asked her.

"No," she said. "My hair has been through enough this week, and you know how much chlorine they dump in these hotel pools, but I wish our pool was big enough for a diving board."

"I have an extra swim cap in my bag," Nicole said.

"We should order room service first and have it delivered out here," Daniel said to Brittany. "You barely ate anything at the barbecue."

Brittany's mouth pursed in slight annoyance. "I had plenty. Just because I didn't pile up my plate three times like others doesn't mean I didn't get enough."

Daniel looked a bit frustrated at her response, which seemed a little odd, but since I couldn't see how it had anything to do with Justin's death, I dismissed it as typical husband/wife stuff. I was just about to ask Nicole about the chocolates, figuring I might get a reaction from Tyler, who had given me a half-hearted wave and remained silent, when my phone signaled a text from Ida Belle.

I looked up and realized she was no longer at the hot tub. In fact, she wasn't in the pool area at all. I queued up the message.

Bryce is in the lobby asking for the suspects.

CHAPTER TWENTY-FIVE

HOLY CRAP! THE LAST THING I WANTED WAS TO BE CAUGHT at the pool with them. I popped up from my chair, startling Nicole and Morgan.

"Sorry. Got an emergency at work and need to go call my boss."

I put my phone on silent and hurried off to the hot tub, where I filled Gertie in and told her to switch to the other side so that her back was to the friends. Then I headed toward the pool entrance, shifting behind the bar at the last minute when I was certain the friends were no longer watching. The bartender didn't even raise an eyebrow as I put my phone to my ear and slipped around the pool screens until I was positioned close enough behind the friends that I should be able to hear anything that happened.

My phone signaled another text.

On his way to the pool.

I texted back.

Took cover and had Gertie turn around. Stay out of sight.

I got back the thumbs-up just as Bryce strode out of the hotel and into the pool area. He locked right in on the friends and stomped their way. Morgan spotted him and mumbled something I couldn't hear to the rest of them and all their heads whipped around to stare. I had to assume the ME had been as good as his word because Bryce looked as though he'd sucked on lemons. His face and neck were flushed red, and I could tell he was clenching his jaw.

"There's been a change," he said. "The ME has declared Justin's death suspicious, so this is now a homicide investigation."

There was a sharp intake of breath by several of them, and they all looked shocked and more than a little scared.

Daniel sat forward and stared at Bryce. "You can't possibly think one of us killed him."

"Of course I do," Bryce said. "Unless you think it makes more sense for some old couple running a B and B to go around murdering clientele."

"No...I..." Daniel fumbled for words, clearly shaken. "You're positive it's murder? I thought it was an allergic reaction."

"It was, but someone suffocated him just to be sure," Bryce said. "So now is the time to come clean and maybe get some leniency."

They looked at one another, eyes wide, but no one said a word.

"Fine," Bryce said. "Who had chocolates with them?"

They remained quiet and I wondered if anyone was going to speak up, but finally Morgan said, "Tyler brought chocolates."

Tyler jumped out of his chair and glared at Morgan. "They didn't have peanut butter in them, and I brought them for Nicole, not Justin."

"He's right," Nicole said. "The chocolates he brought me were filled with more chocolate and that's it. I still have some."

"Please go get them. My deputy will come with you."

He motioned to a skinny, scared-looking guy who'd been lurking in the background and the deputy hurried after Nicole.

"So no one has anything to confess?" Bryce asked, looking around the group.

Daniel shook his head, now clearly angry. "This is absurd. That door was locked from the inside! Tyler and I had to break it down the next morning. How in the world could someone have suffocated Justin when he was locked inside alone?"

I knew Bryce didn't have an answer to that riddle any more than I did, but he just shoved his hands in his pockets and stood there, his gaze locked on Daniel's, pretending he knew something they didn't. It was a common cop ploy and worked on plenty of people, but I knew it wouldn't fly with Amanda.

"Are you arresting anyone?" Amanda asked.

Bryce smiled. "The attorney, right?"

"That's correct, and I'd like to remind all my friends that you shouldn't say anything without representation. If the sheriff would like to question us further, then it can be done at the sheriff's department and with counsel present."

Bryce snorted. "If you're innocent, you don't have anything to worry about."

None of them looked convinced, and I couldn't blame them. As soon as Bryce found someone to railroad for this, he was going to snap on the cuffs and call it done.

Nicole hurried back out with the deputy, who had the chocolates in an evidence bag. He nodded to Bryce, who pulled out his phone and looked at the display. When he smiled, I knew if something had made him happy, it was going to be bad for everyone else.

He looked over at Tyler. "Tyler Dow, I'm arresting you on suspicion of the murder of Justin Barbet."

He motioned to Tyler to stand.

"What?" Tyler jumped up, his eyes wide. "You can't do this. I didn't do anything!"

"Motive, opportunity..." Bryce shook the evidence bag. "And now that I have the delivery system in hand, I think I've got a pretty good case."

"If I could walk through walls, you mean?" Tyler protested.

"Shut up, Tyler," Amanda said. "Don't say a word. Not a single one. I'll get you an attorney. I mean it. Not. A. Word."

Tyler gave her a stunned look as it finally hit him that he was really being arrested. But what I didn't know was if he was shocked to be arrested for a murder he hadn't committed or if he was shocked that he'd committed what he thought was the perfect crime and been caught.

While the deputy placed the cuffs on Tyler, I eased back to the entrance and slipped inside the hotel and around the corner behind a vending machine. I waited until Bryce walked by with Tyler and the deputy, then peered around and spotted them leaving the hotel. I hurried out to the pool wearing my surprised look.

"Did I just see the sheriff taking Tyler out of the hotel in handcuffs?" I asked.

Amanda nodded, a grim look on her face.

"Oh my God," I said. "I'm so sorry. What the heck is he thinking?"

"He's thinking motive and opportunity," Morgan said.

"He's not the only person who isn't sad Justin is gone," Amanda said. "And since none of us can walk through locked doors, his opportunity is no better than the rest of ours."

Brittany bit her lower lip. "Do you think they'll charge him? I mean, with the whole locked door thing..."

Amanda shrugged. "That sheriff is a loose cannon. Nothing would surprise me. If those chocolates Tyler bought for Nicole match what was found in Justin's stomach, then probably."

"But if Tyler doctored a chocolate to try to kill Justin, that means he kept some back from the bag in order to do so," Brittany said. "Doesn't that make it premeditated?"

Amanda blew out a breath. "A case could be made for it, yeah."

Brittany paled. "But that could mean the death penalty."

Amanda nodded.

Brittany's hand flew over her mouth. "Oh my God."

Daniel put his arm around his wife, but it was clear that his Cloak of Control was slipping. Nicole looked as if she was going to be ill. Morgan, as always, looked deep in thought.

"Is there anything I can do?" I asked.

"No," Amanda said as she rose. "There's nothing any of us can do. Except me. I'm going to call a friend and get him down here before Tyler ignores my advice and runs his mouth."

She hurried off and the rest of them rose and silently set off after her.

As soon as they cleared out, Gertie, who'd remained in the hot tub the entire time, waved.

"Can you help me out of here?" she said. "I think I'm waterlogged. Everything is weak."

"It's no wonder," I said as I strode over and helped pull her out. "You've been in hot water with those jets on you for an hour now. You might not get your legs back until tomorrow."

"Serves you right," Ida Belle said as she hurried up to grab Gertie's other shoulder. "Now you know how I felt, except worse. I saw them hauling Tyler out. What happened?"

We sat Gertie in a lawn chair to recover and I filled Ida Belle in on what I'd overheard. When I was done, she shook her head.

"What do you think Bryce got in that text?"

"I don't know. If I had to guess I'd say they lifted a fingerprint of Tyler's in Justin's bedroom."

"Well, he was at the top of our list, wasn't he?"

I shook my head. "Something about it doesn't feel right."

"Uh-oh," Gertie said. "Well, you better figure out what it is before Bryce railroads his next victim."

"I think that's going to be harder than one might think," Ida Belle said. "Bryce still has to explain how the door was locked and the only key inside. And then there's the small matter of how they got in as well. Do you really think Justin would have let Tyler into his room?"

"If he wanted to taunt him, maybe," I said. "But then one would think Morgan would have heard them. Justin was drunk. He probably wouldn't have been quiet about it."

"Maybe Corndog is wrong and there is another key somewhere," Gertie said.

"But how could one of them have known about it and gotten hold of it if Corndog isn't even aware of one?" I asked. "Besides, they didn't even know which room Justin would be in before they got there, so unless they found one of these mythical keys for every door, I just don't see how it could have happened that way."

"What about a 3D printer?" Gertie asked.

"Maybe," I said, "but how would they have gotten it into the house without someone noticing? They all had overnight bags when they left. None of them was carrying something large enough to hold a printer."

"Maybe one of them visited the island before," Gertie said. "Corndog said he leaves the keys in the door. If one of them stayed previously, they could have brought a printer then and made copies of all the keys if the place wasn't occupied, which would be fairly easy to do in the winter and midweek."

Ida Belle shook her head. "That means they'd have to have visited twice before. Once to even learn about the keys and again to haul in a printer. And talk about premeditated."

I pulled out my phone and called Corndog. He put Petunia on speaker, and I told him about Tyler's arrest.

"But we're still stumped on the locked room," I said. "Did any of that group stay with you before this week?"

"No," Petunia said. "And I have an eye and mind for faces and names. I would have remembered if they had."

"Do you think that young man did it?" Corndog asked.

"I wish I knew. Clearly one of them did. I just don't know how."

I disconnected and slumped into a chair, running all the information through my head. Tyler fit—he'd brought the chocolates; he had a multilayered history with Justin and none of it pleasant. But there was something about his reaction when Bryce said he was arresting him that looked like genuine bewilderment. And I hadn't learned anything about his past that led me to believe he was that good an actor.

"If Tyler did it, then it was Brittany looking for that earring," Ida Belle said.

I nodded. "Probably so. Maybe she went in there to try to convince Justin to pay the money he owed."

"But what about the lipstick on the pillow?" Gertie asked. "Won't Bryce go through the evidence now and see it? Surely he'll test it for DNA."

"He should, but since he has his patsy, I'm not convinced he will," I said. "And even if it came back with Brittany's DNA, it doesn't prove anything except that she was in Justin's bed. Unless Bryce finds out about Justin scamming Daniel, he doesn't have motive. Tyler is the easy pick given that Justin tried to frame him for assault, and all of Tyler's accusations to that point would be part of police record."

"Which Bryce could easily access given the current situation," Ida Belle said. "Good Lord. That boy doesn't have a chance with Bryce running this investigation."

"Maybe he did it," Gertie said.

"Maybe," I said. But something didn't feel right.

GERTIE AND IDA BELLE HEADED UP TO OUR ROOM—GERTIE to shower and change and Ida Belle to rinse her feet as she said the chlorine was already drying her skin out. I was too restless to sit closed up in our room, so I went for a jog around the hotel. Exercise was one of the best ways to shake my mind loose when I had a big messy ball of stuff to unwind.

I made two complete circles around the facility and on my third, I spotted Amanda on the smoking porch with her vape. And she was alone. I knew Morgan was the thinker in the group, but Amanda was the observer and from what I'd seen, she didn't miss anything. If anyone could have planned a murder and gotten away with it, my money was on her. But I still hadn't produced motive for her and my gut told me she hadn't done it.

I slowed to a walk and headed toward the hotel, as if I was just ending my run, and then lifted my head as I approached the porch and pretended to just then spot Amanda. I gave her a nod and headed over and plopped on the bench next to her.

"Back on the vaping, I see," I said.

She nodded. "I know it's horrible for me, but it's my stress crutch."

"Plenty to be stressed about right now. I'm really sorry you guys are going through this. That sheriff is an idiot. Maybe he's wrong about everything."

Amanda shook her head. "I don't think he's wrong about Justin's death being a murder. The ME would have made that call, and he's a hack as well—I did my research—but someone suffocated Justin after he had an allergic reaction. Helped things along, if you will. My attorney friend debriefed me earlier and his undergrad is premed, so he can read an autopsy report better than most."

"Oh my God. So Tyler really did it?"

She took a drag off her vape and slowly blew it out, staring across the parking lot. For several long, silent seconds, she didn't speak or even blink, then finally she shook her head.

"That's the problem," she said. "I know he didn't. I went back downstairs that night after everyone had gone to bed. To smoke, of course. I headed for the back porch, but he was already there. I didn't feel like talking so I went to the front. I went back in a couple different times—once to grab water from the library and a couple of times to hit the bathroom. I checked every time—I'm not even sure why—and he hadn't moved. He was on that porch when Justin was killed. The time of death is a fairly narrow window."

I processed that information, then attempted to act as 'Rose' would have received it and stared at her, mouth dropped and eyes wide. "Then you need to tell the sheriff. He'll have to let Tyler go."

She pinned her gaze on me. "And then he'll arrest someone else. And I would have made it happen."

"Oh! Jesus. I hadn't thought about that. So you really think one of you...I mean..."

She blew out a breath. "I wish I didn't, but yeah, it doesn't seem that there's any other option. Corndog and Petunia don't strike me as serial killers, and there's a limited number of suspects, so here we are."

"Do you know—never mind."

"Who did it? I have my suspicions. But I have no proof. The only thing I'm certain of is that it wasn't Tyler." She gave me a small smile. "Or me. If you'll excuse me, I'm going to call my attorney friend and discuss this with him. I didn't want to tell him until I'd mulled it over, but I'm afraid mulling hasn't produced a solution."

"I'm really sorry. Let me know if I can do anything."

She nodded and headed off. I stared across the parking lot, factoring what she'd said into what I already knew. I still thought it was Brittany who had left the earring and likely the lipstick imprint and gone out the window, but had she also been the killer? Or had she gone into Justin's room for another reason and the killer was someone completely different?

I sighed. No matter what, I still had a locked door problem because even if Justin had let the killer in, he definitely hadn't let them out.

I watched as one of the hotel employees approached her car. It beeped as she drew near, and she opened the rear door and popped a backpack inside. When she leaned over, her keys fell out of her shirt pocket and onto the pavement. She cursed and grabbed the keys up before jumping in her car and pulling away.

I laughed out loud. What an idiot I'd been.

But now I knew how the killer had gotten out of the locked room.

CHAPTER TWENTY-SIX

"I've figured it out!" I yelled as I burst into our hotel room.

Ida Belle and Gertie, who were sitting at the table, both jumped and then realized what I'd said and both started talking at once.

"Who did it?"

"How did they get out of the room?"

"Was it Morgan? Those silent types are always a wild card."

"My vote's still for Brittany."

I whistled and they both stopped talking.

"I didn't figure out the who," I said. "Just the how."

First, I told them what Amanda had said.

"You were right," Ida Belle said. "You never quite latched onto it being Tyler and now you know why. Assuming you believe Amanda."

"I do."

"So that's two off the suspect list," Gertie said. "I'm still betting on wild card Morgan, but tell us how the killer got out of a locked room. I'm dying to know."

"I think I can tell you how they got in as well," I said.

"You don't think Justin let the killer in?" Ida Belle asked.

"The more I've thought about it, the less I think so," I said. "Everyone agrees that Justin was beyond drunk, so if someone came after everyone had gone to bed and knocked, why didn't anyone hear them? The amount of noise it would have taken to roust Justin from his half coma should have been heard by the others with rooms nearby."

"Okay, but the key was inside," Gertie said. "And Daniel checked the door to make sure it was locked. If it had just been him, I wouldn't take his word for it, but the others heard Justin lock the door and saw Daniel check it. Do you think they're all lying?"

"Not at all. I think the door was locked when they went to bed, but I think Justin just turned the key in the knob and left it there. I studied the locks before we left, trying to determine if they could be easily picked, and they really can't be, especially by an amateur. But if the key is still in the lock on the other side, then all someone would have to do is use something thin and hard to push it out onto something they'd shoved under the door to collect it. Then simply pull that collection device under the door once the key landed and you have a way in."

Ida Belle nodded. "That makes perfect sense. There was at least an inch of gap between the bottom of the door and the floor. Plenty of room to get something under there."

"But it would have to be something stiff enough to shove under and remain in shape," Gertie said. "And it would have to be something that didn't make a loud noise when the key landed on it and also didn't allow the key to bounce off. Assuming the killer didn't haul in supplies, they would have had to use something from the house."

"They did," I said. "I think they used Petunia's cookie sheet with a towel or dishrag on top."

"Petunia had been looking for her cookie sheet when we first arrived and said it was on the wrong shelf," Ida Belle said.

"Exactly. And what is the likelihood that she'd put it in the wrong place when it's probably been in the same location for decades?"

Gertie gave me an appreciative look. "Genius. Now tell me how they managed to get out of the room, lock the door, and leave the key between the nightstand and bed."

I grinned. "They didn't."

They both looked confused.

"But there was no way to slide the key under the door and reach the location it was found in," Gertie said.

"There wasn't, and if it had been in the middle of the room, it would have been easy to figure out. But the reality is, the killer locked the door from the outside with the key and took it with them. Then the next day, when Daniel and Tyler broke down the door and they all rushed in, they simply dropped it between the nightstand and the bed as if it had been there all along."

They both stared. Then Ida Belle started laughing.

"The simplest explanation is often the right one," she said. "We've been complicating this when the answer was staring us right in the face."

Gertie nodded. "But which one of them did it? They all rushed into the room."

I pulled out my phone. "Let's find out."

Petunia answered on the first ring.

"I have a question for your excellent memory," I said. "I need you to think hard on this one. After Daniel and Tyler broke down the door to Justin's room, I know they all rushed to the bed except Tyler."

"That's right."

"I assume Daniel was standing close to the nightstand

because he checked Justin's pulse. Did Brittany stand next to the nightstand on the other side of Daniel, farther away from it?"

"She stood away from the nightstand."

"Great. Now, when the rest of the friends rushed in, who stood next to the nightstand?"

"Let me think...Tyler had stopped just inside the door after they got it open, and he only inched up to the end of the bed after Daniel said there was no pulse. Morgan was next to him at the corner. Amanda went in right after Brittany cried out and put her arm around her sister's shoulders."

"And Nicole?"

"She was on the other side of Daniel, next to the nightstand."

And just like that, the how made perfect sense.

"Is that important?" Petunia asked.

"Yes. But I can't explain now. I've got to sort this before Bryce railroads the wrong person again."

"I did not see that one coming," Ida Belle said.

"We don't even have a motive for Nicole," Gertie said. "Unless she did it for Brittany and Daniel. I know she circles them like a personal assistant, but murder seems a bit far to take friendships and a longtime crush. And what about the lipstick? And the earring?"

"Brittany had on Nicole's bathrobe when you threw punch on her," I said. "Nicole told me they've always borrowed each other's stuff."

"Like the earrings," Ida Belle said. "You don't think it was Brittany who left that lipstick stain, do you?"

"No. I think it was Nicole. I think she injected one of the chocolates Tyler brought her with peanut oil from the pantry and left it in Justin's room earlier in the day, figuring he'd eat it that night. And I think she removed his EpiPen from the nightstand when she left the chocolate so that he couldn't dose himself."

Ida Belle nodded. "So she let herself into the room later to make sure he was gone, and to put the EpiPen back on the nightstand and take the chocolate wrapper with her. Then she found him struggling to breathe rather than dead and finished the job."

"Exactly," I said. "Then she took the key and locked the door behind her, knowing she'd be on hand to plant it when they entered the room the next day."

"So it was Nicole who went out the window that night?" Gertie asked. "But she wasn't wet."

"She was wearing a robe," Ida Belle said. "She could have ditched wet clothes."

I nodded. "And she had a swim cap. She offered it to Brittany today."

"But she came from upstairs," Gertie said. "And we had every entrance to the house covered."

"We had every entrance downstairs covered," I said. "But she could have just as easily gone over rather than down. Something else that didn't occur to me before and should have. The hallway bathroom was next to Justin's room and the lattice runs all the way over to it. I don't think she was planning on going out the window, but I think she prepared in case she did. And her gymnastics training would have given her the ability."

"So she unlocked the bathroom window and wore her swim cap before she went in Justin's room that night," Ida Belle said and shook her head. "You have to admit, it was almost the perfect crime."

"But why?" Gertie said. "There has to be more to it than avenging Brittany and Daniel. And she couldn't have planned it before they got to the B and B because she didn't know about the keys or the lattice or that Tyler would supply the chocolates."

"You're right," I agreed. "Something changed during their stay. And I don't think it had anything to do with Brittany and Daniel's situation. A murder of passion—which is what this appears to be—is personal. Deeply personal."

"What do you think will happen now?" Ida Belle said. "Tyler's attorney will have to be informed about the pillowcase and will insist on testing. If you're right and Nicole's DNA is on there, then that's all they'd need for reasonable doubt in regard to Tyler, especially if the chocolate in Justin's stomach was the same kind Tyler gave Nicole."

"I wonder why Nicole didn't take the pillowcase," Gertie said. "Or at least swap it out with her own. She was meticulous about everything else."

I nodded. "She might not have noticed. I doubt she turned the light on when she went into his room that night, and she certainly didn't the night I went in after her. She probably wasn't certain about where she lost the earring. All she knew was that Bryce hadn't mentioned it so if she'd lost it in Justin's room, it was still there."

"And he still hasn't mentioned it because Petunia has it," Gertie said. "So as things currently stand, she thinks she got away with it."

"But she knows Tyler is on the hook for it," Ida Belle said. "Do you think she can live with that?"

I shrugged. "I would like to say no, but sometimes people still surprise me."

"Is there anything we need to do?" Gertie asked.

I considered this, then shook my head. "No. The evidence will all come out and the prosecutor will either decide to pursue one or the other or dismiss the entire thing for lack of strong enough evidence against either of them."

"So she'll get away with it," Gertie said. "Justin may have deserved a karmic reckoning, but it really wasn't her place to dish it out."

"No," I agreed. "But that's where we are. And our goal here was to get Corndog and Petunia out of the hot seat. We've done that, so technically, our job is done."

Ida Belle sighed. "This is a wholly unsatisfying end to it all. Except for the part where Corndog and Petunia are in the clear."

"I like it better when there's a chase or explosion and the bad guys are arrested or killed," Gertie said. "Ties everything up in a nice, neat bow."

"I'm afraid there will be no bow-tying on this one," I said. "And it appears that the 'bad guy' was already dead when we started our investigation. That's going to have to be enough."

Ida Belle nodded. "We might as well pack to leave then."

We got our things together and were preparing to head out when someone pounded on our room door.

"Ms. Redding! I need your help!"

I knew that voice!

I gave Ida Belle and Gertie a stunned look as I rushed to the door, threw it open, and stared at a clearly panicked Morgan.

"Nicole is on the roof of the hotel with a gun," he said. "She's going to kill herself. Please help."

CHAPTER TWENTY-SEVEN

I HAD NO IDEA WHAT WAS GOING ON, WHAT MORGAN thought I could do, or why he knew my real name, but I gave him a nod and rushed out of the room behind him with Ida Belle and Gertie right on my heels. He ran for the stairs, and we hoofed it up two floors to the rooftop. When we came out, I could see the friends huddled on the back side of the roof and spotted Nicole standing close to the edge, holding a pistol.

I immediately slowed my pace, not wanting to startle her into shooting someone or jumping. Hostage and suicide negotiation wasn't at all what I was trained for, and Nicole wasn't even a friend of mine, so I had my doubts that I could defuse the situation, but I was going to try.

The others looked over as I approached, clearly confused as to why I was there. Morgan shook his head at them, and Amanda gave him a nod before taking Brittany's hand. Giant tears rolled down Brittany's face, and Daniel stood on the other side of her, his arm around her. Nicole stared at all of them, looking completely spaced out, and I wondered if she'd taken something.

"Is she on anything?" I asked, my voice low.

"I think she took painkillers from our house," Daniel said. "Brittany had some from a recent ACL injury. And that's my pistol."

"Has she said why she's doing this?"

They all shook their heads.

"She's been babbling about a party from high school and a baby," Amanda said.

"But nothing about Justin's death?" I asked.

"No," Morgan said. "You think she did it, don't you?"

I nodded.

Brittany sucked in a breath, and Daniel looked stunned. Only Amanda and Morgan didn't show any signs of surprise.

"Nicole," I said and took a step away from the group. "Can we talk?"

"Don't come any closer," she said, her words slurred. "I know how to use this thing. My dad taught me. All us kids learned to shoot, even the girls."

"It's a good skill to have," I said. "I think all women should know how to use a firearm, but I want to make sure you don't accidentally discharge it and hurt one of your friends. You don't want to do that, do you?"

She frowned and seemed confused. "Of course not. I love my friends. That's why I've got to do this. Because I can't let Tyler take the rap for what I did."

Brittany's hand flew over her mouth. "Oh my God."

"But you don't have to handle it this way," I said. "You left a lipstick stain on a pillowcase in Justin's room. Bryce will have no choice but to give that information to the prosecutor. Let Amanda get you an attorney and handle all of this legally. This isn't the answer."

"Please listen to Rose," Brittany begged. "I love you, Nicole. We all love you. Amanda can fix this. She's the smartest person we know."

Nicole shook her head and stumbled a bit more toward the edge of the building. "I've spent ten years trying to fix this. I thought with Justin dead... But it didn't work."

I'd been inching closer to Nicole as I talked and now, I was only five feet or so away, but she'd realized that, and her gaze locked onto mine. Her eyes widened and her arm flexed. As her finger moved for the trigger, I leaped forward and whirled around, kicking the gun from her hand, praying the entire time that she hadn't gotten her finger in place.

As soon as my foot made contact, the pistol went sprawling and she lunged for it. But I was faster. I dived for her legs and took her down about six inches away from the gun. Ida Belle, who'd been in ready position, scooped up the pistol. Nicole, flat on the ground underneath me, started sobbing hysterically.

I had my murderer but didn't feel a single sliver of joy about it.

Nicole's words came back to me—*Maybe it's best not to revisit the past.*

But I had no doubt that's exactly what had happened. Nicole had been caught up in something that happened with Justin ten years ago, and she'd sought a solution to a problem that had troubled her for a decade.

Then Morgan's words.

Some acts are so egregious that the suffering and the desire for retribution have no expiration.

Whatever Justin had done fit that description for Nicole, and she'd carried her secret all these years. But now it was all going to come out.

And that was the last thing she'd wanted. She'd have rather died than the others find out.

The paramedics and the local police had shown up right after I tackled Nicole. They didn't bother sedating her because she was clearly already under the influence, but they strapped her to a gurney. Based on the way she was holding her wrist, I was afraid I'd broken it when I took her down, but that was the least of her problems. However, the injury and the hysteria were a benefit at that time because they got her a trip to the hospital rather than jail. Houma police took statements from all of us individually, which meant I didn't have to identify myself in front of the others, but since Morgan knew and it appeared he'd already told Amanda, I figured he'd fill them all in eventually.

Brittany had hugged me so hard and long after the paramedics arrived that I thought it was going to take the Jaws of Life to get her off me, but finally, Daniel succeeded in prying her off before he gave me a quick hug and a thank-you. His eyes were filled with tears, and I knew he was just as upset as his wife but was trying to be the strong one.

Amanda, in her calm and controlled way, had simply squeezed my arm and given me a heartfelt thank-you before pulling out her phone to call her attorney friend. Morgan had just given me a grim smile and a nod. When the police were done, we headed back to our room to gather our things. We would still have to go to the Houma PD and give our official statements and sign them, but it didn't have to be today. It was a short drive over from Sinful, and we were all ready to sleep in our own beds.

When we headed out, I spotted Morgan leaning against Ida Belle's SUV.

"I figured I owed you an explanation," Morgan said. "After all, you did save my friend."

"How long have you known who I was?" I asked.

"I thought I recognized you as soon as I saw you at the B

and B, but your cover was so good, I decided I must be mistaken. When you tackled Brittany in the dark, I knew I'd gotten it right in the beginning. But you were clearly in role and I didn't want to interfere with whatever assignment you were on."

I raised one eyebrow at the word *assignment*. "For a guy who 'writes code for a defense contractor,' you have an interesting vocabulary and an odd knowledge of people who live in bayou towns far from Baton Rouge."

He smiled. "I suppose I'm okay telling you, of all people, the truth, but I'm asking for your silence because the others don't—and can't—know what I really do. I'm an analyst for your area of operation with the CIA. And they relocated me to NOLA six months ago, so technically, I'm more in your neck of the woods now."

"That explains a lot. So you've gathered the data for some of my work."

"Yes. Don't get me wrong, I didn't think you being there had anything to do with Justin's death. I just assumed you were on some supersecret mission that I was unaware of."

"Actually, I was on a personal mission. Petunia and Corndog's nephew is a friend, and I was trying to help them out of a potentially bad situation."

He nodded. "Bryce would have railroaded Corndog. I'm sure he's in cahoots with the guy who wanted to buy their house cheap."

"You're the one who sent me the autopsy, aren't you?"

He smiled. "I'll only say that my skill on the web is similar to yours in person—no one ever knows I was there. Why did the ME change his conclusion?"

"It's probably better if you don't know. So Justin died, you didn't think it had anything to do with Corndog making a mistake, and when I turned up, you figured you'd give me prompts, hoping I'd figure out what really happened."

"I'm sorry about doing things that way, but you're right, I didn't think it had gone down like Bryce presented. I had no idea why you were there, and I apologize for trying to take advantage of the situation. I figured if I poked at things enough, you might be curious and decide you had to unravel the mystery."

"Good call," Ida Belle said. "She can't stand not having answers."

"I can't either, which is why I went fishing on the ME's server," he said. "Like everyone else, I had no idea an autopsy had been done. I was just looking for his notes, but that was a real bonus."

"It definitely changed the scope of things," I said. "If you hadn't sent it, Bryce might have caused some good people a lot of trouble."

He sighed. "I have to admit, when I did those things to get you involved, I didn't know it was Nicole. I really thought it was Tyler. He has history with Justin—ancient and recent—and I figured he'd taken an opportunity to even the score. It never occurred to me that it was murder. I figured he was just trying to get Justin sick or give him a scare and then panicked when he died."

I nodded. "I was headed that direction for a bit myself. So out of curiosity, if you'd known it was intentional and that it was Nicole, would you have let her get away with it?"

"Not at Corndog and Petunia's expense. But if they hadn't been a factor and I knew her reason why, then maybe. Whatever he did had to be huge to push her over the edge that way. Nicole simply isn't a killer. Do those sentiments lower my stock?"

"Not with me, but then I'm more inclined to seek justice

than the letter of the law, especially if they conflict. You're a good friend, Morgan. She's going to need one."

He nodded. "Then that's what I'll be. Thank you, Ms. Redding. I appreciate you diving into all of this."

"It's Fortune. And you didn't leave me much choice, especially after sending me that autopsy."

"You're not going to get me back for that, are you? Because I really don't want to be looking over my shoulder the rest of my life."

I smiled. "You wouldn't even know I was there."

"Right."

I patted him on the back, laughing at his clearly uneasy expression. "Don't worry, Morgan. You were trying to help Corndog and Petunia. That's an honorable thing and something that's missing from most people."

He blushed a bit and shuffled, clearly embarrassed by the compliment.

I studied him for a moment, then smiled. "You know, for all your studying human behavior with your shrink friend, you've missed the boat on a couple of big ones this week. And I think you're missing it on another."

"How's that?"

"There's a woman in NOLA—your new hometown—who gets together with a group of women every week for drinks. I know she professes a high level of disdain for men, but I have a feeling she'd set aside some time to have drinks with you."

His eyes widened. "You think?"

I shrugged. "Or you can waste another ten years wondering."

I CALLED CORNDOG AND PETUNIA ON THE WAY HOME. They'd already gotten a call from the state police, who had already stepped in to take over the investigation. So they knew some of what had happened, but were shocked when I filled in the blanks. As much as I could, anyway, because there were still a lot of things unanswered as far as motive was concerned. But their relief was overwhelming and all three of us were sniffing in the car after the call and hearing their sobs of relief.

I sent Carter a text after that, letting him know that the case was solved, Corndog and Petunia were in the clear, and the killer exposed. He greeted us in my driveway when we pulled up. He was on his way out on a call and recognized my expression well enough to hold off on questions, so he just gave me a brief kiss and left.

After the call to Corndog and Petunia, we'd all been quiet on the drive home. I knew we were satisfied that we'd done our job saving Corndog and Petunia from eviction, but bothered by the ultimate outcome. And if I was being honest, I still wanted to know why she'd done it, even though it wasn't relevant to my end of things.

When I entered the house, Merlin gave me a dirty look and stomped off, his flicking tail signaling his opinion on my absence. Feeling restless, I grabbed another beer and headed out for my lawn chairs near the bayou. I'd barely gotten seated when my cell phone rang. It was Shadow Chaser.

"Oh my God, you're brilliant!" he said when I answered. "Brilliant and scary and somehow still gorgeous, although if you ever tell your sheriff I said that I'll deny it. And please don't tell my scary boss either. He's already accused me of proposing to you and I don't need that grief in my life. But thank you! Thank you a million times and more! I don't even know how I can pay you back. I can offer free hotel rooms..."

"Hard pass on that one."

"Good call. But seriously, I have to offer up something for saving my family."

"Given the business I'm in, I'm sure I'll need you to 'unsee' some things in the future. We'll just call it even."

"Deal. You have my undying blindness for all eternity. Even if I have to unsee naked people."

We disconnected and I took another swig of beer and looked out across the bayou. The sun was just starting to set when Ida Belle strolled up.

"Was too restless to rest so I ground up some deer meat and made those jalapeño sausages you like," she said. "I put a package in your refrigerator and another two in your freezer."

"That's awesome and solves my problem about what to have for dinner. Thanks."

She gave me a critical look. "I have a feeling you're not sitting out here because of our case."

I raised one eyebrow.

"Okay," she corrected. "You're not *only* sitting out here staring at slow-moving water because of our case."

I remained silent because I still hadn't quite worked out my thoughts.

"Don't wait as long as I did," she said quietly.

I sighed. "How did you know?"

She shrugged. "Everything that went down in Iran, Maya and Blanchet moving here all cozied up, Harrison and Cassidy before that, and then this case with two long-term instances of unrequited love and far too many secrets for people who were supposed to care about each other... I figure it just added weight to the things that were already on your mind. And I have a pretty good idea just how that mind works."

"Do you have regrets?"

"No. I lived my life on my terms and that's never something that should cause regret. But times are different now—

for women, especially. Old notions of what's right and proper are gone except for the idiots among us. And Walter and Carter are not the same kind of man."

"Walter's a good man. The best."

"Oh, without a doubt. I never once questioned that. But people like you and me, Carter, Harrison, Mannie, and Lord help us all, even Gertie, we're different. Walter should have settled down with someone sweet like Ally, or even a strong, kind woman with a bit of an acerbic tongue, like his sister Emmaline. But he's always loved me, and that's something I didn't give the respect it deserved."

"I get not having regrets, but do you ever wish you would have married him sooner?"

She stared out at the bayou for a bit, then finally shook her head. "I went back several times...after Vietnam."

"To the military?"

She nodded.

"Why didn't you ever tell me?"

She raised one eyebrow.

"Right, classified. Does Gertie know?"

"I'm sure she does. When it comes down to it, I'm sure Walter knew I wasn't off for months at a time looking at potential investments or caring for a cousin he'd never heard of. But suspecting and knowing are two different things. You saw how he was when Carter was MIA. I couldn't do that to him. Better for him to think I was safe somewhere in the US than be worrying day and night not knowing."

"But that was still a long time ago, right? Why not have a relationship when you were sure you were done?"

"Once you're in the business of danger, are you ever really done? Do you have a day in mind when you plan on changing your entire personality and stop taking risks?"

"That's fair enough. So you think Walter would have wanted you to change?"

"Yes. But he never would have asked. The reality is his heart couldn't have taken being my partner during my younger years. It taxes him now even though I don't tell him 10 percent of what we get up to and he's older and wise enough not to ask."

"But you finally said yes."

"Because I finally realized I wasn't being fair to either of us. Walter was never going to love anyone but me and I was the same. We'd both remained untethered to anyone else the bulk of our lives because neither of us could stomach the thought of someone else trying to fill that slot that was only meant for one person. It was time now. It wasn't time before. The circumstances were all wrong for it."

I nodded. "That makes sense."

"It makes sense for Walter and me, but your situation is very different, and you keep that thought in the front of your mind. Carter knows what you're capable of. He admires and respects your ability. Of course he worries. Hell, *I* worry. But he can handle living with it a heck of a lot easier than he can living without you."

I nodded. She'd given me a lot to think about.

CHAPTER TWENTY-EIGHT

THAT EVENING, CARTER GRABBED SOME SIDES FROM Francine's café, and we threw Ida Belle's sausages on the grill. We ate in front of the TV, watching an old Western and talking about anything besides my case. When we'd cleared out the dishes, he sank on the couch next to me and flicked off the TV.

"You want to tell me about it?" he asked.

I nodded and went through everything that had happened, backtracking on occasion to put it all into the correct timeline and perspective. He listened silently and when I was done, he shook his head.

"And you have no idea why she did it?"

"Zero. Not that I expect to—I barely know her—but I don't think Morgan has a guess either, so it must be something really awful if she's kept it quiet all these years, and the first time she sees the guy, she kills him. Keeping things quiet is entirely in her skill set, mind you, given that she's been in love with her best friend's husband for over a decade and Brittany doesn't seem to be aware of that fact. But I have to say, I didn't see her for murder, especially since this one required some planning."

He nodded. "She'll have mental health counseling in the hospital. Maybe she'll get help. I understand you have unresolved feelings about all of this, but it's the best possible outcome given the situation. The guilty party is known and will get medical attention. An innocent man won't be railroaded into prison. Corndog and Petunia are off the hook and hopefully, Bryce's treachery will make the rounds, and he won't be reelected."

"I suppose it's the best outcome given the situation."

But I still didn't have to like it.

After all the drama and sausages, I crashed on the couch with Carter's arm draped over me. He was on the early shift the next morning and we'd almost made him late for work by 'saving time' and showering together. He'd slowed only long enough to dump some coffee in an insulated cup, give me a quick kiss, and get out the door.

It was barely 8:00 a.m. when my phone rang, and I saw Brittany's name in the display. I quickly answered.

"Are you all right? Is Nicole?"

"Yes. We're fine. Before I launch into why I called, I wanted to let you know that Morgan explained that you were a PI and a former CIA agent and were at the B and B undercover to help Corndog and Petunia. He said he'd recognized you from a news story or something but didn't want to blow your cover. Anyway, your tackling me in the dark and kicking that gun out of Nicole's hand certainly made a lot more sense once we all knew. But the bottom line is I owe you a huge thanks for saving my cousin."

"Is she still in the hospital?"

"Yes. I just visited. Her wrist is sprained and they've stabilized her emotionally...well, sort of. She's a bit drugged, but she's lucid. Anyway, she wants to talk to you."

My pulse quickened. "Why?"

"She wouldn't say, other than to stress that it was important. I hate to ask you for anything—you've already given us so much—but I promised her that I would call you."

"I'll see her. I assume I need some form of permission?"

"She's already talked to her attorney. The cops can't question her until her psychiatrist has declared her sound and that hasn't happened yet. But I think it might soon. Before then, it's up to Nicole and her doctors and they said it was okay. Her attorney is fine with it as well."

"What time should I be there?"

TWO AND A HALF HOURS LATER, IDA BELLE PULLED THROUGH the hospital entrance to drop me off.

"You sure you don't want us to wait?" she asked.

I shook my head. "Go grab some sandwiches at Mother's. I'll eat mine on the way home and hopefully provide you with some answers."

She nodded and drove off. They'd insisted on coming with me even though they wouldn't be allowed in to see Nicole. But they hadn't wanted me driving to NOLA and back with only my own thoughts for company. I'd stopped by the sheriff's department to tell Carter where I was going, and he'd given me a hug and kiss and whispered that he hoped I got the answers I needed.

My mind was whirling with possibilities, some rational and others completely wild, so I took a deep breath and headed inside. Nicole was being housed in a locked-down unit, and Brittany was waiting for me in the lobby outside a glassed-in desk. She gave me a quick hug and then I gave the nurse my ID and she buzzed me through. Brittany gave me an anxious look before I headed off, and I wondered if Nicole had told her anything yet or if she was still leaving her best friend in the dark on her well-kept secrets.

I knocked lightly on Nicole's door and heard a faint 'Come in.' I pushed the door open, and Nicole gave me a small smile. She was pale and had dark circles under her eyes. Her usual stylish and beautiful hair hung limply onto her shoulders, but her pupils were normal and she was sitting mostly upright.

"Sorry about the wrist," I said.

She lifted the bandaged hand and shook her head. "It's much better than the alternative. So I'll start with saying thank you. I owe you my life. I was very confused about that, by the way, until Brittany filled me in on your real identity. You're very talented. You and your 'aunts,' who are a genius cover. I have to assume they're not nearly as frustrating in real life as they pretended to be."

"Well, Gertie tries my and Ida Belle's patience daily but much differently than she did on the island. Let's just say she refuses to recognize that with age comes limitations."

"Good for her. Limiting your life only causes trouble in the long run. Take me for example—holding so much in all these years thinking I was protecting myself and now look at the situation I'm in."

She let out a huge sigh. "I asked to speak to you because I wanted to explain."

"You don't owe me an explanation."

"I think maybe I do. If it wasn't for you, I wouldn't be here and people I truly love would have to live without answers. I think that's probably harder than knowing even if the truth is painful."

"That's true."

"I want you to know that I never meant to hurt Corndog and Petunia. I thought the anaphylaxis would be taken as an innocent mistake and nothing more. Since Justin didn't have anyone to push the issue, I thought things would just be crappy for a bit, then go back to the way they were. I had no idea that sheriff would use Justin's death to try to take their home."

"I believe you. No one could have known the direction Bryce would take. Or that Tyler would end up being arrested. I don't know you very well, Nicole, but I have to believe that you had a good reason for what you did. I'd like to understand..."

She stared down at the bed for a long time and when she finally looked back up, she was crying. "He raped me."

I stared. Of all the things I'd thought she might say, that hadn't even been on the list.

"It was at a party right before graduation, a sort of combination graduation and late Mardi Gras, which basically means we were all wearing Mardi Gras colors and masks. I was drinking, but he slipped me something because my memory wasn't right. I'd get flashes of things, but it was like I was looking at everything through a blurry lens, you know?"

I nodded.

"I guess I need to preface the story by saying I've been in love with Daniel since grade school. But I also love Brittany, and Daniel has never had eyes for anyone else. But that night, when things started to fade in and out, I headed for the restroom. There was a line, of course, and the second floor was off-limits, but since the house belonged to a friend, I figured she wouldn't mind if I used her parents' bathroom."

She took a deep breath and slowly blew it out and I could tell the next part was going to be hard for her.

"Daniel followed me upstairs."

I blinked, confused. Daniel?

"He came up behind me as I was about to go into the bathroom and wrapped his arms around me and kissed the back of my neck. I was startled at first, because I didn't know who it was, but then I turned around and saw the team shirts that all the football players were wearing and the purple mask that Brittany had made for him..."

"And Justin and Daniel looked enough alike to be brothers."

She nodded. "Sounded alike too, or maybe it was the drug... Anyway, he told me Brittany was gone and we could finally be together."

She looked down, clearly embarrassed. "I knew it was wrong. Brittany was my cousin and my best friend. She and Daniel were practically engaged, but then I convinced myself that if he would cheat on her then she wouldn't want to be with him. That I'd be doing her a favor if she found out. And then I wondered if by 'gone' he meant they'd broken up. That he'd finally realized she wasn't right for him, and he wanted me instead. I won't say it was all the drug because that would be a lie, but I am positive the drug sent me over the edge into my fantasies."

She took another breath and looked back up at me. "We had sex in the bathroom. He sat me on the counter and...it was my first time. I'd been saving myself—stupid, I know—but I'd always had this hope that Daniel would come around. And it was finally happening."

She frowned. "But afterward, it was all wrong. He just finished and then gave me this cocky grin and said he had to get back to the party. I tried to protest, but he said we had to keep things secret for now or people would take sides, and he didn't want problems between me and Brittany. That made sense, but then, I was so spaced out most anything would have."

"So what happened after the party?"

"I don't remember getting home. My mom found me in a lawn chair in the backyard. She freaked out because I was so out of it and could barely walk, and she hauled me to the hospital."

"They did a drug test?"

She nodded. "They said I had Rohypnol in my system. I swore to the doctors and my parents that I didn't knowingly take anything. Jesus, that was my vegan phase. Why on earth would I take drugs, and definitely not roofies."

"Did they ask you if you'd been raped?"

"Yes. And I lied. I just said I must have blanked out when I got home and fell asleep in the lounger. I couldn't tell them. Brittany is my cousin and my best friend. Our mothers are sisters. It would have torn our family apart, so I begged my mom not to tell anyone."

"No one ever found out about the visit to the ER?"

"Ha. Small town. Everyone found out, but I just told them it was alcohol poisoning. Not like anyone would be surprised by that given the way we were all drinking."

I nodded. "And what about you and Brittany and the others?"

"Everything was the same as before...well, except me. Because of what happened, I avoided her for a couple days in school, which was easy enough with all the end-of-year responsibilities we both had. Since most of them extended into the evening, that bought me more time, but finally, I couldn't stretch it any longer. And I was troubled because I hadn't heard any gossip about her and Daniel's breaking up. That confused me, because usually gossip got through high school in the blink of an eye, so even if Brittany was avoiding telling me, I should have heard whispers of something in the making."

"Because boys rarely keep their thoughts to themselves."

"Exactly. So I headed over to Brittany's house, figuring I'd poke around and see what I could find out. She looked a little stressed but otherwise normal, so I asked if she was feeling okay as she'd left the party early and I hadn't seen her in days, figuring that was her opportunity to share something about Daniel. She said she was fine, but she'd had a migraine at the party, which was why they'd left early."

"They?"

Nicole nodded. "I figured being the dutiful boyfriend that he was, Daniel had taken her home, then come back to the party. I convinced myself that he'd just stretched the truth a little about the breakup because she'd been sick and that he was just waiting until she was better to tell her."

"But it never happened."

"No. They were the same as before—the perfect couple, planning their perfect lives. Daniel would be working for his dad, which he did every summer, but this time, he wouldn't be quitting in the fall to go to school. His dad would be grooming him to take over, and Daniel was going to do online and night classes in business. Brittany had been teaching summer cheer camp to younger girls for years and was already pushing her parents to help her rent a space and equipment to open her own gymnastics studio."

"You didn't confront him?"

"Not until I missed my period. I'd always been like clockwork, but the first couple days, I figured it was all the stress of graduation and waiting for Daniel to call it quits with Brittany. And then one day I saw a woman walk by our house pushing a baby in a stroller and I almost passed out. I drove two towns over and bought three pregnancy tests because I had to be sure. All three were positive."

"But you didn't tell Daniel?"

"No. I went to see him at his house when I knew he'd be alone, and I asked him about him and Brittany, hoping he'd tell me that he was working on it. But his face lit up like it always did when he talked about her. He told me that he was so glad I'd stopped by because he'd been wanting to ask a favor of me. He was going to ask Brittany to marry him and wanted my help finding her a ring."

"That must have been quite a blow."

"I was dumbfounded. He was acting like we'd never hooked up. I started to cry and asked him, 'What about us?' He looked at me like I was crazy, then he got all cautious and says 'Nicole, there has never been an us and there never will be. I've always loved Brittany, and I'm going to marry her and make my life with her.' He sounded genuinely confused, and I started to wonder if he had been so drunk he didn't remember. Or maybe he'd been drugged as well."

"So you never told him about the pregnancy."

"How could I? He'd made it clear he didn't love me. He loved Brittany. If he didn't remember what had happened, then it was no one's fault, right? And if he *did* remember and was just pretending not to, then what would I accomplish by calling him out on it? It would have destroyed our lives and our families. So I told my mom that it was a boy from another school and I didn't want anyone to know his name because his parents were drug users. I convinced them that the baby would be better off being adopted so that he and his parents could never get their hands on it, and that then my life wouldn't have to be ruined."

"I can't imagine that was easy on your parents."

"They were *so* upset. They tried to talk me into having the baby and letting them adopt it, but I couldn't. Everyone would know. And every time I looked at that baby, I'd see Daniel and relive his betrayal. And God forbid, what if the baby ended up looking just like him? I couldn't risk it. And I didn't think I was strong enough to live with all those secrets. They hated it —it was their grandchild, after all—but they finally agreed and we arranged things with my dad's sister in Italy."

"Was it a closed adoption?"

Nicole nodded. "I didn't want to know anything, and I didn't want him to come looking for me, because if explaining now was impossible imagine explaining it twenty years down the road. My aunt took me to an agency over there. It was all legal and all records closed."

"And you started a rumor that you'd fallen for an Italian man and had vexed your parents by refusing to come home."

"Yes. It seemed the best way to avoid questions about my gap year and it worked."

"It must have been hard, though, to remain close to Brittany all these years, being around Daniel all that time."

"At first, it was, but he treated me the same way he always had. That's when I realized that he truly didn't remember. No one can carry on an act every second of every day for years, especially someone like Daniel. I figured he'd been roofied and maybe Brittany as well, which was why she got sick. My own memory was spotty—like flashes of that night, not really a film playback. So I figured it was possible that he didn't recall anything at all."

I nodded.

"Anyway, when I returned from Italy, I pushed it all out of my mind. Locked it in a box and attempted to throw away the key. Brittany and Daniel were about to get married and everything was the way it should be. I went off to university a few weeks later and moved to NOLA after graduation. Brittany and I still saw each other regularly, but it was mostly a girls' thing then. I didn't have to see Daniel, and that made it all easier. And time. After a while, I finally let it go."

"But did you?"

She sighed. "I let that night go. But if you're asking if I'm still in love with Daniel, then the answer is yes, in a way. I think part of me will always love him. But seeing him now doesn't hurt. And he and Brittany love each other. I know they have their issues, but don't all couples?"

I nodded, her story finally clicking with her current situation. "How did you figure out that it was Justin that night and not Daniel?"

"Completely by accident. I guess I've been stupid all this time, still believing it was Daniel that I had sex with, or maybe I just couldn't face that I'd probably been drugged and fooled by some rando who'd been laughing at me ever since. I gave him my virginity. I know that doesn't mean anything to a lot of people, but it did to me. And it's something I can't ever recover."

"It was stolen. Your choice was removed because he drugged you and lied."

She nodded. "That first day after we arrived at the B and B, it was misting on the boat ride over, and we all went upstairs to change. I took longer than usual, and Brittany sent me a text saying Justin and I were holding up the party and to get down to the library. I stopped by his room and knocked but he didn't answer. I tried the door and it was unlocked, so I figured I'd poke my head in and make sure he'd already headed down."

"But he was still there?"

"Yes. Standing right in the middle of the room, naked and drying his head with a towel. He grinned at me when I froze and then he said, 'See anything you like? You did once before.' And then I saw the mole. In a place you could only spot it if he was completely naked. And I remembered seeing it that night. I looked at him and I'm sure my expression was one of horror. He realized that I was just now getting it, and he laughed. He *laughed* at me. Like it was all some practical joke."

Tears slid from her eyes and down her cheeks. "Like he hadn't raped me."

"You could have gone to the police."

"And said what? Proven it how? He'd have just said it was consensual, and I'd have to tell them everything...about Daniel and about my son... I couldn't do it. I couldn't ruin so many lives because of him. But I couldn't let him do it to other women either. All that bragging about his conquests, and I wondered how many had been drugged like I was. How many had wound up pregnant or diseased, and that's just the physical side of things. The emotional is far worse. He ruined my life. I never dated anyone, not seriously. I certainly never had a relationship because after that night, I couldn't trust men anymore."

I sighed because she wasn't wrong. Chances were if she'd gone to the police, there would have been nothing they could do, and she would have blown up a lot of lives to accomplish nothing. And while I absolutely believed things had gone exactly as she'd explained, there was no way to prove it, short of a confession from Justin, who was no longer here. And even though I'd never met him, I was absolutely certain that a man who openly mocked his victim would have never told the truth.

"I'm so sorry that happened to you," I said. "Justin was a criminal but far worse, he was a horrible human being. He didn't deserve friends."

"He deserved to die."

"Maybe," I hedged. "But we can't go around killing everyone who deserves it."

"The world might be a better place if good people did."

I nodded. "Unfortunately, the way the world works now is the good people just have to pay again when they try to fix awful situations."

"I'm going to prison, aren't I?"

"I don't know. That's for you, your attorney, and the DA to work out. But if you haven't already, I think you need to tell your attorney the truth—all of the truth. It's about protecting yourself now. You've spent too much of your life protecting other people at your own expense. And maybe if you'd let it all come out, you would have known the truth a long time ago, or at least that it definitely wasn't Daniel. You could have gotten help. Brittany and Daniel are adults. If their marriage can't handle this, then they didn't have much of one to begin with."

She nodded and swiped at the tears running down her cheeks.

"And I'm going to make another suggestion, which your attorney will probably come around to, but just in case he doesn't—go looking for other victims. Even one or two would be enough to support your story. Because I'm sure you're right. They're out there, and maybe some would be willing to come forward to help you. After all, you gave them closure."

The door opened and a nurse walked in.

"Visiting time is over," she said. "Ms. Lange needs her rest."

I gave Nicole an encouraging smile. "Stay strong. You can still have a life after this, but you've got some work to do in order to manage it."

I rose from my seat and walked out. I hated when I got the answers, but they weren't at all what I wanted. And I prayed that Nicole's attorney was a good one and could figure out a deal that would still allow her a future.

A future free from the burden of one horrible night.

BRITTANY WAS STILL IN THE WAITING AREA WHEN I EXITED the unit. She rose from her chair, an anxious expression on her face.

"Did she tell you about the baby?" she asked.

I stared, confused. "You knew about the baby?"

"When she came home from her year abroad, I knew," Brittany said. "A woman looks different after she's given birth, you know. And if you've known a person and seen them naked your entire life, then you notice it."

"Did you ask her about it?"

"I didn't at first. After all, it wasn't my business, and I figured when she was ready to tell me about it, she would. But we got drunk one night a couple weeks after she came back, and I told her that Daniel and I were talking about trying for kids in the next couple years and she broke down. She told me she'd been drugged and raped by a stranger at a party when she was overseas and had given birth to a baby boy and put him up for adoption."

Brittany swiped at tears forming in her eyes. "I had no idea it had actually happened here...that it was Justin who'd raped her. She left right after graduation, so she wasn't showing yet and she wasn't sick. She was nervous, but I just figured that was about her trip. It was an aunt on her dad's side and one she didn't know very well, so I thought she was just worried about fitting in and all."

"Her mother is your aunt... She never let on that anything was wrong? Never told your mother what was going on?"

"No one told me anything for sure! And I doubt she told my mother. She holds a confidence like religion. And there's no way she'd do anything to hurt Nicole. She thinks Nicole hung the moon. We all do. I hate Justin for what he did to her."

"How did you figure out it was Justin?" I asked. "Because Nicole didn't tell you."

"There was a rumor about that party—that she'd hooked up with Justin that night. I didn't believe it, of course, because Nicole couldn't hardly stand Justin. But then Tyler got all moody and depressed one night when he was drunk, and he told me he'd seen them in the bathroom. Justin was wearing the mask I'd made for Daniel, and they'd all been in their team T-shirts, but Tyler had just spoken to Daniel and me as we were leaving, so he knew immediately who it was."

"But he didn't do anything."

"He said she was into it. They both were. Justin had a reputation... He'd been with a lot of girls, including me. So Tyler just figured Nicole was one more notch on his bedpost, but it broke his heart."

"You never asked Nicole about it?"

"No. Clearly, she was mortified by the entire thing as she avoided me for days. I just assumed she was super drunk and then when she said she'd gone to the hospital for alcohol poisoning, that just confirmed my thoughts. No one ever mentioned that night again. Well, except Justin, who used to taunt Tyler about hooking up with Nicole. Everyone else thought he was lying just to get to Tyler, but Tyler and I knew exactly why he was doing it."

"What did Nicole say about it?"

"That Justin was lying as usual and everyone believed her. Everyone but Tyler and me, that is, but we would never have said anything. And every time I tried to bring it up, she immediately changed the subject. So eventually, I just let it go. High school ended and we all moved on. I guess I figured it didn't matter anymore."

"Justin was a despicable person. I hope you do a better job vetting your friends as adults."

"Ha. Definitely." She teared up again. "Poor Nicole. She's lived with this huge secret all these years. But what I don't understand is, why now? Why wait all these years? Did she not know it was Justin who'd raped her before the reunion? Had the drugs made her believe it was someone else?"

"I don't think it's my place to say."

"You're right—don't tell me. It wouldn't change anything and the less I know the better, right? I mean, legally. I'm going to assume Nicole didn't know before now but somehow found out and she decided to get even. Now I just have to pray that the DA sees it the same as I do."

I had my doubts that the DA would be as accepting of Justin's murder as his victims were, but it was the Louisiana legal system and Nicole had a great attorney. I had no doubt he'd find the best course of defense.

"I wish she would have told me back then," Brittany said. "I could have helped her."

"I don't think she was in a mental state that allowed it."

Especially if it meant Nicole had to admit that she'd thought it was consensual sex with Daniel all this time. But I didn't tell Brittany that. If Nicole's case went to trial, there was a good chance the real story would come out, but if she made a deal, no one ever had to know.

Brittany nodded. "I wish you weren't so good at your job. She might have gotten away with it."

"Do you really think she would have allowed Corndog and Petunia to lose their home because of what she did? Or for Tyler to be railroaded for a murder he didn't commit?"

She sighed. "No. She's just not made that way."

"Then everything worked out the way it needed to."

"I guess so."

"There is one last thing I'd like to know," I said.

"What's that?"

"Why were you really in the kitchen that night? There was water in the library."

Brittany blushed. "I have an eating disorder. I only eat tiny amounts in front of other people, but I knew the leftovers were in the refrigerator, so..."

"You sneaked down for a midnight snack while no one was looking, just like you did with the leftover fish."

The simplest explanation once again.

CHAPTER TWENTY-NINE

I FILLED IDA BELLE AND GERTIE IN ON THE RIDE HOME. They were both dumbfounded at Nicole's story and both hoped the outcome was something other than Nicole spending life in prison. I thought she stood a good chance with a mental health defense, especially if her attorney turned up other victims who were willing to tell their story.

I was happy to have the answers, but the whole situation was sad. After Ida Belle dropped me off, I ended up in my chair in front of the bayou with my Kindle, but I never managed to get more than a paragraph read before my thoughts slipped to other things—like relationships, and love, and how fragile lives truly were.

Carter slipped into the chair next to me just as the sun was starting to set over the water.

"Did you get your answers?" he asked.

I told him what Nicole and Brittany had said. He was silent while I talked, and when I was done, he shook his head, his expression sad.

"That's a horrible story," he said finally. "I know she killed him, but she's also a victim. I hope her attorney can work something out so that she doesn't spend the rest of her life paying for this one thing. She's already paid enough."

I looked at him. "I'm surprised to hear you say that. She did kill the guy."

He shrugged. "It doesn't sound like he was a big loss. Quite frankly, she might have saved some women from being future victims. I'm not saying I condone what she did, but I understand why she did it."

I nodded. "Me too. I just wish I could have managed a better solution for everyone."

He reached over and squeezed my hand. "You saved Nicole's life and Corndog and Petunia's home. You exposed a sketchy ME and a useless sheriff. That's a lot to accomplish in a matter of days."

"I've accomplished more in less," I groused.

He laughed. "Yes, you have. But if you're going to spend the rest of your life trying to one-up your past, I'm going to take out a serious insurance policy on you."

"Really? And exactly how much will it take to console you over my loss?"

He leaned over and kissed me gently. "There is no amount that would console me. But I could spend the rest of my life on a beach in Tahiti trying to drink you into a memory."

I smiled. "That actually doesn't sound half bad. Maybe we need a vacation. A real one—sans terrorists."

"I could roll with a vacation, but I was thinking about something else before that. But first, I want to tell you that I appreciate everything you've done for me these past couple months. The rescue, obviously, was huge, but it's been so much more than that. And I have a feeling that remaining silent while I worked through everything has been harder on you than that rescue."

"You know me too well."

"I do. When I was being held captive, the only thing I could think of was getting back home to you. And then a split second later, guilt would overwhelm me because I knew good and well you weren't going to wait around for the military to take action. I didn't want to be responsible for getting us both killed."

"If you really knew me well, you wouldn't have worried about us dying."

He chuckled. "Touché. But we both know anything can happen, especially in those circumstances... I love you, Fortune. Honestly, truly, deeply love you. And those are words I never thought I'd say to anyone. But you and me, we're endgame."

I felt my chest tighten. "Always."

He reached into his pocket and pulled out a ring with a huge, single stunning diamond. "I figured a marquise cut was perfect for my lady. Fortune Redding, if you and I aren't meant for each other, then we aren't meant for anyone. Will you marry me?"

Fortune's answer to Carter's question and another mystery for Swamp Team 3 coming in 2025.

For other books by Jana DeLeon and to pick up some cool merchandise, check out her store at janadeleonstore.com.